Juliette Hyland began cr
heroines in high school. S
with her Prince Charming, who has patiently listened to many rants regarding characters failing to follow their outline. When not working on fun and flirty happily-ever-afters, Juliette can be found spending time with her beautiful daughters and giant dogs, or sewing uneven stitches with her sewing machine.

Scarlett Clarke's interest in romance can be traced back to her love of Nancy Drew books, when she tried to solve the mysteries of her favourite detective while rereading the romantic chapters with Ned Nickerson. She's thrilled to now be writing romances of her own. Scarlett lives in, and loves, her hometown of Kansas City. By day she works in public relations and wrangles two toddlers, two cats and a dog. By night she writes romance and tries to steal a few moments with her firefighter hubby.

Also by Juliette Hyland

Mills & Boon True Love

Royals in the Headlines miniseries

How to Win a Prince
How to Tame a King

Mills & Boon Medical

Fake Dating the Vet

Alaska Emergency Docs miniseries

One Night Baby with Her Best Friend

Also by Scarlett Clarke

The Prince She Kissed in Paris

Discover more at millsandboon.co.uk.

BEAUTY AND THE BROODING CEO

JULIETTE HYLAND

ROYALLY FORBIDDEN TO THE BOSS

SCARLETT CLARKE

MILLS & BOON

First published in Great Britain 2024
by Mills & Boon, an imprint of HarperCollins*Publishers* Ltd,
1 London Bridge Street, London, SE1 9GF

www.harpercollins.co.uk

HarperCollins*Publishers*, Macken House, 39/40 Mayor Street Upper,
Dublin 1, D01 C9W8, Ireland

ISBN: 978-0-263-32145-6

12/24

This book contains FSC™ certified paper
and other controlled sources to ensure responsible forest management.

For more information visit www.harpercollins.co.uk/green.

Printed and Bound in the UK using 100% Renewable Electricity
at CPI Group (UK) Ltd, Croydon, CR0 4YY

BEAUTY AND THE BROODING CEO

JULIETTE HYLAND

MILLS & BOON

For my girls.

Always chase your dreams.

PROLOGUE

SILENCE WAS A weird thing. Everett Winthrope had spent hours, days, wishing his father would shut the hell up. Now all he wanted was a word, a threat, any kind of acknowledgment.

He'd given up hoping his father might like or even respect his artwork. But as long as Charles Everett Winthrope III screamed, Everett at least knew his father felt some emotion toward him.

Even if it was only anger.

He'd not said a word to his son since Everett called from the jailhouse phone. Technically he hadn't spoken then either. Everett had explained the situation and the charge, and begged his father to come get him.

The line's single click had devastated him. He'd had no one else to call. His mother had been out of his life since birth. His dad was all there was.

Shock, not relief, brought him to his feet when the officer said someone was there to bail him out.

That was almost an hour ago, now.

Was his father going to say anything?

Rain pelted the windows as his father raced down the road. The speeding wasn't unusual. The man never drove anything less than ten miles over, but tonight the rain was splashing against the windshield faster than the wipers could react.

And his father was pissed, so his foot was pressed nearly to the floor of the car.

"Do you know what a damn disappointment you are?"

The words stole Everett's breath. He knew. Had always known. But what was he supposed to say?

I guess silence was the better option.

"My art—"

"Your art is not art. It's childish, meaningless graffiti." The interruption was immediate. His father slammed his fist against the steering wheel, the small red sports car he loved more than anything, slid between the lanes.

"Careful." Everett gripped the sides of his seat as his father's head swiveled toward him rather than looking at the road. "We can fight when we get home, Dad."

It wasn't like this was the first time they'd sparred over his father's disdain for his graffiti work—never mind how well the first ten pieces were received by the public.

I'm anonymous. No one even knows it's a Winthrope tagging buildings in the middle of the night and disappearing.

The line he'd used over and over again hammered in his head. He could say it. Maybe his father was even expecting it. But what was the point?

"You were tagging another damn building."

"I wasn't." Everett glared at the oncoming lights of other cars through the heavy raindrops. That was the real rub. It was pouring. One did not graffiti in the rain. Though that argument hadn't swayed the arresting officer either.

Who would graffiti in the rain? The paint was quick drying but, in a deluge, it would simply color the puddles. All it took was a little common sense but the authorities were not interested in easy facts.

Several buildings had been tagged in the last few weeks, and Everett fit the profile. So…

"You weren't planning on tagging the building?" His father swerved again.

There was no safe way to answer that question. After all,

he'd been scouting. Checking out a location for his next piece. He'd not put a single blip of paint on the building, that was what mattered. Tonight wasn't right for the next Roam piece.

Everett had signed the name to his first piece. It meant freedom. The only time he was free was when the spray-paint can was in his hands. When the image took shape before him.

And it wasn't like he tagged places that weren't in need of a little makeover. The first piece had raised the price of a building for an elderly couple looking to sell by almost 10 percent. His most recent—on a bakery that was struggling—had increased the foot traffic by more than 90 percent.

People came for the art, found a treat shop they loved. The baker, a single mom, no longer wondered if she was making rent.

His work was important and meaningful. But all his father saw was the spray cans. That kind of expression wasn't enough for a Winthrope. No, he was supposed to be on the phone talking to clients. Making money for himself and others that already had so much.

"The police picked you up for tagging."

"It's a bullshit charge." Everett crossed his arms. There was no way it was going to stick. It wasn't illegal to have a spray can of paint. He'd literally been looking at the building wall. In the rain—when no one should have been paying any attention.

He still wasn't sure how the officer had seen him in the shadows with the rain pouring.

Like the cop had nothing better to do than stand in the rain looking for a hint of a crime?

"You're lucky you're a Winthrope. They aren't even pressing charges." His father swerved—again—and this time the wheels of the car came up from the road. But only for a second.

Lucky. That was the word he'd heard all his life. He was

lucky to be born into such wealth. Into a family whose money holdings were so vast they were listed on the top fifty richest families in the world…and that was only the assets everyone knew about.

There were other assets. Holdings in corporate names, bank accounts with trusts named as the recipients. His father once joked that the Winthropes made more money per minute in interest holdings than most of the world made in their entire lifetime.

It wasn't something Everett was proud of. After all, what had he done to earn it? Nothing.

The thing a person had the least control over in their life was their birth. He'd done nothing to be a Winthrope. A simple twist of fate.

"Did you hear me? I said, they aren't pressing charges." His father puffed his chest out, like this was an accomplishment.

"Because they don't have charges to press." How many ways were there to say the same thing? "I wasn't doing anything. And even if I was, I do good work. This isn't crass—"

"It's trash!"

"No." His heartbeat hammered in his ears. This meant something to him. Meant everything to him. "No. It's not trash. I am an artist."

"You—" his father pointed a finger at him as he took his focus off the road, again "—are just a disappointment. You are wasting what the Winthrope name could give y—"

The windshield shattered. Tires screamed. Or had they been screaming before the windshield disappeared? His brain was processing everything but in slow motion.

The car was flipping. Turning in the air, once. Twice…

Boom.

A tree pushed into the side of the car.

There was blood in his eyes. His face was on fire. The

world was spinning. But the car had stopped. That didn't make any sense. His brain was misfiring.

"Dad?" The word felt funny on his lips as he reached for his father. Darkness closing in on the edge of his vision. "Dad?"

Sirens echoed somewhere in the distance. Someone was talking. Or maybe his brain was hallucinating to distract him from the pain he knew he should be feeling all over.

Everett tried to reach for his father again but, before his fingers could find anything, the darkness won.

CHAPTER ONE

SHE SHOULD HAVE set out for Snow Peak Estate as soon as she woke. Cora St. Stevens's hands tightened on the steering wheel as her tires slipped on the mountain pass—for the third time. She didn't dare take her eyes off the icy road but she wished her GPS would say something. Give some indication how close she was to the estate that would be her home for the next three and half months.

Twenty-three miles. That was how many she'd had left to go an hour ago. She should have been there by now. Would have been there, if the snowflakes hadn't morphed into an ice storm.

It was too late to turn around, even if she wanted to. This was her dream job. Sort of.

Her real dream was a gallery with her own artwork. But Cora lacked the talent, so conserving other people's masterpieces was almost as good.

"Tightly controlled" did not begin to describe access to the Winthrope family's Snow Peak Estate, which was rumored in the art world to be the largest private art gallery in the world. Containing pieces the general public hadn't seen in generations.

Including *the* piece…if her research was accurate…that had driven her father mad.

Cora understood her dad's desire, the siren's call of a piece or pieces—to a point. After all, she'd studied every work the graffiti artist Roam had produced around London and Paris. The large pieces always appeared overnight and were signed the same way.

The artist had produced eleven works. Masterpieces. Commentary on the world around them. Then they just stopped. Roam, whoever they were, vanished. It was heartbreaking. More than one blogger and journalist had attempted to trace what happened to the spray can–wielding, brilliant artist only to lose the scent after the last piece appeared on a bakery wall on the East side of London almost two years ago, now.

It was maddening that such a talent was gone. She could see how the chase could consume you. But sometimes you had to walk away. A lesson her father never learned.

Am I any better? I'm chasing his obsession now.

She was too close to the mythical Ringlet Lady to turn around. And the ice storm wouldn't allow it anyway.

This was the path she was on. Completing it was all she could do now.

Her tires skidded. She cried out as the car drifted perilously close to the mountain's edge.

"Who the hell lives up here!" A tear slipped down her cheek but she didn't dare take her hands off the steering wheel as it, and the ones that followed, fell off her chin.

Everett Winthrope was the answer to that scream. Once upon a time, the handsome man was featured in gossip columns surrounded by a bevy of young woman, each one somehow more beautiful than the last. Then he and his father were in a car accident—right after Everett was arrested two years ago.

At least according to the rumors. There were never any charges. Multiple tabloids had attempted to get the arrest record, only to be rebuffed by the police. She'd learned long ago to ignore as many of the *rumors* as possible.

After all, her father, Maurice St. Stevens, was the subject of many lies. Though most lies had some kernel of truth to them.

Whatever had occurred, Everett disappeared after the accident. That wasn't a rumor. The playboy was simply gone from the world. But the Winthrope fortune wasn't.

No. His father had left his entire fortune to the last remaining Winthrope when he crashed that car. And his son had taken the financial reins and grown it by leaps and bounds. The family, or rather Everett, was the tenth richest in the world.

At least according to articles she'd read while researching the position.

The estate's favorite pastime was artwork. Collecting it. Hoarding it. Stealing it away behind closed doors so no one but him could enjoy it.

What was the point of art if it was not enjoyed by the masses?

That argument had been on the tip of her tongue during the interview with Everett's frosty executive assistant, Hannah. The woman had discussed the pieces like they weren't some of the most sought-after art in the world. Cora bristled but kept herself together. Answering every question with the perfect response of an art restorer/conservator.

She wanted this job. Needed it. And Cora was making no missteps. Her ex, Justin, had not-so-subtly pointed out that her apprenticeship under her father was looked down on by so many people—just like her art.

Justin was the creator of masterpieces; she was just his muse. The pretty thing on his arm when he needed it. At least until six months ago.

Cora hated that she'd given him so much of her youth. That his undermining of her self-confidence hadn't been the reason she'd left. That should have been enough, but no, she'd waited until all his lies unraveled.

Four years wasted on the "penniless" artist who was far from it. The art community had chattered on about the lie for a few months, but they hadn't banished him.

No, she was the one in exile. By her choice, mostly, but still. Life wasn't fair. A lesson her father had instilled in her over and over again.

Her life path was different from most in her field, and sometimes difficult to explain in interviews. Cora had grown up at her father's side, holding a paintbrush and conservation tools long before she'd learned to write her name.

The wealthy were groomed from an early age to take over a finance business. Children of actors and actresses often stepped into roles without going through the trenches. The world's rules didn't apply—if you had enough coin in the bank.

If you didn't have the coin, then the world tended to look down on that firsthand experience. Discount it. So she'd gotten a degree, even though her father had railed against her needing it.

Her relations with him never recovered from Cora's insistence on getting an advanced degree in art conservation. He'd bristled at her stepping out, saying he could teach her anything else.

That might have been true, if his mind wasn't so focused on Pierre Alarie's *The Ringlet Lady.*

Besides, even if he'd been in the right state of mind to focus on her education, she'd wanted her degree. Wanted space. Wanted to be Cora St. Stevens, rather than "Maurice's daughter."

Then she'd moved from her father's house to Justin's flat while she got her degree. The moody modern artist made her feel sexy and wanted—when he was in a good mood. When he wasn't, she was less than an accessory in his life.

Her father and Justin had never gotten along. Eventually her talks with her dad had gone from daily to weekly, to every other month, if that. Cora had always figured they'd work it out, eventually. But six months ago he'd had a heart attack. The doctors swore it had been quick, that he probably hadn't even realized.

Maybe it was true…or maybe it was a kindness given to the only family he left behind.

The saddest part was she knew he wasn't thinking of her in the final moments. The paramedics had found the name of the Winthropes' estate on a piece of paper clutched in his hands. Even in death he was focused on the mystery that consumed him.

Now she was on a dangerous icy road—chasing his dream. The only good thing was that after this stint as a conservator at Snow Peak Estate, she'd have enough for a down payment on a flat. And hopefully something she could give to her dad, metaphorically.

But after this, she was done. If *The Ringlet Lady* wasn't in the Winthrope Collection, then this ended her duty. She'd accept what the rest of the art world had told her father for decades: it didn't exist.

Its only known reference was a lone article in one old forgotten newspaper—in October 1929. The US stock market had crashed the week before, so the story was relegated to a tiny column in the back. The art world's position was the journalist, who probably hadn't even bothered to go to the art show, heard that Pierre Alarie had painted women in the nude and they fabricated a story. Alarie had denied the existence in every interview.

But her father swore it was real. That one couldn't describe the beauty of such a piece without seeing it. He also claimed Alarie had never denied the existence, merely said the art wasn't available. When she was younger, she'd been wholly on his side.

Now… Now she wasn't sure, but that wasn't stopping her from risking her neck on an icy mountain pathway.

The manor house came into view, the lights on the front stoop were out. In fact, only one light in the entire place looked lit. If no one was home, she was going to have to either break in or sleep in the car. Because there was no way the aged car she'd bought when she landed in Norway was going to make it back down the mountain in this weather.

Grabbing her duffel bag, she was almost glad that Justin claimed the right to most of their joint stuff, even though she'd paid for it. It made traveling easy. Stepping out of the car, she fought the urge to race to the giant front door. If she slipped and fell there might not be anyone to hear her cries.

Her hair was coated in ice pellets as she pressed against the door chime. Cora's teeth were clattering and her fingers burning in the cold.

"Answer…" Pleading to an ancient wooden door wasn't her finest moment, but she needed inside.

Lifting her hand, she balled her fist and banged against the door. The instructions had been very specific. She was to arrive at Snow Peak Estate today, between the hours of 3 and 5 p.m. It was currently three minutes past five. Three minutes late in this nasty weather couldn't matter.

Please. I have nowhere else to go.

The door cracked open; Everett Winthrope peered out from the crack. She hadn't expected the billionaire recluse to answer, but she recognized him from the celebrity pictures taken years ago.

"Who are you?" The man's deep voice was throaty, like he was unaccustomed to using it.

Cora pushed past him. She could answer whatever questions Everett had from the warmth inside.

"Hey!"

"No." She wanted to hold up her hand for effect but she was too busy rubbing them together to try to bring back some feeling in her fingers.

Everett turned, and she couldn't get a good look at the man. Why was it so dark in here?

"I am Cora St. Stevens. The art restorer you hired—"

"I terminated that contract a week ago." The growl echoed in her soul.

No. No.

She'd taken a sabbatical at the museum for this. An unpaid sabbatical. If her boss had his way she wouldn't return. If Cora had her way, she'd find another place, too. Maybe in Paris or London. Somewhere Justin wouldn't have any reach into the local art world. A place she could re-create herself.

A new life. One designed *by* her, not *for* her. Where she was nobody's muse, but the master of her own fate. She needed this position to make that happen.

But she was not going to show that desperation. "If that is true, you need better staff, because they didn't inform me of such. Which means I am here under the contractual requirements. If you send me away now, you'll have to pay me the full fee of the contract."

Everett let out a scoff. "Money isn't exactly an issue for me, Ms. St. Stevens."

Must be nice. What was it with rich people and not realizing that was not how the rest of the world operated? Justin had claimed to have nothing, the image of the starving artist. None of it was true. He had a trust, a giant safety net. One he hadn't used when they were together, to make "the struggle" more real for him.

She'd scrimped and saved for their apartment, worked

extra shifts at the yoga studio when the water bill was overdue. And he'd had money the whole time.

All of which he'd threatened to use, if she tried to take any of "their" belongings when she left. Her ex's claim of joint property might be flimsy, but it wasn't like Cora had the money to fight his family's high-profile lawyers. Something the jerk had thrown in her face more than once when she'd argued that she'd had just as much right to any of it as he did.

In the end she'd caved. It was easier, even though it stung to grab the few things he hadn't cared about and walk out.

Everything she could claims as hers was in the duffle bag on her back.

And this man's bank accounts made more in interest every second than she made in a year. Still, there was no need to act like her salary was nothing, even if it was to him.

Cora squared her shoulders. Part of her ached to tell him to let her stay until the storm abated and then cut her a check for three and a half months of work. He could afford it after all. But the other reason she was here was to find *The Ringlet Lady*. It was the last thing she could do for her dad.

"It may not be an issue for you, Mr. Winthrope, but I signed my name to a contract. As I see it, I am bound to it until you formally break it. Point me in the direction of my room, let me know where the kitchen and the art gallery are and I will be out of your sight as much as possible."

"I do not want a houseguest." The growl didn't surprise her but she was not backing down now.

"Well, I am not breaking my contract." Despite his use of the word *houseguest*, she knew what she was. This was not her first time in a mansion. She was the help. Cora knew her place.

That didn't change the road's conditions. "Break it formally tomorrow if you like, but you have to house me for the night because there is no way that I can make it back down that icy mountainside."

"Icy?" Everett pulled the door open.

She let out a little squeal as cold blasted through the hallway.

"Why the hell did you drive in that?" Everett swung his full body facing her for just a moment before he shifted his stance, placing one side of his face toward the door.

"As I said..." She rubbed at her temple. Between the stress of the drive and the panic rising in her that he truly wasn't expecting her, a not-so-subtle pounding was starting. "I am contractually required to be here. So here I am."

"You could have died." The hint of worry in Everett's words was more than her ex had ever given.

How pathetic that I stayed his muse for so many years.

"Yes. But I didn't." The trip was over and she really didn't want to contemplate just how close some of her calls had been with the mountain's edge. "Now, if you would please show me my room and direct me to where I can get a cup of tea, I'd greatly appreciate it." Cora picked up her duffel bag and marched toward the staircase. He could show her where she was staying or she'd find a room herself.

She had signed a contract. It had not been rescinded as far as she was concerned, so she was staying for the night. Hopefully she'd be here long enough to close out her father's obsession with *The Ringlet Lady.*

Cora was halfway up the stairs before Everett's brain registered that the woman was serious. She was staying.

Of course she is. I can't throw her into the storm.

She shouldn't have driven up the mountain. The narrow roads were dangerous in the best of times. Tonight—tonight it was a miracle she wasn't a fiery mess at the mountain's base. Leaving tonight was out of the question, and she was likely here for several days, at least.

"Wait." His voice felt weird. He hadn't talked to anyone for longer than a few short video calls since Hannah, his private secretary, had left last week. He and Patrick Lowe, the vice president of Winthrope Wealth Management, communicated daily, but only via email and office chat links.

Hannah was the only one he ever spoke to. She'd dropped all the supplies he'd need for the next few winter weeks and glared at him when he told her that he'd decided to cancel the art restorer's contract.

Turning on the stairs, Cora looked toward him, her head tilted as he stood still in the shadows. "Yes?"

"I'll show you to a room." There had to be one available, right? If not, he could always give her his. Wasn't like he used it much anyway.

"That is the easiest option." Cora leaned against the banister and raised an eyebrow in his direction. "You coming?"

Such a simple question. There'd been a time where he didn't need to be invited to follow a beautiful woman up a flight of stairs. But that man had died with his father. The beast left in his place had been viewed by no one but Hannah for almost three years.

He kept the camera off during all video calls with Winthrope Wealth employees and clients. If they questioned the decision, they never did it within his hearing range.

"Mr. Winthrope?" Cora took a step toward him.

Her furrowed brows warned him that she was worried about him. That worry would turn to pity the moment his full countenance was on display. He'd watched it happen so many times the first year after the accident.

Even a few of the nurses had looked away in the early days. He'd heard them when they thought he was asleep commenting on how he'd been so attractive.

Been.

Such a haunting word.

"Your room is on the right, the family wing. The other... the other wing is off-limits to everyone."

She swallowed as he raised his chin, her gaze going to where people's gaze always went when they first beheld the angry scar that traveled from the top left of his forehead to the bottom of his jaw on the right side. The other scars, the ones covering his chest, his legs—those he could hide. But there was no hiding the damage done to his face.

The fact that the doctors had saved the sight in his right eye was a miracle. Or at least that was what they told him.

It was technically true but the crisp way he'd seen the world vanished that night. The ability to pull color mixes seemingly from thin air based on his mood and the shimmer of the sun was gone.

Colors didn't look right anymore. The shine, the shimmer, the life they'd had—it had vanished. Every piece of art he painted on the wall of his wing was off—no matter how he mixed the colors.

"Is that wing off-limits to you?"

"I was injured in the car accident that took my father's life. I do not discuss the scar."

"I didn't ask about it." Cora shrugged and pointed to the entrance of his wing.

His secret art stash. Roam was gone; everything was just a poor comparison. Yet he kept trying. The wing was where he tried—and failed—to feel alive, again.

"I asked about that."

"Why?" Everett had developed the stock reply about his scars the second he'd stepped out of the hospital. It was *always* the thing people wanted to know. Always, their first, second and third question. If he allowed it.

Until tonight.

He looked at Cora. Took her in. She was at least five-six. Bright red curly hair fell past her shoulders. Deep jade eyes seemed to pull at him as she held his gaze. No one looked him in the eye.

She does.

Heat flooded his body as he looked at her looking at him. She was calling to him just by staring at him. A fanciful thought, particularly on a night where she'd risked her life to get here, but it pulled at him.

She was different.

"Why do I want to know about an entire wing of a giant mansion that I am not allowed to visit? I mean, come on." Cora took a playful step in that direction.

He let out a growl. No one went there. No one but him and the paint pallets that no longer sang to him.

She stopped. "So that wasn't a joke."

"No." He stepped around the red-haired beauty. She was staying the night. And by the look of the storm, a little longer. He didn't need to get to know her, but he could be polite.

Probably.

"This way." He started up the steps and wondered what room to put her in. Hannah had told him she'd prep a suite for the art restorer. But that was before he backed out of the idea. In which suite should he deposit her?

He racked his brain, where might Hannah have selected? Snow Peak had more than twenty guest rooms and ten suites, not counting his own accommodations.

But most were closed up shells that never saw a human.

He probably should have paid more attention. But that lack of oversight was an indicator that he'd never really planned to follow through. He'd let Hannah take care of everything. The hiring. The communications. Everything for the art restorer.

Cora. Her name is Cora.

And Hannah was supposed to handle the contract cancellation and notify the museums she'd contacted that the Winthrope Collection wasn't going on tour after all. The art world was not going to be quiet in their disappointment, but there was nothing they could do about it besides complain.

Everything was too much. Every piece needed appraisal… and inspected to make sure it was in good enough condition to travel. And if not…restored.

A three-month job—just to take the inventory and determine what was fit to go on the road. He figured he could handle having someone here for three months. But in the end, his will had crumbled.

And she was here anyway.

"I… I'm…not sure that there is a bed ready." May as well be honest up front.

"Point me in the direction of the sheets then, Mr. Winthrope. It's not that hard."

He heard the huff in her tone. Not that he could blame her. They walked down the hallway, the lights turned on as soon as they sensed motion. His father had insisted on that little trick, and Everett was forced to admit that it came in handy.

When he slept, it was usually in his office. On the floor. Hannah swore it was penance but the truth was his back felt better on the floor when he woke than in the giant bed he'd once enjoyed.

Another twist of fate he didn't enjoy.

"This door has my name on it." Cora's voice echoed down the hallway and he turned to find her several steps behind him.

"What?"

"I said…this door has my name on it." She tapped on it and offered him a smile.

Before he could process more, she opened the door and stepped inside. "Thank you for your time, Everett. I'm tired. Why don't we meet up tomorrow to discuss the job."

It was not a question. Cora did not need a response from him. She nodded then closed the door.

He smiled. Smiled. Everett reached up, touching his lips to make sure what he was feeling was actually happening. His lips were curved. Not much, but more than they had been in years.

Cora had dismissed him. And if there was a note on the door with her name on it, she'd grabbed it off before stalking inside. So probably not.

Clever, beautiful and unimpressed by him.

Three things that used to be his kryptonite. Three things that, before the accident, would have had him chasing her down to get to know her very well. Three things that no longer mattered.

He put his hands in his pockets, tension pulsing though him. Only one thing ever came close to relieving it. Everett took one last look at the door. Cora was in for the night.

Time to head to his art wing.

CHAPTER TWO

THE LITTLE TEACUP in her drawing was off. She was tired. Exhausted…and the tea in her mug had gone cold long ago. Night one in the Snow Peak Estate was not going as expected.

Everett Winthrope had disappeared from society, but the man was still the CEO of Winthrope Wealth Management. The man was a genius with money management—if the whispered words she heard while repairing or appraising art for the ultrarich were accurate. She'd expected a house manager to answer the door. A quick tour of the grounds with expectations for what she was to do.

Where she was to go.

And not go.

This was not her first time in a mansion with rules on her movements. It was the first time the owner had answered the door. The first time she'd been led down a hallway by a billionaire, clearly flustered by the idea of where to put her.

She'd finally chosen a room at a whim and slipped inside. There were no sheets on the bed. An unsuccessful search for linens was how she found the kitchen. It was well stocked… but it looked like there was no cook.

Did Everett cook for himself? He must, there was no staff here. What billionaire lived without staff?

What *person* lived so alone? Surely it wasn't because of his face. His scar was prominent. The damage the accident caused painfully clear. But Cora couldn't imagine that was the reason Everett had locked himself away.

It certainly didn't diminish his looks. The man was stunning. The scar was unique, and she was certain many women, and men, would find it particularly attractive. A battle wound of sorts.

She tilted her head, looking at the teacup from a different angle and adjusting her sketch a little. Usually adding an image to her sketchbook eased the frustration in her mind. Tonight…tonight it was doing nothing.

"I see you found the kitchen."

Cora jumped and spun on the seat as Everett tilted his head in the bright lights. Yes, the kitchen was large, but Everett was huge. Six foot plus several inches, broad shoulders. Shaggy black hair that fell just over his ears. Large hands that…

Nope. Her brain wasn't focusing on any of those physical traits. It was the stealth irking her. How did he manage to sneak up on her?

"Sorry. I know I can be quite scary." He moved to the teakettle, grabbed the satchel from the tin she'd found and poured his own cup.

She closed her sketchbook, "Sneaking up on people isn't very nice, but this is your home." She watched him shift his stance, pointing most of his scarred face away from her. "Do I make you uncomfortable?"

"Yes."

She'd give him credit for honesty. It was a rare trait. Though softening the blunt tone might have been nice.

"I'll stay away from you as much as possible during your stay." Everett spun the spoon around his teacup—even though he hadn't added anything to it that she could see.

"Usually it's the staff that is warned to keep away." She leaned forward.

The man was a contradiction. A playboy turned recluse. A traditional pretty boy who now had an edge of roughness to him. From life, not the scar on his face.

She'd love to paint him. People were her passion. Capturing their essence. Her work would never hang anywhere, but in this moment, she could see the outline of his features in ink. Or softened by watercolors.

Or maybe even oils—though that was not a medium she'd be painting with anytime soon. Even with the windfall to her bank accounts from this job, there was no way to justify the expense.

Still, a tiny amount of gray mixed with Paris blue would capture the color of his gaze so easily. She mixed it in her mind.

Everett leaned against the counter. In fact, if he could slide into it, she was pretty sure the man would become part of the furniture.

"I'm not used to having people around." He lifted the teacup but didn't take a drink.

"Really? I had no idea." Cora winked, hoping it would lighten the tension radiating off him.

Everett started to turn his head, then shifted so his gaze was away from her.

"Your scar is pretty wicked looking." Cora lifted her teacup, but like him she didn't take a drink. Might as well address the elephant in the room.

"It's hard for people to look at." The soft words vibrated in the large room.

"Pish." Anyone that said such a vile thing wasn't worth knowing. Cora slid off the high chair and moved toward him, not giving him a chance to retreat.

Maybe that wasn't fair, but she was going to be here for over three months, and given the lack of staff, she would go mad with no one to talk to. She'd keep a professional distance but they would need to interact. Besides, it wasn't like the scar made him any less. So he needed to know it didn't bother her.

"Cora..." Everett held up a hand, blocking out the right side of his face.

She ached to pull it away, but she was already pushing a lot in her first few hours.

With the weather he is unlikely to throw me out.

Still, this was a gamble. "It's not hard to look at. *You* are not hard to look at." There was more truth in that statement than she wanted to admit. Everett Winthrope was a hottie.

Dark hair. A chiseled jawline, broad shoulders. The scar was unpleasant only because it was clear how much pain had caused it. And it had to remind him that he'd lost his father, too.

Pictures of her dad could bring tears to her eyes. His favorite song, hell, even pizza—his favorite food—had been banished from her diet after his passing. Somehow it didn't taste good if she wasn't sharing it with her dad.

Justin had called her a baby when she'd broken down over the pizza he'd gotten just before they'd broken up.

But those were things she could avoid to keep the pain at bay, particularly now that her awful ex was out of the picture. Whenever Everett looked in the mirror, he had the reminder that his father wasn't with him.

"I know what I look like."

She almost missed the growly greetings. At least she could get angry at those. These words just made her want to hug him. Tightly.

Cora crossed her arms and barely controlled the urge to stamp her feet. "I don't believe that. I swear, you're acting as though looking at you will make me run away. There is nothing that is going to chase me from the premises tonight—particularly your face."

"How much of that decision is weather based?" There was the hint of a chuckle on the edge of his last words as he lowered his hand.

Good. If Everett was laughing that was progress. Her father had called her his little jester. Justin hadn't had a nickname for it, but he'd recognized her attempts to make him laugh when he was in one of his dark moods. He had not appreciated it.

"No more than 20 percent. Usually it would be none, but you weren't on the road up here. I thought I was going over the edge at least three times." She shuddered, not able to joke about actually getting back on the road.

"Why come up here at all?"

What must it be like to have the world be fine if you backed out of a contract? To cut someone a check for more than a hundred thousand euros because you no longer wanted to do whatever you'd legally bound yourself to?

She wasn't sure how much money one needed in the bank account for that to be true. But Cora knew it was more than she'd ever have.

Rolling her eyes, she shook her head. "Because, unlike someone standing in this room, money is an object of my concern." At least he had the decency to look ashamed of the comment he'd just made.

Good.

"Besides, no one has seen the complete Winthrope collection in generations. This is an art restorer's dream. Since both of us are avoiding actually drinking our tea, I don't suppose you want to show me where the collection is? Save me from wandering the halls tomorrow." She was not going to bring up the fact that he'd wanted her to vacate the premises. Not going to remind him that he'd told her he'd canceled the contract.

And that she'd called his bluff and told him to follow through tomorrow.

Everett looked at his cup of tea, then hers over on the counter before he let out a sigh.

"I suppose, since you're here to categorize the collection and mark any restoration and repair needs, you'll need access to the gallery." Everett set his cup down, his blue crystal gaze holding hers for just a moment. "You need to step back."

She jumped, moving several inches in the initial flight. "Right." Cora nodded. "Right." She'd not realized that she'd gotten so close to him to make her point.

How had that happened? Sure, she was trying to make him more comfortable, but she'd learned the hard way to keep her distance from people. How many times had she seen her father scammed by someone who knew he wanted information about *The Ringlet Lady*?

And Justin…he claimed to love her, called her his muse, used her limited funds then dumped her when he no longer needed to "play" the starving artist role. People wore many faces and most of them were lies.

"This way." Everett headed for the door of the kitchen.

"Wait." Cora grabbed his cup and then reached for hers. "Might as well clean up our mess." Her father had never minded the clutter. In fact, if she hadn't done the cleaning when they lived together and hired a housekeeper to check in on him twice a week after she'd moved out, she didn't doubt that the clutter would have overrun him within weeks.

"I'll get it, Ms. St. Stevens. I planned to come back down here after I show you to the gallery. Leave it. I'll take care of it."

"But—"

"It's two teacups and a kettle, Cora." Everett pushed through the kitchen door and she had no choice but to follow.

* * *

Cora was already here. That was why he'd gone ahead with her idea to see the gallery. Something she definitely didn't need to see if he was canceling the project.

Everett liked her. He was oddly comfortable with her in the kitchen. When she'd stepped up to him and looked at him dead on, he'd thought she was going to cup his cheek. A ridiculous idea—but in that moment he'd craved touch.

It would pass.

She was the first person besides Hannah not to scare at his scar. And Hannah didn't technically count. The older woman had been his father's private secretary and stepped into the role with him when he'd taken over Winthrope Wealth Management.

She'd known him as a boy, rushing into his father's office desperate for attention, and as an angry teen, still desperate but seeking that attention in all the wrong ways.

The man he was today would make his father proud. Hopefully. This man had added much to the Winthrope family coffers. The wealth management firm had a waitlist that would last generations. Access to Winthrope Wealth Management was one of the few things people whose great-great-great-grandchildren would never have to worry about finances couldn't buy their way into.

It infuriated the waitlist, but they never took their names off.

Everett had accomplished everything and more that his father wanted. And he hated the man he saw in the mirror. But he was continuing his father's legacy. Growing it.

No grounds for disappointment—even if his father wasn't here to see it anymore.

"What are your favorite pieces?" Her words were soft, full of awe at the expectation of what was to come.

"I don't have any." Cora's deep sigh didn't surprise him.

The gallery was the thing his father had bragged about most. To clients. Partners. Individuals seated next to him at charity events. Everyone got to hear about the Winthrope Collection.

Sometimes he'd dangle an invite. But to the best of Everett's knowledge, he'd never let anyone besides family into the gallery hall. After all, the collection's unavailability was what made it interesting. The unavailable art a way to boast to those who could have almost anything.

In the year after his father passed, a few pieces every other month had arrived. Deals his father had set in motion before the accident. Not a single piece spoke to him.

But nothing did these days.

"You must have one."

"I don't, though. I didn't acquire any of them. They are part of the family estate. An asset—"

"Art is not an asset." Cora cut him off.

Of course it was. That was a difficult thing for some people to hear, but it didn't change the truth.

The sad thing was that once he would have agreed with her. Hell, he'd realized part of his father's problem with Everett's art was that others made money from it. Sometimes he wondered whether, if he'd used the art studio his father had stocked with the best money could buy to create pieces he could hang in galleries, demand a price for, *then* his dad would have loved his work. Or at least seen it as valuable.

It wasn't possible to argue with a memory, but if he could ask his father's ghost one thing and guarantee an answer then that was what he'd demand to know.

Unfortunately, the pieces in this gallery were assets. He'd not acquired a single piece. They didn't make him feel a thing. They were bought for how much they were worth and how much they *would* be worth, if hidden away for a few decades.

"If you can't see the beauty in the pieces why not share

them with the world? After all, they are still assets—if you think of art that way—when in the care of museum specialists. But then others can enjoy them."

He reached the door of the gallery. He should open it. Should let her walk through and see the pieces. But once Cora was inside, there was no reason for him to seek her out.

"Why are you here, Cora?" He leaned against the door and forced himself to face her gaze. She said she didn't care about the scar—and to her credit she didn't look away. That was far too exciting for him.

"To catalog the Winthrope Collection. Make any notes about restoration needs, and update insurance paperwork. I've done the job for other clients." She recited exactly what was in the contract.

"And what were the reasons those clients were asking for the catalog and insurance papers?" He should just open the door…but he wanted her to think better of him. Weird.

"It varied. They were gathering information to get the estate in order as a patriarch or matriarch was getting up in years." Of course there would be a multitude of reasons she might name.

"I'm thirty-three." No need for a succession plan. Not that there was anyone to leave the vastness to.

"Yes. And at the peak of physical health." She gestured to his body then cleared her throat. Pink coated her cheeks as she bit her lip.

He had to take a deep breath. It had been forever since anyone blushed in front of him like that. If he wasn't careful, ideas might start brewing in his mind. She was here for three and a half months. She was a guest. So what if she was the first person in years to look past his scar, to call him out, to make him smile. "So if not for estate purposes…?"

"Are you actually loaning out pieces? This collection

hasn't been seen by anyone—" Cora laid a hand over her mouth. "I hoped but…really?"

"Exactly, I am not sure what is going, and I will not handle it personally but before parts of it go on tour, I need everything in place. I like my privacy but this is a necessity." *Necessity* was too strong a word, particularly because he'd tried to cancel the contract. But no need to worry about semantics now.

Cora lifted her chin, "I take my nondisclosure agreements very seriously."

"Did you sign an NDA?" There'd been a time where everyone who stepped into the Snow Peak Estate had an ironclad NDA. His father was ruthless with the privacy of this place. Since only Hannah visited regularly and he trusted her, he'd not considered them for a while.

Though anyone dealing with the wealth management company signed one.

"Of course." Cora pinched her nose. "I'm sure you have other things to do—"

"I don't, actually." Everett felt the urge to smile, again. Weird. "Shall we see what is behind the doors together?" He opened the doors and stepped inside, then turned to watch Cora take it all in.

Her green eyes were wide. Her pink lips were open, the perfect little O. Her right hand was over her heart as she slowly looked at the pieces in the entry.

"Ooh."

The room did nothing for him. The art was pictures on a wall. The brush strokes pointless to his gaze. Silent images devoid of meaning.

For Cora they sang. He could almost hear the hum of beauty for her. A spark flickered in his cold soul. It would wither in the empty space soon enough. The flame had a better chance on a glacier surrounded by turbulent waves than in his soul.

The image of a candle in the wild popped into his mind. He could paint it. Bring it to life. Maybe.

So many of the images he'd seen in his mind over the last three years were gorgeous. But he was no longer able to give them breath. They were dull. Half-life creations with no depth. No emotion.

Empty—just like him.

"Everett?" Cora's hand was soft against his. "Are you all right?"

No.

"Fine." He pulled his hand away from her soft touch, all too aware of how much he wanted to feel the connection.

Her eyebrows narrowed but she didn't call out the lie as she looked at the hand that had touched his before pushing them into the pockets of her jeans.

"The sculptures are down the hall. The corridor on the right. The left side contains modern art exhibitions. Not many. Father preferred what he called 'good' art."

"Good is subjective. It's one of the things I love about art. What speaks to one will have no meaning to another." Cora stepped up to an Edgar Degas painting featuring ballet dancers.

"This is the perfect example. There are little girls' rooms around the world with Degas's ballerina prints on the walls. But for me all I see is sadness. I know how much Degas hated women. I know that the life of the ballerinas in these images was the stuff of nightmares. Degas's works make my skin crawl. But they are masterpieces. Someone else seeing this would squeal with excitement."

Cora shrugged and moved on to the next painting.

"Who is your favorite artist?" He wasn't sure why he asked. There was no reason for him to care. The CEO of

Winthrope Wealth Management shouldn't care. These were assets. He'd said it himself.

"Maybe one of their pieces—or dozens given how my family, and particularly my father, collected—is here. I know it's late but if you fancy a certain artist there's a very good chance a piece—or three—is here."

Cora offered a soft smile as she looked down the seemingly endless hallway. "You don't have a piece by my favorite artist."

He should leave it alone. Should, but before he could give his good-night, he heard the words, "There are more than a thousand pieces on this estate. Even if they're obscure, the odds are good that my father found them."

"My favorite artist produced only eleven works and they're on the sides of bakeries and businesses, not in hidden hallways up a mountain."

"Roam." His artist's name slipped from his lips. No. She couldn't mean him. She couldn't.

Cora clapped and spun around. "No way." Her smile was brilliant. The curve of her lips a little uneven. Her cheeks full and her eyes bright. Beauty defined.

If I put her on the wall, could I capture the shades of green in her eyes?

"You know Roam?"

Better than anyone.

"No one knows Roam." He'd made sure of that. A pointless concession to a father who'd never liked the art anyway. "The artist was never identified. Besides he disappeared years ago." Heat was racing up his neck. He did not discuss the side of himself that had gotten his father killed, hadn't uttered the name since the night on that rain-slick road. That part of his life was gone.

He was the CEO of Winthrope Wealth Management. Nothing more.

Cora rolled her eyes to the ceiling. “I wasn’t asking if you knew Roam the person. I am well aware the individual behind the images is unknown. I wrote my university thesis on the artist.”

“Complaining about him tagging buildings.”

“No.” Cora crossed her arms. “Unlike some people, I think Roam’s works are modern masterpieces. It’s why they’re my favorite artist—as I said. Plus, I’ve never owned real estate. Maybe if I did, I’d be ticked off by the impressive artwork created quickly and without being seen. But I doubt it.”

He ached to know what her thesis topic was. Hell, part of him even wanted to pull her into the closed wing of the estate. Show her that Roam hadn’t stopped.

Except that wasn’t true either.

Everett still used his spray cans. But he was a shadow of the artist he’d been. The hints of the fire that had driven Roam years ago were there. It was those tiny echoes that kept the spray can in his hand. Faint wisps of hope he wished would finally die. Maybe then he could finally walk away from the closed-off wing.

“I’m going to walk through here. Get a lay of the land before I start working tomorrow.” She bit her lip and looked down the hall. “Do you want to join me?”

Yes. But he wasn’t going to. Not now. Emotions he’d buried in the twisted wreckage years ago were bubbling far too close to the surface.

“No, thank you. I need to see to some work before I call it a night.” Lies. Everything was done. He finished work early nearly every day. The company practically ran itself now. Algorithms he’d developed to monitor the international markets ran the wealth side, and he had a crawler on the internet that looked for specific words to identify potential start-up companies of interest. He talked to clients—rarely. His father had answered every call to calm their ridiculous fears of losing it all. Everett did no such thing.

He held weekly video meetings with the staff and took conference calls with clients once a week. But mostly his time was his own.

And what have I done with it?

If he stayed here…well, he wasn't sure what would happen, but he needed to be somewhere else. Somewhere away from Cora.

"Good night, then." She nodded and started down the hallway.

"Good night, Ms. St. Stevens." He turned toward the door, very aware that if he didn't leave this instant, he'd find some reason to stay.

CHAPTER THREE

EVERETT STARED AT the computer screen. The spreadsheets showed growth on all the markets. Not a surprise—once you reached a certain stage of wealth, loss was difficult to achieve unless you were reckless.

And Everett was never reckless.

Even when he was tagging buildings, he'd had a meticulous plan. A design he knew he could do in under an hour. He knew exactly which hour would give him time alone. Who would see the image first. Everything.

Picking up the phone, he dialed Hannah's number. She answered before the first ring completed.

"Did the art restorer get there all right? The roads up the mountain must have gotten hit with the storm you had."

"Cora is here. I thought I told you to cancel that contract."

"You did." Hannah was tapping something out. The woman was the loudest typist he'd ever met, but it somehow gave her even more authority. "And I told you that if you want to actually share the works, as you have said repeatedly, then you have to follow through. You grumbled something and walked away. I took that to mean proceed."

That wasn't exactly how he remembered the conversation. "I wasn't expecting her."

"You should have been. The suite next to yours is all set up for her. I cleared it out, put sheets on the bed and made it nice and homey for her."

"So it's not the blue suite?" That was where Cora had stopped last night. His great-grandfather had named the guest rooms after colors. His grandmother had taken it to the extreme and each room was furnished only in that shade. Given that the estate had far too many guest rooms, some of the choices were extreme. No one stayed in the mustard room. No one needed that much dark yellow in their life.

"No. The suite beside yours is the largest. It has an office and to the best of my knowledge it is the only one with sheets. I left the notes on your desk. I swear, Everett, if it's not on a spreadsheet you created you just don't register it anymore. You are more than the CEO. And Patrick Lowe is more than willing to step in. If you'll let him."

More than the CEO.

That had been Hannah's mantra for a year now. She didn't know about his art wing. But it was easy to see the worry in her features every time she was here. She thought he pushed himself too much. Urged him to let Patrick take on more. The vice president was more than capable, but Everett couldn't step away. Not yet. Maybe not ever.

"So you're telling me that my guest slept in a room yesterday with no sheets." He was staying focused on Cora. Hannah's thoughts on his life choice could wait for another day.

"Cora St. Stevens is your employee, not a guest. And yes. I am telling you that she slept in a room with no sheets yesterday. No towels in the bathroom." He could hear Hannah's exasperation and knew she was probably pinching the bridge of her nose.

"Everett Winthrope."

"I'll take care of it." He blew out a breath. He hadn't seen her this morning, but he didn't expect to. Hannah had hired Cora, that meant the woman was beyond professional. She'd indicated she'd worked on multiple estates. He knew the expectation for the "help"—as so many referred to people—was to work without being seen.

She asked me if I wanted to join her in the gallery.

Because he wasn't leaving. She'd said she was staying to get her bearings and he'd hovered. He'd wanted more connection. Needed more. For the first time in forever.

His focus was on how she made *him* feel. He hadn't considered her feelings. If he could go back in time and slap himself, he'd take the option.

She needed a room. A real one. Now.

"You better take care of it." Hannah waited a second. "Anything else?"

"No. Thank you." He hung up and looked around the office that was more his bedroom than the one next to Cora's suite. He ran a hand over his face, hating the taut skin under his fingers. The scar no longer ached; it wasn't bright red anymore either. But it was a reminder of why he was at the helm of this business.

A soft knock echoed at the door.

"Come in, Ms. St. Stevens."

"Good morning. I am sorry to put you out, but…" She bit her lip and straightened her shoulders. "I—"

"Need a room with bed linens and towels?" Everett tilted his head.

Color coated her cheeks and she stared at the floor. "I was so cold last night and you weren't expecting me and I need this job and I just panicked when it was clear that you didn't know I was coming and I…" She balled her fists, then met his gaze again. "I'm sorry."

"You have nothing to apologize for." Everett stood and she took a step back, shock frozen on her face.

He had dated a socialite who told him she never apologized to her staff. He couldn't remember the horrid reason, but that had ended their short relationship. Unfortunately he knew her beliefs were far from uncommon among those whose assets could buy anything.

"I was not exactly welcoming." That was an understatement but at least he was acknowledging the issue.

"You weren't that bad." She grinned. "You did take me to the gallery, ask me my favorite artist, and you cleaned up the tea."

Minor things. And mostly because he'd had a strange urge to spend time with her. It didn't make sense, but as she stood before him, it was still there.

"I spoke with Hannah this morning. She confirmed that the contract was not rescinded and that she set your suite up before she left for the next few weeks. I will show it to you now." He moved toward her.

Cora nodded. "Thank you."

They moved down the hall and he stopped at the blue room. "We should grab your stuff from here and the car."

"Oh, there's nothing in the car. The duffel bag is all I brought."

"You're here for a little over three months. At least." How could she only have one duffel bag?

"At least?" Cora raised one of her brows. Her face focused on him. Just him—not the scar. "Are you already thinking of extending the contract? Nice." She playfully stuck out her tongue but her eyes were downcast.

He chuckled at the silly motion. The rumble in his chest was deep and fleeting. Everett raised a hand like he could catch the laughter. Trap it to figure out how to make it come back on command.

"Why did you only bring one duffel bag for this assignment, Cora?" He opened the door, let her step in and leaned against the doorframe while she gathered the few things she'd brought.

"I assume I have access to a laundry facility. I wear paint

overalls when working. My main equipment is magnifying glasses for basic inventory tasks. Not like I'm expecting to have to go to anything fancy while here, so I packed light." She grabbed the beaten-up duffel and threw it on her back. It was large. Giant even, but there was something about the way she'd answered the question.

That wasn't an answer. It was a statement and there was a hint of something underneath it. Whatever it was, she wasn't going to provide more. And he didn't deserve more.

"Well, if you need anything, ask. I can have it sent."

She pointed to the window. A thick layer of ice coated it and the mountain was snow for as far as the eye could see. "I think I'm the last one coming up that mountain for at least the next few weeks."

"Probably." He moved as she stepped to the door.

"So where is the suite with the office?"

"This way. Right next to my rooms, actually."

"Then how did you miss Hannah setting it up?" She shook her head as she stayed in step with him. "Too focused on CEO stuff?"

"Guess I wasn't very observant." That wasn't true. Or it hadn't been before he took over as CEO. Maybe now he really didn't see anything besides the spreadsheets and coins his father had cared so much about.

"Guess not."

He stopped at the entrance to her suite. "If you need anything, let me know. Seriously, Cora. I mean it."

"I think you do."

The Ringlet Lady wasn't in the gallery. She'd looked at every single image. Nothing looked like the Pierre Alarie piece. Nothing even came close to the descriptions she'd lapped up from her father's long discussions.

She'd sat on the floor of the gallery and wept for an hour.

Unable to control the tears. Swiping them away for what felt like forever as they flowed down her face, oblivious to her commands to stop. She'd said goodbye to the obsession her father had never let go. It was almost like losing him all over again.

Cora was surrounded by masterpieces no one had seen for decades. Masterpieces that spoke to her. Masterpieces that made her cringe. Masterpieces her father would not have appreciated because *The Ringlet Lady* wasn't here.

The last place he'd sought. The lifelong obsession that had cost him so much. It wasn't real.

She'd chased his dream. Followed it to the conclusion he couldn't. And she'd believed it was here. Believed she could give his memory a gift.

The mission was over. Done. Complete yet unfinished.

All the illusions were gone now. The hope. The dream. Dust in her heart.

Maybe her father hadn't wanted certainty. Because once you knew you couldn't unknow that your obsession was pointless.

Standing in the office in her suite, Cora ran her hand over the catalog the Winthrope Estate kept of its assets. The folder was thick but missing what many museums required. This was a list of assets. A ranking of how much a piece might fetch on the market. A boring document with nothing more than the name and potential earning capacity attached.

That's why I'm here.

Her job was to catalog the collection. Group it in a sense that wasn't dollar signs and make notes on what needed restoring so that Everett could do what he wanted with it. Other art conservators would treat this as the highlight of their careers. This was the moment they'd boast over for decades at tiresome dinner parties.

Instead of excitement, she was teary over a painting that

likely never existed. And when she wasn't focusing on the loss of a mythical painting, Cora was far too interested in the billionaire who'd not even really wanted her here.

After the tears finally dried, it was Everett's strong arms and half smile that had her fantasizing. A man she didn't know. A billionaire who lived alone.

He knows about Roam.

The artist completed eleven pieces. Eleven great works before vanishing forever. Her thesis had revolved around the likelihood that Roam had vanished because of family pressures. Each of the eleven pieces had a person or object away from the main image. A man looking through the window at the bakery while others inside looked at a wedding cake. A little girl's balloon hovering above as her mom dried the tears.

It was those touches that drew her eye. Those that made her sure Roam felt like an outsider. Like an accessory to life.

Her professor had told her she was projecting her own issues onto an artist who probably just got bored with a medium. He'd reminded her that bias leaked through all human emotions. He'd even insinuated that Roam might have moved on to something more acceptable—without realizing the irony of owning his bias there.

But her argument was solid—based on the imagery of standing apart—so her professor couldn't fail her.

Graffiti as a medium was misunderstood by many, a point she'd made in her thesis. Even the artists who were well-known in the medium were unknowns to most of the world.

Yet, Everett knows Roam's work.

That was a first. Justin thought her obsession with the artist was funny. A cute add-on conversation with his friends. Looking back at it, it was a way to make fun of her not being serious enough. Just like her art wasn't serious enough.

He'd picked on her chosen medium, watercolors, as pointless and "commercial." Like the goal of selling your work was somehow bad.

Ironic considering how many people purchased Justin's works these days.

She gathered the catalog. It was time to get started on the job she'd been hired for. Time to fully let go of her father's mission.

Starting down the stairs, she looked to the closed-off wing. A few paintings hung down the corridor. Frames visible.

Could The Ringlet Lady *be there?*

Cora tilted her head as she mentally counted at least six large frames. Surely a nude woman wasn't hanging in the forbidden hallway. It was wishful thinking.

But something was pulling at her. Begging her to walk toward them. To just make sure *The Ringlet Lady* wasn't there.

"Cora?"

She jumped and turned to find Everett staring at her. "Oh. You scared me."

"You're not the first to tell me that. Sorry." Everett tilted his head, turning his face so the scar wasn't quite as visible.

"*You* are not scary. But you do seem to have a very light foot. Good for sneaking up on people." Cora started down the stairs. She needed him to know that. He was a mystery. But he wasn't scary.

She looked back at him. His blue eyes held her gaze, and now her body wanted to move closer to him. Tall, dark hair, bright eyes. He was delicious. Someone should paint him.

Focus.

"I was lost in my own world."

Everett didn't comment as he pointed to the catalog under her arm. "Heading to the gallery?"

"Yes." Where else would she be going? "But before I do…" She pointed to the hall. There were images there. The odds were minuscule, but she had to ask. "Do I need to catalog the images in that hall?"

"No." He shook his head, crossed his arms. His blue eyes seemed to darken as he looked at the wing. "That wing is off-limits."

He'd said that—in nearly the same growly voice last night. But that was before she'd walked the gallery and not found what she was looking for. "I know. But I can see the picture frames. I'm here to catalog the estate and all its assets as you say." No matter what they were, they had some value.

"There is nothing of any value in that hall."

She hated to push. It wasn't her job. However, her father had died with "Snow Peak Estate" written on a note in his hand. She had to at least try. "With all due respect, I am a trained conservator. You might have a hidden gem—"

"No! Do the job you were hired for. That is the only reason you are here." Everett turned on his heel and headed for his office. "If you go into that wing, I will throw you off the estate. Contract or no contract."

The slam of his office door echoed in the empty hall.

"Right." Cora squeezed her eyes closed. She was here for a job. Last night was an aberration. Everett had chatted about Roam. Asked her about her favorite artist. He'd seemed interested. Actually interested. Not listening for a weakness to poke fun of.

This morning he'd seemed genuinely upset to realize that she was in unfortunate accommodations—because of her own actions. He was kind, to a point. The art wasn't his focus, it was the catalog. She needed to remember her place.

She was staff. Apart. Seen not heard.

She'd grown up in houses like this. Standing beside her father, looking longingly at the children around her. But she'd never been allowed to play with them.

Since her dad passed, she hadn't really belonged anywhere.

Her knees buckled but she didn't fall. Straightening her shoulders, Cora headed to the gallery. At least among the paintings she was in control.

Cora examined the Jackson Pollock *Number 5, 1948* through her magnifying glasses. The attached headlamp let her know the painting was in excellent condition. Unlike many of the artworks in this gallery, the Pollock was less than a hundred years old and had never been subjected to serious elements. It was as close to the way Pollock intended as possible.

The painting was last known to have sold in 2006 to a private collector. It was the only Jackson Pollock in private hands. If Everett made it available, museums would fight for the collection for this one piece alone. And there were so many others.

His father had purchased the piece for 140 million dollars, but the decades off market and behind closed doors raised the price. If it went to market today it would likely fetch at least two hundred million, maybe four hundred. An asset indeed.

She gazed down the hallway and tried to keep the panic taking control of her lungs. *Overwhelming* did not begin to describe the scale of the task.

It was the second piece she'd looked at in the six hours she'd been here. The first was a pencil rendition by Manet behind glass that had some wear on the edges of the paper but overall was in decent shape. The fact that Manet and Pollock were hanging next to each other showed how little care the Winthrope family had used when structuring this gallery.

His description last night was accurate in its simplicity. There was a room of sculptures. A room of modern art exhibitions and a nearly never-ending gallery of art. All seemingly hung in the order they were purchased. Despite its fancy lights and temperature regulations, this was a storage facility. A gallery in name only.

And there was no way she was going to get through more than fifty of the pieces in three months. And even that was an extremely lofty goal assuming everything she looked at was in excellent condition.

Something she knew wasn't the case from her cursory search for *The Ringlet Lady*.

Which meant Cora needed to talk to Everett. Set realistic expectations. Go over his actual goal. If he planned to lend out pieces, they could work out a theme. She could pick the ones that would be best. Make sure they were ready to go. And recommend a team come in to handle restoration for works that needed extra TLC.

Cora stood, stretching. Her stomach rumbled; a reminder that she hadn't had anything besides tea and toast hours ago. All right, first step: food. Next stop: Everett's office.

I could always stop there first. Get it over with.

Her stomach complained again and she was grateful for the reason to put off seeking Everett out a little longer.

Stepping into the kitchen she let out a sigh at the sight of Everett's back. Damn, the man was fine but why the hell wasn't he in his office?

Didn't all wealth management CEOs live and breathe spreadsheets, stocks and figures?

He has no staff, so he has to make his own meal.

Still. He could make it some other time.

It's his home. I'm the interloper.

"I have a stew going in the Crock-Pot and there are cold cuts in the fridge." Everett didn't turn around as he kept chopping something next to the sink.

"Thanks. I'll just grab a quick plate and get out of your hair." She needed to talk to him. Planned to talk to him. Now was a good chance but she needed more planning than walking in on him in an apron with the kitchen smelling of stew.

It was too fanciful. Too out of place. She needed this morning's beast not last night's growly but fine billionaire.

"That isn't necessary." Everett's voice was soft, the edge from hours ago gone.

A man who cooked was her kryptonite. Her father had never cooked. He claimed her mother had before she passed. Cora was less than six months old when her mother was struck by a drunk driver while out on her bicycle. She had no memory of the woman.

Her father had done his best but making dinner was not in his skill set. As soon as she was strong enough to pull open the fridge, feeding herself became her responsibility. Hell, she even had a burn on her upper arm from reaching over steam at ten because she didn't realize the danger.

Justin had cooked for her on their second date and she'd fallen for him hard and fast. Only to realize later she was holding her heart over the steam doing her best to ignore the burns he caused.

"Oh, but I need to get back to the job I was hired for." It was a petty response. She should probably feel bad for saying it. But she didn't.

Instead she headed for the fridge. It was well stocked, of course. She grabbed an apple, some grapes, cucumbers and hummus. Must be nice to get fruit and vegetables up a giant mountain no matter the season. She planned to take full advantage of that while she was here.

"Cora, I shouldn't have said what I did."

"No. You should have. I'm the help. It's a position I have been in most of my life. I know the rules. The fact that you don't have other staff doesn't change that. I have a contract. I will stick to it. However, in a few hours we need to talk actual expectations. Because this is not doable with one person in three and a half months. Even working seven days a week."

"Seven days?" Everett stepped away from the stove. His

apron was stained. Not dirty. Just stained from use. So the billionaire really did cook his own meals. Fascinating.

And he was apparently unaware of the particulars of her contract. "Yes. Did you read my contract?" If her life hadn't been in such shambles she might have negotiated for one day off a week. But probably not. She'd needed to see if *The Ringlet Lady* was here and one did not walk into such a private collection by seeming difficult. Even if you were just asking for humane conditions.

"No." Everett crossed his arms, his gaze falling to his shoes.

"Well, you're a busy man." She held up her plate. If she stayed any longer, she might start to feel bad for him again. He had every opportunity. Had the money.

Yes, he had a scar. Yes, he'd lost his father.

But millions of people would like to be where he was. With his resources.

"I'll find you later. Have a good day, Mr. Winthrope."

Cora's contract was a nightmare. It demanded ten-hour workdays Monday through Friday and half days on the weekends. That schedule hadn't been legal since workhouses were abolished.

How had this even happened?

Everett rubbed the dull ache at his temple as he leaned back in his chair. This was his father's contract template. The man had always boasted that anything done at Snow Peak Estate could be done in three months. Everett had considered it one of his father's most annoying brags.

And I didn't bother to look at the estate contracts when I took over.

Not that he'd had much reason to. The staff at Snow Peak had all either taken an early retirement package or his offer of job placement in one of the many estates his family owned around the world. He had a cleaning crew come in once a quarter to deep clean the largely empty property but that was a one-week job for a large team.

When Hannah had asked how he wanted to proceed with the art conservator hire, he'd said a standard contract—without bothering to look into what was standard at Snow Peak.

Cora had laughed when he'd mentioned extending it. Probably because the wage she was receiving meant she'd be comfortable for at least two years following the three-and-a-half-month stint.

A huge payout didn't make the contract right. Hell, the courts would probably even side with Cora if she wanted to push it. Though contract work was still woefully misused by many companies. And it would require a lawyer to take the suit. No small task given how fierce the team he'd assembled to protect Winthrope Wealth Management was.

He took one more look at the offending document then stood. Cora had said she needed to talk to him. It had been hours since she'd taken the fruit and veggies from the kitchen. The stew he'd prepared was ready for dinner tonight. He'd made sure of that.

Stepping into the gallery, he was pleased, and more than a little disappointed, to find her workstation abandoned. She should be done for the day. Should have found somewhere else to be.

But, man, he'd been looking oddly forward to finding her. Weird considering the difficult talk they needed to have. And the apologies he owed her. He'd not been welcoming.

This morning he'd been downright beastly. She'd asked about his art wing and Everett had panicked. Told her to do her job. He'd been a tyrant.

And she'd called him on it at lunch. Cora hadn't cowered.

She'd addressed him and put him in his place. It was refreshing. Exhilarating.

The Jackson Pollock was on her easel. A turned-off lantern attached to the frame and a pair of glasses on the floor.

He picked them up, noticing the extreme magnification they offered.

"Careful. Those are very pricey and I doubt the estate has an extra pair." Cora's voice carried down the gallery as she walked up the long hallway. Her focus was largely on the tablet in her hands.

"Surprised you noticed I was holding them given your focus." Everett tapped the tablet and pulled his hand back as a small frown crossed her brow.

Hands to yourself, man.

Even little ones knew that lesson. His attraction to her did not give him rights to encroach on her space.

"Sorry, Ms. St. Stevens. I touched your tablet without thinking. I've been out of social settings for years. I guess I'm rusty on my interactions with other people." He let out a sigh.

"You are. But you also have a ton of money and that means people look past it." Cora held her hands out and he placed the glasses in them.

"Most people would have given me a platitude." He liked that she hadn't.

Cora tilted her head. "Do you want platitudes? I was kind when I first got here—a day ago. I reached out and you put me back in my place. I'm here to do a job. I'll respond to you the way you want. I got the feeling it wasn't with platitudes."

Words were darts. The reason there was the saying that the pen was mightier than the sword. A weapon might kill you, but words, they could shred your soul and leave you a walking ghost.

"I want you to be you." Everett breathed the words out

while he stared at the Pollock. He'd never been a fan of Pollock's splatter paintings. He understood the expression of movement and the abstract art, but for him they never did much.

Cora let out a soft sigh. "Who are we really? Does any person truly know themselves?" Her brows furrowed and she pointed to the painting. "So we need to chat about the actual job. Your assistant wasn't overly clear in the scope of this work when I was hired. There is no way to do this in three and a half months, even with the schedule I agreed to."

"Why did you agree to that?" The question popped out but he wanted to know. Almost as much as he wanted to know why she'd offered the insight into not knowing herself.

How often had he felt unmoored in the world? A man floating on the expectations of his birthright while desperately seeking his creative function. Succeeding in the world's expectations hadn't offered him any more belonging than his creative side.

"Money." Her gaze hit the floor.

That was a lie. Or at least not the whole truth. But he was already pushing too much.

"Cora—"

"What is your goal with sending the art out?" She looked back at the tablet, made a few notes, then looked up at him.

"What?"

"What is your goal?" Her eyebrows narrowed as she gestured to the collection. "Are you hoping to highlight certain works? Do you want to show off the pieces most people thought they'd never see? Do you want to highlight particular art movements?" Cora pointed to the Pollock.

"This is the only Pollock held in a private collection. You have other pieces that are similar—"

"I know there are pieces here no one has seen. And no, I

am not looking to ship those out to highlight what the Winthrope Estate has hoarded."

"Why am I here, Everett?"

He hated that he was the only one with access to work that he knew others craved. Yet sending them out…part of it felt like a betrayal to his father. That was dumb and it shouldn't matter. He and his father hadn't exactly seen eye to eye on most things.

He'd taken on the legacy of Winthrope Wealth. This…this was something he needed to do.

"Because my assistant failed to cancel the contract?" He raised his brows, hoping the words came off like the joke he intended. Though it was true, too. If Hannah had listened, she wouldn't be here.

And he was very grateful Cora was in the gallery.

"Everett." Cora took in a deep breath. "What do you want me to do with my schedule? I can start at this end of the gallery and go one by one. I might, and it is a huge might, get through fifty or so paintings. But that depends on condition, age and—"

"You won't get through that many." He understood little of the art conservation world. But he knew that people spent years with one painting. Yes, his family's assets were well maintained. The gallery had top-of-the-line climate control but that didn't mean everything was in good condition.

If she was doing a good job—and the woman before him would do a great job—each piece would get at least two days. The older works considerably more.

"You really didn't expect someone to show up." Cora rolled her neck. "I get that."

"Do you?" Somehow, he couldn't imagine Cora locking herself away. The woman was funny, kind, gorgeous. She had to be the life of any party she attended.

"When my dad passed I—" she looked down the gallery

"—I locked myself in his place for three weeks. I claimed I was cleaning it, readying it for sale, but really, I was hiding."

Cora's jade gaze met his. "And I liked it." Tears coated her eyes. "I liked it a lot. I could have stayed there forever."

"Why didn't you?" He'd craved solace after his father's parting. Demanded it. Isolated himself away and everyone told him he'd hate it. He should.

But that wasn't his truth. It was easier to stay out of sight. To leave everyone behind.

"Because the world is full of hard days for everyone. Every human experiences loss. Whether you have billions in the bank or nothing. It is the human experience none of us can avoid. Life has meaning because it's fleeting. The world's colors change with grief but they are still beautiful. So I put my armor back on, I stepped into the world and now I am in the most restricted gallery in the world. That doesn't happen if I lock myself away."

Cora gestured to the gallery. "I am standing in that gallery with a billionaire finance bro who plans to do something with the artwork that he has no feelings for."

"When you say it like that, it sounds so bad." Everett playfully rolled his eyes to the ceiling.

"Come with me." She tilted her head and walked down the hallway.

He followed. This was not why he'd come. They needed to talk about her contract. Needed to renegotiate it…in her favor. But the command, the straightforward talk, it was what she'd given him the moment she walked into the estate. And it was impossible not to be drawn to it.

"Look at this." She pointed to a Manet.

He looked over the piece. It was like many of Manet's images. Loose brushstrokes, the world a little fuzzy. "What am I looking for?"

"A feeling."

"A feeling?" He crossed his arms and looked at the image. "I feel astonished that so many people like this type of art. My father loved Manet, Monet, Degas, Morisot…any of the European Impressionists, really."

"Is that astonishment and judgment because of your father or the painting?"

He opened his mouth then closed it. He'd never considered that his feelings were tied to his father. Taking a deep breath, he looked over the image, trying to see it with fresh eyes. It was one of Manet's two known self-portraits. He wore a tan suit, had a paintbrush in his hand and was looking slightly to the side.

"He feels off." The words fell from his lips.

"Off. Interesting." Cora's voice was a meditating sound as he gazed at the self-portrait.

"It's weird that he's in a suit. He's painting. When I paint… when I painted as a child, I mean… I got paint everywhere. It's almost like he's saying I'm here and this is me. I am in control." Everett cleared his throat. "Well, that was a lot of rambling words."

"They weren't rambling and you're right. It is different to be in a suit. It made you think. Once pieces leave an artist's studio they belong to the world. The feelings they engender belong to the world. So, what feelings do you want to send out? And how many paintings? Because there is only one of me."

"There is only one of you." The words were a breath, an ignition to the tiny flame she'd started when she first arrived. "I need some time to think on it. But not the Pollock. I know people really like him, but…"

"It's fine that you don't."

"But umm…this one." He pointed to the Manet. "I want this one in the collection."

"All right. I will put this one on the list and find some

complementary pieces. Now, what did you actually want to discuss?"

"Dinner. I have the stew ready. So, let's go eat." He pointed to the door.

"I'm not sure that's a good idea. I'm on contract."

"Yep. We're discussing that, too. But you and I are literally the only ones here. So, have dinner with me?"

"All right."

CHAPTER FOUR

CORA LOOKED AT the closed door to Everett's office. What Everett was she going to get today? The unsure of himself, scarred man who looked at the Manet painting yesterday with clear eyes for what she suspected was the first time. Or the gruff beast who'd opened the door and told her not to worry over the pictures hanging in the off-limits wing.

Last night they'd sat at the small kitchen table and said basically nothing. She'd waited for the conversation he said he'd sought her out for. But she was also very aware of how much she'd given away in the gallery yesterday.

Not intentionally. The words had just popped out. No one had asked why she'd hidden away after her father died. And no one had asked why she reemerged. She'd stepped back into her small studio at the Fredrick's, a New York–based auction house serving individuals with more money than they could spend in three lifetimes, as though nothing had changed. Gone back to work and continued with her life. The world kept spinning even though she was bereft.

Of course, it was unlikely that job was waiting for her when this was over. The only reason they'd let her take the sabbatical was because she was coming here. Fredrick's was hoping that more than one piece would come up for auction and they'd have inside information.

Her boss had not hidden his surprise when she'd announced that she'd taken the job and asked for the sabbatical. Her work had fallen after her breakup and her father's death, how could it not?

She'd seen no indication that Everett planned to sell anything, which meant Fredrick's wasn't going to get anything on its auction block. She wasn't even completely convinced he planned to loan the art out.

The door opened and she jumped back. Everett raised a brow and leaned against the doorframe. *Relaxed Everett today. Good.*

"How long were you planning to stand outside my door?"

"I don't know. I hadn't decided yet. Maybe you should go back inside and we will see." She started to stick her tongue out then thought better of it.

Everett smiled. It wasn't a giant grin and there was no one who'd describe it as "beaming" but it was there.

Her insides shifted as she looked at him. The man was moody, but hot as hell. And when he looked at her with that soft gaze, her legs weakened just a little.

Once upon a time, the man had dated most of high society and she could see why. He was...disarming. When he wanted to be.

"I was coming to find you."

"You were?" That was a dumb statement. He'd told her last night that they'd table the discussion on her contract until today.

"Yes." He winked, then stepped back into the office and showed her to a soft chair. The room was unexpected.

It was clearly his office but it wasn't the shades of gray she'd expected. There was color everywhere. Bright. Fun. Not the stereotypical billionaire financier setting.

"Who designed this room?" They'd understood color theory so well she was jealous of the faceless designer. Pieces that most wouldn't have chosen, fearing clash, were next to each other, complementing the brightness.

"I did."

"No way." She leaned forward and pointed to a brilliant blue vase. It had crocheted flowers in shades of orange and purple. "You chose that?"

"It's hard to get fresh flowers up here."

"I mean, I get that. Though, flowers are so…" She tried to think of a word besides *amazing*. Her dad had gotten her flowers for every birthday. She'd pressed the last ones he'd ever sent in the back of her sketchbook.

Justin had claimed flowers were a waste of money. Good for nothing. The moody artist was constantly riffing on things she loved and Cora had stayed. Happy to feel part of something.

Of course when she'd found him in bed with a beautiful blonde there'd been rose petals everywhere. He swore it was an art exhibit. That was sad enough but it was the flower petals on the bed. The bright red petals that had made her angriest.

She'd packed her bags that night. Letting him keep whatever he wanted.

"What is your favorite flower?" A simple question but she didn't have a good answer.

Cora couldn't say, *Whatever my dad got me*. Which was always what was on sale given how he sunk so much of his money into finding *The Ringlet Lady*.

Which doesn't exist.

That sad thought brought her back to reality. Last night their conversations had started with work and somehow they had ended with her forcing him to discuss the feelings a Manet self-portrait gave him.

An image she'd picked because it was one of her favorites. It wasn't considered by critics to be his best work but she loved the juxtaposition of the palette of paint in his hands and the nice suit. No artist painted in dress clothes but it was like he was making a statement to the world.

I am here. I am worthy.

She had no idea if Manet actually thought those things. Those were her hopes and emotions coming through. And when Everett had commented on the suit…she knew herself. If she wasn't careful, it would be far too easy for her to develop a crush on the man.

Grumpy and unavailable was her type after all.

"We aren't here to discuss flowers." She pulled her tablet out of the side bag that she carried with her while working. Pulling up her contract, she took a deep breath. The contract already required more working hours than any she'd ever had. But the paycheck made it worth it.

Mostly.

Still, there were only so many hours in the day.

"Adjusting my contract is allowed one time but I have to approve it."

"Understanding contract law," Everett said, leaning on his hands, "that is very…" he paused and a hint of red crept up his collar "…beneficial."

She was nearly certain he'd been about to say something else. Something with a little heat under it?

Or I'm just reading far too many spicy romances.

"I can't work more hours, Everett."

"Your damn right about that. This contract is atrocious. Today is Saturday and that means it's a day off. Sunday, too. And the week is only eight-hour days."

Cora opened her mouth but no words came out. "Everett, I already have too much in front of me in the gallery. If I cut back my hours…"

"You are cutting them back. That part isn't up for negotiation." Everett waved a hand. "And as for the many, many paintings and drawings in the gallery—"

"Don't forget the sculptures." She hadn't meant to interrupt. Hadn't meant to thrown in the little jest. It was just easy, and she was rewarded with another not quite full smile.

What would Everett look like if he really smiled? Really gave in to humor or fun?

Brilliant.

"The statues—how could I forget?" Everett winked and then AirDropped a contract onto her tablet. "The new contract outlines the expectation that you will select twelve pieces that are in good condition. Ready to go out now."

"Twelve?" That was doable.

"Well, technically thirteen. The Manet self-portrait is going. So twelve more." Everett tapped the pen in his hand, "If you have leftover time, then we can determine what else the gallery needs based on the length left on the contract."

"Any chance that includes rearranging the gallery?" Might as well shoot her shot while Everett was in a good mood. Yes, the Winthrope Gallery was a family selection but it was horribly organized. No thought. Just pictures thrown on a wall.

"Fine." Everett waved a hand like changing one of, if not the most, elusive galleries in the world was no big deal.

"Twelve pieces, plus the Manet." Cora ran over the items on the contract that had changed. Everett had marked the changes in red, that made it easy at least.

The hours were changed. The job description outlined to reflect what he wanted. And the payment. She was no longer being paid by Winthrope Wealth Management. Now it was a trust but that wasn't what was holding her eyes.

Cora stared at the number on the screen. The amount she'd agreed to was substantial—the new amount. It would change everything in her life. For three and a half months, that couldn't be right.

"The payment..."

"Will come from my father's estate's trust." Everett leaned closer, a spark in his eyes.

"I thought he hoarded artwork. Would he appreciate using the trust for me to ready pieces for transport?" She and her father had had their differences, particularly when she moved into Justin's place. He'd said the man wasn't good enough for her. A painful truth her ears hadn't wanted to hear and her heart hadn't been ready to accept. But she wouldn't tarnish the thing he loved most.

Of course since *The Ringlet Lady* didn't exist that wasn't even possible.

"Oh, he'd have hated this idea." Everett's deep chuckle echoed in the room. "He'd have railed against it and claimed that it was somehow lowering the value of the pieces."

"No. That isn't the case. In fact, sending some out might increase their worth if you choose to auction them."

Everett waved a hand. "I have no doubt that's true. But the main reason I want the trust paying you is purely selfish."

Cora looked at the contract. "I don't understand. I mean I won't turn down the increase in salary."

"You are here for three and a half months. Trapped for at least half of that. The mountain will be too treacherous to leave for at least the rest of this month. You are unable to travel to see loved ones during this period on your off days. The salary should reflect that loss."

"I don't have anyone to spend the days with anyway." She bit her lip as she continued to scroll through the document. No other changes seemed evident.

"I'm not in control of the trust. So, you'll be my guest, while working for the trust."

"Guest?"

"Guest." Everett crossed his arms as he leaned back in his chair. "I will admit that I've had little practice in the art of hosting for three years, but you aren't the help. You are a guest at Snow Peak working on behalf of my late father's trust.

"Are the changes acceptable to you?" Everett opened his hands and nodded to her tablet.

"Yes."

"Great. Use the stylus to electronically sign it, send it back to me and then, you are free for the rest of the weekend."

"To do what?" Cora signed the document and put the tablet back in her bag. "I don't mean that rudely, it's just. I, umm… I know where the kitchen is, the gallery, your office and my bedroom. And I know to stay out of the other wing."

Having free time was nice—in theory—but, if she had nothing to occupy her time then what was the point?

Everett clapped his hands and stood. "Right. First thing a host should do is show their guest around. And there is one place I think you might really enjoy."

Everett took a deep breath as he led Cora out of his office. The contract was signed. The trust was paying her. The wall of employer/employee was down.

In Cora's presence he seemed to breathe easier than he had since the accident. Maybe before. She didn't look at him and only see the scar. Didn't address him with the sycophant subordination that seemed to come when your bank account had so many zeros.

It was refreshing.

"So there is a library through here. I prefer to read on my device so unfortunately it doesn't have any new releases." Everett pointed to the closed doors that he rarely stepped through.

"I also read on my tablet. I loaded more than a hundred audiobooks and podcasts on it before coming. I like to listen to them while I'm examining the paintings."

There was one place he wanted to show her. The room he thought she'd likely spend much of her time in. So he didn't bother opening the library doors.

"What do you listen to? Art history?"

Cora wrinkled her nose. "Do you only read finance books?"

"No. Sometimes I also read books on leadership." He was trying to break the cycle of dictatorial leadership that his father had brought to Winthrope Wealth Management.

"Leadership…ooh." Cora's giggled. "Is there a lot of room for leadership here by yourself?"

"No." He laughed, too. Without explanation it did sound ridiculous. "There are online forums discussing ways to survive three years at Winthrope Wealth Management."

"What!" Cora stopped and crossed her arms. "I thought Fredrick's was bad, but our online forums are only about surviving the first year."

"In a weird way, it's nice to know it's not just Winthrope Wealth Management."

"It shouldn't be any place." Cora tilted her head and pointed at him. "So you're reading leadership books and hiding away from the actual office."

Another sentence full of darts. The woman spoke truths. "I have instituted several policies and fired the managers with the worst survey results. It's a slow process."

"One that might go faster if you were in the London or Paris offices." Cora's jade gaze caught him. "Why aren't you in the London or Paris offices?"

"I could also be in the New York office." Pink coated her cheeks as he pointed out the office she was leaving out. The office in the city she'd come from.

"You could." Cora cleared her throat. "So, why aren't you?"

"I don't know." Everett looked at the giant entry door of

Snow Peak Estate. The first year of his recovery traveling had been spent in hospital. So many surgeries and physical therapy appointments.

The second year—the second year he was getting used to his new normal.

Now three years later, he didn't have an excuse.

Her palm brushed his. The heat of her touch traveled up his arm and burst through his chest. He looked down at her.

Cora's eyes were bright, hopeful. Sea green with flecks of amber in the center and hints of sapphire on the edges. He could re-create that color of her eyes. Throw them up on the wall. He knew it.

"Come on. I want to show you the studio."

"Studio?" Her mouth opened and he stared at her lips for a split second before forcing his gaze away.

"You think a family obsessed with art collection doesn't have an art studio?" Everett enjoyed the near skip Cora did next to him.

"Not that it gets any use. I don't think my father ever stepped into it."

"Did you?"

"Yes." The admission was out before he could think it through. "I was instructed in most of the classic methods. Oils, acrylic, gouache and ink."

"And none of them spoke to you?"

"I didn't say that."

"You didn't have to. It's in your tone. The grumpy Everett." Cora smiled.

"Grumpy?" He looked over at her, enjoying the smile on her lips.

"Yes. You are very moody." Cora playfully rolled her eyes.

"I prefer the term *brooding*." Everett hit her hips with his and immediately stepped to the side. The action was unintentional.

He'd been an excellent flirt when he was in college and then after. But he'd always planned it out. With Cora things just seemed to come to the surface. Easily and without thought.

Because I've locked myself away.

It wasn't her. Or rather it was. But only because she was the first one to breach his walls. Right?

"Brooding. Moody. Two sides of the exact same coin. The point," she said and tapped her hip against his, "is I can tell by your tone that you aren't interested in those mediums."

She was right, but it was a little disconcerting that she could read so much from what he thought was a simple statement.

"Did you ever try graffiti art?"

"Yes." There was no point in lying. "I really enjoyed it for a few years but then…" The words died away.

"The accident?"

"That was part of it." Everett pursed his lips as they walked up to the studio.

"What was the other part?"

"My father wanted me focused on other, more productive, pursuits." His stomach turned as he remembered those final moments. The words confirming that he was a disappointment.

He wasn't now. But his father never saw the man he'd become.

The studio door came into view and he was grateful for the reprieve he'd get.

"What's your favorite medium, Cora? I saw the pencil drawing the first night."

"Oh, that was nothing."

"It was an impressive rendering of the mug."

"The handle was off and the dimensions," Cora shrugged. "I was tired and just goofing off in my sketchbook."

"You didn't answer my question." Everett grabbed the door handle and leaned against it. "What's your favorite medium?"

"Watercolors is what I use most. And I love oils." She looked at the door behind. "But I rarely got to use them."

"Why?" Damn, he wanted to stuff that question back in. Oils were notoriously expensive. She had exactly one bag of belongings and had agreed to a nightmare contract. It wasn't rocket science.

"Cost prohibitive. Plus, I grew up in other people's homes. Rich folks don't exactly want a child or teen who isn't their own playing with paint that will stain everything." There was laughter in the words but her body held none of the glee. "Watercolors are easy to clean and store."

"Well, there are tons of oil paints in here." Everett opened the door, enjoying the showmanship motion. The room was bright. Windows covered all three sides looking out to the mountain on which the estate rested.

"Oh."

He watched Cora taking it in. The raised hand on her chest. The parted lips, the huge eyes. It was like that first night in the gallery. Watching her, getting to see the reaction to what was ordinary to him through her eyes. It was life changing.

"How are you not in here all the time?" Cora walked to the easels set up in the center of the room. Four of them, waiting for artists that never came.

"Finance stuff." Numbers, spreadsheets, bank information. For some people those things sang. For him…for him it was the responsibility he'd inherited on that slippery road three years ago.

"Everything you might need." He walked over to the wall and opened the first cabinet showing off every size canvas possible. "Canvas…" he opened the cabinet next to it "…watercolors…" Then he pulled open the one next to it. "Oils."

Cora moved to that cabinet. "These are all just housed here. Just sitting?"

"Yes." He grabbed two canvases. "Paint with me?"

Cora took one of the canvases from his hand. "You do not have to ask me twice." She put it on the easel and then walked to the oil cabinet.

"Wow." Her hand reached out, hovering just above the paints. "There are so many."

"My art instructor was allowed to purchase and use whatever he wanted to teach me. The man used that perk of the job to the fullest extent." Everett grabbed a pallet of watercolors and took them over to the easel beside Cora's setup.

"Watercolors?" She asked the question without turning her gaze from the oils. "That's a classic paint medium. But you didn't mention it."

"My instructor thought water paints were for girls. I disagree but it meant that my instruction in them was cursory at best." He walked to the water station, filled a mason jar with water for cleaning his brushes and a spray bottle for keeping the paints wet. "Watercolors are playful. I don't have to think with them. I can let the water do the work."

If he wasn't using spray cans for graffiti this was the medium he gravitated to. His instructor, a reed of a man whose eye was always on the mistakes Everett made, had hated the medium.

As a child and teen, Everett assumed it was because the man wasn't very good at it. And he wasn't but, with the wisdom of adult eyes, he suspected the frustration went far deeper. Most likely there was a lover or friend skilled in the medium who wasn't teaching "rich brats."

Or maybe he was just an ass.

He set up his station and started to drag his brush along the canvas. A shade of green that was almost the exact shade as Cora's eyes. He mixed it again, smiling as she set up a palate of oils and started working herself.

This was the best way to spend an afternoon.

CHAPTER FIVE

EVERETT HAD PAINTED last night. The spray can alight in his hands. Last night he enjoyed creating, again. *Finally*. The image easy to pull from his mind to the wall. Yesterday had been as close to perfect as possible.

Painting in watercolor while Cora mixed oils and worked slowing on a landscape. They'd said very little. Two artists just working side by side.

And he hadn't been finished. His mind racing with ideas to cover the walls of the wing off-limits to everyone but him. After eating dinner with Cora, he'd grabbed his spray cans and spent hours letting the image take shape.

A woman at an easel.

Cora at the easel.

She was in profile and he, Roam, was standing off to the side holding a spray can. Watching.

It was the first true Roam piece he'd produced in years. The colors were vibrant. The picture of perfection.

Today was Sunday. Another day off. Though he'd check his email after coffee and breakfast.

Stepping into the kitchen he was surprised to see Cora at the center aisle, a bowl of yogurt pushed to the side, a cup of coffee in one hand, as her pencil moved swiftly.

She wasn't paying any attention to him. All her focus was on the page before her. The art was calling to her.

Just like it had to him last night.

He wasn't going to interrupt that. He had no plans for the day. So he leaned against the wall and just watched her. Her tongue pushed out from her lips as she tilted her head and squinted at the paper.

Everett couldn't see what was on the paper, but whatever it was had Cora enthralled.

Taking a deep breath, she smudged a line then closed one eye, then the other. After a second she repeated the process with the other eye. Artists had their own processes. He clicked a pen while looking at a building or wall.

Did the pen have any meaning? No. But if he wasn't clicking it while planning the piece there was no way to birth the piece. There was no way to explain the need, it simply was.

She looked up, pulled her head back and offered a small smile.

Cora's smile was the best way to start the day.

"Good morning, Everett."

"What are you working on?"

"Oh, nothing." Cora closed the sketchbook, pink cresting across her cheeks.

"Are you embarrassed of sketching?" They'd spent all day in the studio yesterday. His watercolor had been an expression of green. An abstract playing with the color. Nothing fancy but it was fun. Cora had stood at her easel all day, too.

So there was no reason to worry over a sketch.

"It's just not very good." Cora looked at the teacup. "I sketched the mug the first night I was here, and the handle was wonky. Now it's the side."

She stuck her tongue out at the teacup on the counter.

"Can I see it?"

Cora shrugged and flipped her sketchbook open.

The image on the pad was perfect—technically. "It's fine."

"Yep. That is what Justin always said." Cora closed the book, stood and moved to the sink to rinse the cup. "'It's fine, Cora. Fine. You don't have the spark and that's fine.'"

She said the words in mock tone that he suspected was Justin's—whoever that was.

"That was a lot of *fine*s."

"Yep. Four little letters." She held up her hand, showing four fingers. "F-i-n-e." Cora wrapped her arms around herself after spelling out the offending word. "I hate that word."

"Then I apologize for using it." He'd meant no harm. The teacup was technically well-done. It didn't have spunk or spark, but it was a quick sketch of a teacup she had no attachment to.

"No." She bit her lip as she looked at the sketchbook. "It's my problem."

Everett stepped up to her, leaning his body on the counter beside her. Not touching but close.

"Just because your instructor thought you had no spark doesn't mean they're right."

"Justin is my ex-fiancé." She let out a little chuckle. "I can't imagine him teaching anyone."

"Your ex-fiancé?" Her ex-fiancé, the man she'd planned to spend the rest of her life with had told her she didn't have the spark. The bastard!

"Yep. I walked in on him six months ago banging the neighbor. He said it was an art exhibit and when I called bullshit on that, he blamed me for my distance after my father died the month before. Then I found out he'd lied about other things..." She closed her eyes, leaning her head back against the cabinet.

He didn't think, Everett just wrapped his arm around her. Cora stepped a little closer, her head resting on his shoulder. They stood there, not moving for several minutes.

The scents of mint and rosemary invaded his nose as he held her. Her breath slowed and he felt her choke back what he feared was a sob.

When she finally stepped away there were tears in her eyes. "Sorry. I don't remember the last time someone gave me a hug."

"I don't remember the last time I gave one, if that makes you feel better." Hannah wasn't a hugger and no one else ever came to Snow Peak Estate.

"No. It doesn't make me feel better, it makes me feel sad for you."

Everett didn't want to pull on that thread. "So why a teacup?"

"Huh?" She shook her head, then looked at the sketchpad. "It was here."

"Is that what you like to draw or paint? What's there?"

Cora's brows furrowed and she stepped around him. "I'm going to the gallery. I want to look at the sculptures. I haven't really had a chance to take them in."

"Take them in like you're looking for one or two to send out?" Everett had meant it when he told her the weekends were hers.

"No. I don't think there's any sense in sending those out. Cost prohibitive for the museums, space…" She waved a hand. "But I want to take them in, as an art lover."

"Artist," Everett corrected. "You are an artist."

"I just—"

"Nope." He put his hand up to stop the argument he could see from her expression was brewing. "All artists are art lovers. Not all art lovers are artists."

Cora stuck her tongue out. "Want to come to the gallery with me?"

"I need to see to a few things in the office. I'll catch up with you."

Cora grabbed her sketchbook. "Don't work too hard. It's an off day, remember." She waved a hand as she walked out of the kitchen.

Everett watched her go, took a deep breath enjoying her lingering scent. Then he shook himself. Cora was his guest. He was comforting her. And comforting did not include enjoying her fresh scent.

The sculpture was unique. That was the best way for her to describe the Ristzo steel piece. It was titled simply *Air.* She didn't see how the bent metal pointed at the ground was air, but the artist was the one who got to title it.

Cora looked at her sketchbook and flipped it open to what she'd been working on this morning. Not the teacup. She'd done that the other day. A small lie because she hadn't wanted to tell the truth.

Everett's face was captured perfectly on her page. It was the best work she'd ever done. His eyes, his lips, the scar. It was perfection.

She'd stared at his eyes, smudged his lips just a little.

Like they'd just been kissed.

That was what Cora had thought when she closed one eye and then the other. It was a process that she'd started as a little five-year-old with markers at the kitchen table. At least according to the lore her father had liked to tell.

For her, a piece she cared about wasn't truly done until each eye had individually approved the image. Justin had roasted the idea so much she'd tried to break the habit and never managed it.

Everett had watched her do it. He had to have if he'd been standing there for long. And yet, he'd expressed concern and an artist's appreciation.

That was not going to help her find a way to keep her distance.

I don't want to.

And it had nothing to do with the fact that he was the only other living creature in this place.

Yesterday they'd worked in the studio for hours. His watercolors were an expansion of green that seemed at odds with the snow-covered mountains around them. He'd made light conversation but their time had been spent creating.

And with no judgment.

He'd nodded at the mountains she was re-creating in the heavy oil paints. Told her he liked the shading and the angle of light coming through. Offering no criticism.

Then they'd had dinner. The man was hot. He cooked. He was an artist.

And a finance bro.

Her mind seemed intent on bringing that fact up. It wasn't one she should overlook. They were not in the same class.

She wasn't quite a soot-covered fairy-tale princess—but Cora and he came from very different backgrounds.

Doesn't mean I can't enjoy his company.

Looking around the sculpture gallery one more time, Cora stood and stretched out the muscles in her back. Cold marble floors were not so nice to thirty-year-old backs.

Reaching her hands above her head, she moaned as some of the tension left her.

"Now I want a hot cocoa and my e-reader." The sculptures didn't respond.

She walked past Everett's office door and saw the glow of light under the door. This was the light she'd seen the night she showed up at Snow Peak Estate. The room he spent nearly all his time in.

Technically he'd told her that Saturday and Sunday were not workdays.

She'd been with the sculptures for over four hours. Time

seemed to disappear for her in the presence of art. But that meant there was a good chance Everett had "checked his email" for four hours, too.

Cora started toward the door, then paused. Nope. She had a better idea.

Cora knocked once, careful to keep the tray in her left hand balanced. She didn't wait for Everett to call out, the cocoa was warm now. She was the only other person in this mansion; he knew who was at the door.

And the point was to get him away from his desk.

He was looking up when she entered, and a smile crossed his lips. The biggest one she'd seen yet.

"Pencils down!"

He chuckled, pointing to the computer. "I'm not using pencils."

Cora stuck her tongue out as she laid the tray down and handed him the cocoa. The silly face she'd made with her father had always annoyed Justin. He'd called it immature. Which it was.

But everyone needed something fun, and Everett clearly didn't mind.

His fingers brushed hers and heat that had nothing to do with the cup of hot cocoa raced up her arm. Everett held her gaze for a moment.

Probably wondering why she was just standing next to him.

Grabbing her own cup, she took it and sat on the edge of the giant desk. "It's Sunday. Aren't the banks and markets closed?"

"It's Sunday here. But the markets in Australia and New Zealand opened about thirty minutes ago, Tokyo and Hong Kong will open soon. Have to have the market on open orders ready."

"Those are a lot of words." She had a savings account—with basically nothing in it. Finance for Cora meant enough money to pay the rent, her bills and, if she was lucky, a fancy coffee every few days.

"Market on open orders are just what they sound like. Orders that have to be completed as soon as the market opens. I watch each foreign market and place those orders in the next opening markets based on trends." There was no sense of satisfaction in the words. It was almost a recitation.

I asked a basic question. He is answering.

"Why don't you have someone else do it? I mean, you are the CEO I know but, I mean..." She wasn't sure what she meant.

Everett started to reach toward her knee, like he was going to lay his hand on it. Her body tensed, aching for the touch with a pinch of worry about what it meant.

Nothing.

He looked at his hand, like the appendage had grown a brain of its own and was acting out. Everett pulled back.

Hopefully her face didn't show any of the disappointment radiating through her body.

"I have algorithms set up to track the markets. Most of the trades I initiate are done based on those, but the opening markets... I just like to monitor them. Maybe that's weird."

"Is that what your dad did?" Cora lined up her conservation tools the same way as her father. It was an afterthought. Something she hadn't even realized she was doing until he'd passed.

"My father tracked every market on a giant whiteboard in his office. Even when computer technology made the method inefficient, the board was there."

Everett looked at the computer and then to an empty space in the corner.

"Was that where he kept his whiteboard?" she asked, pointing.

"No." Everett let out a chuckle that was missing the humor. "My father never worked here. He was always so focused on the business. I lived here with nannies, a governess and staff. He visited."

"And your mother?"

"Gone before I could remember."

She laid her hand on his shoulder. He looked at it, then at her.

"I hate finance." The words were so quiet she knew they hadn't meant to be heard. He probably hadn't even meant to say them. Words that he'd buried in the back of his mind and the depths of his heart.

"What do you like?"

Everett looked at the computer. "Hot cocoa with a smart artist."

"Art conservator." She hopped off the desk.

He followed and grabbed her hand.

Cora turned, her breath catching as his other hand took her free one.

"You are an artist, Cora, *and* an art conservator. Two things can be true at once." He squeezed her hands.

Time, space, thoughts, all of it evaporated as his blue gaze held hers.

He's going to kiss me.

Cora started to lean toward him and Everett pulled back. She barely managed to catch herself.

What is wrong with me?

She reached for the hot cocoa cup. Maybe he hadn't seen her slip. She bit her lip and looked at the computer. "I think you should have Sunday off, too."

There was no reason to wait for a reply. She needed to go somewhere else. Anywhere else. Find a way to kick the unexpected feelings for Everett from her system. It had been a busy week. A weird week.

They were snowed in, in a giant mansion. But this wasn't a fairy tale. No Prince Charmings and damsels in need of rescuing resided here.

"Don't work too hard," Cora called out as the door closed.

CHAPTER SIX

HE'D ALMOST KISSED her three days ago. Three days and a lifetime. He'd retreated, or maybe she had. Either way they'd barely seen each other since Sunday.

Everett went days…weeks sometimes…only communicating with people through the computer or Hannah when she was at the estate. Three days was nothing.

Except it felt like a lifetime.

And it ended now.

Cora had been in the gallery all day. It was past dinnertime. Past time for her to be done for the day. He raised his hand to knock on the door, a bit of a weird feeling considering it was his gallery.

It's her space.

For now at least. Almost a whole week of the three and a half months was gone.

When she was gone it would still be Cora's space. Maybe she'd want to stay on. The gallery could be a full-time job for her for the next several years. Having her near wouldn't make his crush on the artistic beauty vanish, but it was better than life without her.

Maybe he could bring up extending her stay.

Or maybe not.

Before he could knock, a scream echoed from the gallery. He was moving before his brain could fully figure out what might be happening.

"Cora?" No one was at the entrance. His feet had a mind of their own as he raced to the end of the gallery.

"That is the last known sound of Britney Lowes. Many sleuths argue they can hear a man's voice behind the scream, but vocal analysis has ruled that out. What do you think happened, Tara?"

"What?" Everett took a deep breath. Cora was looking at a painting he didn't remember seeing. The magnifying glasses were on the tip of her nose and she was holding a tiny scraper. Wholly absorbed in her work.

The words and scream were coming from the gallery speaker system. He'd given her access but somehow expected music to echo from them. Or an audiobook of some kind.

"Cora?" He didn't want to make her jump with the scalpel.

She tilted her head and drew back from the painting. Reaching into her pocket, she pulled out the speaker system remote and hit Pause. "Are you okay?"

"No. Yes. But no. I ran in here because I heard a scream."

"Oh. Sorry. I didn't realize the speakers were that loud." She put the cap on the tiny scalpel and took the glasses off her nose.

"You listen to true crime while looking at art?" In his mind it was classical notes that floated through galleries like this. Or maybe it was pop music in the modern art area, but bloodcurdling true crime—it didn't compute.

"I love true crime. I read all sorts of books on it when I was growing up, if I hadn't gone into this, I always thought forensic science would have been the path I took. But Dad…" She shrugged as the words dropped off.

It had been impossible to shake the responsibilities placed on him by his father. The fact that Cora had experienced the same saddened him.

If she hadn't, she wouldn't be here.

"What's in the basket?"

The question brought the actual purpose of this visit back to his brain. He was a little surprised that he'd held on to it in his sprint to rescue Cora.

"Picnic." He pointed to the painting. "Work is over."

"Are the markets closed?"

"Ouch." He playfully covered his heart. The US stock market didn't close for another hour but the trades for his clients were in and he'd done most of the morning's trade requirements for the Australian markets that opened in a few hours.

"That ouch wasn't a no."

Her stomach let out a loud rumble.

Color coated her cheeks and she let out a sigh. "Don't suppose that basket has a blanket? The gallery floor isn't designed for comfort."

The basket was huge. His first nanny had loved picnics. As a child they'd spent hours playing outside during the cool summers. He'd thrown snowballs at her, then come inside to a warm picnic in the giant basket.

He opened it and pulled the blanket out. "I'm pretty sure I thought of everything."

"Wine?" She giggled.

"Of course." He laid the blanket out. "What picnic doesn't have wine?"

"I think a lot." Cora settled herself on the opposite end of the large blanket while he pulled food out of the basket. "If working late gets dinner delivered by a handsome deliveryman, this really doesn't make me want to end my day on time."

Handsome. He bristled a little at the dig. "I'm not handsome." He had been. Before the accident. Now most women, most people, turned their gaze away from him.

"Yes, you are." Cora grabbed the wine bottle and started uncorking it.

"Cora, I know what I look like. You don't have to offer

me a pity statement." Everett grabbed the fruit tray he'd put together and placed it between them without looking at her.

"Why would you think that's a pity statement? How insulting to both of us."

Everett looked up, stunned to find fire dancing in her eyes. He opened his mouth but no words found their exit.

"You are very attractive. Yes, you have a scar, a large one, I'm not denying that, but it doesn't diminish anything about you." Cora grabbed a grape and popped it in her mouth.

"Thank you." It was all he could think to say. "I guess, I saw so many people turn away in the early days—" The words came out and he swallowed, trying to stop the torrent.

It didn't work. "I was everywhere before the accident. Traveling, attending meetings and events."

"A different lovely lady on your arm at every event."

Heat coated his cheeks. "I'd love to claim I was young, and I was, but I was a playboy."

"You could have it again." Cora poured a glass of red, handing it to him, before taking a giant sip from her own glass. "Ladies would fall at your feet, scar or not."

"I didn't enjoy it that much then. I did it mostly because it made my father angry. He isn't here to get mad or react, so…" Everett shrugged as that truth fell from his lips.

Even in the darkest moment, he'd rarely thought of why he'd pushed his father.

"You're allowed to be angry with him." Cora set her wineglass down and moved a little closer to him. Not quite touching, but close enough that if he shifted, they'd brush hands.

"I'm not angry." He moved, his pinky touching hers. She didn't pull back.

"Really?" Cora looked at him, her mouth so close.

His mind was racing with thoughts twisted together. Cora, her words, his father…it was a wild twist that should be out of place.

"I was mad at my dad. Still mad sometimes. He was so focused on something he could never find," said Cora.

"Fortune?" Everett leaned back against the wall, grinning as Cora followed. "That was what my father chased. All he chased."

"Even with all the money in the world?" Her head was tilted just a bit. A little more and she could rest it on his shoulder. That would make the night even better than hearing her thoughts on his handsomeness.

"Some people are never satisfied." There was no amount of money that would ever be enough for his father. He'd grown the investment business. Enriched his father's clients more than they could imagine—added so much coin to the Winthrope bank accounts seven generations could live off it without lifting a finger.

Of course he was the last generation.

Even with all of that, Everett knew that if his father had survived the crash, their billions wouldn't have been enough.

"I often wonder what would have happened if my father found *The Ringlet Lady*." She sighed and her hand slipped a little closer to her shoulder.

He could put his arm around her. Pretend to yawn and stretch like some teen boy on his first date at the theater.

"He wanted to see *The Ringlet Lady*?" To the best of his knowledge his family had never let the picture leave the estate.

"Yes. It's this painting that doesn't exist, but he was so certain. It was his obsession."

"*The Ringlet Lady* exists." He hadn't set eyes on it in years. But it was in his office. Behind a fake wall his grandfather had installed.

"No." Cora shook her head and sat up. No way she was resting on his shoulder now. "Dad spent his whole life convinced the artist—"

"Pierre Alarie." Everett stood and reached out a hand. This was a way better topic than his father. "It's here. I know it well."

Her hand was so warm in his as he led them out of the gallery.

"You know the painting? Really? This isn't some weird joke."

It would be a weird joke. "Sure. It's hidden in my study."

"Hidden?"

"Well, family lore says my great-grandfather hung it above the fireplace in the room but my grandfather didn't want a naked picture of his mother hanging in his office." Everett opened his study and pulled her toward the false wall in the corner.

"His mother?"

Everett chuckled. "Not all of the Winthropes have been hermits snowed in on a mountain several months a year."

"That is a choice you're making." Cora raised a brow and squeezed his hand. "Is the painting really here?"

He pushed on the side of the cabinet, heard the latch click and pulled the door open. There she stood. In all her glory. Quite literally.

"Oh, my God." Cora's free hand was covering her lips, and the one in his palm tightened so much he was a little worried about his fingers snapping but he didn't dare pull away.

She reached a hand out, but pulled back before she touched it.

He took the hand still holding his and lifted it to the frame. "It really is here." His thumb brushed her wrist as he guided her hand along the edge of the frame.

"It's real. It's real." She let out a little squeal and turned.

Her lips were on his and vanished before his brain could wrap itself around the motion.

"Sorry."

Everett was not going to accept that apology. "Cora." His hand grazed her cheek, so soft. "You don't get to apologize for kissing me."

Pink colored her cheeks. "Maybe I was apologizing because it was so short."

Everett leaned his head toward hers. "That apology I will accept." His lips skimmed hers. The touch barely there.

Cora let out a soft moan, stepping closer to him.

Her hands were around his neck, her body molding to his.

His hands gripped her hips.

"Kiss me."

Her plea broke him, and his lips captured hers. Everything was mythical. The touch. The smell of her. The feel of her lips pressed to his.

Her mouth opened and took the invitation. Wine, honey and Cora. A perfect blend of taste.

When she stepped back, her gaze was focused on him completely. Then her stomach let out a vicious growl.

He couldn't stop the laughter bubbling up. "As much as I want to explore what just happened here, we need to get more than a few sips of wine into your belly. You can investigate *The Ringlet Lady* tomorrow."

"Tomorrow." She looked at the painting, but her gaze quickly shifted back to him. "Tomorrow."

"Tomorrow."

She touched her lips as she made her way to Everett's office. Last night. Twelve hours ago. So little time but it felt like forever since he'd kissed her.

I kissed him first.

That was true. It had been quick. Her soul had filled with so much excitement and it burst forth when she saw the painting her father had craved.

The knowledge that it was real. That it wasn't for nothing. That coming to Snow Peak had been the right choice.

All of it had rushed through her at once. She'd spun and pressed her lips to his without thinking. Stunned and wanting more when she'd stepped back.

She'd fallen asleep to thoughts of his mouth capturing hers. She'd woken with the realization that somehow their talk last night had gone from her asking about his dad to a discussion of hers.

Once more she'd given more of herself and he'd added very little.

It doesn't mean anything.

The news that *The Ringlet Lady* was real was more exciting. It made sense.

The tingle of suspicion that Everett always found a way to shift the topic away from him buzzed in her brain. It was fine. It was two kisses. One of them a showstopping number but it didn't necessarily mean anything.

What if I want it to?

That was a thought for later. It was time to get started on the day. And today she was examining *The Ringlet Lady.* With any luck Everett would let her move it to the gallery and put it on the list to send out. The art world would ignite with the news.

And it would vindicate her father.

Pushing open the door, she nearly dropped the tool set she planned to use to exam *The Ringlet Lady.* Everett was on the floor. A pillow under his head, a blue blanket that did not cover his chest tossed over his body.

His bare chest.

Scars covered nearly every inch. The wound on his face was stark, but these—these indicated how close the world had come to losing him.

She set the tool kit down slowly and moved toward him.

Why was he on the floor? The man had a room next to hers. Hell, it was a suite. Probably the largest one in the whole giant mansion.

Yet he was on the floor of his office.

Cora knelt beside him, brushed her fingers over his cheek. The bristles of his beard rubbed against her thumb. "Everett?"

"Mmm-hmm…? Cora…" The words were slurred.

"Everett. You're on the floor."

"Cora?" His eyes snapped open and he sprang up and immediately winced. "Ugh. Oh. Damn."

He leaned back on his elbows, sucking in deep breaths, his eyes pinched tight.

"Roll over." She gave the order but was a little surprised when he followed through. She placed her fingers at his waist, searching for the pressure points.

"Take a deep breath, this might hurt before it helps." She waited just long enough to hear the intake then dug her fingers into either side of his spine.

Everett let out a grunt that turned to a moan. "An artist and a masseuse."

"This isn't massage. It's acupuncture. Sort of. I got tired of hearing my ex complain about his low back pain so I got him an appointment. He didn't take it, and I'd already paid for it. So…" She moved her thumbs just a little. "The woman who put the needles in me was kind enough to give me a little knowledge—that until today I've never actually used."

Justin hadn't really wanted relief. He'd wanted to complain about how his art was making him suffer.

"Well, bless her." Everett sighed. "Thanks. My back feels better and it even loosened my hips a little."

"Do you trust me?" Cora bit her lip as she looked at his butt. There were pressure points there that would help his hips.

"Of course."

"Take another deep breath." She moved her thumbs quickly and found the points to help his hips and applied the pressure.

"Dear God. Oh."

She didn't dare stop. Everett was hissing and moaning as she put as much pressure as her fingers could handle onto his pressure points. It wasn't enough—the man's hips were tight as hell. And not in the good way.

"You need yoga."

"Very funny." Everett let out another hiss as her right thumb pushed harder.

"It's not a joke. Yoga can open your hips. I've practiced for years. I mean technically I'm a certified instructor, though I only ever substituted." She'd become an instructor accidentally, signing up for the six-week intensive as a challenge during a particularly turbulent time in her relationship with Justin.

Substituting had paid their bills more than once when his art wasn't selling.

"So you're a yoga instructor." Everett sighed as she watched the left side of his body relax. Now if only his right side would follow suit.

"No. I—"

"You are an instructor. Just like you are an artist." Everett shifted, but she didn't let up on the pressure point.

"I—"

"I'd say don't make me get up, but I am still not sure I can, Cora. You are an artist. You are an instructor. Why is that so difficult for you to say?" He huffed and she was certain it was about her, not the tension in his back.

"I don't know." It just was. Her father had told her that her art wasn't good but that they didn't have the connections to make her great. Which just meant she wasn't good enough. Justin had reinforced that idea.

Yoga was something she did because she enjoyed it. The

instructor course had been a happy accident. "I guess sometimes when you hear it isn't good enough long enough, hearing someone say it is is uncomfortable."

Her thumb was beginning to scream from all the pressure but she felt the release and the happy sigh from Everett just as her digit started to give out.

"Good thing you're in a better position now. Not sure my thumb could have taken much more. We'll have to do this a little every day." Cora sat back on her heels and rubbed the sore digits.

"Won't complain about your hands on my body—ever." Everett rolled over, his blue eyes blazing.

"If you can make sexual innuendos then I think you are definitely feeling better." Cora stuck her tongue out as she stood and offered him a hand.

Everett took it and pulled himself up but didn't let go. "I think I was far too direct to call that innuendo."

His thumb ran along the soft spot on her wrist, each stroke sending a tiny spark up her body.

"If we weren't snowed in—" she raised her chin as she grinned at him "—I'd suggest a first date."

A piece of hair fell over his eyes as he tilted his head. "I thought our picnic was the first date."

It was hard to focus when a hot shirtless Everett was standing in front of her. She swallowed the ball of desire as she shook her head. "A date requires one of the parties asking the other out. Otherwise it is just two people sitting on the floor of an art gallery chatting."

Two people who'd kissed, but that was a minor point. At least in this argument.

"Well, then." Everett offered a small bow. "Will you go on a date with me this evening, Cora? We can't leave the estate but I have a pretty good idea to make it memorable."

Any date with Everett would be memorable. She had no doubt of that.

"Yes, on one condition." She looked to the blanket he'd lain under last night. It was tossed in a ball, but it was well used. This was not his first night on the floor.

Last night he'd dodged the questions about himself. Shifted the conversation. She'd given so much of herself and he'd managed to evade every personal question.

"Condition?"

"Why were you sleeping on the floor?"

"Afraid you'll have to join me in the odd habit?" There was a hint of bitterness under the humor.

"No. I'm concerned that you were on the floor, but I want to know why. I want to know something about you that isn't facts and figures." She had a crush on him. Their kiss last night would keep her dreams satisfied for months. If he couldn't give her something real, that was fine for friends and colleagues, not for dating.

She wasn't going to be blindsided by a man. Not again.

"You know how tight I was this morning?" Everett looked at the floor, then his desk, then the fireplace. Pretty much everywhere but at her.

"I was just digging my thumbs into your ass, so yes, I recall."

"That directness. It's so…hot." Everett looked at her, the hint of heat in his cheeks.

She was glad someone finally liked it. "Avoiding the question?"

"No." He scratched his head. "Hannah swears I sleep on the floor as penance. No matter what I tell her."

Penance. What would he be punishing himself for?

"My face didn't take all the damage in the accident." He gestured to his scarred chest. "Just the damage that most people see."

She wanted to tell him he wasn't damaged. Because it was clear by his tone that he thought he was, but, if she interrupted, Cora knew he'd never finish.

"My back, the bed, it…it just doesn't work. I wake up in more pain and the irony isn't lost on me that a billionaire sleeps on the floor of his office."

Cora grabbed his hand and pulled him forward. She wrapped her arms around him. "I suspect you are not the only billionaire that sleeps in his office. Though you might be the only one that sleeps there because your bed hurts your back."

"So you're willing to go on that date?"

Cora let out a fake exasperated sound. She was holding him, shirtless, and kissing his cheek. The answer was obvious. "Yes. Though it better be somewhere that isn't fancy, because I didn't bring any dress clothes."

"That is something easily rectified." Everett kissed the tip of her ear.

"We're snowed in, Everett."

"I know." He kissed the top of her forehead and stepped back. "I should get ready for the day. Can't stay topless all day."

He could. She wouldn't complain. Luckily, she kept that thought to herself.

CHAPTER SEVEN

CORA WASN'T SURPRISED there was wear on *The Ringlet Lady*. Hiding a picture behind a wall in an office wasn't exactly the right environment. On the bright side, hidden in the wall meant it hadn't had direct sunlight.

Unfortunately that was about all the good she could offer about its location.

"Is it in terrible condition?"

She didn't turn around. "Too early to tell. There is a small tear on the right side. Looks like something hit it at the same angle over and over. Maybe a nail?" Cora ran her hand along the wall and found the offending location quickly.

Damn. She should have used a flashlight to prove the point. The broken wood was sticking farther out than she'd imagined. Her finger was already bleeding and it felt like there might be a splinter imbedded.

"Cora?"

"Not a nail. A large piece of the wood is broken behind it. Guess care for the hiding place wasn't top priority. It's sticking out and hitting the edge of the painting. Given how far out it is, I'm a little surprised it didn't do more damage. Don't worry I didn't get any blood on *The Ringlet Lady*." She started to put her thumb in her mouth, but Everett's hands were on hers before she could lift it to her lips.

"I'm not concerned about some painting, Cora." Everett looked at her fingers. "You need to get that cleaned."

"It's a little scrape and maybe a splinter." It was on the pad of her thumb and going to be sore for several days but in the grand scheme a minor injury. She'd find a Band-Aid at some point to keep it clean.

"Cora, there is no telling how long that broken section has been there. There might be bacteria. Hell, the paints might have lead in them."

"Oh, they absolutely do." Everett's thumb brushed over her wrist and there was little her brain wanted to focus on besides his soft touch. "Given the age of the paints and type, it was a drying additive."

"Cora." He held her hand for just a moment longer then walked to the desk and opened the bottom drawer. As he set the small first aid kit next to the computer, she let out a giggle. Seriously, a first aid kit for a scrape and a tiny splinter.

Justin wouldn't have noticed her pain. Her father would have told her to make sure the blood didn't get on the painting.

"Everett, I've been around old paints, rusty nails, broken wood frames and everything else that comes with archival work since I was able to walk. Probably before that." Her dad had liked to joke that the first black eye she'd ever gotten was from racing into the gallery and hitting the edge of a frame that was being carried.

He also liked to recount how the people carrying it had not been pleased with her or him. It had cost him that job. She didn't have the memory of the black eye, but the shame that she'd cost him a job had stuck with her every time he told the story.

"I take it that means injuries were not a big deal."

She shrugged. She was standing here. Fine. Mostly. "I lived."

"The fact that those injuries were not treated does not

mean this one shouldn't be." He held out his hand and she dropped her palm in it.

"Why do you have a first aid kit in your desk drawer?" She winced as he sprayed an antiseptic cleaner. "That stings."

"I know. Sorry." He kissed the top of her head.

The action brought tears to her eyes. Stupid. It was dumb.

"You okay?"

"Yeah. It just stings. And I'm not used to anyone taking care of me."

"Well, there is a splinter in here, so…" He grabbed the tweezers out of the kit. "Deep breath."

He pulled the splinter out on the second try. "The kit doesn't have any fancy Band-Aids, so just flesh tone will have to do." Everett took the tape off the Band-Aid then secured it on her finger. "All better?"

"Yes." She pulled her wounded hand to her chest. How did such a tiny thing feel so monumental?

"Since that's over, I think it's time for the surprise."

"Surprise?" Cora turned as he walked back toward the office door.

"Sure." He held up an outfit bag, looking ever so proud of himself.

"What is that?"

"A dress." Everett passed it to her. "For tonight."

"Why do I need a dress, Everett?" Her stomach dropped as she felt the weight in the bag.

And why do you have a woman's dress just hanging out?

"You mentioned not having a fancy outfit." Color was creeping up his neck. This was meant to be a surprise, she understood that.

And I am ruining it.

"My father let a fashion designer stay at Snow Peak for three months years ago. They created several fashion pieces that were used in gallery photography pieces." He pushed a hand through his hair. "No one has ever worn them."

"How were they photographed, then?" It didn't make sense but then she'd seen some unusual things in the homes her father had worked in when she was growing up.

"Hanging on strings." Everett pointed to the bag in her hand. "That one was always my favorite and it…well, I just thought. But wear whatever you want tonight. Jeans. Sweats. Nothing at all. Nope that was…"

She stepped up, pressing her lips to his. "Thank you." It was a very kind gesture, and she'd overthought the meaning. Justin had had ulterior motives. That didn't mean Everett did.

"You're welcome. But again, wear whatever you want. I'll pick you up at the base of the stairs tonight at seven." He offered her a small bow and turned.

"Aren't you working?"

"I am. But mostly on my phone today. Handling some meetings with clients and such. You stay, check out the piece you looked for for so long." He lifted a hand and headed out.

Cora set the dress bag on the couch he had in the office. She turned toward the painting then looked back at the bag. She hesitated only a moment before pulling the zipper down.

"Oh." A lavender dress, with flowers, birds and butterflies sewn into the lace overlay, greeted her. It was gorgeous. The finest thing she'd ever seen. A true work of art.

And a reminder that this wasn't real. Not truly. They were snowed in. Enjoying each other's company. But when the snow melted. When the work was finished. She'd go back to whatever small flat she could find and he'd do whatever it was he did in this giant house all alone.

They were from different worlds.

But tonight…tonight she was going to enjoy every minute of the temporary fairy tale.

* * *

Bong. Bong. Bong. Bong. Bong. Bong. Bong.

Everett had never paid attention to how loud the grandfather clock in the entryway was. The piece of furniture had stood in the exact same place for longer than he'd inhabited the earth. A fixture that now clanged in his head.

Where is she?

The dress had been a mistake. Or rather the delivery was a disaster. If he'd thought about it a little more, maybe he wouldn't have watched her face go through the roller coaster of thoughts. One of which was definitely *which ex's dress is he giving me.*

The dresses were payment for use of the space. The fashion designer and photographer had taken all but three of the pieces developed in the months in residence.

It was the only time his father had opened Snow Peak Estate to anyone besides family and staff. His father had planned to hang the dresses in the gallery. A unique find after the gallery showcases.

Unfortunately, the six showings and multiple purchases of images was not grand enough for his father so he'd tossed the dresses in a storage area and forgotten about them. Then Cora had made the not-so-offhand remark about not having fancy clothes for a date.

There was more behind the statement. More behind the one large duffel bag. More that he didn't know.

But I want to.

If she came down the stairs in the overalls he'd seen her in all month, he'd melt. It was Cora he was fascinated by, not the clothes on her body.

She appeared at the top of the staircase and Everett felt the world still. She was *beauty* defined. Her red hair was done in a beachy-wave style—loose and light. Aching for fingers to run through it.

The dress was artwork. And Cora was the masterpiece. The bodice hugged her perfectly. The birds embroidered on the skirt seemed to sing with joy at fulfilling their purpose.

Like the universe knew she'd be here someday and created the perfect thing for her alone.

"Sorry I'm late." Cora offered her hand to him as she reached the landing.

"Worth every tiny second of waiting." Everett pulled her hand to his lips. "That dress was made for you."

"It wasn't, though." She blushed as she stepped back. "But it is the most beautiful thing I've ever had on my body."

She spun slowly; the back was a lace-up corset. "I don't think I got the bow on the back right. That was why I was late actually. I kept retying it. Then I figured to hell with it. I was going to get a cramp in my neck if I kept trying."

Her hair fell over her shoulder as she looked back at him. "How does it look?"

The bow just above her perfect butt was the last thing he was paying any attention to. But no one would have guessed she'd done it herself while looking in a mirror.

That was the image he was going to paint on the wall the next time he went to the closed wing. Cora—in this dress—looking at the bow. He could see it so easily.

"You are perfection."

"Nope." She spun and kissed his cheek.

Before he could argue that point, she continued, "So where are we going dressed so fancy?"

"This way." Everett held his hand out. He'd spent most of the day in the kitchen. Working up a meal that would taste good on the warmers in the library. He'd lighted the room, set up the stereos. Tonight was his and Cora's.

He opened the library door and watched her enter the candlelit room.

"Oh." Her free hand went over her mouth. "Now I am glad you didn't show me this room on the tour." She dropped his hand as she stepped into the room.

The candlelight caressed her features. This was another painting. All the walls in the closed-off wing were going to be Cora. His masterpieces. Memories of her.

He pulled the remote out of his pocket and hit two buttons. A soft tune hummed in the room. "Oh…"

"May I have this dance?" He offered a small bow, enjoying the grin spreading on her face.

"I feel like Beauty in the fairy tale." She put her hand in his and he wrapped his other arm around her waist.

"Does that make me the Beast?" He spun them in a wide circle.

"You are not a beast." Cora ran her hand down his cheek. Her fingers brushed his scar but she didn't recoil.

"In your arms I feel like that might actually be true." Everett skimmed his hand up her back, pulling her a little closer.

"Everett."

This time it was his turn to silence her rather than touch the uncomfortable subject. He bent his head, capturing her lips. She let out a little moan, pressing her hips against his as they moved in sync around the room.

When the song shifted to a faster beat, neither pulled away or adjusted the dance's speed. He simply held her. Reveled in the moment, the majesty.

Finally her stomach rumbled, and she giggled.

"Not sure there's a less sexy sound than a stomach going off in the middle of a dance." Cora's lips brushed his.

"I made us dinner and then kept you spinning around the room for over an hour." Good thing he'd set up the warmers his father had insisted on purchasing despite never inviting more than a few people to the estate.

"Has it been an hour?" Cora looked at the mantel clock as she wrapped her arm around his waist. "Time moves slowly when I'm in your arms it seems."

"It stands still for me." He kissed the top of her head and led her to the small table he'd set up on the other side of the library. "I promised you dinner and I plan to deliver."

"Are you going to serve me as well?" Cora squeezed his waist with her hand as she gazed up at him. Her green eyes sparkled.

He took a mental snapshot. A memory he wanted forever. Needed forever. "Of course."

Everett guided her to her chair, pulled it out, then planted another kiss on the top of her head as she sat down.

"For the first course, we have baked feta with sesame seeds and honey, with a sourdough bread I made." Everett put the plate in the center of the table and sat down across from her.

He tore off a piece of the sliced sourdough, dipped it in the feta cheese and lifted it to her lips. "It's salty and sweet with the warm comfort of bread."

Cora took the offered morsel, ate it and closed her eyes. "Mmm. That is delicious. You could have the whole meal be that."

She pulled another piece off, dipped the bread and held it out to him. "The chef needs to eat to."

Heat bloomed through him as she held it to his lips. He opened his mouth, the sweet honey touching his tongue first. Cora's thumb grazed his chin as she pulled back.

"Cora."

"I do like it when you say my name." She wrapped her fingers through his and leaned forward on her free hand. "No one has ever said it the way you do."

He leaned forward, mirroring her. "How do I say your name?"

"Like you like it." She squeezed his fingers.

"That statement makes me want to punch someone. Who on earth said your name like they didn't like it?"

"My ex was a piece of work. He didn't think it sounded fancy enough. Which should have been one of the first clues I had that he was hiding who he really was." She laughed. "But that's a story for a tenth or so date."

"Think there will be a tenth or so date?"

"I guess we'll just have to see." Cora grabbed another piece of bread and put it to her irresistible lips.

Everett had never been on more than five dates with a woman. The society setups had never meshed well.

And he'd been a playboy. Meeting and moving on in his youth.

But he wanted a tenth date with Cora. Wanted to know what date twenty looked like. Thirty…fifty…

Damn he had it bad.

"Time for the second course, miso soup." He brushed his lips against hers, then stood and prepared the dish.

"Wow. What is the main dish and the dessert?" Cora lifted the soup to her lips as he sat back down.

"After this is seared scallops with brown butter and lemon pan sauce."

"Fancy."

Everett chuckled. "It sounds fancy but it is just a simple pan meal."

"Take the compliment, Everett." She rested her hand on his knee. "You've earned it."

Compliment.

You've earned it.

Words his brain blanked on processing. Still, they were nice to hear, even if he wasn't sure he fully believed them.

"We have to go grab the peach ice cream with caramel bourbon syrup I made. Or I could grab it and bring it in."

"Nope." Cora wrapped her fingers through his again. "We go together."

We do.

CHAPTER EIGHT

THEY SPUN AROUND the room as the clock struck midnight. "It feels like the hours whisked by and we never made it to the kitchen." Cora's arms were wrapped around his shoulders, the candlelight flickering away.

"Do you want dessert?"

"I do."

But not ice cream.

Cora lifted on her toes and pressed her lips to his. His fingers slipped up her back the way they had since he'd heard the soft moan it elicited after dinner.

Her body was a live wire. It craved one thing.

Everett.

"Why don't we blow the candles out and get something sweet?" His words were warm against her ear.

She shifted her hips just a little, enjoying Everett's quick intake of breath. "Sounds like an excellent plan." Cora headed to one end of the room, blowing out the candles while Everett headed to the other side and did the same.

When she reached the final candle, she waited for him. He stepped to her side and they blew it out together.

Only moonlight filtered through the glass panes. "Dessert time." Cora grabbed his hand and headed toward the door.

"Whatever the lady wants." Everett chuckled.

The lady wanted something very specific. She got to the stairs and started up.

"Ice cream is in the kitchen, Cora."

Turning on the top step, she raised a brow. "Do you want ice cream, Everett? Or a different kind of dessert? Besides… I thought I got to choose?"

He stepped on the first step with her and pushed a loose curl behind her ear. "You do get to choose."

"Fantastic." She grabbed his hand and guided them toward his bedroom. For the last hour all she could think of was sliding that coat off his shoulders, undoing the tie and kissing her way down his body.

She opened his room and grinned as he flipped the light on.

"You are so beautiful, Cora. So gorgeous." Everett beckoned her to turn around. "Let me help you undo that bow you worked on so long."

His lips trailed kisses along her bare shoulder as soon as she turned. "Careful. The dress is art after all."

"*You* are art." Everett's tongue darted along the base of her neck.

Her knees weakened.

I'm not even undressed yet and I'm already burning with need.

His fingers pulled at the corset ribbon and she felt the dress loosen. She gripped her top so it didn't crumple to the floor.

"Having second thoughts?" Everett pulled back and turned her. "It's fine."

"No second thoughts. But the dress."

"Is a dress." He ran his finger along the edge of the bodice.

Her breasts ached at the simple touch but the dress was both dress and art. The idea of just dropping it, even for the sexiest man she'd ever stood before, made her art conservator heart ache.

"Everett—"

"It's fine." His hands lowered to her hips. "Let go. I will

catch it carefully. Then you can step out of it. We can lay it across the couch I have. Though that does mean I can't set you on it and worship your body there."

She bit her lips as tightness flooded her lower region. The man found the exact right blend of helpful and erotic words.

"Thank you." Cora stepped out of the dress. She'd worn black panties but no bra because of the way the dress was made. As soon as she was out of the dress, she lifted it gingerly and took it to the couch.

When she turned, all her attention was on the man who was still fully clothed before her.

She moved in front of him and slipped his jacket off. There was no reason *it* couldn't just drop to the floor. As Cora undid Everett's tie, he cupped one breast, his thumb rolling over her nipple.

Cora hissed as he moved to the next.

"Your breasts are very sensitive." His thumb raked over her nipple.

She nearly ripped the button off his shirt. Her lips brushed against each inch of skin she slowly revealed as each button was undone. His chest was scarred. Tiny marks, longer ones, flesh-colored stitches that marked where he'd been sown back together.

His breath caught as more were revealed. "I know they aren't much to look at."

No. He was not going to worry over his scars. Not tonight. Not with her.

Cora pushed his shirt off his shoulders, shuddering at the magnificence beneath. She traced a finger along the longest scar on his side, then bent her head and pressed her lips to them one at a time. "You are so perfect."

Her legs were wobbly with need. Her body on fire, but she didn't want to rush this.

As she reached for his belt, Everett's hand grabbed hers.

"I'm already about to lose myself. And there are so many things I ache to do first. The couch is taken, so the bed will do."

"Wha—" She was in his arms and then being deposited on the edge of the bed before she could think. She sank into the mattress as Everett encircled her waist and pulled her to exactly where he wanted her.

She wrapped her legs around his waist, enjoying the color in his cheeks and the quick breaths coming from him.

"Black panties are my favorite," he murmured, his hand floating along her thigh.

"That was fortunate, then." She ran her hand along his chest. Scars covered it, but for once they seemed far from Everett's mind.

He dipped his head, suckling one nipple then the other as his hand slipped ever farther up her thigh.

"I'll let you in on a little secret, Cora." Everett's thumb slipped under her panties, finding her bud.

Stars exploded. Lightning echoed in her soul as she bucked against him. "Everett."

"Any color on you would be my favorite."

"What about no underwear?" Her breath caught as a finger slipped into her.

"You are a little minx. I love it." The pressure was building and he still didn't have his pants off.

"Everett." She panted against him as he kept the pressure exactly the same, coaxing her, calling her toward oblivion.

As she started to crest, he captured her mouth, kissing her as she rode through the ecstasy.

Cora was always beautiful. Cora panting as he stroked her to completion was beguiling. He was bursting and still wearing his pants.

If she'd undressed him, he'd have spent himself already. And he still had so many plans.

Slipping his fingers from her, she watched as he put the finger to his lips. He'd craved her taste for days. Weeks… maybe since the moment she'd forced her way into the estate and not cared about the scars crossing his body.

"Everett."

"You taste so good." He reached under her lovely bottom and dragged the panties down her legs and dropped them on the floor.

"Everett."

"Lay back, Cora." She gasped but followed the command.

He'd meant what he'd said about worshipping her on the couch. They'd shifted the location but that didn't mean any of his plans were changing. He was going to spend as much time kissing her, licking her, imprinting her into his memory as possible.

Feathering kisses along her inner thighs, he reveled in every moan. Running his hands up her abdomen, he found her nipples and stroked them as his tongue found her core.

He licked her, nearly losing himself as her legs wrapped around his head. A man could spend his entire life kissing Cora St. Stevens and it wouldn't be enough.

"Everett."

His name on her lips. His hands on her body. There had never been a better night.

"I need you."

He pulled back, dropped a kiss between her legs and grinned as he looked at the siren on his bed. "You have me."

"I need you, all of you. Please. Please."

The second "please" broke every bit of restraint he had. He reached into the top drawer of his nightstand, grabbed a condom, then freed and sheathed himself.

Standing at the edge of the bed, he positioned himself to

her. "Cora." He breathed her name as he slid into her. Her legs wrapped around his waist, pulling herself all the way to him.

Tonight was heaven and he never wanted it to end.

Cora was in his arms. Snoring lightly, her naked body draped over him. His lower back was on fire. He wanted to hold her all night. Wanted to wake up next to her, wake her with kisses and orgasms. She was the only thing that could keep him in a bed.

"Everett?" His name was slurred on her lips.

"Shh. Go back to sleep." He ran a hand along her back and kissed the top of Cora's head. Tomorrow his body was going to feel terrible, but it was a price his soul was willing to pay.

CHAPTER NINE

CORA STRETCHED AS she pulled her overalls on. Her body should feel amazing. Everett had ensured her pleasure over and over again. She should be loose and relaxed.

She reached her arms above her head and tried to work the knot behind her shoulder blade out. No wonder he preferred the floor.

Right now, she wanted Everett, coffee and a pain tablet. In that order.

Cora grabbed her supply kit and headed for his office. She was going to spend the day with *The Ringlet Lady*, ensuring what she already suspected. The painting could travel as soon as the tear was mended.

This was the piece every museum would clamor for. The piece that would bring art tourists from around the world. It would make the collection even more of a must-see.

She opened the door and was glad to find Everett behind his desk, not on the floor.

"Good morning," he stood and walked to her, pulling her close. "Did you sleep well?"

"No." She kissed his cheek. "My body aches."

"Did I—?"

She put a finger over his lips. "You were wonderful. It's your bed."

"It's the finest mattress money can purchase. I've had it for years."

"And slept on the floor." Cora yawned and pointed to the coffee cart. "I need coffee."

"I used to sleep great in it." Everett let her go and followed her to the coffee cart. He waited while she poured and doctored her drink before following suit.

"*Used* to is the key word there." Cora yawned again. Today was going to be a long day. "I assume that was before the accident."

Everett shifted. His shoulders slumped a little, his gaze focused on the other side of the room. That moment in time had altered his whole life.

She understood that. A different person had entered the vehicle than the one pulled out by emergency personnel.

"Why do you still have a bed that doesn't do what you need it to do?"

"Because it's the best. I don't want to brag about how much it cost, but—"

"I am sure it is more than my bank account has ever seen. But that doesn't matter." The bed in her suite was great. The nicest she'd ever slept on, but it was also firmer.

"Cora, it's fine. You sleep and I will deal with the pain."

"Or, since I slept like crap in the bed, too, we sleep in my bed tonight." She raised her cup of coffee to her lips.

"Your bed?"

"Yes. There is a couch in my suite, too. Assuming you weren't making up stories about worshipping me on the couch."

Everett put his coffee down and reached for hers.

Cora held up a hand, drained the cup, then handed it to him.

He laughed as he set it next to his and pulled her to him. "I very much was not making that up." His hand gripped her butt.

"Overalls aren't the sexiest outfit." Cora was aware that

the dress she'd worn last night was a fairy-tale moment. This was Cora without the magic, without the money, without the pretty gown that turned heads.

"I disagree." Everett's lips brushed her cheek before moving down her neck. "You in anything is sexy as hell. But the best outfit…is your birthday suit." He nipped at her ear.

She wrapped her arms around his neck.

His computer started ringing.

"Damn it."

"Meeting time. The CEO is in demand." She kissed his lips quickly, then stepped back. "I'd planned to spend this morning looking at *The Ringlet Lady.* But if I'll be in the way…?"

"You won't be." Everett said the words as he moved behind his desk. "Good morning, Ian. I saw the numbers."

She watched him for a moment. The man was in command behind the computer. But he didn't fit there. Cora wasn't sure why she was so certain of it. But it was like he was playing a role.

Like he was trying to force himself to be there. He was in command, but something was off.

He rolled his neck and she caught the grimace he was quick to hide. She looked at the painting. The whole reason she was here. Her father's obsession.

But there was something else she needed to do. *The Ringlet Lady* had hung there for decades, another few hours weren't going to matter.

Everett looked over at *The Ringlet Lady.* The painting was standing open, and Cora's supply bag was next to it. But she'd disappeared during his first call.

And the calls had poured in this morning. Insecurity in the American markets was upsetting the global shares. He wasn't concerned. The markets shifted. That was what they did.

There might be a downturn here and there, but the amount of money his clients might lose was pocket change for them.

That didn't stop their panic, though.

"Everett." Cora opened the door, the overalls gone. She was in dark gray yoga pants and a bright pink sports bra.

His mouth watered as he monitored the pain in his back. He could lower her onto the couch in here. There would be pain but...it was worth it.

"Come on."

"Oh, I don't think I want to go anywhere." He walked around the desk. As he reached for her, she stepped back.

"Nope. I went to the gym and found two yoga mats. There isn't a space there, too much unused equipment, so we're going to be in the foyer. I went through your closet, found some workout shorts and a white T-shirt." She tossed them at him. "It's yoga time, I'll give you a moment to get changed." And then she was gone.

He changed quickly and strolled through the door. "I feel like after last night, you could have stayed for the show. Unless you were worried it might lead us to the office couch instead of the yoga mat." Everett winked as he watched the color rise in Cora's cheeks.

Her breasts turned the exact same shade when he lavished them with kisses.

"We are working on your hips today." Cora gestured to the mat, then stepped to the one opposite it.

Everett nearly made a quip about her enjoying his hips last night but thought better of it. She was here to help him. He wasn't sure this would work any better than the physical therapy or shots the doctors had given him, but he was willing to try.

Mostly so he could easily spend the night with her in his arms.

"All right, what are we doing?"

"First, child's pose." She sat on her knees then moved her hands forward, her head resting on the floor, her arms outstretched. It looked easy enough.

As soon as he got on his knees and started inching forward, he groaned. Cora's head rested on the floor; he could barely get more than five inches off the ground. "Ugh."

"All right, sit back up." Her hands were on his shoulders in an instant. It wasn't until they made the connection that he realized how much he needed her help to slide back up.

"You make that looks so easy." He let out a breath, stunned at how his heart was racing from such a simple move. And there was no room to blame the sexy woman next to him.

"I have practiced for a long time. You, sir, are stiff as a board—and not in the good way." She winked. "So cat cow pose, and then some hip openers and we will end in child's pose again to see how different you feel when you forced them to open for the first time in years."

A commanding woman. So enticing.

"You lead, I'll follow."

He slid into the final child's pose and let out a soft sigh. His head was nowhere close to the floor, but it was closer than it had been. And the pain was now a subtle stretching that was almost delicious.

"Man, this feels good." Everett let out a groan. "I mean…"

His eyes filled with tears. *What?*

He wasn't upset. It didn't hurt, but suddenly they were dripping down his face no matter how hard he tried to blink them away.

"There is a theory that we keep unwanted emotions in our hips. I'm not sure how scientific it is, but I have seen more than one person break down in a session. There's no shame in it." She ran a hand along his back. "Breathe through it."

Everett let out a sob. Anger, sadness, annoyance that the tears wouldn't stop, all rushed through him.

"Gah."

"Breathe or start talking," she said, gentle but commanding.

"Talking about what?" The words were hisses through his teeth.

"Whatever you need to say. There are no rules here." She moved back onto her mat, resumed her child's pose.

"There isn't anything to say. Nothing to point out." The words were a lie. His heart screamed at him to say something different. But he wasn't going to break. Not now. Not ever.

And not in front of Cora.

"Okay."

"Okay. Just okay." Seriously, how could she be so relaxed about it. He was a melting mess and she wasn't going to push?

"Yes, just okay. You are in control, Everett. If you don't need to say anything, let the tears flow. The science on tears is well studied. They are stress relievers, so let them flow if you have no words."

Oh, he had words. They were bubbling up in his chest, shouting to echo into the foyer.

"I was a disappointment to my father. 'You are just a disappointment.' Those were his final words to me." The words escaped the chains he'd wrapped around them after the accident.

No one knew that. No one knew the anger his father had passed with. No one knew how much his son hated those final words.

"So much about that night is a blur. The authorities asked me all sorts of questions. What was happening, was there anything in the road, any reason? I remember so little about that night, but I remember those words.

"I'm so mad at him." He sucked in a breath, hoping that

forcing air into his lungs would stop the words from leaking out. So angry and so desperate to prove him wrong. How did that make sense?

"Understandable. I'm mad at him, too." Cora breathed through her nose and let it out in a heavy breath.

"You didn't know him. You can't be mad at someone you've never met. Can't be pissed at the dead."

"Oh, you absolutely can. I assure you." Cora let out a small laugh.

"He was yelling at me in the car. Yelling and driving so fast. If he'd paid attention, if he'd not lost his temper…"

I might be whole.

He barely managed to catch those words. He'd said plenty already. The tears kept coming but the words stopped as they stayed in the pose for what felt like forever.

"Take one more deep breath, Everett."

He followed the order even though he didn't want to.

"Now sit up and flip over to your back." She did the same.

He watched her close her eyes as she stretched out on her mat.

"We end in Savasana, or 'corpse pose.' Arms out, body heavy, breathing slowly, I want you to lie as still as possible."

He breathed, his body coming back into alignment. The emotions that had overwhelmed him a minute ago were stuffed back in the hole in his soul he hadn't looked at in years. The hole he never wanted to look at.

After a few minutes of quiet, interrupted only by the soft inhales and exhales of the two people on the mats, Cora broke the silence.

"Start moving again by flexing your fingers and feet, until you feel ready to sit up."

He heard her move long before he finally opened his eyes. Part of him was hoping she might roll up her mat and be gone when he looked at the world again.

Coward.

When he finally opened his eyes and sat up, Cora was seated on the mat, looking at him. “How do you feel?”

You. Not your back.

It was a subtle question. An impressive one that left him many options.

“My back and hips feel much looser. Thank you.”

“We should do this every day. At least until I leave. That way you can loosen everything up.”

Leave.

The word was hammered into his brain. She was still leaving. Of course she was. Not for another few months, but still.

There was a timeline. An end point. There was time before her, and there would be time after her.

His chest tightened on the despair that thought unleashed. At least he had the tension he’d released to blame his frown on.

“I can’t say that I want to do it every day, after the display you just witnessed.” He turned to the left, his back and hips cracking, then repeated the motion on the right. Wow, he hadn’t had that level of rotation in years. “But I also can’t claim I don’t already see improvement.”

“Great.” Cora stood and offered him a hand. “Then it’s a standing date.”

“A standing date.” He grabbed her hand, stood, then pulled her close. “Just one of many, I hope.” He ran a hand down her cheek, unable to keep from touching her.

“I look forward to all of them.” She stood on her tiptoes, and brushed her lips against his.

CHAPTER TEN

SHE HADN'T COME back for *The Ringlet Lady* after their first yoga session. Hadn't asked about his breakdown. Hadn't pushed any of the hard topics over the last few weeks. She'd just been there. A constant.

Cora had simply accepted the angry words he'd level at his father. Somehow that made them easier to bear.

Time was slipping through his fingers. This whole week he'd been wrapped up in the market downturn in the US, the resulting Asian markets' instability and finally the European. Sometimes it felt like if the American market sneezed the rest of the world prepped for everything to break. It rarely happened.

And if it did, the people he kept accounts for would be well insulated from the worst of it. Something all of them had needed to hear over the last week. The requests to talk to him were pouring in, though his staff was keeping him fairly protected. Though there'd been four they'd passed through when the clients became unmanageable.

But the hiccup in the market meant he was trapped at his desk far more than he wanted. Which meant he and Cora met for yoga, dinner and slept in her bed, which was far more comfortable than his own. But he'd missed the easy words and run-ins.

Today was Saturday—finally. She'd said last night that she was going to spend the day in the art studio. So he was going to see what she was up to. What creation was coming to life under her delicate fingers.

His phone buzzed as he stepped in and he glared at it before he met her gaze over the canvas. She raised an eyebrow and frowned as he held up a finger.

Everett tapped the earpiece. "Yes?"

"Mr. Goff for you, sir."

Before his assistant could say anything else, Benjamin Goff screamed, "What the hell are you going to do to mitigate this nightmare?"

"I do not appreciate yelling, Ben." The man was the relatively new heir of a fashion house fortune and prone to overreacting. His mother, God rest her soul, had had an intimate knowledge of the fiscal markets. If the woman hadn't been so focused on keeping Ben's father from running the fashion house into the ground, she would have managed everything herself.

Her son was not nearly as capable. "If you want to start over, fine, if not, that is also fine. However, I will cancel your account with Winthrope Wealth Management. I am certain other firms would be grateful for your business."

"Whoa. I didn't mean. Wait. No need to be hasty. I just logged in and saw the account. A hundred million in a week lost. I panicked. Sorry."

Saw it. Panicked and decided to yell. The sign of a great leader for sure. Everett rolled his eyes to the ceiling. Dealing with clients was his least favorite part of a job he absolutely hated. He did it as little as possible.

He took a deep breath then spoke as calmly as he could. "A hundred million when you are worth over ten billion is nothing."

He saw Cora's eyes widen and she shook her head.

Everett stepped out of the room to calm Ben. There was no reason to disrupt the work Cora was accomplishing for a man-child who had no boundaries. He talked the man off the proverbial cliff and wasn't surprised when Ben didn't bother to thank him.

When Ben was off the line, Everett reached out to the weekend secretary to let her know not to push any more phone calls through. He'd had enough of people with more than enough money worrying.

Besides, he'd lost most of the week to this mess. So, right now he was going to focus on Cora.

He stepped back into the room. "Sorry about that."

"Why does the CEO answer calls for the company? I thought one of the benefits of sitting in the corner office, at least metaphorically, was that you didn't get the angry phone calls." Cora didn't look up from her canvas.

Everett wished that was true. Wished he could turn the phone off. When his father was still alive, he'd told him to plan for someone else to take the reins when he was ready to give them up.

Then his father was gone and the void needed someone. Everett had never wanted the title. It was stifling. It provided no joy. Yes, he was good at it but being good at it didn't mean he looked forward to any of it.

"When people have their sureties with Winthrope Wealth, there is an expectation of access." The words were right. Hell, he'd heard his father say them so many different times. Usually in a boastful tone.

"I do put more boundaries in place than my father." The man had lived attached to his phone. His father had had every generation of mobile phone. His investments in cell technology had increased the Winthrope family portfolio exponentially.

But the look on Cora's face was anything but impressed. He understood.

"What are you working on?"

"Nothing important." She stepped back from the painting. Looked at it with one eye then the other and shrugged.

"Of course it's important. You're working on it." She was always so quick to push away her work. Cora was talented. If she trusted herself, her work would truly glow.

It was a lesson his college art instructor had told her students all the time.

If you love it, others will, too.

He'd thought that was fanciful, until he'd put the first Roam art up. He'd loved the graffiti and the world had loved it, too.

"It's just a picture. Nothing important and it's not very good, anyway. Decided to play with my favorite—watercolors."

"Why do you do that? Knock your own work down before anyone has even looked it over. You—" He looked at the painting and felt his mouth fall open. It was a self-portrait. Sort of.

Cora's face was obscured and she'd shaded the hair so it could be anyone with red, blond or brown hair. An imaginary creature anyone could self-insert into the painting. But the dress. The purple dress she'd worn on their first night together—the one she'd laid so carefully on the couch—it stood out in all its glory.

Draped down the stairs in a way that hadn't actually happened. It looked like it belonged on the cover of a book. She'd captured every little intricate detail. With watercolors. *Impressive* did not begin to describe the painting.

The tiny birds and butterflies looked elevated in paint, despite lying perfectly flat against the paper. The hint of three-dimensionality stole his breath. She was a master.

A master who'd never shown off her work.

"Wow." He crossed his arms and took it all in. A few classic pieces had moved him, items hung in studios and galleries for all to see, but this was the first he'd had the privilege to view before anyone else. "Cora."

There were no words. No words for the majesty she'd created. "This should be in a gallery." People would stand in front of it. Art collectors would discuss the watercolor medium and how the artist had chosen it. Historians would remark on the faceless woman and what she meant to the artist. Some would be right, most wrong, but art's meaning was twofold.

And he'd argue that the meaning that mattered most was the one perceived by the viewer, not the one intended by the artist. It was the meaning that stood the test of time.

"There is no need to say such things. It's fine. But hardly worthy of a frame, let alone a gallery."

"Excuse me?" He couldn't believe what she said.

"It's just fine, Everett. I mean I like it. It's nice. A pretty painting."

He waited, not wanting to interrupt, hoping she'd elaborate.

"I can see how some might like it. Those that buy things to make them feel good or because it's pretty."

That was the whole reason to own art, if you weren't amassing it as part of a fortune.

Most people owned art that spoke to them. That made them smile, or laugh, feel good. There was nothing wrong with that.

"As the owner of one of the finest galleries in the world and certainly one of the most exclusive, I think I have a very good eye for what belongs in a gallery. This does. It breathes on the canvas."

"You didn't purchase any of the art in the Winthrope Collection. Unfortunately for you, I remember you claiming that nothing in there spoke to you." She tapped her nose, depositing a bit of lavender watercolor pigment on the end of it.

He walked to where they stored rags, grabbed one, soaked it in water, then gently wiped the color from her face.

"Then all the more reason to trust what I'm saying here. If none of those pieces speak to me—"

"Then I know that this isn't very good." She lifted on her toes and kissed his cheek. "It's all right. I've heard it all before. 'It's cute. Simple. Blasé. A waste of paint. Cheesy. Chintzy. Pointless.'"

He laid a finger over her lips. Everett had heard more than enough. His father had said so many similar words. Directed at him they stung. Knowing that someone had said it to Cora brought every shade of red into his vision.

"Who?" It was the only word the anger in his system would let through.

"Who?" Cora tilted her head.

He took a deep breath. "Yes. Who? Who told you such lies? Your dad? Your art teacher? Your ex?"

Her cheeks darkened on the last one.

"It doesn't matter." Cora pulled away.

"The hell it doesn't." Her painting was a once-in-a-lifetime piece for most people. And she'd done it in a day. Sure, she'd used an air dryer to quick dry the colors, but she'd painted it fast and beautiful. There were professional artists who'd give anything to do the same.

"Who?"

"You sound like a beast when you growl like that." Cora started to reach for the paintbrushes.

"Cora!"

"My ex. Justin Patrick. I was his muse."

"His muse?"

"Yes. I stood for him, at least in the early days of our relationship. His pieces are abstract but have a human element to them. It's hard to describe if you haven't seen them."

"And he told you your work was cheesy, chintzy, worthless." Justin Patrick better hope he never crossed Everett Winthrop's path.

"He does know something about art and its worth. His work in displayed in galleries all over New York. Justin is an ass but he knows what is marketable. Knows what people want. What hangs in galleries.

"Even the scandal earlier this year was easy enough for him to weather. In fact, seems to have only increased his notoriety. No such thing as bad press and all." Cora grabbed the brushes and took them to the sink.

He leaned against the counter, his arms aching to hold her while his brain screamed for more information.

"What was the scandal, Cora?" It had involved her. He could tell from the tightness in her shoulders, the hunch in her back.

"He rose up through the art scene as the starving artist. The 'make it on your own' story—though 'make it on your own with your girlfriend's paycheck' was more accurate." She blew out a breath.

He suspected the only reason she wasn't banging the paintbrushes against the walls of the sink was because she was trying to maintain some decorum. Something she definitely didn't need to do for him.

"You were the girlfriend whose checks he lived off."

"The muse and the girlfriend." Cora sighed. "The fool easily played."

"Cora."

She ignored him. "He's everywhere in New York these days. No one cares that he is actually a trust fund baby. That the starving artist line was all an act. Hell, he even said in an interview that it was a long game performance act to show that anyone could do what he did." This time several brushes did slam against the edge of the sink.

"I take it you paid for everything, probably worked more

than one job, too." It wasn't really a question. He'd run into more than one grifter in this life.

Hell, more than one social media influencer had begged followers for money for rent or groceries or utilities only to later be caught owning their flats and having far more funds in the bank than the people they were collecting from. It was a horrid fraud—particularly to play on the woman you claimed to love.

"Why do you think I'm a yoga instructor? Art restoring pays well, once your name is well-known, but until then…" She shrugged.

Until then she'd supported them on barely there funds and hard work. She didn't have to say the words for him to hear them.

"A reporter showed up at our place. All the receipts in tow, wanting a comment for her story."

So her ex hadn't even bothered to come clean himself. That didn't surprise Everett. Cowardice was a rampant issue with grifters.

"I stood there while she recited everything, already fuming from him bringing home a pizza the night before. Pizza. The thing my dad and I ate together for years. The thing that every time I smelled it after he passed, I lost my appetite and burst into tears."

No pizza. Done. That was an easy enough sacrifice.

Her words kept coming. "He came home as I was standing at the door with the reporter—learning the last four years of my life were a complete lie. Do you know what he did? Can you even guess?"

"Laughed." It was something he'd seen time and time again when people were caught in lies. Most denied it, or apologized, begging for another chance. But some—the truly horrid—took pleasure in the truth being out.

You didn't lie to the woman you shared a bed with for years and not laugh when the truth finally came out.

Cora nodded but still didn't turn from the sink. "Exactly. Laughed. Even the reporter who'd discovered the worst was stunned by that. I told him to get out. Screamed that I'd paid for everything and I never wanted to see him again. And he laughed—again."

The paintbrushes hit the bottom of the sink and she let out a sob that echoed through the studio.

Another sob followed by a nervous giggle that rocked her body. "Laughed. Told me that he owned everything."

"How?"

"I'm not sure. Not even sure if it was true, but he had the lawyers and the trust fund and the truth was out so I wasn't needed anymore. I took what he couldn't claim, couch surfed for a few weeks on my girlfriends' couches and then came here."

"Sounds like Justin Patrick is a twat." One that he very much would like ten minutes alone in a room with.

Now she did turn around.

"Twat." She leaned against the sink. "What a deliciously accurate word for that jerk."

"Exactly. So, why is it that his opinion on your art matters?"

Cora opened her mouth, then closed it. She cleared her throat but still no words came out.

"That wasn't a rhetorical question, honey." The endearment slipped through his lips. Her lips twitched. Not quite a smile but after the conversation they'd just shared, that wasn't surprising. "Why does his opinion matter at all?"

"He is the most successful artist I know." She sucked in a breath. "Some of the others we hung out with have had a few showings but Justin made it. The playing poor was a gimmick he didn't need, but it worked. And now he's the 'it' artist in the city."

"And you being more successful than him was something

he wouldn't want. So he put you down. Come on, Cora. Go look at your portrait without the eyes of the artist. Look at it as though you were its restorer, or the curator."

"It's not that easy." She crossed her arms but headed over to the painting.

He knew that. The Roam image on the side of the bakery had a tiny line that was off. The first piece he'd done. The blue of the sky he'd painted was all wrong. The fifth—he could make a mental list of flaws for days. Nitpicking your work was a habit every artist he knew had.

But the ability to step back, and he had with his work, to see it as someone else might—it gave a new perspective.

What Justin had feared was the talent of the woman he lived with. He'd seen her work and Everett knew beyond a shadow of a doubt the man hated her for her talent. Such a little man to see his partner as a threat. He'd diminished her flame rather than build it up.

"It is good." Three little stilted words. "I mean, it still needs work. I plan to add shimmer to the edge of the dress when everything is fully dry. I used the portable air dryer you have in here, but even with watercolors it's best to let them rest. At least for a few hours."

"It is beyond *good*, Cora. And Justin knew it."

She looked at the painting one more time, then looked to the door. "I fancy some food. What about you?" She took the apron off and draped it over the chair beside the painting.

This conversation didn't feel over, but they could reattack it another time. "All right. Let's get you some food."

"Good morning." Everett rolled on his side and pulled her to him.

This had been their routine since he started sleeping in her bed. Everett woke first, always. Waited until she woke then pulled her into his chest. If there was a better way to start the day, Cora never wanted to find it.

"Morning." She ran a hand along his chin, enjoying the stubble underneath her fingers.

"Any plans for the day?" His fingers trailed up her back as he nuzzled against her neck. The feel of his stubble on her chin sent lightning through her entire body.

"I plan to spend the day in your office. I haven't had that much time with *The Ringlet Lady.*" She'd looked it over enough to establish it could travel, once the small tear was rectified. But every time she'd headed for his office, she'd gotten distracted.

Usually by the man currently doing his best to drive all thoughts but those about him out of her mind.

And it was working.

In their free time, Everett watched her paint. Oh, sure, he'd claimed he was painting, too. And there were a few acrylics splashed across his canvas but most of the time he'd watched her.

Exclaimed over her pieces. The watercolors come to life. She nearly believed him when he called them masterpieces.

"I like it when you're in my office." His hand cupped her butt and pulled her leg over his thigh, giving him easy access to exactly where he wanted.

Exactly where she wanted him.

His thumb pressed against her bud and she rocked against him. "What do you want for breakfast?"

Everett asked the simple question then bent his head to suckle her breasts. What was this madness?

Everyday talk between enjoying her breasts. Why did that turn her on so much?

"Toast and coffee." Her breath hitched as he slid a finger into her. "Everett."

"Toast and coffee. Mmm-hmm. I could have guessed that."

His teeth brushed her nipple and she arched her back as his finger found the spot he seemed to know instinctively would send her over the edge.

Less than a month in his bed, and Everett knew her body better than any lover she'd ever had.

His manhood pressed against her belly, but when she reached her hand to cup him, he pushed it back. "Morning time is my time, darling."

Darling. Honey. Sweetie.

The man was trying all sorts of nicknames out on her and she was loving each one of them.

Love.

The word struck her brain as his lips captured hers.

Love.

Good God. She was falling in love with Everett Winthrope. That wasn't possible. This was a wild three-month affair. A fantasy. A fairy tale.

His tongue danced with hers. A waltz only they knew the steps to. Choreography felt rather than learned.

"Cora." His mouth slipped down her throat. His fingers still driving her ever closer to the edge. "My sweet."

"Everett!" She arched her back as his tongue trailed its way down her body. Each feather kiss barely there but leaving a spike of heat with each motion. "Everett."

"I do love how you say my name when I'm about to make you come." Everett replaced his fingers with his tongue as he wrapped her legs around his head.

She raked her fingers through his hair, anchored to this world by him and him alone. "Everett!"

Cora felt him smile against her as he drove her over the edge. Her body needed him. Needed him—all of him now.

Luckily, he was inclined to agree. Everett rolled onto his side, put on a condom and hooked her leg back over his hip as he slid into her, filling her.

"This is the best way to start a morning." Cora brushed her lips against his, moaning as he pushed her over the edge again.

"I agree."

"No. No. I know what the market is doing. I know it looks like it might crash. Yes. It might." Everett rolled his neck as he tried, for what felt like the hundredth time since she'd come into the office, to calm someone panicking on the other line.

Cora was mentally designing a patch for *The Ringlet Lady*. She didn't have the supplies here, but the weather had finally broken three days ago.

She picked up her tablet and added to the list of supplies she'd started her first day here. The last two months were going to fly by. She'd begun the process of alerting museums and galleries that part of the Winthrope Collection would be available for exhibit.

It wouldn't go on the road for at least a year. The large galleries and most impressive museums had their collections scheduled one to five years ahead of time.

"No, I understand." Everett blew out a breath as he slammed the phone down. "Ugh."

She didn't understand market fluctuations. Her father's legacy was a rented flat, paintbrushes and a wall that looked far too much like it belonged in a movie about a conspiracy theorist losing their mind than an art conservator.

His estate had not even covered all of his debts. The only thing he'd left was grief and a gratefulness that she'd been his daughter. Even if it had been difficult at the end.

"I don't know how much I can offer but is there anything I can do." She wandered over to the desk and wrapped her arms around Everett's neck.

"The American market crashed while I was on that phone call." He took a deep breath. "Three of the start-up companies

I invested in filed for bankruptcy twenty minutes ago and more will follow if the crash lasts more than a few months."

"Are you worried?"

"No."

She was pretty sure that was a lie. "Then what do you need to do?"

"I need to go to London. For at least a week." He was tapping his fingers on the edge of the chair. Stepping back into the viper pit had to be unnerving after years away. Everett leaned back in his chair, glaring at whatever was on the computer screen.

A week. Seven days.

At least.

It was what he needed to do but she couldn't pretend that losing a moment of their limited time together didn't sting.

"We can leave tomorrow."

We. We...

Had her heart just inserted herself into the trip?

"We?" Such a foreign word on her lips. Cora had never been part of a "we." Even in her long-term relationship.

Everett's head snapped up. Was he realizing that he'd invited her along unintentionally? Or had her heart forced her brain to hear something that truly wasn't there.

"I assumed you'd want to come. Uh...given our..." Everett stood and started to walk over to her but only made it around his desk before the phone rang.

He turned to look at it then turned back to her.

"I'm not answering. I'll call whoever it is back." The force of the words was sexy as hell.

Putting her first. No one, not even her father, had done that. Hearing those words from the man she was falling in love with was a bigger turn-on than she could ever imagine.

But she was not going to interrupt this with kisses. Not yet.

"Given our…?" She gestured between them as he stepped closer.

"We've never discussed this, Cora." Everett raised his hand like he was going to cup her face but only ran his thumb along her cheek before dropping it.

They'd never even broached the subject. They'd lain in each other's arms, whispered secrets and pains, but never discussed the future.

It had felt almost off-limits. A foreign, distant thing that if not acknowledged, then couldn't be stolen from them.

"We haven't." She swallowed and stared at him.

"Come to London with me. The work will still be here." His blue gaze was fire as the phone chimed, but he never looked away.

"People will ask why you have an art conservator with you." That was easier to say than *What am I to you?*

"I wasn't planning to bring you as an art conservator." He leaned against *The Ringlet Lady*'s frame and raised a brow. "I had planned to bring you as my girlfriend."

Cora swallowed as his tall frame leaned toward her. The man was fantasy come to life.

"Girlfriend?" Her grin must be massive. Her feet might float off the ground if they weren't weighed by the pure lust of his body so close to hers.

"Girlfriend." Everett's hand cupped her cheek. "Is that all right with you?"

"Yes." The whispered words were out as she closed the tiny distance between them. Her lips had barely captured his when the phone rang—again.

He grabbed her ass, gave it a quick squeeze, then pulled back. "We'll have some free time in London. Promise."

"We better." Cora winked as he sat back down at the desk.

The moment his magnificent backside was in the chair,

his whole demeanor changed. It was a weird sight to watch the mask fall into place.

Cora shook her head. It was a tough day. He was adjusting. Years of watching Justin's moods shift had trained her to look for minor things that might become major. But Justin's issues and mood swings did not translate to Everett.

They were going to London. As boyfriend and girlfriend. And her duffel bag had nothing appropriate for anything more than standing in an abandoned art gallery.

"Oh, no." The words slipped out.

"I'll have to call you back, Patrick. Cora, what's wrong."

"Oh." She stepped around the painting. "Sorry, you didn't need to hang up. I…"

"Patrick is more than capable of handling things. I'll call him back in a minute. What's wrong?"

"Not sure I should go to London. I don't have—"

"Anything you don't have we will get in London. I figured we need to stop by the shops anyway."

"Because I have so little." That stung. It was true. But it still stung.

"We can get anything you want, but I specifically thought some new lingerie might be nice." He winked then sighed as the phone's ringtone echoed in the room.

She set her tools down, walked over and kissed his cheek. "I'll get out of your hair so you can handle the worrywarts."

"I'll order the helicopter and we'll leave tomorrow morning—assuming the weather holds."

Order the helicopter. Buy whatever.

It wasn't like she needed a reminder that they came from such different worlds, but those words clouded her brain. "Sounds good." Cora swallowed the tiny pinch of worry that this was all too much.

CHAPTER ELEVEN

CORA SMOOTHED THE black dress and tried to figure out a way to make it seem like she belonged in the room with people whose watches were worth more than everything she'd ever owned. The dress…and dozens of others…had been at the London apartment when they'd arrived this morning.

This morning.

Outside the cocoon of Snow Peak Estate it was far too easy to remember who she was. Who Everett was. And why their relationship probably didn't work in his world.

She was an outsider. The interloper that had no idea what role she was supposed to play at this—this party?

Party wasn't the right term. It wasn't happy enough. *Business meeting* was too formal for whatever this event was.

Uncomfortable. It's uncomfortable.

Cora looked at the shoes someone she'd never seen had laid under the dress for her. They fit like a glove. The perfect shoe. Somehow procured without her ever stepping foot inside a store.

Money. Power. Prestige. Those were access points. Access points Everett had. Access he was leveraging for her.

"You look out of place." A young woman with long blond hair and a black dress very similar to Cora's passed her a glass of something alcoholic.

It was a painful truth, but there was no reason to argue it. Cora took the glass but didn't take a sip. There was almost as much liquor floating around this place as money. Everyone was a little tipsy. Except her…and Everett.

She wasn't sure of his reasons for sobriety. But Cora already felt like an outsider, no need to add alcohol to the system. Still, she raised the glass to the woman. "I'd like to pretend it isn't obvious but I've never been much of a liar."

"Don't hang out with this crowd if you aren't able to lie, honey." The woman took a deep sip of her drink. "Alyssa Cooper. Wife of Lord Pembrooks. When he remembers he's married."

Cora had no idea what she was supposed to say to that. Luckily Alyssa didn't seem to need a response.

"So you are Everett's new doll." She looked Cora up and down, not bothering to hide the critique.

"Doll?" Heat was trapped in her cheeks. She wanted to argue. Wanted to say that was ridiculous. But she was wearing an outfit wholly picked out by his staff. Including her undergarments.

"Before the accident he had dozens of dolls. Beautiful women, well-dressed, educated, and gone before the next event." Alyssa pointed to the drink she'd brought Cora and asked, "If you aren't going to?"

"Oh, sure." Cora passed it over. "I am not a doll." The words were awkward but she needed them out. "I'm an art conservator."

"Impressive. Who's your favorite artist?"

"Roam. They're a graffiti artist who—"

"Who defaced buildings around London before giving it up." A man who was probably Lord Pembrooks stepped next to Alyssa, wrapping his arm around her waist. A possessive claim that Alyssa didn't seem to enjoy.

Everett put his arm around Cora, too, but it felt protective. Safe. An anchor in this high-society storm.

"He didn't deface them." Cora looked to Everett, hoping

he'd say something. When he didn't open his mouth, Cora continued.

"Roam's pieces are masterpieces. The buildings' occupants—"

"Don't know enough about art to really matter." The man let out a sigh. "These parties are always so boring, don't you agree, Winthrope?"

"They are a necessity." Everett pulled her a little closer.

"Why?" Cora pretended not to see the horrified look cross Alyssa's face before she hid it behind her glass.

"What?" Everett looked at her, but it was the CEO looking at her now. His eyes were shadowed and the mask she'd seen at his desk was fully in place.

"Why are they necessary? What is anyone getting out of this? Besides drunk." It wasn't diplomatic. In fact there were dozens of ways she could have asked the question now popping into her mind. But it was already out.

"Everyone is here to be seen." Lord Pembrooks didn't bother to hide his sneer. "Which is good since some haven't been seen in far too long."

"I wasn't asking you." Cora didn't look away from Everett. "Why are *we* here?"

"To be seen." Everett's fingers squeezed her side. Was he trying to tell her something? Or was that squeeze just a subtle shut-up sign.

Justin had done that when she'd said something he didn't like. Cora didn't appreciate the subtlety now. If Everett wanted her to do something different, he needed to say something.

After all, she'd been given no instructions for this. There'd been no time for it. She'd seen him for all of ten minutes before this event.

They'd landed. He'd kissed her, told her he'd see her at the apartment and that everything she needed should be there. Then he'd gone to the office.

She'd gotten ready for the event only because Hannah had sent a note to the apartment and a staffer had told her when to be ready.

"And it is good to finally see Winthrope. His father would be very disappointed in him hiding away in Norway at the top of some mountain for years. Though given the scar—" Lord Pembrooks gave a small shrug but there was far too much satisfaction in his features.

He tensed beside her and now it was her turn to squeeze him. Though she was looking forward to Everett telling Lord Pembrooks off.

Silence hung in the air as it dawned on her that Everett wasn't going to say anything. The man was a drag. Everett was brilliant with finance. Funny. Romantic. These people trusted his company—trusted him—with their financial well-being.

And Pembrooks was insulting him to his face.

"I suspect if people were less inclined to mention people's physical appearance, then he might have come off the mountain sooner." If he wouldn't defend himself, then she would.

Alyssa coughed but it didn't hide the laugh.

"Your father would not have liked her." Lord Pembrooks cleared his throat and pointed to a group in the corner. "Good, Cox is here. We should say hi."

Cora was grateful the lord was about to take his leave. The feeling was short-lived as Everett kissed her head and followed the ass to the small group of men dressed alike in the corner. Each raised their glass as the two slid into the gathering.

"Right." Cora looked at Alyssa.

"You get used to it." The woman's features were soft now.

"I won't tell you that it doesn't sting, even after a decade, but you do get used to it."

"I doubt I'll be around long enough to get used to it." Everett had barely acknowledged her this evening. They'd gone from being inseparable to ghosts at a party before the earth had made one full rotation of the sun.

"I bet you will."

Cora let out a laugh that had no humor in it. "And why would you think that?"

"Because you are the only one he's ever brought to a gathering like this. Dinner dates, parties, those are easy. This, this is part of him. You might not realize it, but that is no small accomplishment."

Being ignored didn't make her feel like she'd won anything. "Is that a prize? I thought I was a doll."

Alyssa's cheeks darkened and she bit her lip. "I shouldn't have said that. I hate these, too. The dolls were a joke, not a very funny one, for when he was younger. I'm afraid when I'm nervous, I can act like a real jerk. And I'm always nervous at these. Even after a decade as Lady Pembrooks I feel out of place."

Alyssa looked at the now empty cup in her hand. "I shouldn't drink so much. It loosens my tongue."

"Why don't we get some fresh air? In fact—" Cora looked over at the gaggle of rich men talking about who knew what "—why don't we get out of here completely?"

"Leave?" Alyssa looked over at the husband she'd complained about the moment she walked up and shook her head. "I can't."

She could. But Cora wasn't going to force her.

"Well, I can." She reached out and squeezed Alyssa's hand. "I hope your night gets better."

Cora looked over to Everett one more time. Her heart

screamed to go to him, tell him she was leaving. But he was busy doing whatever this was.

"Cora?" Alyssa held up her phone. "I know we've been here ten minutes, and I was a bit of a bitch when I first walked up, but any chance you want to exchange numbers. I just… I think maybe we could be friends."

"The mean girl who is actually a girl's girl." Cora grabbed her phone. "That is what you are. You should let her out more often." Cora exchanged digits with Alyssa, then headed for the door.

Cora stepped into the cool night air, wrapping her arms around herself. A driver materialized out of the dark, "Would you like to go somewhere, Ms. Cora?"

"Yes." She offered the driver a smile. "But I think I'll walk. Thank you."

"Does Mr. Winthrope know where you're going?"

"Mr. Winthrope didn't even know I was there. He'll be fine." Cora hated the catch in her throat. "Have a good night."

She was in London. There were dozens of places to go. Dozens of things to see. But right now there was a side of a bakery she wanted to sit in front of for a little while.

He was back here. In London. The chaos and backstabbing. He'd dreaded it from the moment he'd realized it was necessary. If Cora hadn't squeezed his hand as they stepped onto the helicopter, Everett might have called the whole thing off.

And part of him wished he had.

Tonight was exhausting. Everything he'd feared…and more. From the stares to the impolite chat, to the reminders that his father would have done something different. To Pembrooks's direct statement that he'd disappointed his father's memory by hiding. Everett had hated these events when he'd accompanied his father, and hadn't missed them during his three-year exile. An observation many of the attendees had pointed out.

Most with no delicacy. Unfortunately, now that he was here, Everett understood why his father had attended. You learned a lot. Particularly after the alcohol had flowed for hours. Information he needed to know.

Arthur Cox was bleeding money between his mistress and the wife who refused to grant the divorce. Oliver Hampton was gambling like the funds he had were infinite—something Everett might have said was true when his parents controlled the fortune. And Emma Patrill's daughters were trying to hide her dementia diagnosis but their mother had already been scammed by three different individuals. The time to step in was fully past but the daughters were struggling to get the mother's lawyer to move forward with the paperwork.

Probably because he was scamming the woman, too. All of these were things Winthrope Wealth needed to know to adequately project wealth growth. And given the nature of the information it also wasn't something clients were inclined to share freely.

The first two clients had issues he'd adjust for in order to safeguard as much of their finances as possible. The Patrills… well, that lawyer would be getting a personal phone call from Everett. If that didn't move the paperwork forward, then he'd initiate fraud charges.

And then there was Ben Groff. The idiot he'd yelled at weeks ago was making noises about trying to oust him from the CEO position. It would probably go nowhere…but he had to head it off.

All the necessary information he'd gathered didn't change the drain on his battery. What he wanted now was to get Cora, go to the apartment, take a nice hot shower—preferably with her—climb into bed, sleep for several hours, then wake her with sweet kisses.

A solid plan. Assuming he could locate her. The crowd had thinned.

And it wasn't that large to begin with. Where is she?

"If you're looking for your doll—"

"Cora is not a doll." Everett rounded on Alyssa, the wife of Lord Pembrooks.

The blonde raised an eyebrow. "Hmm. Good. That means what I told her wasn't wrong."

"What did you tell her?"

Alyssa had been fun, once. Lord Pembrooks was not exactly the loving type. She'd married because of family pressure. Something far too many wealthy individuals expected from their offspring.

Romantic love was the stuff of fairy tales when you reached a certain level of society.

Love.

The word rattled his brain.

Love.

He loved Cora. He wasn't sure when it had happened or how. But he loved her. He didn't want what so many of the people he knew had. He needed her.

"I told her, she'd be around awhile. Assuming you don't screw it up."

Everett didn't want to waste time playing games. "Where is she, Alyssa?"

"She left." Alyssa pointed to the clock on the mantel. "Two hours ago."

"Two hours?" How was that possible?

How did I not notice?

"Asked me to go with her. Wish I had." Alyssa cleared her throat. "Don't mess it up, she's going to be so fun."

He had no plans to mess any of this up.

I didn't notice she was gone. Not the best start, Everett.

Milo, his driver, would know where she was. Probably headed back to the apartment. He couldn't blame her.

Stepping out to the pavement, he was glad when Milo opened the door for him. "Did you see Cora into the apartment?"

"Ms. Cora walked."

"Walked? No. What? Walked to the apartment? That's over three miles." The shoes he'd had purchased for her were soft leather. Comfortable, but not designed for city hikes.

"I don't think she was headed to the apartment, sir." Milo looked at his watch. The man was very good at his job, but Everett could sense the frustration behind the cool smile. "She left here an hour and forty-three minutes ago."

"An hour and forty-three minutes?" Such a precise statement was a dagger to his heart. She could be anywhere.

"About that." Milo gestured to the seat. "Where shall I take you, sir?"

Where would she be? The city was huge but it was late. The museums were closed, the shops, the food…bakery…

"I think I know where she might be." He gave the address and hoped he was right.

She was barely visible in the dark. Cora was sitting on the bench the bakery had set up for the last piece he'd done. The wall was lit, but Cora was coated in shadows.

"I missed you," Everett said when he walked up to the bench.

"Not for a while, you didn't." Cora didn't look at him. "Sorry. That was—"

"Earned." Everett slid onto the seat beside her, hating how ramrod straight her shoulders were. He'd hurt her.

Unintentionally. But still.

"How did you know where to find me?" Cora didn't look away from the last image he'd ever put out for the public. A man standing in front of the bakery, looking through a window at a happy couple picking out a wedding cake.

Everett had seen critics call it an odd choice. They'd wondered what message he was sending with the piece. There'd been no message. He'd painted what he'd seen walking past the bakery one day. He'd been out scouting a new location—for a piece that never made a debut—and found the bakery's perfect wall.

A couple had been trying cake inside. The groom picking up the little pieces and feeding them to the bride. He'd stood on the walkway for several minutes, soaking in the strangers' happiness. Then he'd had to paint it.

"You've talked about this painting. It's the major discussion point for your thesis. It made sense that you'd come see it." Everett put his arm around the back of the bench and tried to ignore the pain of her not leaning into him.

"I love this painting. And I hate how upset Roam must have been when they painted it." Cora let out a sigh.

"Upset? Why do you think Roam was upset?" He hadn't been. Not if memory served. Life changed forever three weeks after this went up. So the memories were all a little jumbled.

"He's outside looking in on happiness. As an artist he was always apart. I think that's why I like the works so much. I spent so much time apart—like tonight." She turned, the talk of artists over.

"I'm sorry."

"Why do you have to be there? And I do not want to hear the phrase 'to be seen.' Because I know you dreaded coming. You barely made it onto the helicopter." She crossed her arms, her body still pulled away from him.

She saw so much. Knew him so well. "You're right. I didn't want to come. Still don't like being here. But it is to be seen, but more so to hear what the gossip is. And as the alcohol flows the information turns from a trickle to a deluge." He quickly relayed the main things he'd learned tonight.

"You really think the lawyer is in on the scam, too?" She scooted a little closer to him, not touching, but closer.

"I do. Their reluctance to act doesn't make sense otherwise." Everett let out a sigh. "And Ben Groff is going to cause problems. There were probably other items of interest, too, but unfortunately, I only have one set of ears."

"Except you don't. You have two." She pointed to her ears. "Assuming you trust me to listen, too." This time she scooted close enough to lean her head against his shoulder.

"Of course I trust you enough." He trusted her with his life. He loved her. Sitting in front of this painting. His painting, her in his arms. It felt like everything was right for the first time ever. "But I assumed after tonight, you'd never set foot in another event."

"If I understand the reason and the point, I will happily attend—provided we spend at least a little time together."

That was such an easy ask.

"Done." He kissed her head and took a deep breath as he looked at the painting he'd completed just before his accident.

The man looking through the window was sad. It wasn't possible to see his face. But the hunch of his shoulders, the stance, the otherness in the face of love—he was the artist and he'd not seen it.

"Do you want to know who Roam is?" The question was out before he could think it through.

"There was a day when I would have jumped at the answer. Sought it out and tracked every clue that might lead to the revelation, now, though…" She kissed his cheek.

"Roam wanted to be anonymous. Whatever their reason, it was important to them. So no. I guess I am not looking for that answer. Not anymore."

Why did that answer burn? His secret, the thing no other

living person knew. He wanted her to know. But she was no longer searching.

Everett could still tell her. But the words he was nearly sure he was going to share a moment ago were gone. And she was right—he'd wanted anonymity. Craved it. Needed it.

So in the end, he didn't say anything, just squeezed her tight.

CHAPTER TWELVE

"HI, HONEY."

Everett set Cora's tea on the side table next to the watercolor palates she'd lined up in the small studio he kept in the London apartments. He stepped behind her and nearly spilled his tea as he stared at her creation.

It was a watercolor version of the bakery piece.

"I know it's a poor companion."

"No. It's better than the original." Those weren't kind words because she needed a boost. The art was better than what he'd hung on the side of the bakery wall. There was more depth to it.

She'd captured the otherness of the man at the window. It was perfection.

"It is not better than the original." Cora grabbed the tea he'd brought and warmed her fingers but didn't lift the mug to her lips.

"It is. Roam would agree."

Cora rolled her eyes. "Do you like it? And I mean like actually like it. Not because you're sleeping with me."

Everett stepped behind her, wrapping his arms around her waist. "I like it a lot. It's got a depth to it that the Roam piece doesn't."

"That's probably just the medium shift. Watercolors and spray cans are very different after all."

"The medium is different but the talent is so clear." Everett kissed her cheek, and slowly ran his hand down her stomach.

"You better not start anything you don't plan to finish." Cora laughed as she bent her head back to kiss his cheek.

"I always finish what I start." Everett undid the top button of her pants and groaned as his phone rang through his earbuds.

"I heard that." She whispered and stepped away.

"Everett Winthrope. Yes, I saw the news. I have checked all the indicators. Your assets are fine. There's going to be a loss moving forward but think of the joys of investing when money is cheaper. Crashes provide opportunity, too."

He pinched the bridge of his nose as the client unleashed their frustration. "Enough. I am not going to be berated and I will not allow you to berate my staff." He took a deep breath as the client struck one more blow.

"You're right. I am not my father."

Not my father.

He'd taken pride in that line a few weeks ago. Now he felt like a failure saying it.

The line clicked and Cora reached for his hand, squeezing it. "The markets aren't recovering as fast as the clients hoped."

The downturn was likely here for at least a few months, maybe even a whole year. His clients wanted the markets to continually climb, but that wasn't possible. Something none of them wanted to hear. "I've heard more than once that my father would have handled this better."

That was the part that stung. He and his father hadn't been close. He'd died in the car yelling at Everett. But he'd prided himself in the last three years that he was continuing the legacy. Growing it. Making it better.

What if I'm not?

"Would he?"

"What?" Everett had expected a small consolation. A simple statement that of course he wouldn't have done it better. This woman was always surprising him.

"Would your father have done a better job? Deep down, what do you think?"

"I don't know. Maybe he'd have seen something I didn't. He'd have invested differently, and he'd be very focused on protecting the Winthrope name. It was his primary concern." The irony that it was Everett carrying on wasn't lost on him.

"The Winthrope name is a name. It holds no real meaning other than what you assign it. So your dad might have done it differently and better?"

"He would have been wholly focused to contain it. No distractions allowed." As soon as the words were out, Everett wanted to pack them away.

"I'm not sorry to be a distraction." Cora raised both her eyebrows, then winked. It was absurd and so cute.

He was pretty sure she made the joke to lighten the mood. "You are not a distraction—or at least not a bad one. My father...well, the clients don't have an option. It's me or the highway." Because he was not going to let a takeover happen.

No matter how much Ben, Lord Pembrooks and the group they were gathering wanted it.

"Ever consider it not being you?" Cora lifted the teacup and took a sip.

Yes. "No."

"You could hire—"

"It's me." Everett kissed her cheek as the phone rang in his ears again. He pointed to it. "See...always me."

"Doesn't have to be," Cora called as he headed for the door.

"I'll see you in a couple hours. That painting is fantastic. I'm hanging it in the gallery and you are not arguing with me."

Cora took a deep breath as she started toward the group of women huddled in the corner. She'd promised Everett she'd help in these outings, even though she was positive after this morning that he didn't want to run the company. He was doing it for his father.

I drove up an icy mountain to find a painting my father was obsessed with.

Did she really have a place to judge? Everett was busy listening to a group on the other side of the room, but she wanted to know what gossip these women were discussing.

"Hello." Cora smiled as she slipped into a small opening between two women during a lull in the conversation.

The head-turns of everyone reminded her of Justin's "friends" when she stepped into their conversations. The outsider. The unwanted.

Breathe. And stop projecting.

"I wasn't aware Everett was dating anyone." A brunette with deep brown eyes didn't hide the glare. This wasn't like her interaction with Alyssa.

Breathe.

"Dating the help. I guess the rumors about him are true." A short blonde, whose roots were showing, let out a laugh.

She let the dig roll off her shoulders. It wasn't the first time someone had referenced her station.

It won't be the last either.

That cold truth washed over her. If she was Everett's partner there would always be those that looked at her like these women did.

"What rumors?" Cora took a sip of her drink. It was a nonalcoholic beer that the bartender had joked no one ever ordered before putting it in her cup.

"Oh, you don't need to worry about those, I'm sure you won't be around long enough to watch the board attempt to remove him." The blonde giggled as she leaned in closer to the brunette.

It was not lost on Cora that no one had introduced themselves.

"Why would the board want to remove him?"

"Because he isn't his father. He hides away and does everything via algorithms rather than networking. I mean, who invests in unknowns." The brunette rolled her eyes.

"The people who invested in Apple, Facebook, Google and others might disagree with not investing in unknowns. Apple started in a garage." Cora plastered a smile on her face as she tried to keep her cool.

"He gets upset when people call him. I mean, I know my father used to talk to his father at least three times a week. Charles Winthrope was always available."

"And calming." Another member of the group chimed in.

"Is Everett not making you money?"

"Of course he is. That is what Winthrope Management does. But it's how he's doing it that's rubbing people the wrong way."

That was the most ridiculous argument she'd ever heard for removing a CEO. The complaint was that "he is making us money but not interacting with us and placating our whims."

"Excuse me, ladies." Everett stepped up. "I need to steal Cora away. I do hope you don't mind."

They all made a few fake complaints about loving her company.

"That was an interesting conversation. We need to talk, Everett." He needed to know the plan. The intrigues afoot.

"Later. I need you to meet someone first." Everett was nearly bouncing. He was excited. At this event, he was actually excited. It was nice to see.

"Who?" This was the man she loved. The one filled with life that had nothing to do with what so many in this room wanted him to be.

"It's a surprise!"

The room parted as they moved through it, but she saw more than a few glances and rolled eyes. These people disliked him. They were plotting against him. Fire poured through her. This was such a joke.

"Everett, the board is plotting to remove you as CEO." She hissed the words in his ears.

"I know." He swallowed. "I'm not living up to the expectations my father gave."

"Everett—"

"No. We're not discussing it here." He held up a hand. "Mathias, this is the watercolor artist I told you about."

"Your girlfriend." The man tilted his head. "I thought you meant a real artist, Winthrope."

Why did everyone only call him by his last name? It was off-putting.

Probably by design.

"She's the one who painted the images I showed you on your phone. The ones you said belonged in your gallery and asked how much they were up for when you thought they were for sale. Cora St. Stevens." The words were clipped, as he raised a brow.

Images on his phone?

He was showing off her work. If she hadn't already been in love with him, that would have sent her tumbling all the way over the edge.

Mathias looked over Cora. "St. Stevens. Any relation to the crazy conservator convinced that *The Ringlet Lady* was real?"

So this was the game. Put down something you loved because it didn't come from a source you respected. If Cora wasn't floating on the knowledge that Everett was showing off her works it might upset her. But nothing was going to bring her down in this moment.

"Maurice was my father. And he was not crazy—hasn't anyone explained to you that society doesn't appreciate that language anymore? It's judgmental and rude." She felt Everett stiffen beside her. This was an opportunity. For her.

And I'm throwing it away.

But opportunities from people that started conversations by insulting others was not a win. Not in her book.

"And *The Ringlet Lady* does exist. It was hiding at Snow Peak Estate but it will go on tour with additional pieces late next year." Her final gift to her dad. A way to make people like this realize they'd been wrong.

"No. It won't." Everett kept his tone even. "The painting is real, though. My great-grandmother posed for it."

The ringing in her ears nearly drowned out the screaming in her head. *The Ringlet Lady* was real. They'd never discussed it. He said she could pick the pieces. It could travel. Sure, it needed a minor repair. He knew how much it meant to her.

To her father's legacy. How could Everett…

Her throat was tight and there were going to be tears. But not here. Not in front of these people.

"It's a nude, is it not?" Mathias raised a brow. "A nude Alarie spoke of only once and said was his lover."

There was a glitter in his eyes that turned her stomach even more than Everett striking down the idea that the portrait would travel.

Nudes were in museums around the world. The human body was gorgeous in all its forms and artists from the dawn of time had captured it.

"Correct," Everett stated. "Cora's work is what we are here to discuss, though."

Her work. Like she'd want to discuss it with this man—particularly after Everett had killed the idea of *The Ringlet Lady* traveling.

"Her watercolors are cute." Mathias crossed his arms. "But *The Ringlet Lady*—"

Cute. Justin had used the same word. It had nearly destroyed her when she heard it from him. From Mathias, the four-letter word didn't matter at all.

"*The Ringlet Lady* is not up for discussion."

Of course it wasn't. In this room of millionaires and billionaires, only what they wanted to discuss was on the agenda.

"Cora's work has depth and imagination. You stated only twenty minutes ago—"

"Everett, I have a headache." Cora had seen these conversations before. There was no winning here. Mathias probably thought her paintings were excellent. He likely even made musings about hosting them in a gallery. But that was before Everett revealed they were hers.

Before it was discovered that she was the daughter of Maurice St. Stevens. A man who'd contacted everyone he could and even some he shouldn't have been able to reach about a painting that until tonight, no one besides him had said was real.

These people weren't her friends or colleagues. They never would be. And they weren't Everett's either.

"A headache?" Everett looked at her. "I see."

He turned his attention back to Mathias. "I will send you the proofs of her paintings."

"You will not." They were hers. Period. If she was going to show them, it would be on her decision.

"Your father would not have liked her."

She thought she'd wear that as a badge of honor. Cora turned without bothering to give a farewell.

"I'll admit that didn't go great." Everett sighed as they slid into the back seat of the car.

"It did not." Cora crossed her arms.

Two days in London and it seemed like they were falling

apart. Two business events. One she'd left early and the other where an idiot had insulted her artwork.

"Mathias thought your work was magnificent."

"Not magnificent enough to overcome who I am, though." Cora let out a sigh. "Why on earth were you negotiating my paintings with him?"

That was a misstep. He'd been so excited to show her that someone else viewed her work the way he did. He'd acted without thinking. "It happened so quick. I'm sorry."

"Do you really have pictures of my work on your phone?"

Everett grabbed his phone and opened it immediately. A picture of her at the easel was the background.

"You have me as your background?"

"I love this picture. You're so focused, though both of your eyes are open." She punched his shoulder and he chuckled.

He flipped through the images. He'd captured each of the watercolors she'd done. Each and every one.

"You're so talented, Cora. I just had to show you off." He kissed the tip of her nose.

"It's hard to stay mad when you say it like that." She brushed her lips against his. "But there is something else we need to talk about."

"Yeah, the company."

"Oh." Cora nodded. "Yes, that."

Everett looked at her for a moment. Was there something else she wanted to discuss?

He waited a moment but when she didn't say anything, he started, "I'll need to focus on making sure they can't oust me." Everett hadn't planned for that. The vultures were circling.

He'd stayed at Snow Peak for too long. And all he wanted to do was head back there now. Cocoon himself and Cora away from the rest of the world. Sink back into the universe where only they existed.

"You are the CEO and the owner. How is it even possible for them to remove you?" Cora laid her head on his shoulder.

"I'll always have a controlling share, but it is possible for the board to leverage votes and force me to appoint someone else. It never happened to my father."

"Why don't you let them do it?"

Everett's heart jumped. He could just let others take over. That had been his plan before the accident.

"What would I do if I wasn't at the helm of Winthrope Wealth Management?"

"Anything you wanted." Cora put her hands on either side of his face. "Anything. You could paint—"

"You are the painter, Cora." He ran his thumb over her lips, before kissing them. Drinking her in.

"Spoiler alert, Winthrope." She raised her brows. "Art is not pie. We can both be artists—support each other. Or you can do anything else. Start another business. A charity foundation. Start a rock band."

"I have no singing voice, Cora."

She rolled her eyes. "The point is you don't need them."

"Winthrope Wealth Management was my father's dream." His inability to connect with it was why he was a disappointment. It was why his father was dead.

"But is it yours, Everett?" Her hands were warm on the side of his face.

She was looking at him. Waiting for his answer. An answer he knew deep in his heart.

"Yes."

Lies.

Cora blinked and laid her hands back in her lap. "Really?"

No.

His heart screamed at him to tell the woman he loved the truth. Show her the closed-off wing. Take her to each Roam exhibit and claim them, even though she'd told him she didn't want to know.

"Yes. I owe it to my father."

"That isn't the same thing as it being your dream." Cora was looking at her hands as she quickly raised one to push away a tear.

She took a deep breath.

He held his own. Was she about to end this? Tell him it was too much? He couldn't blame her if she felt that way.

It would kill him, but he wouldn't try to hold her if she wanted out. This life…it came with so much privilege, but that didn't mean there weren't thorns sticking out on the rose.

When she looked back at him, her eyes were clear. "All right, if it is your dad's dream you want to follow, I'll help. But I am never ever, ever going to enjoy these events. And you are not allowed to sell my paintings without talking to me first."

It was so much more than he deserved. "I love you." The words slipped out. It wasn't the best time to come clean with that announcement. She deserved fanfare and more than an argument in the back seat after a work event that went sideways.

But the words wouldn't stay buried. "I love you, Cora St. Stevens."

Cora smiled and put her hands back on his cheek.

"I love you, too. Obviously, if I'm willing to go to these stuffy gossip parties masquerading as work events." She let out a giggle before his mouth captured hers.

She loved him. That was worth more than all the money in his accounts.

CHAPTER THIRTEEN

THEY WERE HEADING back to Snow Peak Estate today. Finally. A week and a half playacting for the rich and spoiled individuals who were only worried about expanding their ever-growing bank accounts was infuriating. And somehow it was Everett's fault that the accounts weren't growing at the constant rate they expected.

If only they could live on the millions or billions they already had.

"Yeah. Yeah. I know." He walked up, kissed her cheek, but his eyes were far away. His ears focused on whatever new complaint someone was lodging.

In an attempt to hold off the hostile takeover, Everett had made himself available to anyone and everyone. He'd gone from the reclusive CEO who only handled pressing issues to a man anyone could reach.

Anyone but me.

Cora bit her lip as the jealous thought tore through her. This was temporary.

Still, it had been like this all week. The only time they'd had to themselves had been late at night and first thing in the morning. They'd made use of that time with their bodies instead of with words.

She hadn't even brought up *The Ringlet Lady.* Every time she tried, there was a phone call. Or a rough day. It was always something.

Everett was having a rough time. Battling for a company he didn't want.

It's his father's dream.

She'd chased her father's dream to completion. Why did it bother her so much that Everett was doing the same?

Where does it end?

Cora sucked in a breath, trying to force her lungs to expand. That was her concern. She had an end point. A place to stop.

Would I have stopped if The Ringlet Lady *wasn't at Snow Peak?*

She wanted to believe she would have. Cora had promised herself. A promise that was easy to keep because it was completed.

"I'm heading back to Snow Peak, but we'll be doing regular trips to London. I've got requests in to update the video equipment in my office. You'll be able to reach me whenever."

Whenever?

He couldn't mean that.

Everett clicked off the phone and grabbed her luggage—or rather one of her luggage bags. She was heading back to Snow Peak with far more items than she'd arrived with. "Ready?"

"What did you mean by 'whenever'? Who can reach you whenever?" He had to mean that metaphorically. Had to.

"A client. I guess I didn't realize how often my father was in contact with them. What they expected. Or I guess maybe I did." He looked at his phone, a frown crossing his lips that vanished before he looked at her.

"Because he only had time for clients?" It was easy to see the answer. And she knew it hurt.

After all, her father had missed so much because of his search for the painting in Everett's office. She'd stood in front of him once, told him she thought he loved the chase for the painting more than her.

In her father's defense, he'd been horrified. He'd apologized and promised to be more present. A promise he hadn't been able to keep.

Had Everett's father even managed that? She suspected not.

"He wasn't great at balancing the business and family. My mother left before I was born. My father won custody—or bought me, I guess. Paid her to vanish from his life…and mine. I went looking for her as a teen but she'd passed with cancer by the time I located her." Everett carried her bag up the stairs to the private jet.

"That is terrible." She'd never met her mother either, but her father had talked about her with such love. Cora knew if it was possible, she'd have raised her. She'd never doubted that she loved her.

Everett had had two parents who'd prioritized everything over him.

She waved to the pilot then took her seat beside him. At least in the air, he could have an excuse to turn the phone off. Sure, he could be reached via Wi-Fi, but there was no expectation he be available when they were thirty thousand feet above the ground.

"I'm so sorry, Everett."

"It's fine. Or I mean it's not. But I have had more than two decades to deal with the fact that she didn't want me." He looked at the window.

Cora grabbed his hand, squeezing it tightly. A mother who'd left him in a home with a man who saw him only as a legacy. No wonder Everett was so focused on living up to whatever myth his father had created.

But it wasn't healthy. His father hadn't had a partner to help him balance. Everett wasn't going to slide down that path.

"Speaking of balance," he muttered as the phone rang and she watched him hold up a hand.

Less than ten days after they'd said I love you and she already worried she was second to everyone else that had his cell phone number. There was no way to pretend it didn't sting when he answered it no matter what they were doing.

He finished up the call as they started down the runway.

"Are you going to talk on that thing the whole time we're in flight?"

Or do I get some of your time?

Everett closed his eyes and reached for her. "I'm sorry, honey. I've been fending off the takeover."

"I know." She didn't understand. The man was happiest when he wasn't dealing with the company issues. But for now, it was what he needed.

She watched the clouds out the window then took a deep breath. Balance was off the table, at least for now. Might as well bring up the other elephant in the room. "Why don't you want *The Ringlet Lady* on tour? That piece would bring so many visitors. It would—"

"It's my great-grandmother in the nude." Everett held his hands out. "She had an affair with Alarie. He painted her and showed it off only once. My family bought it to keep people from looking at it. To keep the tongues from wagging and laughing."

There was a myth that historical individuals were such prudes. The truth was that humans had been stepping out on their significant others since the dawn of time.

People decried divorce rates harkening back to a time when people loved each other and stayed married. Never mind that most of those unions were required because women weren't allowed to work or have their own autonomy. Many of those unions were stoic not loving.

And at the level of wealth the Winthrope family operated in, it wasn't like most people married for money.

"People have affairs. It happens. More than anyone wants to discuss."

"I know." Everett shrugged. "Tale as old as time."

So the affair wasn't the sticking point. "Did you know her?" Cora had grown up in museums and galleries. The nude body didn't cause her any consternation. There were nude portraits in nearly every art exhibit.

But she wasn't related to any of them. At least not that she knew of.

"No. She'd been gone for decades by the time I was born. I don't think my father knew her either." Everett stretched the seat out and put his hands behind his head.

"The painting is a masterpiece. Her hair covers her breasts and—"

"Cora. She is naked. Yes, I know it's art. I know nude bodies have been part of art since the dawn of time. However, you heard Mathias. That's just one example of what people will say."

"And you care what people will say?" Cora ran her hand along his knee.

"I don't want to."

Then don't.

Words so easy to say but hard to follow through on.

"I understand." She did. It hurt that the image he wanted to protect meant her father didn't get his full redemption. It was one thing to say the painting was real. Everett's word carried a lot of weight—in the world of the wealthy.

In the art world…in the art world his statement that it existed might convince a few people. But most would demand proof. And until it was delivered, they'd say he was covering for the woman he was sleeping with.

Maurice—the man driven mad by a mythical painting—would be the memory her father left. The legacy he carried forward. It hurt, but it wasn't completely inaccurate. It had been her father's sole purpose and he'd died not knowing.

She did, though. And that would have to be enough.

"Thank you." Everett kissed her cheek and closed his eyes. "I think I might attempt a short nap."

"Of course." She nodded and went to grab her sketchbook. There were a ton of emotions pouring through her and she needed them out. Needed them on paper. Some place where they couldn't hurt.

Two days back at Snow Peak Estate and he felt like he'd seen Cora less than he had when they were in London. How was that possible? Part of the reason he'd wanted to come back here was to give them more one-on-one time.

In London he was always on his phone or in some meeting. The same was true here, too.

But she never came into the office now. Before they'd left, she'd spent at least an hour or so in there. Investigating *The Ringlet Lady* or chatting with him. Sitting on the edge of his desk.

He'd expected her to be in there yesterday. He knew she had picked up the supplies to fix the rip in the corner while they were abroad. Yet, no Cora yesterday or this morning.

Opening the gallery door, he wasn't surprised to hear the podcast blasting.

"She always told her friends not to say she lit up a room after she died. But when it happened it was all her best friend Suzy could think to say. That and she was sure her ex-boyfriend was responsible. She said it to anyone who would listen and even those that wouldn't. And in the end it was Suzy's persistence that landed Brad's jail sentence."

"At least this one has a happy ending." Everett smiled as he took in Cora. She was back in the oversized overalls that were just as, if not more, enticing than the fancy outfits Hannah had selected for her in London.

"Happy? She's dead." Cora didn't change her position on the painting she was examining.

"I just mean that it's solved. The last one you were listening too was unsolved." Everett cleared his throat. Why was he so nervous? He slept next to this woman every night.

She hit Pause on the podcast from the remote on her hip. Still, she didn't rise and meet his gaze.

A gulf had formed between them in London. He thought they'd easily close it when they got back. But it was deeper now.

"I thought you'd be in the office today. Repairing *The Ringlet Lady*." He knew she was frustrated that he didn't want the painting to go out on exhibit.

But letting the painting out—it just wasn't an option. The comments. The snide remarks. His position was already precarious enough.

"It isn't going on tour. There's no reason for me to fix it. I put the repairs needed on the list I'm keeping for the foundation." The words were so matter-of-fact. So distant.

"Cora, you looked all over for it."

"No. My father looked all over for it. I found it. Mission complete." She stood and rolled her hips.

Mission complete.

There was a bite to those words.

He moved and ran a hand over her lower back. "You are so tight." He pushed a thumb into her lower right side.

She hissed as his thumb rotated around the knot.

"We should start yoga again."

"I waited for you yesterday and this morning." The words were soft. The implication clear.

Damn.

"I didn't realize we were…" His words faltered. They'd

had a routine before London. Wake, yoga, coffee, shower. Then start the day.

He'd hopped out of bed the last two days to an inbox full of "critical" emails and voicemails. He'd made coffee at the bar he kept in his office. And buried himself in work.

"Tomorrow. It's a date." He kissed the top of her head.

"Don't make promises you don't plan to keep." She turned and looked at him.

"I—" His phone buzzed and he grabbed it. "It will only be a minute."

"Right." Cora nodded. "A minute." She kissed his cheek and headed farther into the gallery, hitting the remote and restarting the podcast.

That wasn't necessary, he'd only be gone a minute or so.

He stepped outside; he didn't want to explain to the client why a murder saga was blasting in the background.

"Right. I understand the flexibility in the market and your personal investor can adjust to lower risk, but that also means the gains are smaller." Everett rubbed his forehead. There was a pulsing vein in his temple as he repeated the same thing for the billionaire on the other end.

"No, I am the CEO, not your personal investor. I make suggestions to the investors. No, I cannot be your investor solely." He pinched his eyes closed and tried to keep the angry words he wanted to throw at the woman on the other end in check.

"Because if I'm your personal investor, everyone else will expect that as well… No. I do not believe you will keep that between us. You will tell just one or maybe two people and then they will want the same thing, swear they can keep it between us, and before I know it, I'm running every single account." Everett sighed as the phone call finally ended.

He didn't have to look at his watch to know that he'd been

gone for hours rather than minutes. How had his father handled this?

He didn't.

Everett had had a pattern. He'd set up the algorithms, answered phone calls infrequently and it had worked.

And it had nearly led to a hostile takeover.

How was that fair?

It wasn't.

The phone rang again. He thought about throwing the earpiece across the room, but resigned himself to the necessity.

"Any chance you have time for dinner?" Cora's smooth, sweet voice on the other end of the line was a balm to the day's tedium. There wasn't a hint of nagging or sadness—though she'd be within her rights. It was just a simple question.

And a reminder that he'd promised to see her this afternoon and lost the entire day.

"You do not have to call me on the phone to get my attention."

"Today would demonstrate otherwise."

"Touché." Everett stood and hated how tight his back was. He shouldn't have skipped yoga.

He headed into the kitchen and smiled as she held her hand out. He laughed and put his hand in it.

"Nope." She squeezed his hand and then pointed to his phone. "I need that and the earpiece that goes with it."

"Cora."

"Everett." She matched his tone. "You need a break. You clearly won't give it to yourself, so I am giving it to you. Now pass them over."

He held his phone and earpiece out, hating how hard it was to watch her hit the power button.

She put a plate in front of him and then took the other seat.

"Thank you." He dug into the pasta dish.

"You're welcome. It's nothing fancy."

"Don't do that." Everett reached over and grabbed her hand. "You made a great meal. It doesn't need to be fancy."

"Well, good thing the hermit CEO who refuses to poke their head out of the office isn't picky about what I fix for dinner." She tapped his nose.

"You should come into the office tomorrow. Work on *The Ringlet Lady*."

"No. I have to get the other projects heading out ready. Those take precedence." She swallowed and looked away from her plate for a moment.

"You could come to the gallery for lunch. Take a break."

"I'll do that."

She smiled but it didn't quite reach her eyes.

"Cora?"

She met his gaze. "Yes."

"I love you." He meant it. Meant it to the depths of his soul.

But what if it wasn't enough?

"I love you, too."

They spent the rest of dinner in an ever-widening silence.

CHAPTER FOURTEEN

CORA LAY IN bed and tried to pretend that Everett would be right in. That he'd come to bed. That today, unlike the six days they'd had back at the estate, would be different.

I lay awake waiting for Justin for years.

She'd waited so long for him. For something to change. And in the end, he'd taken everything.

Everett isn't Justin.

Her heart cried as her mind beat out that even if he wasn't the same, he wasn't here with her. He said he loved her but she'd taken a back seat to a company he hated—even if he wouldn't admit it.

She slipped out of bed, brushing a tear from her eye. It was past time for him to come to bed.

And if he doesn't?

Cora shuddered as she stepped into the hall. They had to talk. He was trying to please a ghost. A ghost whose habits had nearly destroyed the son trying so hard to emulate him.

The gulf between them couldn't get wider. Now was the time to build a bridge across it.

She slipped into his office and frowned at the empty room.

"At least he isn't sleeping on the floor."

Cora walked over to the desk; his phone was lying on it. Another good sign—but one that didn't offer any indicator of where he was.

She yawned and went in search of the man she loved.

Twenty minutes later she'd exhausted all of his usual haunts. Staring at the base of the stairs she looked at the closed-off wing. The off-limits area. She'd meant to ask what was there when they got back.

Meant to ask if it was still forbidden to the woman he loved.

But I was worried about that answer, too.

This was a crossroad, literally. Forking right, heading back to her room, would take her down the path she'd walked over and over again since coming to Snow Peak Estate.

Left. Left took her into the unknown.

Her feet moved before her heart had time to war it over with her brain. She wanted to find him. Needed to find him.

The carpeted hallway looked just like the other side. The doors to each room closed, hiding whatever was there. If she had to open each of them this was going to take a while.

What if he isn't here?

A low thumping from the end of the hall caught her ear. Or maybe it was just wishful thinking but she headed toward what she thought was the sound. Her steps picked up as she heard the rock music coming from the last door.

When Cora reached it, she thought about knocking but she wasn't sure he'd hear her over the loud music.

It was a ridiculous excuse, but she didn't want him to tell her to go away. Whatever was happening on this wing…

She grabbed the handle and opened the door before her brain could find any reason to walk away.

Colors were splashed on the walls. All the walls. Bright. Happy.

Everett was standing on a ladder at the end of the room. A giant mural coming to life under the spray can in his hand.

A mural of her. Just like the one on each of the other walls.

One was her eyes. One was her at an easel. One was her in bed, sheets tastefully draped over her.

It might be flattering—if she'd known.

Her hand was at her throat. Words were trapped. Emotions tumbled, crashing into her heart as her brain tried to make sense of what her eyes were seeing.

Everett was painting.

Graffiti.

His style was bigger now. More defined than it had been on those buildings years ago but the art was unmistakable. The style purely unique.

"Roam." She was an expert in the graffiti artist. Probably the only expert on the vanished artist.

His spray can halted. The music on the speakers stopped. So this room had a sound system like the gallery.

Of course it does, Cora.

What a dumb thing to think of in this moment.

"Cora." Everett turned to come off the ladder. "This wing—"

"If you're about to tell me that this wing is off-limits, you better suck those words right back in. I have been ignored for days now. I have waited for you at dinner, in bed, on the yoga mat. I have called you to schedule an appointment. An appointment with the man I love. So if you are about to tell me this room is off-limits, don't."

Everett pushed a hand through his hair. "I kinda thought you might be excited to know who Roam is. Though when I asked you if you wanted to know you said no."

No. He was not putting that on her.

"I didn't think it was you. You should have told me. Should have shared this." She gestured to the walls with her on them.

She'd said no when the person was faceless. No when she thought Everett was asking a hypothetical. Not *No, I don't want to know the man sharing my life is the artist I've been fascinated with my whole adult life.*

"Fair." Everett set the can down and looked at the walls. At least he wasn't going to argue that point.

How could he have hidden this? A secret persona.

And how had she fallen for two people who hid so much of themselves?

Another man who used her as a muse without pulling her into his world. Her heartbeat was pounding in her ears as her brain screamed that she'd been tricked again.

Everett is not Justin.

She was not going to force everything on him.

"So, you are Roam." She needed to hear it from him. Hear the reason.

"Yes. My father didn't approve." Everett closed his eyes, communing with a man who wouldn't answer.

His artwork was amazing. So beautiful. A gift from the universe that he was hiding in a mountain estate.

"You should share this. Maybe not the one of me in bed. But you should share this with the world. It's your calling."

Everett stepped toward her.

But she stepped back. "I mean it, Everett. You've talked about my art as though it glows when you are painting giant masterpieces back here."

"Your art does glow. It is the masterpiece and this is…" He looked to the wall and shrugged. Shrugged!

"This is just a weird hobby."

Hobby. He called his art a hobby.

"How dare you?" Cora marched over to the image of her painting. "This is gorgeous."

"Because of the muse."

Muse. A term that she didn't want. That was not a gift she needed.

"Everett, you should be showing this off. Claiming—"

"And disgrace the Winthrope name!"

Disgrace. How could this disgrace anything? And if people found it disgraceful then they were not worth any of the precious time a person had in this world. "You are the one that gets to determine what the name means. You. You are the only Winthrope left."

"Because my art killed my father." Everett sucked in a breath as he stared past her.

"What?" Cora was moving now. "He was driving—"

"He was picking me up from jail. I got caught scouting."

"Scouting. How—?"

"I don't know, Cora. I've never known. The charges were dropped because they were baseless but still. My dad was on the road that rainy night because of me. He picked me up, told me what a disappointment I was—"

She'd never understood the term *seeing red*. Until right now.

"*You* are not a disappointment Everett Winthrope. That was wrong on levels that cannot even be described." If she could patch a call into the afterlife, she'd give Charles Winthrope more than a piece of her mind.

"You saw the clients." He looked past her again. Was he seeing an imaginary group of rich idiots whose opinion he cared far too much about?

"You get to decide what disappointing the Winthrope name means. *You*. Not the clients. They don't matter. If you drop all of them, others will step forward. And if they don't, who cares. You have more money than you could possibly spend in three lifetimes. You have the gift of time—to do what you want without fear of making the rent or paying the bills." She ran a hand over his cheek.

"You get one life, Everett. One life for yourself." How could he hide this? How could he not want to scream to the world that he was Roam. That he made things that mattered.

"Yeah. You get one life, too, and you are wasting it as an

art conservator when you could be creating art. I'm not the only one dimming my gift."

Her heart cracked and she felt like she might crumple to the floor. "I am not wasting my life. And my job is an important one."

"It's not the one you truly want, though, is it?" Everett pointed to the wall, to her at the easel.

"Unlike you, I have to worry about bills. I have to pay rent." The funds in her account were enough these days, but only because she'd driven up an icy mountain.

"My art is hidden, Cora, but so is yours. You could do both—artists do it all the time. Work a day job while pursuing their passion. But you let your ex diminish your flame."

"Fine." That was true. She could agree to that. Justin had destroyed more than she wanted to admit. "But you are losing yourself in a ghost's expectations."

"No. These embarrass the Winthrope legacy."

"The Winthrope legacy? The company?" How weird to think of a company that produced nothing as a legacy. A company he hated helming. A company he'd clearly run from once.

No man called their son a disappointment because he was waiting in the wings to follow in his footsteps. Everett had wanted out once and his father had hated that.

"Yes."

"But only the Winthrope legacy, right? Not the St. Stevens—"

"Is this about *The Ringlet Lady*?" Everett shook his head. "It's a painting. Nothing more."

Nothing more. Nothing. "That painting—its existence—is my father's legacy. My family, my father was called crazy. A word that is considered a slur by many in the mental health world. That painting is real and it's here. He will go down as a mad conservator because the Winthrope legacy demands that it stay hidden."

"The company—"

The company. Of course. "You don't have to say anything else. I get it. I know my place. It's the legacy that matters." She looked around the room at the pieces no one would ever see.

"Cora. It's my father's, my family's legacy. I can't tarnish it." Everett's words washed over her.

Cool and empty. She was so empty. She didn't have words. There was nothing to say. Nothing that wouldn't send them farther into whatever abyss they were careening toward.

"I'm going to bed." She pushed a tear off her cheek. He wasn't going to join her. She wasn't sure why she was so sure of it, but deep down she knew they'd broken something tonight.

Cora turned, hating the knowledge that Everett wasn't chasing her. Wasn't calling after her. She'd fallen into a fairy tale all right. But she knew the originals. Those stories were far from the happily-ever-afters the modern versions depicted. The old stories were meant to teach lessons.

Don't step out of line. If you fall in love with the Beast, you will get hurt.

Lesson learned.

Everett groaned as he pushed himself up from the floor. How had he thought this was preferable to following Cora to their bed?

Because I am a damn coward.

He'd stood in the room where he'd painted her on each wall and wanted to kick himself. She'd come to find him. Discovered his secret and told him what he'd expected her to say. That his work was great.

Masterpieces.

Words he'd longed to hear from his father. Words he'd never hear. His cell buzzed and Everett pulled a hand along his face.

He'd take the call. Look at his email and then go find Cora. Apologize. See if there was some way to push past last night.

How?

He answered the phone and sat behind the desk. When he looked up, hours had passed.

Because of course they did.

He needed to find a way to balance this. Cora deserved that.

The phone buzzed again, but he put it in his pocket without answering and headed to the gallery. He needed to see her. Needed her.

No murder podcast was playing. Maybe that was a good thing.

"Cora?" The gallery was silent.

Empty.

He looked at his watch. Not quite three. This was where she should be.

His stomach dropped. As he moved farther into the gallery. She wasn't here. He knew it.

The estate was huge. So why was panic building in the back of his brain. She hadn't left. She hadn't…

Everett ran to the art studio, knowing she wouldn't be there. Once that was confirmed he raced to her room. The room they'd shared for weeks now.

The bed was made. The clothes he'd had purchased for her lay on it, folded. The painting of her in the dress on the steps was propped up on the pillows, a note underneath it.

No. No. *No.*

"Cora!"

He fled the room. This wasn't happening. He raced to the

front of the estate knowing what he'd find but not willing to believe it.

Her car was gone. It was only when he saw that, that he accepted the truth.

Each foot was lead as he made his way back to her room. His body crying out with each heavy step.

He grabbed the letter and sucked in a breath as he tore it open.

Everett,

Forgive me for doing this via letter. I fear that if I tried in person I'd lose the will to do what needs to be done.

I wish you the best with the company. I really do. But I can't watch you bury your dreams to chase your father's.

You are not a disappointment. You are so much more than you give yourself credit for. I only wish you could see it.

Sorry. I promised myself I wouldn't lecture via the written word.

Thank you for letting me close the mystery of The Ringlet Lady. Even if only I know the truth, my father can rest knowing he chased something real.

Good luck,

Cora

There was a tearstain over her name.

How long had she been gone? How long was he alone here without realizing it?

Hours. Hours.

He'd worked. Answered calls, emails, taken meetings, never realizing that the woman he loved had left him. His phone buzzed again and he headed back into his office. But he didn't answer the buzzing monstrosity.

Instead, the moment he entered the office he slowly moved to the cabinet containing *The Ringlet Lady.* The portrait his great-grandfather had purchased to keep out of the public eye. A picture hidden in a wall so people didn't see it.

They hadn't destroyed it, though. They could have. It would have been easy. No one would have known. Maybe they hadn't been able to destroy such a work. Alarie was a master.

His great-grandmother was standing in the nude. The artwork was incredible but, as he looked at it now, it was the woman's gaze that caught his attention. Her eyes looked at the painter, her lover. Alarie wasn't visible but it was obvious her gaze was for him.

A lover who society said she couldn't marry. A lover cursed to ignore the piece he'd crafted with skill and love. A love denied.

His phone buzzed. Why did the damn thing never shut up?

Because I always answer.

Everett looked from the desk to the art and back again. Legacy. What did the term mean?

Whatever I want it to mean.

But taking that step, leaving everything he'd been raised for…what his father had died cursing him for…

The phone continued to buzz.

"What."

"Is that how you answer? I guess you actually don't care what your clients think. Maybe I should look into that vote on the board again…" It didn't have to be a video call for Everett to know Lord Pembrooks was sneering on the other side of the line.

"Maybe you should." Everett chuckled.

"Laughing, Winthrope."

"Yep." Cora had stated the obvious last night. He could

kick whomever he wanted out. Others would fill their place. He had a waitlist generations long.

Or he could let another take the helm. He still had the controlling interest.

Everett could choose.

One life. He had one life. And he planned to spend it with Cora St. Stevens. But first he had to make a few changes.

CHAPTER FIFTEEN

"I CAN'T BELIEVE it's here!"

Jack Anderson, the curator at the London gallery, had squealed over *The Ringlet Lady* the first time Everett had called. And several times more since the piece had been hung on his wall this morning. It had taken him three weeks to get this opening scheduled. Lightning speed in the art world, but forever when you were parted from the one you loved.

It was opening to the public tomorrow. But tonight a few select people were invited to the preopening.

And he was praying that Cora was in the crowd. Alyssa had promised she'd asked Cora to come with her. But she wouldn't force her.

Gossip had spun quickly when he'd started looking for Cora. It hadn't taken him long to hear the rumors that she was at Lord Pembrooks's apartments. Not that the lord graced those doors. No, she was a guest of his wife, Alyssa.

Everett wasn't sure how that friendship had spun up. Another failing of their brief time in London when he'd become so focused on Winthrope Management that he'd lost the most important person in the world.

Less than a month and so much had changed. For starters, he was no longer the CEO. Patrick was the obvious choice. The vice president knew the ins and outs of the business. He was respected by the employees. And he was Everett's choice. The board had no reason not to vote for his choice.

He was free. It gave him more time to do what he pleased. To organize this. To be him. For the first time in his life. The only thing missing was the woman he loved.

"I still think we should have repaired the tear." Jack pouted at the tear in the corner.

The tear Cora had marked so delicately. The tear that according to Jack was an easy fix. One that could be handled in a day or two.

Everett hadn't wanted to wait. Besides, there was only one person in the world who was going to fix that tear. If Cora didn't want to…

He didn't want to think about that. This had to work.

It had to.

"And these," Jack said, pointing to the two other canvases making their introduction tonight. "These will be what people talk about tonight. *The Ringlet Lady* will bring them in, but this…"

He stopped in front of Cora's masterpiece. The watercolor of her on the steps in the purple dress. Jack had seen it and squealed as loud as he had with *The Ringlet Lady*.

"This will be all people talk about. I suspect if you change your mind and put a price tag on it, it will fetch a lovely price."

Everett was not changing his mind. "No, Jack."

The curator shrugged and moved to the other piece. The other was Cora, too. Though her face was obscured behind the easel.

He'd re-created the image hanging on the wall in the art wing—mostly. Without her at Snow Peak, this version had deeper blues. The hints of his brokenness clear. If you knew him.

The giant graffiti canvas took up almost an entire wall at the back of the gallery but it was the name in the corner that was most important. Roam. His name. His outing. His work—in a gallery.

"I still can't believe you're Roam. I figured this gift was gone from the world for good."

Jack tilted his head and sighed before moving to unlock the gallery doors.

It nearly was.

Alyssa was practically dancing as they walked up to the gallery. If she hadn't been so excited about attending this very exclusive event, Cora would have demurred. But Alyssa had answered her call when her car had broken down less than three miles from the turnoff outside Everett's estate.

Like the universe itself was chastising her for leaving a note and running.

Because she had run. Three weeks in London, licking her wounds in Alyssa's apartment, had made it very clear that she'd panicked. Rather than taking a deep breath and trying to work anything out, she'd fled.

Because staying and getting hurt would destroy her.

And yet she'd gotten destroyed anyway. Because Cora was lost. She'd picked up the phone so many times to call Everett. To explain, to build the bridge she'd wanted to build the night she'd discovered his secret.

But every time she picked up the phone, she'd stopped. What did you say after such a fight? After fleeing down a mountain? When you realized the arrows you aimed at the man you loved could take you down, too?

After all, she was chasing her father's dreams just like Everett. Her father never painted for himself. All his skill was directed to repairing others' works. And that was fine.

But Cora… Cora wanted more. And that should be fine, too. But stepping out of your parent's shadow wasn't easy.

"This is so exclusive!" Alyssa wrapped her arm through Cora's. "I think it will perk your mood right up."

"Alyssa. I know the definition of *sourpuss* currently has my picture next to it, but I am not sure one gallery invite is going to snap me out of it." There was no way Cora could express the gratitude she had for the woman who'd answered her sobbing call. She hadn't known who else to call. She'd dialed Alyssa on a whim and bawled when a driver arrived, took her to a private airport and then to the Pembrooks London apartments.

Alyssa had meant it when she said she thought they could be friends. And they were.

"I think this one will. Like I said, very exclusive." Her friend winked then giggled.

Cora rolled her eyes, "Exclusivity isn't a huge draw for me."

"It is tonight." Alyssa squeezed her hand and opened the gallery door.

The painting was hanging in immediate sight. People were mulling around it. Looking it over. Talking.

Tears blurred her vision as she stared at the group standing in front of *The Ringlet Lady.*

"Cora?" Alyssa's voice was miles away as she stood, rooted to the entrance.

"Everett?" She turned her head, blinking the tears away. He had to be here. He had to be.

Alyssa patted her hand but didn't let go. "There's another painting you're supposed to see first."

"Is he here?" Cora's voice caught as she whispered the thing she wanted most.

"Yes." Alyssa patted her hand again and pulled her toward a painting that had drawn more crowds than *The Ringlet Lady.* Her painting.

"Oh—"

"Don't get too excited." A middle-aged white man stepped up. "Jack Anderson, gallery owner. That piece is not for sale. I have had more than twenty offers so far. And no, not even for three million pounds, Lady Pembrooks."

"Three million pounds." Cora put her hand over her chest. "Three million." For her painting. No.

"I tried the moment I saw it, but I'm hoping I might convince the artist to sell." Alyssa hit her hip against hers.

"Much to Alyssa and Jack's dismay none of the three pieces here is for sale. Despite the numerous offers that have been made." Everett's voice was soft in her ear.

"Everett."

He held up a hand before she could say anything else. "There is one more. In the back, it's too big to be out here."

"Everett." She put her hand in his and knew before they walked back that it was a Roam piece. His work. In a gallery.

It was similar to the picture of her standing in front of an easel. Cooler, though, sadder.

"This three-piece collection is called *Cora's Collection*." Everett pulled her hand to his lips. "Because without you, none of them are ever seen by anyone and that would be a tragedy."

"Everett."

"Cora, I am so sorry. You were right. I locked myself away and turned myself into a man I thought my father would like, even though I hated the creature in the mirror. Then you came and set that beast free. Except I was scared to leave the cage." His hand brushed the tears away from her cheek.

"I stepped away from the CEO position three weeks ago."

No. She loved him and she thought that best, but she wanted him to choose it. Not because she forced his hand. "Everett, you—"

He laid a finger on her lips. "I did it for me. For the life I want. Patrick will do better than me as CEO, anyway. And I'm still on the board. Not gone completely."

Was she dreaming?

"I love you, Cora St. Stevens. I love the art you create and I love the man I am when I'm with you."

His fingers brushed her cheek and sparks flew down her spine. He was here. He was really here.

"Everett." She hiccupped and threw her arms around him. "I love you, too. But you aren't the only one that needs to issue an apology."

She kissed his cheek, then stepped back. "I locked myself away, too. Not to the same extent, but my talent, my dreams. Chasing them never seemed right. I was buried under my father's expectations, too. Until I showed up on your door and everything changed. And then I let a few stressful weeks jade everything."

"I was a pretty big louse in those weeks." Everett kissed her cheek.

"I wasn't exactly perfect either. I fumed rather than speak my piece and then burst and ran when I couldn't hold it in anymore. I'm sorry."

"Forgiven. But you're going to have to help me fend off the buyers for your watercolor."

Everett laughed as Jack held up another slip and mouthed, *Four.*

Cora shook her head. "You'd think they'd all be back here looking at the Roam piece."

"It's good. Really good. But nothing compares to *The Woman in Purple*."

"*The Woman in Purple*? That's what you named it? How boring!"

"And what would you have named it?" Everett dropped a soft kiss on the end of her nose.

"*Beauty from the Beast's Perspective.*" Cora looked at him. "After all, it's how you saw me that night."

"Not true." Everett pulled her closer. "I was paying far less attention to that dress. But you're right, that is a better name."

EPILOGUE

HER FIRST ART SHOWING. The first real one that was only Cora's work. *Pride* didn't begin to describe the feeling in his chest as he watched people move from watercolor to watercolor admiring his wife's work.

"This is so fancy," Alyssa cooed as she wandered next to him. Cora's unlikely best friend had stood beside her at their union and cheered on every single piece of art she created.

Though Cora still refused to sell *Beauty from the Beast's Perspective* to her friend. Alyssa had collected more than her fair share in the divorce agreement with Lord Pembrooks last year and she'd hired Cora to help her procure all sorts of things that she liked for her new apartment.

"She deserves this." Everett agreed that it was fancy. Several galleries had bid for a chance to be her debut location. Cora St. Stevens-Winthrope was a star.

"Look at how many people came!" Cora clapped as she walked up to Alyssa and Everett.

"Did you think they wouldn't?" Everett pulled her into his arms.

"Of course she did. Even after all this." Alyssa rolled her eyes. "I'm going to go schmooze the attendees because I can tell from the look in your eyes, you're about to do that Cora and Everett lovey-dovey thing."

"Lovey-dovey thing?" Cora raised a brow.

"Yeah. We do that." He kissed her. These last two years

had been perfection. He'd chosen his replacement then stepped aside as CEO of Winthrope Wealth. He was still on the board with a controlling interest—in case anyone got any less-than-bright ideas. Though after he'd dropped Pembrooks, and the others threatening to oust him, the rumblings had ceased. The openings had filled up from the waitlist in less than twenty-four hours. After he let Alyssa take her ex-husband's place on his books, he'd heard more than one whisper that other spouses were thinking of following Alyssa's path. Good for them. Life was too short to be unhappy.

Something his wife continued to teach him.

Cora had convinced him to open a studio specializing in graffiti art. So far he'd sought out new locations twice because the classes kept filling up minutes after opening.

"My own gallery showing." Cora leaned her head against his shoulder. "I never thought this was possible."

"The first of many." He kissed the top of her head.

"I think I'll need to take a little break."

"Break." Everett pulled Cora in a small room to the side with no painting. "Honey, this is going to be a success. There is no reason you have to take a break."

Cora giggled and pulled his hand to her belly. "Well, we've been doing other things with success, too."

Everett looked at his hand on her belly and bit his lip. "Cora."

"I realized it this morning. I'd planned this whole elaborate thing. I was going to paint a picture and show you but—" her lips brushed his "—I couldn't hold it in. Plus, if anyone offers me champagne to celebrate." She raised both her brows in that playful manner.

"If Alyssa thought we were lovey-dovey before—"

"Oh, she will avoid us all night." She kissed him deeply. "I love you, Everett."

"I love you, too."

Everett captured her lips once more. They needed to go out and mingle soon. But for a moment longer he was going to drink in the color and life that was his wife.

And their son or daughter.

* * * * *

If you enjoyed this story,
check out these other great reads
from Juliette Hyland

How to Tame a King
How to Win a Prince
Fake Dating the Vet
One-Night Baby with Her Best Friend

Available now!

ROYALLY FORBIDDEN TO THE BOSS

SCARLETT CLARKE

MILLS & BOON

To my mom and husband.

It was a mad dash to the finish line,
but you made it possible.

CHAPTER ONE

Eviana

PRINCESS EVIANA ADAMOVIÇ had less than a second to register the wave coming at her before it hit. She sucked in a shuddering gasp as chilly rainwater splashed her face and soaked the left side of her body. Brakes screeched as she bit back a curse.

You have got *to be kidding me.*

Her neighbors waking her up at five o'clock with a very loud argument over someone's flirty coworker had been the first sign that today wasn't going to go according to plan. Her early wake-up had been followed by her coffee machine sending a cascade of much-needed caffeine down the front of her cabinet after she'd overfilled it.

And now… Eviana looked down and sighed. She'd picked one of her best suits for today, a couture black blazer and pants with Louboutin pumps. It was now soaked through. A splash of mud on her white blouse added an extra flair to her debacle of a morning.

A car door slammed.

"Are you all right?"

The voice wrapped around her, deep and masculine. She raised her head. And froze.

The man standing in front of her was both unbelievably handsome and incredibly intimidating. Dark red hair combed back from a broad forehead. Strong slashes of cheekbone above a beard cut to precision along an angular jaw. A three-piece suit expertly tailored to follow the broadness of his shoulders and accommodate his impressive height. He stood nearly a foot taller than her.

Deep blue eyes fixed on hers. Something flared, a look of surprise, perhaps, before a shutter dropped over them.

"Yes." A brisk wind swept down the road and pierced her now sodden coat. "Just…chilly." She glanced down at her shirt again and grimaced. "And dirty."

"I apologize. I didn't realize how deep the puddle was."

Scottish, judging by rolling *r*s and melodic cadence of his words. But there was a blunt roughness in his voice that, coupled with the hardness in his face, told her he was in just about as good of a mood as she was.

"It's…fine." It wasn't, but the man had stopped when most would have just kept driving.

"How much do I owe you for the suit?"

"It'll wash out." She patted the maroon-colored leather bag she'd thankfully had on her right side. "And I have a change of clothes, too."

"Can I drive you somewhere?"

Her head shot up in surprise. "Excuse me?"

He gestured to the empty street. "Few taxis at this hour. The bus won't be by for another twenty minutes."

"You're not trying to kidnap me, are you?" she said, only half joking.

He stared at her for a moment. Then one corner of his mouth slowly curved up.

Vau. A different kind of shiver traced its way down her spine. If the man could stir that kind of reaction with just the hint of a smile, what would a real one do?

"No, I'm not trying to kidnap you."

Don't even think about it.

But she was. It wasn't just the man's good looks, although

that certainly didn't hurt. No, there was something…compelling about him. That bare-bones smile, a distinct contrast to the tension that rolled off his muscular frame, the faint darkness in his eyes.

Cold reality smothered temptation. That and one of the palace's many rules filtering through her mind:

Princesses do not ride alone in cars with men unless they are related by blood or serving in a security role.

"I appreciate you stopping. And offering a ride. But I'm only a block away from my office. And," she added with a smile to take any potential sting out of her words, "I would probably give my brother a heart attack if I accepted a ride from a stranger."

Again that twitch of the lips that made her stomach do a long, slow roll. "Your brother sounds like a smart man."

"He is."

Although if Nicholai knew everything she was up to, from the tiny apartment she'd rented to walking to work with only a private bodyguard following nearly a block behind, he wouldn't have a heart attack. He'd fly to Scotland and drag her back to Kelna without a second thought.

Her mystery man pulled out a black leather wallet. "At least let me give you money for dry cleaning."

The man was clearly wealthy, from his bespoke suit to the gleaming black Rolls-Royce parked just behind him. But she couldn't do it. Not when she had a walk-in closet full of clothes back at the palace, dresses and skirts and blouses from designers around the world.

"I really do think the mud will come out."

He held out a banknote, the value of which made her eyebrows shoot up.

"Take it."

Her eyes narrowed at the insistence in his tone. She'd been

spoiled the last two months, living her life on her own terms. Having someone tell her what to do to rankled.

"How about you offer me a tenth of that for coffee and a pastry?"

"Are you always this stubborn?"

"Yes." She cocked her head to one side. "Are you?"

His fingers tightened on the banknote. Then, slowly, he tucked it back into his wallet.

"Yes."

The resignation in his tone tugged at her.

"Here."

He held out a much more reasonable amount, although still double what she had suggested. Eviana started to reach for it, then stopped as an idea flared. It was a ridiculous idea. But as she stared at her handsome stranger, longing wound its way through her veins.

Could he hear her heart pounding as the idea sank its roots deeper? See the pulse pounding in her throat? She'd invited plenty of men to join her for coffee before—parliamentarians, ambassadors, visiting dignitaries, wealthy businessmen.

But they'd all known who she was. Never had she invited a man for personal reasons for…well, anything.

A princess is never bold.

Except she wasn't a princess. Not right now. She was just Ana Barros, intern for a boutique public relations firm in Edinburgh. Princess Eviana wouldn't have been able to invite a random stranger to coffee.

But Ana could.

Her heart galloped in her chest. "I'll accept it on one condition."

One eyebrow arched up. "Oh?"

"You let me buy you coffee."

His lips parted as a V appeared between his brows. "What?"

She nodded her head toward the row of buildings that lined

the street with what she hoped was a casual gesture. The windows of one glowed with yellow light, beckoning early morning commuters and random passersby to stop.

"Braw Roasterie. They make the best cortados."

"I stick to black coffee."

"They make that, too."

"Why?"

She bit back a grin. Beneath his grumpy tone, she sensed that Mr. Rolls-Royce was flustered.

"You look like you could use it. That and five minutes of sitting with nothing to do."

His lips parted slightly before he looked over his shoulder at the coffee shop. For one moment, she thought he was actually going to say yes.

Then he glanced down at his watch. "I should get going."

Disappointment lanced through her. He struck her as the kind of man who kept a rigorous schedule, one that didn't allow for situations like splashing chilly puddle water on a pedestrian. She wanted to push, to encourage him to break free for just a few minutes.

But she wasn't going to be that person, wasn't going to push. She knew all too well how it felt to be pushed. Besieged. Cornered.

"All right. Thanks again for stopping."

She started walking.

"Wait." She turned back just in time to see him hold up the money. "You forgot something."

A princess exhibits gratitude and grace at all times.

She grinned at him. "I said I'd only accept it on one condition. So no, I didn't."

The surprise on his face almost made getting drenched worth it. She gave him a friendly wave and kept walking.

Helena, the head of the palace's public relations department, would have had steam coming out of her ears if she'd witnessed Eviana decline a gift. A thought that added an extra bounce to Eviana's step as she moved down the sidewalk.

It felt good, so good, to just…be. To talk with a stranger without monitoring every word that passed her lips. To tease, invite, converse without wondering if Helena or one of the public relations minions was going to show up outside her door later and provide her with a detailed list of what she'd done wrong. Even if the man behind her had refused her invitation, just the fact that she had been able to invite someone to coffee without worrying about photos being taken and splashed across social media was a win.

Not to mention, she thought with a small smile, getting to talk with a very handsome man for a few minutes. No expectations, no pretenses.

She almost glanced over her shoulder. One last look.

And then decided not to. She could have done without mud and rainwater. But her interaction with the Scottish stranger had been a pleasant anomaly in the midst of a chaotic morning. One that had made her feel both normal and more like… like a woman, she decided with a satisfied smile. Something made all the more precious with the few weeks she had left before returning to her former life.

Perhaps, she thought as she opened the door to Braw Roasterie and inhaled the rich scent of roasted coffee beans, her morning had turned out just right.

CHAPTER TWO

Shaw

WARMTH SPILLED OUT from the open doorway. A group of men and women in suits poured out of Braw Roasterie onto the street, talking and laughing even as they all checked their watches.

Shaw stood back, eyes trained on the woman sitting in the corner of the shop, her attention focused on a notebook as her pen darted across the page. She must have changed while he'd parked his car and walked back. Instead of the black pants and white shirt he'd glimpsed beneath her raincoat, she now wore a bright yellow skirt and an ivory blouse dotted with blue flowers. He'd talked with the woman for less than five minutes, but the outfit she had on now seemed more…her. Vibrant, colorful. The cascade of blond hair falling down her back seemed more natural, too, versus the tightly wound bun that had been at the nape of her neck.

Although a downside of her hair hanging loose was that it partially obscured her face—a stunningly unique face that had made him look twice when he'd gotten out to check on the pedestrian he had unintentionally drenched on his early morning drive. *Ethereal* was the first word that had come to mind. Wide-set green eyes, a bow-shaped mouth, romantic features offset by a pointed chin that hinted at defiance. Her easygoing acceptance of the whole incident and declining of the money had struck him, too.

Not just struck him, he admitted as the crowd cleared and he moved toward the door. Intrigued him. Enough that he'd pulled into a parking space and sat, deliberating on his next action for a solid five minutes before he'd succumbed to his curiosity and walked back to the coffee shop.

He didn't do things like this—spontaneous meetings with random people he met on the street. He barely came out of his office at all.

What am I doing?

He didn't have an answer. Only that driving away from the woman who had rejected his money and bounced off with a smile and a cheeky wave had seemed like the worst possible thing he could do.

Numerous scents hit him at once as he walked into Braw Roasterie. The earthy boldness of coffee underlined with chocolatey sweetness. Freshly baked bread and rich butter. Soft music played from hidden speakers. Gleaming wood tables played hosts to wrought-iron chairs. A well-maintained shop, one that he had passed by for years.

He squared his shoulders and moved toward the blonde woman's table. His dating life had been stagnant the past few months. But just last year he'd dated a corporate lawyer for nearly five months and a software engineer for a Fortune 500 company the year prior to that. Women who had been interesting enough yet just as focused as he was on their careers, on things other than what most people wanted out of relationships: love, marriage, family. Those things he had zero interest in. He didn't want, or need, anyone in his life. Not when getting the Harrington Foundation back on track required his full attention. Not when the last person he had trusted had taken his trust and ripped it to tatters, along with the reputation of the organization he'd dedicated his life to creating.

Yet in the span of a few minutes, this woman had crawled under his skin. She might have been pretending that she didn't know who he was, but he'd bet half his fortune her lack of recognition had been genuine. Her casual grace, coupled with that impish defiance, had been a breath of fresh air. He normally surrounded himself with competent, emotionally removed individuals. A strategy that had served him well.

Perhaps too well, he mused as he sidestepped a sleepy-looking couple pushing a stroller. He'd kept people at a distance for so long that one encounter outside of his normal routine had upset his balance. Had made him think there was something special about this woman to the point that he had backtracked and was now seventeen minutes behind schedule.

Just five more minutes. Five minutes to talk to the woman, prove there was nothing unique aside from an unusual encounter early in the morning, and move on with his life.

A light, floral scent floated beneath the homey smells as he drew near. His shadow fell across her table. She looked up…

And smiled at him. Not the teasing grin or sassy smirk she'd given him earlier but a true smile, one that made her eyes crinkle at the corners. As if she were genuinely happy to see him.

His world shifted.

"Hello."

Her voice, regal and composed yet warm and layered with that musical accent he couldn't place, pulled at him. Made him long for something he hadn't even realized he'd wanted.

"I decided to take you up on your offer."

She stood, the brightness of her smile matching the eye-popping yellow of her skirt. "I'm glad. Cortado and a black coffee?"

"Just the coffee."

"How about I order you both and if you hate the cortado, then you have the black coffee to fall back on?"

Phrased like that, and accompanied by that smile he couldn't stop staring at, he simply nodded.

Dhia, what was wrong with him?

She moved to the bar and ordered two cortados and a black coffee. Her butchered attempt at Gaelic had him pressing his lips together and looking away as the barista laughingly coached her through the phrases.

He handed her the twenty-pound note he'd offered earlier, which she accepted with a thank-you as she slid it across the bar and told the barista to keep the change.

"Not many people bother to learn Gaelic," he said as they moved off to the side.

"I love the sound of it. It's unlike any other language I've learned. I've only been learning for six weeks. I sound atrocious," she said with a laugh.

"But English is not your native language?"

"No." She hesitated, the barest pause. "Croatian is my first language. I also speak Italian and a little bit of French."

"And how does a girl from Southeastern Europe end up here?"

Another hesitation, along with a slash of pink along her elegant cheekbones.

"Taking a break from home," she finally said.

Her answer surprised him, as did the fatigue in her voice, the quiet sadness on her face.

Like looking in a mirror.

"Stepping away is never easy."

She drew in a deep breath, then slowly released it. When she looked at him, the sparkle was gone, replaced by a maturity that altered his previous impression of a sunny young woman who had known little hardship.

No, this woman was someone far more dangerous. Someone who had experienced hardship and overcome. Someone dynamic and complex and interesting.

Someone he wanted to know.

"No, it's not. But sometimes necessary."

Necessary. Crucial. The only way to survive when the life you knew shattered in the blink of an eye.

For twenty years, Shaw had had no problems keeping everyone at arm's length. When the doctor had come out to tell him his mother hadn't made it—the same doctor who had brushed aside Shaw's concerns the week prior when his mother had gone in for a checkup with a *trust me, she's fine*—a switch had been flipped. He'd mentally drawn a line that separated him from the rest of the world. To this day, he'd never been tempted to cross it. Never been tempted to let feelings past the wall he'd built, stone by stone, in the weeks after his mother's death that separated the boy he'd been and the man fate had fashioned overnight with one cruel blow.

Yet for the first time in two decades, words rose in his throat. A desire to share with another human being. One he had a gut feeling would understand more than anyone he'd met in a long time. The challenge of the past few months. The stress, the frustration, the deep-seated grief at realizing his decision to step away from the foundation had cost so much.

"Two cortados and a black coffee!"

The barista's boisterous announcement broke the spell. Shaw stepped back. A small move, but he saw the confusion in the blonde woman's eyes, followed by the smoothing of her features. Unnerving to watch, although he'd been accused of doing the same thing himself—hiding his thoughts and emotions behind a mask.

"I hope you enjoy your drinks."

He frowned. Still her voice, still soft and flowing. But the cheerful energy had disappeared, replaced by a smooth, practiced cadence that sounded…bland. Colorless.

"Thank you."

Shaw reached for his drinks at the same time she reached

for hers. Their hands brushed. The faintest touch, but it shot through him like a bolt of lightning. He forced himself to grab the cups and face her. Judging by the twin splotches of color in her cheeks, she'd felt it, too.

He allowed himself a moment. Just one moment to imagine what he would do if life was different. If life hadn't taught him at a young age that trust was not something to lightly give nor receive. If his former friend and colleague hadn't destroyed years of hard work. If he was capable of offering anyone more than the wealth he'd painstakingly built over the years.

A fantasy. One that would never be. Six months later and he was still staring down the barrel of a crisis that had no end in sight. A crisis he had created by giving a grain of trust to someone he had thought qualified to lead, to do what he couldn't. Even if Zach hadn't dragged the foundation to the edge of annihilation, Shaw had no interest in breaching the wall he'd carefully maintained for so long. A wall that kept him immune to pain and heartbreak.

No one would ever be worth the risk of that kind of pain again.

"Enjoy the rest of your day."

He didn't wait for her response. He stalked outside, hands wrapped around the cups, his steps firm and determined. The farther he got from the shop, the more the band of tension around his chest loosened. It was like coming out of a dream. One where, for a moment, he'd been tempted to ask a woman on a date. Not for an event, not for mutual companionship, but because he'd wanted to get to know her better.

Sun broke through the clouds as Shaw reached his car. He breathed out. The strain of the last few months, as well as poor sleep, had left him vulnerable to emotions he rarely experienced. It was only natural, he told himself, that an odd encounter with an attractive stranger would have sucked him in, made him behave out of character.

As he started the car, he glanced at the two cups he'd placed in the cup holders. Then, slowly, he raised the smaller cup to his lips. Rich espresso and sweet milk hit his tongue, an indulgent blend that made his black coffee seem bitter and boring.

With a frustrated sigh, he set the cortado down and picked up his coffee. His life didn't need change. At least his personal life. He had been content before this morning's events. And as to the professional aspects, the meeting he had scheduled two hours from now would hopefully be a step toward getting the Harrington Foundation back on track.

Content, he told himself as he pulled away from the curb and kept his gaze fixed on the road ahead. *I'm content.*

He ignored the little voice whispering *Liar* as he drove away.

CHAPTER THREE

Eviana

THE OFFICE SPACE for Murray PR was the size of a large walk-in closet. Big enough for Kirstin Murray's L-shaped desk, two tufted leather chairs arranged around a small coffee table and Eviana's own tiny desk shoved up against one of the two windows. The wall behind Kirstin's desk was taken up by a glass dry-erase board, the surface covered with scribbles, notes and schedules. The other wall featured framed photos of Kirstin's clients to date.

Eviana hummed to herself as she flicked on the lights and savored the small flicker of joy she always felt walking into the office. When she'd finally decided to take up her brother on the offer of a sabbatical, he'd suggested somewhere lush and tropical. The Seychelles or Belize.

But she hadn't wanted a mindless vacation. She'd needed a place where she could breathe, yes, but also a place she could explore herself, regain her confidence, maybe even learn something that would help her handle the ever-increasing demands of royal life.

Demands she wasn't sure she could handle.

She moved to the windows, crossing her arms as she gazed out over the country that had been her salvation. When she'd searched for relaxing destinations, there had been the usual results for beaches and mountain resorts tucked away from prying eyes. But seeing pictures of the rolling green hills of Scotland, the white sandy beaches, the winding cobblestone streets…it had called to something in her. Traces of home evident in the history, the old architecture, yet still somewhere completely new.

Kelna would always be her home. But after her time here, Scotland would rank a close second.

She glanced down at the street below and smiled when she glimpsed a familiar figure seated on a bench across the street. The one stipulation her brother, Nicholai, had demanded when she'd asked for a few months off had been a bodyguard. Jodi was not only an incredible bodyguard but seemed to understand Eviana's need for space, for a simple life without the trappings of palace royalty.

A soft sigh filled the quiet of the office.

Poor little princess.

It felt wrong. This discontent, this looming sensation of dread as her July deadline drew near. She'd been granted twelve weeks. The first eight had gone by in the blink of an eye, although she didn't regret a second of how she'd spent them. Having the chance to live independently, to work and apply herself, to not only do things right but make mistakes without the palace watching and critiquing her, was something she had desperately needed.

She glanced back at the planning board. At the words written cockeyed around schedules, names of contacts and random ideas jotted down during meetings. It was utter chaos.

And she loved it.

Everything at the palace was regimented, even more so in the months leading up to and after her father's passing as she'd taken on new duties. There'd been days when she'd been scheduled down to the last minute. No flexibility, no room for error.

At first, it had been a godsend. The frenetic pace had left

her tired and tumbling into bed at the end of long days that had sometimes stretched into even longer nights. It had also left her with little time to remember that her father, her *otac*, was dying. Once he'd passed, she'd thrown herself in even deeper, ignoring the warning signs slowly piling up. But as the meetings had increased, as she'd tried to maintain a diplomatic face at the ever-increasing number of public engagements she'd been requested to attend, the stress had pressed in on her. Strained her to the breaking point.

Until she'd broken.

Eviana scrunched her eyes shut, swallowed. One deep breath, then another.

You are more than a crown.

How many times had her soon-to-be sister-in-law Madeline said that to her in the last year or so? Encouraged her to speak her mind, to let her personality shine through? Something that was easy for Madeline to do when she'd been raised to be independent and strong, not an ornament loved by her father but essentially raised by the females on the palace staff. Women who had encouraged Eviana from as far back as she could remember to be proper. Graceful. Regal.

A small smile curved her lips as she imagined Madeline's face if she ever shared the differences in how they'd been raised. Madeline was one of the best things to ever happen to their family. Eviana loved her brother with all her heart. But until he'd met Madeline, he hadn't let anyone help, had hoarded the numerous duties he'd been saddled with as their father's health had steadily declined. It hadn't been until he and Madeline had shared an illicit kiss in the gardens and made international headlines that he had finally confronted his inability to ask for help.

Yet the improvement in her and her brother's relationship had come with a price. Namely her increased involvement in palace affairs.

Eviana turned away from the window and stepped over to her desk. Nicholai hadn't asked—she had volunteered. Kelna was growing rapidly. Between the new seaport and the increased media attention from Nicholai and Madeline's upcoming wedding, their hidden gem of a country had become the focal point of international interest.

That, too, had come with a price. One that demanded so much more of her, of Nicholai, even of Madeline. Their time, their effort.

What if I can't give enough?

The thought whispered through her mind, a cruel taunt that slowly pulled up a memory she'd tried to keep buried deep. It had been nearly three months now. But the hot sting of embarrassment, the nauseous ball of shame in the pit of her stomach as she'd stumbled through a speech in front of dozens of Kelnian business owners, the flood of tears she had barely kept contained until she'd made it back to the receiving room.

There had been no triggers. Nothing concrete she could put her finger on when Helena had followed her into the room and demanded to know what had happened. One minute she had been fine and the next she hadn't.

The coverage had been thankfully minimal, no doubt smoothed over by Helena's minions working in tandem with the media to spin a story about a tired, grieving princess. But it had been enough of an incident that Nicholai had told her to take some time away.

Eviana sank into her chair. When she returned to Kelna, she would not only be returning home but coming back to a list of even more duties and responsibilities she'd never before contemplated. Speaking at galas, military processions and national holidays, something Nicholai or their father had previously done. Serving as the patron of numerous charities, not just her select few that currently revolved around healthcare. Hosting visiting dignitaries, especially when Nicholai was in other meetings or taking some much-needed time off with Madeline. Duties he insisted he still trusted her with, even if she didn't trust herself to do them.

Or you don't want to do.

Her shoulders drooped. Dueling doubts plagued her even as she moved through this fantasy of a temporary life away from the spotlight. Had she failed because she wasn't capable of leading? Or worse, had she faltered because, deep down, she was selfish and didn't want to follow the rules of her own country? Didn't want to do what so many had done before her and pledge her identity to the crown?

If this morning was any indicator, she'd pick the latter. When the handsome stranger had shown up, the leap in her pulse had been far too strong to excuse as simple excitement. No, she'd been interested. Very interested.

Except where could it have gone? A few dates before she disappeared back to her life in Kelna while she pretended to be someone she wasn't? A one-night stand?

Princesses do not have one-night stands.

Imagining that on Helena's lengthy list of rules brought a much-needed smile to Eviana's face. As much as the man's abrupt departure had stung, it had been a reprieve. She never should have invited him to coffee in the first place. The invitation hadn't been rooted in throwing caution to the wind or living life to the fullest.

It had been rooted in desire. Arrogance. A momentary lapse in judgment.

At least I won't have to see him again.

Footsteps sounded outside the door.

Kirstin breezed into the room, silver hair pushed back from her angular face with a red headband.

"Good morning, Ana!"

Whether it was the events of the morning or Eviana's dip

into the past that had left her emotionally raw, she couldn't contain her flinch at the use of the name she'd been using ever since she'd landed in Scotland. It was a nickname, one she had faint memories of her mother using. But she was using it, and her mother's maiden name, under false pretenses.

She shoved her misgivings to the side and smiled at the woman who had become not only her boss and mentor but a good friend.

"Good morning." She glanced at the oversized coffee cup in Kirstin's hand. "Rough night?"

"More like I couldn't sleep." Kirstin beamed from ear to ear as she set the coffee cup down and punched a button on her computer screen. "We have a meeting with the Harrington Foundation!"

"That's wonderful!"

Kirstin's smile dimmed a fraction. "You have no idea what I'm talking about, do you?"

"No," Eviana said with another small smile, "but judging by your reaction, it's big."

"It's bigger than big. This is what I've been waiting for. The account that will catapult Murray PR to the top."

Excitement clashed with a faint sense of foreboding. One of the reasons why she had applied for Kirstin's internship was because she worked with smaller organizations, ones primarily based in Scotland. Eviana's risk of exposure was minimal.

God, how self-absorbed can you be? Her friend had just gotten incredible news, and here she was, worried about herself.

"Okay," she said with enthusiasm to cover her lapse, "so fill me in—everything I need to know, and most importantly, where do we start?"

A knock sounded on the door.

"Oh, goodness." Kirstin nervously smoothed a hand down her blouse. "He's here."

"Who?"

"Shaw Harrington," Kirstin hissed. "Hedge fund extraordinaire and the founder of the Harrington Foundation."

Eviana glance down at her outfit. The bright yellow of her skirt suddenly seemed garish, the little flowers on her blouse childish.

"I'm sorry, Kirstin. I had on a suit and—"

"You look great." Kirstin gave her a look, one that told Eviana to not get so deep inside her head. "If he doesn't pick us because you're wearing a fantastic skirt, his loss."

Another knock sounded. Kirstin opened the door, but with the way the small space was angled, Eviana didn't get a glimpse of legendary Shaw Harrington.

"Good morning, Mr. Harrington. Thank you for coming to us."

"You're welcome."

Eviana froze.

There's no way...

"Ana?"

Kirstin glanced over her shoulder and gestured for Eviana to join her. "Mr. Harrington, I'd like for you to meet my intern, Miss Ana Barros."

Each step reverberated through her body as her heart sank in her chest. She knew even before Shaw Harrington came into view what he would look like, from the broad forehead and sharp blade of a nose to the dark blue eyes that widened a fraction as she came around the door.

His eyes flicked to hers, then fixed on her face. Shock flared for a single moment and then disappeared just as swiftly.

The man who had splashed her with rainwater, whom she had flirted with on the street, was her boss's potential new client.

Definitely not my best morning.

CHAPTER FOUR

Eviana

EMOTIONS TANGLED IN her chest, the strongest being nervousness that she had spoken so frankly and freely with a prospective client who apparently had the power to change the course of Kirstin's business.

Unsure if he would want their impromptu morning meeting revealed, she offered him a polite smile. "It's nice to meet you, Mr. Harrington."

He stared at her for a long moment, eyes narrowed, suspicion evident on his face.

"Good to see you again," he finally said with an emphasis on the last word.

Kirstin glanced between the two of them, concern deepening the slight wrinkles on her forehead. "Do you two know each other?"

"We met this morning at Braw Roasterie." Eviana kept her voice even, her tone pleasant. "Happenstance."

Shaw continued to watch her with that razor-sharp glint in his eye. She returned his stare with what Madeline teased her as her "resting royal face." Amiable yet devoid of any true emotion.

A princess never lets the world know what she's truly thinking.

That wasn't just one of Helena's rules. She'd heard them

plenty over the years—from her father, from Nicholai, from well-meaning parliamentary members and public relations representatives. She'd hated it as a child. Yet at some point she had accepted it as the way things simply were and had done her best to keep herself contained. Hidden.

Coming to Edinburgh had been like waking up. Stretching her wings for the first time. It had been freeing to scrunch up her face when she'd tried a food she hadn't liked or laugh without thinking about how she might look on camera.

Slipping back into a role where she concealed her thoughts, even for just a moment, made her feel…uncomfortable. Self-conscious. Having that taste of freedom for the past eight weeks, the liberty to explore who she was and express herself without reservation, made putting that mask back on nearly unbearable.

But necessary. Whoever Shaw Harrington was, he was the ticket to Kirstin's success. Yes, this morning he'd relaxed for a few minutes. But he'd pulled back so quickly, retreated into that intense professionalism he was exuding now. An intensity that filled up the tiny office space and made Eviana feel like she couldn't catch her breath.

"Yes. Happenstance."

Muscles twisted and knotted in her back at the suspicion coating his words. She bit back a retort and fought to keep that serene smile on her face.

"It's a bit tight in here for three people," Kirstin finally said, even as she cast another worried glance between her potential new client and her intern. "I'll make us some tea, and we can have our meeting in the rooftop garden. Eviana, would you escort Mr. Harrington up there?"

Eviana grabbed her notebook, squared her shoulders and escorted Shaw out of the office and down the hall to the elevator.

"Fortuitous our meeting like that this morning," she said conversationally as she pressed the elevator button.

"Yes."

She glanced at him over her shoulder, then nearly flinched when she realized how close he was. A spicy, smoky scent wrapped around her, one that made her pulse beat just a tad faster.

"You sound suspicious."

"I am." He held up a hand as her eyes narrowed. "I'm the one who splashed you. I'm not thinking this is some devious campaign to get my business. It's just...odd. I wasn't expecting to see you again."

Surprised and, judging by his dark tone, not happy that circumstances had brought them together again. Whatever moment of camaraderie they had shared in the coffee shop had disappeared as soon as he'd made the decision to leave.

The elevator doors opened. Eviana stepped into the car, trying to ignore the ugly twist in her stomach as Shaw followed her and the doors shut. She'd talked with the man for less than ten minutes. She was leaving in four weeks. Oh, and he was about to be Kirstin's new client. Multiple reasons why she shouldn't be interested in him, why his easy ability to step back from whatever had passed between them shouldn't hurt.

But it did.

Later. She'd examine her feelings later. Right now, her personal views didn't matter. What did matter was doing whatever was in her power to land this contract for Kirstin and give something back to the woman who had taught her so much.

The doors opened. Eviana breathed in, unable to keep the smile from her face as she stepped out onto the rooftop garden. Crisp air greeted her, tinged with a hint of sea salt drifting in from the bay. Morning sun had chased away the gray clouds and left a spectacular blue sky overhead.

Whoever had arranged the garden had done phenomenal work. Golden-brown wood planks hosted flower beds teeming with orchids, wild thyme, bell heather and Scottish bluebells. White patio tables with matching chairs were arranged across the roof, providing little pockets of privacy for people to conduct business, along with a few picnic tables and lounge chairs for those seeking a break from the workday or a place to eat lunch in peace.

Or enjoy the view.

Edinburgh Castle stood proudly against the summer sky, over one thousand years of history behind those stone walls. It had been one of the things that had drawn Eviana to Edinburgh as she'd tried to decide where to take her sabbatical. It was somewhere new, somewhere far enough away that she could have a few blessed months of being just Ana. But there was that comforting familiarity in the winding cobblestone streets, the cry of a seagull, the castle on the hill. A blend of new and old.

"Have you visited the castle?"

Shaw's voice sounded just behind her. Invisible fingers squeezed her lungs as she tried to suck in a quick breath. She'd heard plenty of Scottish accents since she'd arrived in Edinburgh. When she'd first heard his voice, she'd thoroughly enjoyed the breathlessness the deep masculine tone had caused, the uptick in her heart rate.

But now it was a problem.

"I did my first week here. Hopefully I can go again before I return home."

"And when is that?"

Slowly, she turned. He was standing a few feet behind her. Plenty of space. But it might as well have been a few inches given the little electric pulses traveling through her veins.

"The end of July."

He blinked. "A month away."

"Yes."

He took a step closer. She stood her ground, threading her fingers together as she gazed at him like he was simply another human being and not a very attractive man wreaking havoc on her control.

"And where is home exactly?"

"Southeastern Europe."

There was that twitch again. The tiniest movement of his lips. The ache from earlier returned in full force. What on earth had happened to this man to make him put up such a stalwart front? To eschew something as simple as the pleasure of a smile?

"I want to reassure you, Mr. Harrington," she said, directing his attention away from any more personal questions, "that I will be able to maintain a professional attitude throughout your working relationship with Ms. Murray."

Even if I find you ridiculously attractive.

"Is there a reason why you wouldn't be able to?"

His cold tone shocked her out of her lingering attraction. Made it easy to move down the path of professionalism. The man might've looked like a god, but his personality was more like…

Helena.

She bit down on her lower lip hard. So hard she wondered if she'd drawn blood. But it was better than laughing out loud at Kirstin's potential new client.

Talk about an attraction killer.

"No." She inclined her head. "I just wanted to reassure you that my familiarity this morning is not how I conduct myself in a professional environment."

His eyes flickered over her face. For one pulse-pounding moment, she had the impression of Shaw looking past her mask. Of seeing the woman she truly was, the one who invited strangers to coffee and preferred living in a tiny apartment in Edinburgh.

The one who couldn't, or wouldn't, help lead her country.

She swallowed hard. His gaze moved down to her throat.

"Here we are!"

Eviana had never been so grateful for tea in all her life. Kirstin walked toward them with a silver tray in her hands, complete with three steaming mugs. They sat at a table near the railing. Eviana set her notebook on the table and pulled a pen out of her skirt pocket. Taking notes would help her focus on the job at hand and not on the man sitting less than a foot away.

A man who, despite his icy demeanor, saw far more than most.

"I was just briefing Eviana on your request when you knocked." Kirstin placed a mug in front of Shaw. "Let's start with you providing us with an overview of what brought you here."

Silence reigned. Slowly, Eviana looked up. Shaw was staring at the castle, shoulders tense, jaw firm, lips thinned into an angry line. At first glance, he looked furious. As if whatever circumstances that had brought him to Murray PR had also brought him to the edge of the control he seemed to prefer.

But the longer she looked, the more she saw. The shadows beneath his eyes spoke of restless nights. The faint frown between his eyebrows implied a deep-seated worry beneath the anger.

And as he turned his attention back to them, she saw grief in his gaze.

CHAPTER FIVE

Shaw

MORNING SUNLIGHT BATHED the sandstone walls of Edinburgh Castle. The walls blended into the cliffs beneath them, creating the illusion that the castle had been fashioned from the plateau that held it above the city.

Unreachable, unbreakable.

He had thought the same of himself. Yet the past few months had revealed that his self-image had been rooted in pride. Pride and a fixation on the end goal that had blinded him to the things happening around him.

Things like betrayal.

Out of the corner of his eye, he saw Ana look at him. He didn't see so much as feel her concern, as if she could sense his mood.

"Five years ago, I founded the Harrington Foundation."

In honor of my mother, he silently added.

For her. It had all been for her, for what they'd almost had and lost.

"I obtained a degree here in Edinburgh and attended graduate school in New York. My internship turned into a job at a hedge fund company. After my success in New York, I wanted to establish a fund that would support charities, specifically ones that focused on helping people become independent or overcome major challenges that upend normal life."

"The list of organizations you support is extensive."

Kirstin rattled off a list of charities in the United Kingdom and the States. Compared to the other two firms he'd met with, Kirstin was already demonstrating a level of knowledge that far exceeded the others. That he had reached out at eight o'clock last night and she was prepared just over twelve hours later was another mark in her favor.

He nodded in her direction. "Even though I resided in New York up until recently, when I founded the charity, I wanted it to first benefit the people in the city I spent most of my childhood in."

Except for those two years. Those two years when he'd thought that he and his mother had finally overcome, would never have to worry about putting food on the table or having a roof over their heads again.

"I created a board of trustees and turned over most operations to them, including the formation of a small marketing team and an accounting department. It was suggested that I continue to serve as CEO, but I am not what I would describe as a people person."

A slight noise sounded to his right. But when he glanced at Ana, her attention was focused on her notebook, her pen flying across the paper much as it had this morning in the coffee shop.

"I'm generally a private man. This makes it difficult for me to market the foundation and solicit the kind of donations we need to not only maintain but expand our operations. That's why I recommended they hire someone else."

Anger punched through him. Most days he could dismiss it, and on the rare occasion it rose up, he could usually control it. But there were moments like this, when the reality of the challenges he faced confronted him, that he struggled not to let it show.

"I recommended someone I met at Edinburgh University, Zachary White."

It was an accomplishment, he reminded himself, that he could say Zach's name out loud without letting his disdain show. A man he'd known had been spoiled and naive about the world beyond the gilded existence he'd grown up in as the son of a pharmaceutical developer. But still a man who had possessed the skills and affability Shaw did not. One who had made him believe he would do Shaw's vision proud.

Ana's pen continued to scratch across the paper. Did she have any knowledge of what had happened? Had she heard the rumors? Did it change what she thought of him?

Stop. It didn't matter what Ana thought or didn't think. What mattered was, if he chose Murray PR, that she would do her job and do it well.

"Ten months ago, Zachary came to me. He wanted to expedite our fundraising by investing some of the foundation's funds. He wanted my opinion before presenting it to the board. It was a good idea, and it's not an uncommon practice among charities, but the investment he initially identified was questionable."

To say the least.

Shaw had barely had to glance at it to recognize it for what it had been: a scam.

"I encouraged him to speak with the board but to avoid that investment. Instead, he used his exceptional public-speaking skills and charm to persuade the board it was a good investment, then chose to sink half the foundation's funds instead of the five percent he'd been approved for into a hedge fund through an offshore account in the Cayman Islands." The anger seethed in his chest, pulsing in time with his heartbeat. "We lost over one million in savings, along with over two dozen donors who had made substantial gifts in the past two years, when the news broke."

He looked at Ana then. She didn't hesitate as she continued to write and take notes. Her face remained impassive, her demeanor tranquil despite the bombshells he had just dropped.

"Where does that leave you now?" Kirstin asked, redirecting his attention away from her intern.

"The investigation was completed on Wednesday. The board of trustees, the charity, and I have been found innocent."

Just saying the words out loud brought a much-needed sense of calm.

"Congratulations."

He nodded to Kirstin. "Thank you."

He, of course, had known all along that he'd had absolutely nothing to do with Zach's foolish investments. But to hear it stated in court, to have it on record that he had not been involved, had loosened a band wrapped around his chest. Had given him hope that perhaps things could still be salvaged.

"Zachary, on the other hand, is facing numerous charges. The trial, of course, won't happen for quite some time. But now that I've officially been cleared, I want to move forward with a campaign to entice our donors to reinstate their financial support."

"What is your primary goal?"

Ana's voice flowed over him, soft and soothing.

"The long-term goal is to reestablish our reputation and move past this. But in the short term, my primary goal is to reconnect with some of our highest-profile donors."

Or rather, he thought darkly, ex donors. The people who had withdrawn their support and fled as soon as the Harrington Foundation's name had been dragged through the mud by the worldwide press.

Part of him understood. As a hedge fund manager, he'd often made difficult decisions on where to invest and where not to invest. But the part that didn't, the man who had reviewed the lengthy list of commitments they wouldn't be able to fulfill without a quick return, was furious. The people who had kept the foundation afloat were extraordinarily wealthy—far wealthier than him. They owned private planes, numerous villas scattered around the world. They knew the work the foundation did, the people it helped start new chapters and get on their feet. It wasn't worth enough for them to stand up to the court of public opinion.

Which brought his fury full circle back to the one man who had caused it all. A man he had hand-selected based on hard facts and, over time, had even trusted to a certain extent.

This was what trust led to. Volatile emotions that impeded judgement. The tightness in Shaw's neck twisted harder and harder until he almost couldn't move.

"Not to be rude," Ana asked quietly, "but why are you doing this? Why not a member of the board?"

"Given that they approved the investment, we all agreed it would be best for them to stay in the background for now. They're innocent—" a fact he'd had confirmed by an extensive private investigation of his own "—but they still made a mistake in not fully vetting Zachary's choice of investment, as well as not having safeguards in place to catch his mistake until it was too late."

Guilt pricked his conscience. The board had told him several times they'd been expanding too quickly, that they'd needed to slow down, hire more people, evaluate their procedures as they'd grown.

But he hadn't wanted to slow down. And now he was paying the price.

"The board also thought that as founder, I might be able to resurrect our reputation faster than a new hire, someone with no ties to the foundation."

Kirstin nodded. "Smart."

He gave her a tight smile. "Except the reason I declined the role of CEO in the first place is because I am not a people person. I don't converse well with strangers. I understand the board's thinking, but I'm concerned about the execution."

More like he anticipated complete and utter disaster unless he had a professional on the sidelines helping him through. Reaching out for help from a public relations firm was the last thing he'd wanted. Assuming they survived this, the foundation would be adding its own PR director, if not a small team.

But right now, he needed immediate action from someone who had experience with this sort of catastrophe. Someone like Kirstin Murray, who had worked for an international news organization in London for years before moving to Edinburgh and starting her own firm. A firm where she took on cases for small organizations. Even though the Harrington Foundation had been on an upward trajectory, they had a staff of fewer than two dozen people. The majority of operations were centered in Edinburgh.

If Kirstin could come up with a better campaign than some social media proposal like the last firm, one which included him making a video for TikTok, he would hire her on the spot.

"What are your thoughts on connecting with the donors?" Kirstin asked.

"Something private."

His tone was firm and brooked no refusal. That was an area the first firm had failed on. They'd suggested gala fundraisers, giveaways, splashy events that would only draw more attention. Later, yes, when the foundation was back on its feet. But the last thing he needed right now was to have images of high-profile elites dancing and drinking as the foundation failed to send money to those in need.

"Like a private dinner."

Shaw glanced at Ana, then nodded at her suggestion. "Yes. Something where I can speak with them one-on-one, establish trust. Provide data and answer hard questions they may feel more comfortable asking without an audience."

Ana frowned slightly. "Data is great. But with something of this magnitude, you'll need to personalize it, too."

He gritted his teeth. "I know. That's why I'm here. I don't do personal."

She pressed her lips together as if she were trying to suppress a smile. When he narrowed his eyes at her, she ducked her head.

"Given what you've shared, I'm confident Ana and I can come up with a proposal to meet your needs." Kirstin smiled at him. "I can have it to you within two days."

"Tomorrow morning by eight."

Kirstin arched a brow as Ana's head came up. "Eight?"

He started to stand. "If it's not possible—"

"It is."

Surprised, he and Kirstin both looked at Ana. She glanced first at her boss, then at him, her chin raised, her expression determined.

"We can have a detailed proposal to you by eight tomorrow morning."

Kirstin's lips curved up with pride before she tilted her head to the side. "I agree. We just need the names of the donors who are your highest priority."

Shaw stared at them both for a long moment. Then he nodded. "I look forward to your proposal."

"Thank you. I'll walk you out," Kirstin offered as she held open the door.

Shaw gave Ana a brief nod as he left. She gave him that slight smile again, one that made him feel as if she'd grouped him in with the rest of the world and shut him out.

The notion burrowed under his skin and stayed there, an irritating itch that persisted down the hall.

"Your intern is very bold," he observed as they walked to the elevator.

"Don't let her fool you," Kirstin said with a fond smile.

"She professes to be a novice, but she's a natural communicator. I've learned a lot from her as well. And," Kirstin added as the elevator doors opened, "I really believe with my experience and her insight, we can bring the foundation back on track."

As the doors slid shut and the elevator descended, Shaw let out a harsh breath. The thought of hosting a dinner, of trying to make friendly conversation as he worked to reassure some of the wealthiest people he knew to resume their donations left his body wound tight.

You'll need to personalize it, too.

A fist grabbed his heart, squeezed. Sharing his mother's story—his story—would no doubt entice some donors back.

Nausea curdled in his stomach. His mother had worked so hard, fought for so long to give him everything she could. She hadn't lived to see the success he had achieved. But everything he did, he did for her. For her memory. If honoring her meant pushing outside his comfort zone, then he would do it wholeheartedly.

But he refused to share her sacrifice.

Another image flashed into his mind. One of Ana seated at the table in the café, blond hair falling over her shoulder, that slight smile on her face. He'd vowed that morning to forget her, to not let one encounter upset his focus.

But now, as he walked out onto the sidewalk, he couldn't deny the flicker of interest that lingered, the desire to know more about the audacious young woman.

Except if you hire Murray PR, she'll essentially be your employee.

He shoved thoughts of her smile out of his head. Whether or not he hired Murray PR, he intended to stay as far away from Ana Barros as possible.

CHAPTER SIX

Eviana

A SHRILL PING yanked Eviana out of her much-needed sleep. She and Kirstin had stayed at the office until nearly nine o'clock perfecting the proposal Kirstin was going to deliver to Shaw Harrington. Due to Eviana's early wake-up call the previous morning, her mood was less than charitable toward her unknown caller.

Grumbling under her breath, she grabbed her phone and was about to decline the call when she saw the name on the screen.

"Kirstin?"

"Ana." Her boss's hoarse voice came through the line. "I'm so sorry to call you so early."

"No, don't be. What's wrong?"

"My mother..."

Cold fingers wrapped around Eviana's heart and squeezed. Kirstin's primary reason to move to Edinburgh and start her own firm had been to move in with her aging mother who was slowly losing her mobility. Eviana had never met her, but Kirstin had frequently shown photos of them having in-home movie nights, dining at local restaurants or taking slow walks through Leith or along Portobello Beach.

"Kirstin..."

"She's alive."

Eviana's breath rushed out. "Thank goodness."

"But I don't know..." Kirstin's voice trailed off. "She fell overnight." Her voice caught, broke. "I slept right through it. I didn't find her until an hour ago."

"It's not your fault."

"But—"

"It's not," Eviana interrupted firmly. "You were with her. Who knows how much longer she may have gone without help if you hadn't been there for her?" She gentled her voice. "You love her, Kirstin. You're a good daughter."

Kirstin sucked in a shuddering sob. "Thank you, Ana."

"You're welcome. I'd feel the exact same way, but I'm not the one in the middle of this, so I can tell you you're doing far more than many would. Focus on your mom. Text me updates, but other than that I don't want you to worry about anything at work."

"I just...the Harrington Foundation proposal. I hate putting all of that on you."

Katastrofa.

Eviana scrunched her eyes tight. Of course. Her resolve to keep Mr. Rich and Moody at arm's length was off to a rousing start.

"You're not putting this all on me." Did her voice sound normal? Like she wasn't inwardly cursing or her pulse hadn't shot up beyond a healthy limit? "You're taking care of your mother, which is where you need to be. And I'm stepping up to do the job you've been training me to do."

The words barely left her mouth before doubt flooded her veins. Hadn't she said similar words to her brother? If this was a bakery in Leith or a bookstore in the Grassmarket, she would have no problems. But was she capable of leading a project of this magnitude? Of working alongside a man who had captured her imagination even as he unsettled her with his coldness and intrusive perception?

Another muffled sob from Kirstin answered her unspoken questions. It didn't matter if she was capable or not. She would make this work.

"I won't let you down, Kirstin."

"I don't know what I'd do without you." Kirstin let out a deep, shuddering sigh. "Thank you, Ana."

Eviana sat there in bed for a solid minute after Kirstin had hung up, the phone in her hand as she stared at the wall.

The memory came back, stronger than yesterday. She could feel the paper beneath her fingers, the glossy folder underneath that held the speech written for her by someone else. Could still see the sentence that tripped her up. The one she'd stumbled over as the words had come out of her mouth because it had sounded nothing like her. There'd been so many gazes trained on her, watching her slow descent as heat had crept up her neck and pierced her skin to settle behind her eyes as she'd fought past the sudden lump in her throat.

She'd been sitting in a chair with a bottle of water in the reception room, trying to figure out what had happened, when she'd overheard Helena out in the hall.

This never happened with His Highness.

It didn't matter whether she'd been speaking of Nicholai or the late king. Neither of them had stumbled. Faltered. Failed.

Why that speech? Why that event? Even now she couldn't pinpoint the reason why she'd slipped. The not knowing was the worst. When would it strike again?

Her fingers tightened around the phone. What if it happened with *him*? As she was trying to help her friend achieve her dream?

Panic flared. She closed her eyes, mentally reached out and wrapped her hands around it. Squelched it. She had failed before. But she'd learned a lot since. She was also unencumbered from the restrictions that had constantly made her question herself.

She would not fail now.

She glanced at the clock and sighed. Just after five thirty. She tossed back the covers, stood and stretched. She had to be at the Harrington Foundation office by eight, which meant she should aim for seven thirty in case of traffic or some other unforeseen event.

Like getting splashed by a hedge fund millionaire.

Really, she thought as she padded into the living room and pulled back the curtains, this was an opportunity. A chance to use what she'd learned working for Kirstin and couple it with the confidence she'd developed living as Ana. A confidence she hoped to somehow bring back with her to Kelna.

She wrapped her arms around her waist and watched the sun rise above the horizon. So many unknowns still lingered. Fear fluttered like trapped butterflies in her chest. But she also had resolve. Determination. A friend who needed her.

And a client who desperately needed her help.

Eviana turned away from the window and dove into what had become her morning routine. Opening curtains, putting the kettle on, doing a few stretches in the tiny living room. The four apartments on her floor would have fit into her bedroom at the palace back in Kelna. But she loved it, from the trio of curved windows that overlooked the street to the carved trim that separated the cream-colored walls from the ceiling. The faded coloring added to the historic charm. She loved making tea in the comfort of her kitchen, a room so small she could stretch out her arms and touch both rows of cabinets. No worries that someone would interrupt her precious alone time to whisk her away to yet another scheduled event.

Her head thumped against the cabinets as she leaned back against the counter. Was she capable of this? Could she be the princess her country needed her to be? That her brother and Madeline needed her to be?

She wouldn't go back on her promises. But *dragi Bože*, there were days when it felt impossible.

Eviana shook her head as she reached across the narrow space and pulled the teakettle out of the cupboard, then turned to the tiny sink to fill it. Right now, she needed to focus on the Harrington Foundation and how she was going to work with one very attractive, very cold-mannered millionaire. At least she'd proven to herself whatever attraction she'd experienced wasn't going to interfere with their working relationship. She'd slipped into "royal mode" easily once she'd realized he was a potential client. Years of training had made it second nature even if she despised the mask she wore.

There had been the added element, too, of not wanting to attract Shaw's attention. Not only was Shaw her potential client and therefore temporary employer, but she couldn't get involved with anyone. She'd made a mistake inviting him to coffee, yes. But engaging in an actual affair was one line she had not crossed.

Even, she admitted with a small grin as she placed the kettle on the stove, if she dreamed of it.

A pleasant warmth stirred in her belly at the memory of how he'd looked at her when she'd pitched her idea. When she'd first uttered the words "private dinner," she hadn't missed his body tensing, his eyes narrowing. But as she'd talked, the tension had eased, replaced by one of interest and respect.

She blew out a breath. Shaw was a man who noticed details, things out of place. He'd already heard her unfiltered. Letting small glimpses of her personality show through every now and then wouldn't be the end of the world. But the rapport and camaraderie she enjoyed with Kirstin would not be acceptable.

The teakettle started to whistle. She would do her job and do it well, seeing Shaw only when she had to and conducting herself professionally when she did.

Two hours later, Eviana walked into the glass-enclosed lobby of the Harrington Foundation. An elegant building with a stone facade, it hosted three levels of offices, meeting rooms and a conference room on the top floor next to Shaw's office.

She pressed the button for the elevator.

"Good morning, Miss Barros."

Warmth pooled in her belly as that deep, rough voice sounded just behind her. She turned slowly, giving her a few precious seconds to compose herself.

"Good morning, Mr. Harrington."

Once again, the man looked as if he'd stepped off the pages of a magazine. Navy suit with a matching vest and a black tie. His dark red hair was combed back again, not a strand out of place, as he stared down at her.

She resisted the urge to fidget with her own hair, wrapped in a tight bun at the base of her neck. But as Shaw continued to gaze at her, she had a frantic thought that he was peeling back the layers she'd carefully hidden behind, stripping her down until she had nothing left to hide behind.

Coward.

The thought had her raising her chin and straightening her shoulders.

Respect glinted in Shaw's eyes before he nodded to the elevator. "Going up?"

No, I was just admiring the elevator.

She bit back the dry reply and gave him a small smile. "Yes."

His eyes narrowed, but he stayed silent. The elevator doors opened a moment later, and they stepped in. Eviana breathed in deeply, a mistake she instantly regretted as Shaw's scent wrapped around her. Smoky wood and spice, hints of something wild that contrasted with his buttoned-up appearance.

"Kirstin texted me this morning and said she would not be able to attend the meeting," he said.

"I see."

Part of her almost wanted him to dismiss her, to tell her he had no interest in meeting with an unseasoned intern. It would make things so much simpler.

But that wouldn't be fair to Kirstin. And another part of her, the defiant part that rattled in the box she'd stuffed it into long ago, wanted to see this project through.

"Kirstin assures me that even though you're just an intern, you're immensely qualified to fill in for her and walk me through the proposal."

Eviana gritted her teeth. Yes, *just* an intern.

"I'll do my best, sir."

Silence fell between them, thankfully broken a few seconds later by the doors opening. Shaw gestured for her to exit first, then led her down a carpeted hall toward a gleaming wood door with a gold plate affixed to it.

Shaw Harrington, Founder.

The door swung open. Eviana's mouth dropped open. One wall was comprised entirely of glass. Less than a quarter of a mile away, the steep, craggy slopes of Castle Rock stood proudly over the city, topped by the majestic stone walls of Edinburgh Castle. She'd thought her view of the castle was incredible. But it was nothing compared to this.

She moved toward the windows, entranced. "How do you get any work done?"

"You get used to it after a while."

"I don't see how."

Shaw cleared his throat. Eviana turned, inwardly wincing as she yanked herself away from her daydreams. Another trait that separated her from her brother. Performing in public came easy to Nicholai, whereas she felt like she always had to be on guard, to ensure she was acting with propriety and decorum.

"I'm ready for your proposal, Miss Barros."

Her proposal. It might as well as have been, since she was presenting her and Kirstin's plan to the man who, as her boss had said, could make the future of Murray PR.

No pressure.

Eviana pulled a leather folder out of her messenger bag and handed it to Shaw before taking the seat across from his desk.

No pressure at all.

CHAPTER SEVEN

Eviana

"TELL ME ABOUT your proposal."

The butterflies flapped wildly in her chest. With one sudden push she was back on that stage. But instead of facing down over one hundred people, she was looking into just one pair of arctic blue eyes.

I will not fail. I will not fail.

"You'll begin with individual meetings with two of your donors who have suspended their contributions." She paused, inhaled quickly. "Roy Miles and Olivia Mahs. Your top two donors, and from what I found online, they have strong relationships with several other key donors.

"Meet with Roy and Olivia. Persuade them to renew their donations." As she spoke, her voice strengthened with conviction. "Then in three weeks' time, you will host a private dinner for a dozen donors who are no longer contributing to the foundation. Assuming Olivia and Roy agree to recommit, invite them to be a part of the dinner and serve as unofficial cohosts. Have them share why they decided to resume."

The man didn't even blink. "And after?"

She swallowed hard even as she kept her spine straight and her expression placid. He might not have been jumping up and down for joy, but at least he hadn't tossed her out.

Yet.

"It's going to take time." The words reminded her of the countless times she'd sat by hospital beds, holding hands and offering encouragement tempered with reality. It had been one of her favorite duties, the simple act of connecting with her people, of seeing them smile and supporting them through some of their most challenging times. A role she had loved, and one she drew on now as she continued. "But getting funds flowing back in while reestablishing trust is the first step. After you achieve that, then look ahead to hiring a new CEO, increasing public donations and investing in publicity once you have the support of your former donors. Their recommitment would be a huge selling point."

Shaw's lips tightened a fraction. "Given their faithlessness, I'm not holding my breath."

Eviana hesitated. "Since Zach was the primary link to those donors, it makes their withdrawal more understandable."

"Agree to disagree."

The man's words could have frozen hell. As a princess, this would have been an occasion where she continued on, politely ignoring his breach of manners.

"You don't have to like it. But if you can't understand it, you'll struggle to convince them to come back."

Eviana blinked. *Did I really just say that?*

Apparently she had because Shaw sat back, his thick brows drawing together as he regarded her with curiosity. Curiosity, she noted, edged with irritation if his tense jaw was anything to go by. Few people probably dared to challenge him. But if he couldn't handle constructive feedback, then it didn't matter whether she was here with Kirstin or working alone. Murray PR was successful because Kirstin encouraged her clients to do hard work, not just strive for the perfect image with no substance underneath.

Eviana waited, hands folded in her lap, heart thumping.

"Acknowledged."

She barely kept her composure, fighting back a grin of triumph as she inclined her head to him. "Thank you."

"Did you summarize all of this?"

"It's all listed in the proposal," she added with a nod to the folder.

Shaw opened the folder and started to flip, reading each and every single page. Eviana sat as she had done so often in meetings, ceremonies, events where her mere presence had been the only requirement. That and not functioning, not doing anything that might invite criticism.

Twice Shaw glanced up, his eyes flicking to hers as if to gauge her level of irritation at his thoroughness. She simply smiled in return. Fifteen minutes was nothing compared to a four-hour military ceremony or the six-hour economic forum she had sat through last year to allow Nicholai to track down Madeline in Kansas City and properly propose.

At last, Shaw sat back in his chair. Even in a more relaxed pose, the perpetual tension gripping his body was evident in the taut tendons of his neck and the firm slash of his lips.

"I don't like special events."

Her heart sank. She'd botched it.

"However, I'm willing to make an exception with this proposal."

Elation surged through her. "Thank you."

"I'll expect you and Kirstin to start tomorrow."

"I'll be happy to start as soon as you need me. Kirstin…" Eviana paused. "With Kirstin's family emergency, I will be your primary contact for the next couple of days and—"

He sat forward in his chair, the action almost like a lunge with how quickly he moved. "I thought she was only detained for the meeting."

Eviana lifted her chin as irritation flickered through her

at his accusatory tone. "I'm telling you now before we begin any work."

The beat of silence that followed spoke volumes, as did the gathering anger in his eyes. "I understood her to only be gone today, not for the beginning of a campaign. An omission on both your parts that borders on a lie."

Eviana opened her mouth to retort, then stopped. Given what he had just gone through, she could understand his reaction. "I won't say I'm sorry if the alternative was you declining to meet with me in the first place knowing Kirstin would be unavailable at first. However, I will apologize if my actions hurt you in any way."

Shaw blinked in surprise. Then, he slowly leaned back in his chair. Fingers drummed on his arm rest once. Twice. "Apology accepted."

The words sounded almost wrenched from his chest. But he didn't strike her as the kind of man who normally accepted apologies.

"I have reservations," he said.

"Understandable."

"Is there any possibility of Kirstin returning in the next week or two?"

Again, Eviana hesitated. "I don't know. I'm happy to convey whatever information she's comfortable sharing. But as I referenced earlier, it's a family emergency, one that is ongoing."

The royal in her told her to stop there. But the friend in her, the passionate soul that had been allowed to thrive these past eight weeks, pressed forward.

"I will say I greatly admire Kirstin. Having the opportunity to work with someone like you is something she has been pursuing ever since she opened her firm. Yet when someone she loves needed her, she went." She nodded to the folder. "The proposal in front of you is the result of her nearly thirty years of experience in the field. Even though I would be the one to get it started, it's a plan created with her expertise and knowledge. And," Eviana added with a bravado she didn't feel, "she trusted me to carry on her vision."

Shaw slowly turned his head and gazed out the window at the castle. "Trust is not a commodity to be shared lightly. Or at all," he murmured so quietly she almost wondered if she imagined it.

"Anyone would hesitate after what happened."

"Even before Zach…" His voice trailed off, and he shook his head slightly. "I am making what is, at least for me, a very difficult decision."

Her lungs constricted. Had she misread him?

"Of the three firms I have consulted so far, yours is the only proposal that seems to have truly taken into account the situation and my personal requests for as much privacy as possible. I would like to hire Murray PR."

Eviana sat, frozen in her chair. Giddiness rose up inside her like a bubble about to burst. Finally, Kirstin would get the chance she deserved. And she had helped. Not just with the proposal, but with selling Murray PR's services to Shaw. Instead of backing down and following rules and protocols, she'd taken a leap of faith and relied on the confidence she'd been slowly building to advocate for the firm. A move that had paid off.

"You won't be disappointed," she said.

Shaw held up one finger. "I am throwing a clause into our agreement."

He could throw whatever he wanted to. Eviana was determined not to let this opportunity pass her by.

"If I am not satisfied with your performance at any point in the next two weeks, I will cancel the contract at no cost to myself or the foundation."

"I'll want to confirm that with Kirstin—"

"Yes or no. Right now, or the deal's off."

Pressure slammed into her as her confidence evaporated, insecurity and doubt quickly filling the vacuum. This should have been Kirstin's call. Eviana had no business making decisions of this magnitude.

Yet what other option was there?

"Miss Barros—"

"Done."

She'd talk to Kirstin later. If Kirstin disagreed, she'd wire for money from home to cover any penalties. She wouldn't have her friend pay for her mistakes.

That hint of a smirk played about his lips. "Let's hope you're not overly confident in your abilities."

Eviana inclined her head to him as she stood. She didn't like being backed into a corner by a man who thought he could simply order people about. She had met plenty of people like him.

But this was the first time she could deal with someone like him and do it on her terms. Another building block for her confidence.

"I'm not." She leaned into her frustration and resentment as she gave Shaw an uncharacteristically sharp smile. "I'm just realistic."

CHAPTER EIGHT

Shaw

"MR. HARRINGTON?"

Shaw glanced at the speaker on his desk. "Yes?"

"Miss Barros is here."

It had been three days since Ana had strode into his office with that serene calmness overlaying a spine of steel. The proposal had impressed him, as had Ana's alluring combination of confidence and sheer audacity.

The plan she and Kirstin had prepared was a good one. He'd thrown out his stipulation about her performance more as a challenge to see how she would respond. That she had taken him up on it without so much as batting an eyelid told him that while Miss Barros might've been an intern, she was either an exceptionally confident one or she had prior experience that made her overqualified for her current role.

Which begged the question, he thought as a knock sounded on his door, why was she interning for a small public relations firm? What had brought her here to Scotland?

"Come in."

His chest tightened as Ana walked in. Like the last meeting, she was wearing black pants, a white shirt and a black blazer. Almost identical to what she'd been wearing when he'd accidentally splashed her. A far cry from the colorful ensemble she had changed into. That bright yellow skirt had seemed more…her. She wore her suits well, with a grace and maturity that women far more experienced would envy. Yet it seemed…out of character. Like a colorful painting had been muted.

Good God, stop.

She was a woman, not a piece of art. And he was a man with a mission, not some smitten teenager. Ana had stayed true to her word and maintained a professional demeanor in every interaction they'd had. That he was struggling to keep a leash on his own errant thoughts clung like an irritating burr to his already shortened temper.

"Good morning, Mr. Harrington."

He dismissed the uptick in his pulse as her soft accent floated over him. "Miss Barros."

She slid a folder across his desk before sitting across from him. "Roy Miles has agreed to dinner. He has availability tonight, tomorrow and early next week before he and his wife leave for Kenya."

Shaw didn't bother to hide his scowl as he flipped open the folder. The foundation needed people like Roy. People who had grown up with wealth, who wallowed in it and were always looking for an excuse as to where to spend it.

But that was also the problem with people like Roy. They were capricious, full of their own importance and subject to random whims.

Just like Zach.

I did it for the foundation, he'd said.

No. Zach had done it for himself. He hadn't liked being told no, had been so convinced of his own superiority that he had plowed forward without thinking about how his actions would affect anyone else in his orbit.

"Where is this meeting taking place?"

"The Dome. Upscale restaurant, a staple of Edinburgh's dining scene. The kind of place that will impress Mr. Miles and has the added benefit of being a favorite of his wife's whenever they're in Scotland."

Shaw gave her a brief nod. Impressive. "What night are you free?"

Perhaps it was petty, a result of his own inability to stifle his attraction, but he couldn't help but enjoy the look of surprise on her face.

"Excuse me?"

"As I mentioned in my initial meeting with you and Kirstin, one of the things I struggle with is developing and maintaining personal relationships. I need someone with me as a sort of…"

"Buffer?"

"Exactly. Someone who can be on standby to assist, to add the personal touches that I struggle to exhibit."

A trait he had never regretted. Not until he had been confronted with the reality of how much he had come to depend upon Zach's affability.

"As I'm sure you're aware," he added with a pointed gaze, "many major organizations have their own public relations departments and representatives who accompany their executives to a variety of events to do exactly that. A gap in our current structure, but one we will eventually rectify."

Twin blooms of color appeared in Ana's cheeks. It was gratifying to see those touches of humanity in the woman who had ensnared him with her spontaneity and sunny outlook on life, only to retreat behind a bland mask.

"I am aware of the role many PR executives play."

She paused, her eyes flickering to the side. Was that fear on her face? Something uncomfortable twisted in Shaw's gut.

"Is everything all right, Miss Barros?"

Her attention jerked back to him. "Yes. I'm just surprised that with your concerns the other day about dealing with just an intern you would trust me with something of this magnitude."

He blinked, then struggled to suppress a smile. She had

parroted his words with a formal primness that most would have mistaken for simply repeating what he'd said. But he didn't miss the flash of irritation in her eyes.

"I had concerns. You alleviated them enough for me to choose Murray PR. Until your boss is available, I expect you to fill in the roles she would have served in."

She sat there, staring at him.

"Is this no longer a suitable arrangement?"

He hadn't realized it was possible for her to sit up even straighter, but she did.

"No, Mr. Harrington. I'm just surprised. I'm free tomorrow."

"But not tonight?"

A slight frown drew her brows together. "I can make tonight work if you require it."

Jealousy unfurled in his chest, unexpected and heavy. "Do you have a date?"

"As I said, I can make tonight work if needed."

It should come as no surprise that a young, attractive, self-assured woman would have men interested in her. The fact that he loathed the idea as much as he did, however, was a knot he was not prepared to untangle.

"Tomorrow is fine," he said. "Please make sure to wear something formal."

"Of course."

"Give me your address, and I'll pick you up at seven."

"I'll catch a taxi," she said.

He glanced up. "I would prefer to pick you up."

Fire flashed in her eyes as her chin came up. "And I would prefer to take a taxi."

He sat back, steepling his fingers as he regarded her with a gaze that had made men twice his age quake in their boots back in New York. Ana, however, simply returned his stare. He shouldn't admire her show of strength. Zach had defied him, too, and look where that had led. Shaw had learned a valuable lesson—that while he might have kept himself impervious to personal relationships, he'd slipped when it came to professional ones. Had extended too much trust without even realizing it until it was too late.

"Why do you not want me to pick you up?" he asked.

"I like being in charge of myself."

Her answer seemed genuine, truthful. He was projecting his own experiences onto her. Memories of a time when he'd lied about his age to secure a job and help his mother pay the seemingly endless list of bills that kept them trapped in poverty.

His gaze darted to the photograph in the silver frame on the edge of his desk, angled so that only he could see it. Red corkscrew curls in a wild cloud about his mother's face. Her lips were parted in laughter, her blue eyes sparkling. A student photographer from the university had captured it on a rare day off when she'd taken him on a picnic to the park.

It was the only picture he had of her. If the office caught on fire, it would be the one thing he would save.

When he looked back up, Ana was watching him, curiosity on her face. Curiosity and a hint of empathy in her green gaze. An empathy he didn't want or need.

"While your personal preferences are noted, I will pick you up, Miss Barros. I will not be tethered to the irregularities of a taxi schedule," he said. "When I tell Mr. Miles and his wife that we will be there at seven, I want to ensure we'll be there at quarter till."

"Understood."

Her voice was polite. No change in her expression. But he could sense the disapproval, the irritation in her clipped movements as she pulled the pad of paper closer to her and jotted down an address.

"Do you have availability in the morning to review our strategy?" she asked.

"See my secretary on the way out. She'll schedule you."

He turned his attention to his computer screen. He was being rude. But the longer she stayed in his office, the more he wanted to turn the picture around, to show her the woman who had fought tooth and nail to provide him with a better life. Who was the heart and soul of the Harrington Foundation and everything he was trying to achieve.

But he didn't.

"Goodbye, Mr. Harrington."

His fingers tightened on his computer mouse. He stared at his screen until the words blurred and he heard the click of the door closing. Murray PR had been the right choice. In the two meetings he'd had with Ana, she'd proven to be everything Kirstin had said.

She wasn't the problem. He was.

He stood and stepped to his window. He'd grown up with Edinburgh Castle standing guard over the city. Over time, it had become one of those symbols he barely glanced at. It was always there, would always be there, at least for his lifetime.

As he stared at the stone walls, the stalwart cliffs holding up hundreds of years of history, he saw it through Ana's eyes. The tradition, the majesty. He envied her outlook on life, her ability to appreciate the little things he so often missed as he marched forward, so determined on where he was going he often forgot to look around at where he was.

He turned away and moved back to his desk. Yes, life would be better if it were all sunshine and rainbows. But he'd grown up in the real world, one where he had known hunger and cold and judgment. His mother had been a constant blessing that many in his position had not had. It was because of her that he had become successful, that he was now in a position to help others. He would not lose sight of that purpose, not for anything.

Or anyone.

CHAPTER NINE

Eviana

EVIANA SMOOTHED HER hands down her skirt as she stared at her reflection in the full-length mirror. She had attended balls, weddings and a slew of formal dinners ever since she'd been five years old.

She had never felt more nervous than she did right this moment.

The black dress she had chosen, a Gucci gown with a full skirt, square neckline and straps tied off in tiny bows at the shoulders, was a little much for a supposed intern. But in her mind, it was worth the risk. Not only for Murray PR, but for representing the Harrington Foundation and clearing this first hurdle.

If there was a small part of her that hoped that Shaw would be impressed, so be it.

She tucked a blond strand back into place. It had been over two months since her bodyguard, Jodi, had suggested she dye her hair to give herself even more freedom of movement. That, along with the bangs across her forehead, had so far done its job. Not that many people in Scotland had even heard of Kelna or its royal family. But it still gave her a degree of comfort, a safety net that allowed her to move about Edinburgh as if she were truly just a civilian living her life.

She sighed. To date, Jodi's presence had been comforting,

a reminder that she had someone here who knew her deepest, darkest secrets and would do anything to protect her. But tonight it made her feel…false. A reminder that she was living her own odd version of a fairy tale. One that would soon end.

Her phone buzzed, drawing her out of her reverie. When she saw Shaw's name on the screen, her heart leapt into her throat.

Three minutes away.

Their meeting this morning had gone well. Almost perfect. She had laid out the key talking points she thought might persuade a man like Roy Miles to resume his donations. Shaw had agreed to all of them and delivered a couple of practice speeches for her to review. Much better than yesterday's face-off over him picking her up, she thought with an irritated tug on one of the bows at her shoulders. Although the meeting today had been frustrating in a different sort of way. As Shaw had gone over talking points with her, he'd impressed her with his depth of knowledge, the dedication he felt for the work the foundation did.

A sigh escaped. The man wasn't just a spoiled millionaire playing around with charities. Beneath that seemingly impassive exterior beat a passionate heart. It was subtle. One had to realize that Shaw Harrington was not just a cold block of ice to even identify the signs.

It would be so much easier, she thought as she snatched her shawl and clutch off a chair, *if he was simply a jerk*.

Easier to ignore the attraction that had resurfaced with those glimpses of the man behind the mask. The deepening of his voice, the softening around his eyes as he spoke of the Harrington Foundation and the work it did. The pride in his voice as he mentioned the success rate of a charity in

Inverness that helped low-income families receive paid job training.

She shook her head as she headed toward the door. Instead of mooning over him, she needed to think like a professional—how best to use those glimpses to further the cause of the foundation. If she could just help people see that side of him, share whatever it was that drove him to work so hard, the donors would come back, arguing over who got to pledge the most money.

But for whatever reason, he wouldn't. Which was why she was here.

Her phone dinged again. She glanced down at her screen and smiled.

Good luck tonight!

Kirstin had checked in regularly, offering insight and suggestions to the plan as she went along. With her mother moving from the hospital back into her home but still needing help moving around their apartment, Kirstin had been far too busy to return to work. She had called and had an extensive conversation with Shaw this afternoon, too. All Kirstin had said was that it had gone well, that Shaw had been very understanding regarding her mother and he had reported being pleased with Eviana's work.

Which was good because even though she'd seen a bit more humanity today, he was not the type of man to give praise lightly or converse in a friendly manner. Although, she conceded as she locked the door to her flat and started down the stairs, it had been a good test of her ability to continue working in a tough environment.

A smile lit her face as she stepped out onto the stoop. She'd persevered. Instead of constantly being on edge, evaluating her every move, she'd simply focused on her work. If doubt crept in or if her gaze had occasionally strayed to Shaw's handsome profile, she'd pushed through.

Tonight would be a good night. Not only a potential milestone for the foundation and Murray PR, but a personal one, too. A test of the work she'd done, both to develop as a professional and to personally overcome her lingering insecurities.

A far cry from helping to run a country. But each step was progress.

Her phone dinged a third time. Her smile disappeared as she saw the name.

Nicholai.

Slowly, she tapped the screen.

Hey. Hope you're enjoying your sabbatical. It'll be good to have you home.

She stood there, staring down at her phone as she fought against an onslaught of emotion. She missed her brother. Missed Madeline. Her country, the people who had supported and loved the royal family through thick and thin.

But there was grief, too, the kind of grief that came from knowing when she returned home, it would never be the same.

And beneath it all—the pain, the loss, the confusion—lay the worst emotion of all: fear. She hadn't even lasted a year with her new duties before the worst had happened. One failure might be excused, especially given her father's recent passing. But what if it happened again? Two more times? How many times before she not only lost faith in herself but her people did, too?

"Ana."

Her head snapped up. She'd been so caught up in her own miserable musings that she'd missed the black car pulling up to the curb.

And missed Shaw getting out of the car.

Warmth spread through her. Dressed to perfection in a black tuxedo and crisp white shirt, his beard had been trimmed and his hair combed back to showcase the angular planes of his face.

But it wasn't just his attractiveness that caught her attention. No, it was the glimmer of worry in his eyes as he moved towards her.

"Are you all right?"

Royal smile.

"Yes." She slid her phone into her clutch. "Just a text from home that surprised me."

Acutely aware of his gaze on her, she descended the stairs with slow steps.

"I'm fine."

If he had accepted her casual dismissal of the moment, it would have been so easy to move on with the night. But instead Shaw leaned forward, his intensity magnified tenfold as he directed it squarely at her.

"Sometimes the most painful things are the small things. They rear their head when you least expect them."

Her throat closed. She didn't want this man to understand her on such a deep level. To understand her unlike anyone else ever had.

And yet, she thought as she met his stare, *he does.*

"My father passed away last year. This trip has been valuable in so many ways. But it's also been an escape. Just thinking about going back home is…" She paused, trying to find the right word. "Hard." Her voice broke. Not much, but enough to convey the depths of her grief.

Instead of stepping back or chastising her, Shaw's gaze softened even further. "It's never easy."

"No. It's not."

She broke eye contact and glanced around the street, taking a moment to compose herself and mentally letting go of the tension Nicholai's text had ushered in.

"Thank you for listening."

Shaw nodded as his features relaxed and he gestured toward the car. At some point during their conversation, a chauffeur had gotten out and stood guard by the passenger door. But as he reached for the door handle, Shaw waved him aside. He opened the back door and gestured for Eviana to climb inside.

As she moved forward, Shaw held out his hand. She took it, partially out of habit, partially out of instinct.

Their fingers brushed. The world shuddered. Stopped. Such a simple contact, similar to the graze of fingers when she'd handed him his coffee days ago. Except this time, his hand wrapped around hers, a firm, comforting weight that sent tendrils of warmth through her body. Her breath caught in her throat. She looked down at his hand engulfing hers, then slowly raised her gaze. Shaw stared at her. Aside from the warm pressure of his hand on hers, he was so still he could have passed for a statue.

"Hvala vam."

It took a moment for her to realize she had thanked him in Croatian. Flustered, she climbed into the limo. His hand tightened on hers for a heartbeat.

And then he released her without a word.

The limo ride was quiet, tension pulsing between them like a living thing. Eviana kept her eyes trained on the passing scenery. Normally she would enjoy the sights, the stone architecture, the gardens and green spaces dotted throughout the city.

But she saw nothing, registered no details as the limo moved through the night. All she could think about was the man sitting opposite her. The man who was essentially her boss, who held her friend and mentor's fate in his hands. Who prized honesty and despised any type of deception. If Kirstin ever found out Eviana's identity, she would be shocked, yes, but would probably also find it fun, an adventure of sorts having a princess work for her. If Shaw found out, however...

Eviana suppressed a shudder. At the very least, he would cancel the contract with Murray PR. For a man who claimed to have little ability at building and maintaining relationships, he made her want to confide in him, to show him the woman she was.

But it wasn't meant to be, she firmly reminded herself as the limo pulled up outside the restaurant. While he might've felt something similar to what she was experiencing, his fury at her deception would eclipse any attraction.

The chauffeur opened the door, and Shaw got out. Even if he could get past her real identity, there was the matter of... well, everything else. Everything about her life, her real life, was the antithesis of what Shaw wanted for himself. Public scrutiny, constant demands on her time. The man she married would have to accept her duty to the crown and be accepted by the people of Kelna.

Shaw extended a hand to her. She mentally braced, then placed her hand in his. She'd maintained walls her entire life. Whatever spell she had fallen under when it came to Shaw Harrington needed to be broken and broken fast—before she made a mistake that would hurt her friend or herself.

Or both.

CHAPTER TEN

Shaw

WINEGLASSES CLINKED INSIDE the cavernous space of the Dome's main dining room. Curtains trimmed in gold brocade shut out the night and created an intimate atmosphere despite the numerous tables arranged throughout the room. Chandeliers gleamed overhead as waiters moved around the tables, carrying silver trays laden with caviar, brisket and Scotch pie.

Across the table, Roy Miles tossed back a hundred-pound glass of whisky like he was at a London rave instead of an upscale restaurant.

"Excellent choice," Roy repeated for the fourth time.

At just over fifty years old, he kept a trim physique and skin bronzed to such a degree it hinted at help from a tanning salon. His suit was from Savile Row, his watch a Rolex.

Shaw understood, at least to some extent, investing in quality. The clothes he wore, the car he drove—all of it was an investment. The clients he worked with trusted someone who gave off a certain appearance. The same could be said of the people who donated thousands to the Harrington Foundation. Quality made an impression.

But Roy was also a prime example of how money could be wasted.

Shaw forced what he hoped looked like a smile onto his

face as he held up his own glass of whisky that he had been nursing for the past twenty minutes.

"Thank you."

Roy's wife, Victoria, was engaged in a quiet conversation with Ana. The two had hit it off almost as soon as Shaw and Ana had walked into the restaurant. How Roy had ended up with a woman like Victoria, a retired veterinarian with silver-blond hair wrapped into a simple braid and a kind smile that reminded Shaw of his mother, was a mystery.

But Roy had also been one of the most prolific donors to the Harrington Foundation, eager to have his name attached to what he'd seen as a rising star in charity work. That Zach had met Roy at some celebrity event in New York City and plastered Roy's photo across the foundation's social media and brochures had no doubt helped.

Unfortunately, Roy's obsession with status did not mesh well with the fallout from Zach's choices.

"How's business?"

Not the most engaging question Shaw could ask, but it was at least an attempt to engage with Roy instead of point-blank asking him to resume his donations. Out of the corner of his eye, he saw Ana glance at him and give him a slight encouraging nod before returning her attention to Victoria.

He'd never relied on the approval of others. But the small acknowledgment soothed some of the restless energy coursing through him.

"Excellent," Roy boomed. "The wife and I just bought a ranch in Montana."

Shaw tried, and failed, to keep the frown off his face. "A ranch?"

"Yep." Roy raised his hand to signal the waiter for another glass. "Four hundred acres set against the Rocky Mountains. I forget how many cattle. And a four-thousand-square-foot ranch house complete with its own sauna and hot tub."

"Dear," Victoria said with a patient smile on her face, "let's not brag."

"Let's!" Roy shot her a toothy smile. "How many times have I told you I thought I would make an excellent cowboy?"

"Plenty," she replied dryly.

"Perhaps to you, but not to these two lovely people."

Shaw's hand tightened around his glass. The audacity of the man to sit there, to brag about his spending even as charities floundered to support people desperately in need, made him want to toss the contents of his very pricey drink into Roy Miles's face.

"Congratulations." Judging by the warning look Ana shot him, his voice had come out just as growly as he'd intended.

"Thank you." A waiter set another glass of whiskey in front of Roy. "As much as I'm enjoying this dinner, you didn't just ask me here to lavish food on me."

Finally.

"The investigation has officially concluded in New York." Shaw tempered his voice, strove for professionalism and confidence. "The Harrington Foundation, the board and I have all been cleared of any wrongdoing."

Roy didn't even look at him, choosing instead to survey the array of Scottish cheeses on the platter in the middle of the table.

"Given that we are no longer under suspicion," Shaw continued as he focused on a point over Roy's shoulder instead of the irritating man himself, "I wanted to ask you to consider resuming your donations to the Harrington Foundation."

Roy used a fork to spear a piece of brie. "I'm glad to hear you've been cleared, not that I had any doubts. But it's all—" he waved his fork in the air and nearly sent the cheese sailing across the dining room "—so recent. I know your group does good work. I admire that. It's why I donated in the first place."

You donated because Zach sold you on the idea of being a knight in shining armor, come to save people beneath you.

"But I'd like to give it a little bit longer," Roy said just before he popped the piece of cheese into his mouth. "Let things die down a little more. Let's revisit this in a few months."

It was a wonder Shaw didn't break the glass in hand.

Ana and Victoria had stopped talking, their attention now fixed on Shaw and Roy. Victoria sent her husband a narrow-eyed look. But Roy's attention was focused on spooning a generous amount of caviar onto his beef. Each motion ratcheted up Shaw's simmering anger.

"Have you thought that being the first donor to renew his donations might make its own statement?"

Ana's serene voice floated over the table. Roy glanced at her, then smiled, his eyes warming with appreciation at her beauty.

Shaw's anger heightened as it twisted into an ugly mass inside his chest. Ana looked lovely, yes. Stunning. When he'd seen her on the stoop of her apartment building, strands of curling blond hair framing her heart-shaped face and wearing a dress that looked tailor-made to her petite figure, he hadn't even bothered to excuse away the surge of attraction.

So he could understand other men looking, too. But not the way Roy was, like she was a prize to be won.

Ana's eyes flickered to Shaw. The tiniest shake of her head made him forcibly relax, mentally unwinding each muscle as he sat back in his chair. He didn't want to trust her, didn't want to turn things over to her completely.

But until he got himself under control, he had no choice.

Roy's avaricious leer disappeared as his expression turned thoughtful. "Can't say I thought of it that way."

"The Harrington Foundation continues to do good work."

Ana spoke gently but firmly, a blend that Shaw envied. It reminded him of Zach in that she spoke as if she'd been with the foundation for years instead of just a few days. But whereas Zach had relied on a blindingly white smile and charm, Ana radiated quiet authenticity.

"Even with the lack of funds," she said, "they've continued to make substantial contributions and support as many charities as they can."

Shaw forced himself to sit still and let her do what he had hired her to do. Roy was giving her more eye contact in the last thirty seconds than he had given Shaw in the past ten minutes. It was a struggle to turn things over to her, to not interfere. But trust issues or not, he knew his own weaknesses. And he was coming to learn more about Ana's strengths. Strengths he both envied and admired.

"Worthy efforts, Miss Barros. But," Roy said, his eyes flicking to Shaw before refocusing on Ana, "I lost a lot of money when this thing blew up. So did associates I recommended the Harrington Foundation to. We thought we knew Zach White. We trusted him." He faced Shaw then, his eyes suddenly hard, all traces of the partying buffoon gone. "I don't know you, Shaw Harrington. No one does. Learning that that donation was lost is not something I'm going to get over easily."

"Zach is gone." Shaw's voice whipped out over the table. "That will not happen again."

"How do I know that?" Shaw didn't give Roy any ground even as the older man leaned forward and pointed a finger at him. "You want us to trust you, trust your foundation, but you've given us nothing except some statistics to smooth over what happened."

"Mr. Harrington is an honorable man."

Shaw's head snapped around at Ana's voice.

What on earth is she doing?

"I know you don't know Mr. Harrington well, but the fact that he believed in something so much that he invested, and continues to invest..."

Her voice trailed off as her gaze collided with Shaw's. It

was more shock and fury that kept him mute. How had she found out about his investments? Worse, how many times had he told Ana over the past few days that he preferred his privacy? That he wanted to persuade the donors based on the merits of the foundation and not his personal life?

Ana cleared her throat. "That he continues to invest his own funds speaks volumes."

Her last words fell flat, her confidence gone. Shaw knew he'd taken a bad situation and made it worse with his reaction. But he couldn't see past the betrayal. A minor incident compared to Zach's treachery, but a betrayal nonetheless. His ongoing donations would be a matter of public record, including the sizable chunk he had invested six months ago. But she hadn't asked his permission to share that detail, had gone against his specifications for privacy.

Roy glanced between Shaw and Ana with renewed interest even as Shaw's blood curdled in his veins. This was what he hated—being looked at like a specimen, being the center of attention. Once a small detail was revealed, people wanted more. They wanted to dig deeper and deeper until they had the whole story of how Shaw Harrington had grown up in the slums of Edinburgh, bouncing from place to place while his mother had worked herself to death trying to provide for them. How he'd used his own money to start the foundation and do what another charity had failed to do for him so long ago.

His lips curled into a slight sneer. The perfect sob story. One that, if Ana continued to share these little tidbits, would eventually be revealed. The thought of having his mother's sacrifices used as marketing fodder cranked up the heat on his simmering anger and turned it into a fire that burned away any remaining patience. He'd trusted Ana for all of five minutes, and she'd gone rogue in less than three. No matter how the rest of this hellish night proceeded, he would either make his conditions crystal clear with no more second chances. Better yet, maybe he should fire Murray PR and be done with Ana altogether.

"Something to consider, Miss Barros. Now," Roy said as he picked up his fork and knife again, "tell me more about yourself, my dear. Are you enjoying your time in Scotland?"

Ana glanced at Shaw as if to confirm that he wanted her to follow Roy's lead and drop the conversation. For the first time since he'd met her, worry gleamed in her eyes. Uncertainty drifted across her face. Something twisted in his chest at causing her discomfort. It twisted even tighter at the thought of having to fire her.

And then he dismissed his ridiculous emotions. Feelings had no place in business.

He managed to make it through the rest of the meal, mostly because Roy did the majority of the talking. Finally, after what had to have been the longest hour of Shaw's life, Roy stood and leaned across the table.

"Thanks for the meal, Shaw. I'll be in touch."

I doubt that.

Shaw acknowledged Roy's statement with a nod of his head. Victoria was much friendlier, coming around the table to offer him a hug. She did the same to Ana, whispering something into her ear and giving her a light squeeze on the arm before following her husband out of the restaurant.

Shaw sat back and watched as a waitress cleared the remnants of their meal. Ana, who had been mostly silent since her attempts to salvage the pitch, kept her gaze focused on her glass of wine until the waitress left.

"What was that?"

To her credit she didn't flinch, even though he flung the words at her with the force of an arrow whistling toward its target.

"Me trying to persuade a client."

His discomfort returned, along with a heavy dose of guilt

that beat its fists against his defenses. It only made him angrier, as did her refusal to meet his gaze.

"No." Shaw leaned forward and placed one hand on the table, his fingertips pressing down into the tablecloth. "That was you violating a direct order not to share any private information."

Her head snapped up. He barely resisted moving back from the sparkling fury in her eyes.

"No, it was me doing the job you said you would trust me to do." She leaned in, closing the distance between them as her confidence returned in full force. "I didn't share anything that's not public knowledge."

"It might be available to the public," he growled back, "but that doesn't mean I want it bandied about. At what point did you forget my specific request for privacy?"

She set her wineglass down so hard the ruby liquid swirled dangerously close to the rim.

"On the first charge, not only are your donations a matter of public record, but it was included in a statement from *your* foundation to the press three months ago."

Cold flooded his veins. "What?"

Ana pulled out her phone, tapped something on the screen and handed it to him. Shaw read through the article, his body tensing as he got to the last paragraph.

Shaw Harrington is committed to maintaining the foundation and keeping it solvent throughout this crisis. Mr. Harrington has donated a significant portion of his own funds to cover as much of the deficit as possible for the current operating year.

"I didn't approve this."

He glanced at the date, then bit back a curse. He remembered that day. It was the day Zachary had shown up to his office in New York. The week before Shaw had decided to rent out his penthouse and return to Edinburgh for the foreseeable future. Zach had managed to bluster his way past the secretary on the first floor, but Shaw had alerted security before he'd made it off the elevator. The guards had hauled him away as he had shouted out Shaw's name. The image of Zach being tossed out of his office had made its rounds on social media in the evening news. Shaw had told his marketing department to handle the subsequent press.

"I didn't know."

The excuse sounded lame even to his ears.

"I shared information I thought you had already approved. And," she added as she leaned forward once more, color high in her cheeks, "this is the kind of information that makes a difference, that changes someone's mind. You heard what Roy said—you can't do it solely on the basis of what the foundation does. Not anymore. Not after their trust has been broken."

"You don't think I know that?"

Heads turned their way as his voice rose above the din. One woman with dark blond hair in a long braid and dressed in a simple black suit seemed to take an especially strong interest in their conversation as she stared at him over her shoulder. She turned away when he glared at her.

"This is not the time or place for this conversation," he said.

"Obviously." Ana stood and tossed her napkin onto the table with an uncharacteristic lack of finesse. "Although I will say this, Mr. Harrington—you're asking these people to trust you, yet you trust no one but yourself. I don't know how you expect to make any headway when all you're offering is a one-way street on your own terms. Oh," she added with a sweet smile laced with daggers, "and in case you forgot, you hired a *public* relations firm. Something to keep in mind if we proceed."

The truth of her statement punched him in the gut. He gritted his teeth, consciously aware of the heads still turned in their direction. "We can continue this discussion in the car."

Ana paused, then looked down her nose at him. "No."

Blood roared in his ears as she continued to look down at him as if he'd been the one to do something wrong. As if she were the boss, not him.

"Excuse me?" The two words sounded as if they'd been pulled through a steel grater.

"I said no. You didn't trust me to do my job tonight." She held up a hand as his lips parted on a retort. "Yes, I faltered. But that was after you interfered. Had you not, I might have been able to make more progress with Mr. Miles." She grabbed her shawl off the back of the chair. "Now, if you'll excuse me, I would prefer to discuss this in the morning once we both have the chance to cool off."

Before Shaw could respond, Ana turned and walked out the door. He nearly followed her. But he didn't. Following would be a sign of weakness, chasing her down when he was the one who had hired her. He might give her a second chance, one he didn't extend to many. Knowing how she had gotten the information about his donations helped ease some of his anger. But she still should have talked to him, cleared it before she'd gone off script.

"Would you care for another drink, sir?"

Shaw looked up at the waitress, then down at his nearly empty whisky glass. "Tempting, but no, thank you. Just the check."

Slowly, everyone else returned to their meals, leaving Shaw alone at the table.

Usually he preferred it this way—no one to depend on but himself. But as he glanced once more at the door Ana had walked out of, he didn't feel strong.

He just felt alone.

CHAPTER ELEVEN

Eviana

EVIANA WALKED OUT of the restaurant, each step heavier than the last. But she pushed through. She didn't want to see Shaw, couldn't bear to let him see the swirl of emotions spinning inside her chest like a cyclone. Embarrassment, anger, frustration.

And above all, fear. Fear that the last nine weeks had been nothing more than slapping a bandage over the fact that she wasn't capable of being the kind of leader her brother was, the kind of leader their father had been. Leaders who exhibited diplomacy and confidence, who didn't let angry glances and self-doubts prevent them from doing what needed to be done.

Of all the nights to let her heart speak instead of her head.

Her phone vibrated in her pocket. She pulled it out, her stomach sinking when she saw Kirstin's name on the screen.

How's it going? Can't wait to hear all about it. Still going to be out for a few days at least, but I know you're representing Murray PR well!

Eviana swallowed against the sudden thickness in her throat. Instead of doing well, she might have just torpedoed the entire contract by jumping into the verbal fray instead of doing what Helena had always encouraged her to do.

Sit. Observe. Be quiet.

Roy, for all of his bluster, had proven to be a far shrewder individual than she had expected. She'd observed him all evening, taken in by his obsession with fine whisky and high-priced food.

But when push had come to shove, Roy had shoved back. Hard. It had been challenging to sit off to the side and watch Shaw struggle to connect with the man.

She had met plenty of men like Roy before. Parliamentary members, CEOs from the companies trying to court Kelna's growing business and shipping sectors, dignitaries. Shaw was confident in what his foundation had to offer. But he certainly had not been lying when he'd said he struggled to showcase the personal side of the Harrington Foundation. To accept his role, even if it was temporary, as the face of the foundation.

Yet she had also seen other details, ones she had grown adept at noticing in her years of sitting on the sidelines. The way Shaw's eyes had followed the spoon as Roy had dumped caviar onto his plate, almost as if he'd been mentally calculating how much each spoonful cost, weighing it against the financial need of the people his foundation supported.

Shaw might not have been the most personable man. But he was certainly an honorable one. Roy had a point, yes. It was his money and his choice as to where to invest it. She had struggled with whether or not she should speak up, say something.

And then she'd remembered that this was the kind of role that she would be called upon to fill again and again in the coming years. She would have to speak up, even when she was unsure, even when she wasn't confident what the right thing to say was.

At first, when Roy had turned his attention to her and Shaw had remained quiet as she'd spoken, she'd felt brave. Confident. Feelings that had evaporated when she'd seen Shaw's face harden, felt the walls slam into place. Eviana had wanted to pursue her conversation with Roy, to share some of the facts and statistics she had compiled that demonstrated the true impact the Harrington Foundation had had over the past five years. That and the ongoing challenges since the fallout over Zachary White's fraud. Challenges that had left hundreds, if not thousands, of people struggling to make ends meet.

Irritation swelled. She'd been doing the right thing. Roy had been listening to her—maybe not on the verge of changing his mind in that exact moment, but certainly closer than he had been with Shaw making stilted conversation and failing to contain his glower. But the fury in Shaw's eyes when she had met his gaze had made the words dry up in her mouth.

The rest of the dinner had been just as awkward and humiliating. She'd sat there like a rock, questioning every other word she'd come up with. All her hard-won confidence gone in the blink of an eye.

Or rather, she thought mutinously as she moved down the sidewalk, in one glare from a controlling millionaire.

A breeze blew down the street and whipped an errant curl across her face. She brushed it aside, the cool air soothing some of her ire. Unfortunately, that left her with the fact that even though Shaw had overreacted, she had failed at her job. Shaw had told her multiple times he didn't do well in those types of situations.

Embarrassment pulled at her limbs, crept under her skin and slid through her veins with an icy coldness as words from the past flickered in her mind.

This never happened with His Highness.

"Excuse me?"

A small voice sounded from a dark doorway to her right. She squinted. A young woman shuffled out, a stained blanket wrapped around her shoulders.

"Could you spare some change?"

Eviana smiled gently at her as she reached into her clutch. "I can. What's your name?"

"Catherine."

The girl's eyes were clear but nervous as her gaze darted around.

"What are you doing out here?"

Eviana held out several bills. Catherine's eyes widened.

"Lost my job. Left my boyfriend."

"I'm sorry."

"Don't be." Catherine grinned as she accepted the money. "He liked to smack me around, and my boss was a nut job."

"Then congratulations." Eviana paused. "There's a shelter near here. One that offers clean beds for a night."

The young woman's nose scrunched up. "I don't want charity."

"Not a charity. Just a place to rest while you get back on your feet."

Catherine tilted her head to the side. "Yeah. Maybe."

"Something to think about," Eviana said gently. "Have a good night."

She'd only made it a dozen feet or so down the sidewalk when she heard her name.

"Miss Barros!"

She turned her head as a car pulled up. Her heart dropped at the familiar leering grin of Roy Miles as he pulled a cherry-red BMW convertible up to the curb. Victoria offered her a wan smile from the passenger seat.

"Mr. Miles."

He beckoned for her to approach the car.

Will this night never end?

"A word of advice. There's a significant number of homeless in Edinburgh. Some of them need help. But the city has ample shelters to help them." Roy's eyes flickered toward the doorway behind Eviana. "If you give handouts to everyone you see, you're going to go broke very quickly."

Eviana's eyes moved from the Rolex watch on Roy's wrist to the gleaming polish of his convertible. She focused on those details as she fought against the rising tide of anger. Not just anger at this odious man and his utter lack of empathy, but years of standing on the sidelines, watching every word she said and never stepping up for anyone lest she make a bad impression.

Not anymore.

"Mr. Miles," she said, "I gave that girl twenty pounds."

"Which is kind, but—"

"Your Highland Wagyu beef with caviar cost nearly four hundred pounds."

Roy reared back, his expression hardening. "How I choose to spend my money—"

"Yes, I know and respect your ability to make your own choices." *Even if you are a colossal donkey.* "Just as I'm asking you to respect my choice. There are weeks where I have spent double and even triple the amount I just gave that girl on coffee. On coffee," she repeated, not bothering to hide her disdain. A disdain for not only him but herself as she reality of what she was saying hit hard. Of how she had judged this man even as she'd engaged in similar actions. "I would be lying if I said I gave money to every single person I saw. But if I feel drawn to do so, I will."

Eviana started to walk off, then stopped. *Might as well go all in.* She turned and folded her hands demurely in front of her as she arched a regal brow. "Those shelters you mentioned? Two of them are partially funded by the Harrington Foundation."

Before he could respond, she turned around again, intent on walking away and putting as much distance between her and Roy Miles and Shaw Harrington and the whole mess as possible. Hard to do when she ran right into somebody standing just behind her.

"Oh, excuse me…"

Her voice trailed off. Shock rooted her to the spot, swiftly followed by horror. Shaw stood in front of her, hands tucked into his pockets, watching her with an unreadable expression.

If he hadn't intended to fire her after their exchange back in the restaurant, it was a certainty now after the way she'd spoken to one of his top two donors.

Behind her, she heard Roy's car take off down the road, leaving her alone with one ticked-off millionaire.

"I suppose you heard that exchange."

"Most of it." Bland tone, blank expression. No clues as to what he was thinking.

She looked up at the sky and shook her head. "What are the odds?"

"The odds of what?"

Even though she would have preferred to crawl into a hole, she lowered her chin and met his gaze. "The odds of me finally saying something that needed to be said and you walk out and hear most of it."

He tilted his head to one side. "Do you think I don't approve?"

She threw her hands up. "I don't know what to think, Mr. Harrington. You hire me, tell me that yes, trust is hard for you but you think I'm capable of doing the job that needs to be done. Then, the very first time I try, you're furious. And that was just over sharing one small detail that was public information released by *your* organization. Essentially telling one of your largest donors that he's acting like a dobber isn't what most public relations professionals would do."

One corner of his mouth twitched. "Dobber?"

She narrowed her eyes. "Are you laughing at me?"

"I don't laugh."

She snorted. God, Helena would have a fit if she could see Eviana now. "That I can believe. One of the many words I picked up from Kirstin."

"I didn't hear you expressly call him that."

"I was thinking it," she retorted as she looked down at her watch. All she wanted was to get home and under the scalding hot spray of a shower. For the first time in weeks, she craved her suite back in Kelna. The marble Jacuzzi tub with its trio of bay windows overlooking the palace gardens that provided a partial glimpse of the sea. A place of refuge. One she had sought numerous times, especially over the past year.

"Look, I need to get going if I'm going to catch a bus—"

"Let me give you a lift."

She pinched the bridge of her nose. "Shaw, I don't want to talk anymore tonight."

Eviana could feel it coming on, that heaviness pressing on her, wrapping around her like a stranglehold. She could fight it. Would fight it. But it would be so much easier if Shaw wasn't there, watching her struggle with an unseen weight he couldn't even begin to fathom.

"Not talk. Just a ride."

She glanced down at her phone. Waiting for the bus would take at least five minutes, and that was assuming it was on time. The ride would be another thirty. Walking would easily put her at forty-five minutes to an hour. Riding with Shaw, however, would get her home in less than fifteen.

A sigh of defeat escaped her lips. "All right."

The chauffeur brought the car around. Shaw opened the door and she slid in, sinking into the depths of the heated leather seat. She leaned her head against the window and watched the buildings of Edinburgh pass by once more. The silence between them lasted all the way to her apartment.

At last, the car pulled up in front of her building.

"I'll walk you to the door," he said.

"It's not a date, Mr. Harrington." She didn't even care that she sounded snappish. It was like a dam had burst and she was no longer capable of maintaining any sort of pretense.

"No." Shaw rapped once on the glass partition between the front and back seats, then opened the door himself. "But it's the right thing to do."

Her hand slid off her own door handle as she forced herself to wait for him to circle around the car. She didn't want him to be nice to her. It was so much harder when he was kind, when he let her see those bits and pieces of who she suspected he really was.

He opened the door. Sensation still danced in her belly, but she was prepared this time to accept the hand he offered. True to his word, he walked her up the stairs to the front stoop as she pulled her key out of her clutch.

"My office, tomorrow, nine o'clock."

She nodded. Whatever the consequences were from her actions tonight, from her failed attempt to sway Roy Miles to renew his donations to being caught speaking in an unprofessional manner, she would handle whatever came her way with diplomacy and maturity.

"Nine o'clock," she repeated softly.

Shaw stared down at her. The longer he looked, the more her exhaustion melted away. A fluttering sensation flared, deepened, transforming into an awareness that made her lightheaded. His gaze moved down to her lips. She leaned forward, just a fraction, but enough to break whatever spell had settled between them as Shaw took a deliberate step back.

Mortified, she turned away as she jammed the key into the lock and twisted.

"Ana—"

"I'm sorry."

She walked into the hall and turned to close the door behind her. Shaw brought his forearm up and planted it against the door.

"Ana."

She looked down, unable to bring herself to meet his gaze. "Don't. I—"

"I'm sorry."

Her head jerked up. "What? I—"

"That was unprofessional of me."

She sucked in a shuddering breath. "I didn't exactly respond in a professional manner myself."

"It won't happen again."

A protest rose to her lips, then died just as quickly. He was right. It couldn't happen again. For so many reasons, ones she had repeated to herself multiple times over the past few days.

The true question she needed to ask herself, if he didn't choose to fire her in the morning for insubordination, was if she would be able to separate these personal feelings from the work she had promised to do.

"I know," she said. "And I… I won't…"

"I know."

It was too dark to tell what emotion flickered in his eyes. Surely it couldn't be regret. A man like Shaw didn't strike her as someone who regretted things very often. He made decisions and stuck by them. She envied him that certainty, that ability to move forward without constantly questioning himself.

"Good night, Miss Barros."

The coldness spread and wrapped chilled fingers around her heart.

"Good night, Mr. Harrington."

She closed the door and locked it, the sound of the dead bolt turning echoing in the empty hallway.

CHAPTER TWELVE

Eviana

EVIANA ENTERED THE ELEVATOR, a cortado in one hand and a black coffee in the other. The heat from the cups warmed her fingers. If only it could take away the chill that still clung to her after a night of tossing and turning.

She'd wanted to call Madeline. Tell her everything, from the failed meeting to that dreadful moment when she'd revealed the depth of her attraction to Shaw as she'd swayed towards him…only to be rejected.

Not just rejected, she thought as she barely resisted the urge to tap her foot against the floor, but rejected *nicely.* Why couldn't Shaw have been his usual brooding, borderline rude self? Why did he have to be kind in a moment of complete and utter humiliation?

Madeline would have made it into a joke. Offered words of encouragement and commiserated with all the goings on in Edinburgh. It had been a shock to realize how little interaction Eviana had had over the years with people other than palace employees, her father and her brother. She'd considered the people she'd worked with for the hospital charity friends. But once she'd gotten to know Madeline, she'd realized she'd never had a true friend, one she could share absolutely anything and everything with without fear of rejection or judgment.

But that would be placing a great pressure on her future

sister-in-law. Madeline wouldn't tell Nicholai where Eviana was and what she was doing if Eviana asked it of her. But putting her in that position, especially as she shouldered some of the duties Eviana had left behind for her sabbatical, would be unfair.

So instead, Eviana had taken a steaming-hot shower and sipped a cup of tea with a dash of honey just before lying down. She'd gotten some sleep but had been awoken around 2:00 a.m. by a racing heart and a highlights reel of her most embarrassing moments from the day flashing through her head. It had taken an hour of rolling this way and that, giving her pillow a few solid punches, and finally reading a few chapters of a mystery book she'd picked up to get back to sleep.

The elevator doors slid open, revealing the long hallway leading down to Shaw's door. She caught a glance of herself in a gilded mirror hanging on the wall and grimaced. The dark moons beneath her eyes stood out even more against her pale blond hair. She'd applied a heavier hand with makeup to make herself look at least somewhat awake. Her movements had been slow and sluggish as she'd pulled on her usual black blazer, black pants and a white shirt.

Better than a zombie, she comforted herself as she continued on. *Barely, but better.*

At least she'd left a little time for a coffee stop. The first sip of her cortado had steadied her somewhat, a liquid refresher to bolster her before she faced her judgment.

She stopped outside Shaw's door, sucked in a breath as she conjured up an image of steel doors slamming shut on last night with her stupid crush locked firmly behind them.

Dramatic, much?

One more deep breath. Then she knocked twice. Footsteps sounded behind the door. Her pulse started to pound as the door swung open. Dressed in his usual three-piece suit, this one a charcoal gray with a black tie that made him look every inch the imposing hedge fund manager he was, Shaw gave her a nod.

"Good morning."

At least he wasn't firing her before she even crossed the threshold.

"Good morning, Mr. Harrington." She held out the coffee. "A peace offering."

Shaw glanced down at the coffee. His lips curved. Had she walked into an alternative universe by mistake?

"Thank you. Come in."

Still confused by his almost smile, it took her a moment to register what was on his desk. A cup of coffee with Braw Roasterie's logo on it and a smaller cup with the same design.

"Is that for me?"

"Yes."

She tried, and failed, to hold back her own smile. "Great minds." The tension in her shoulders eased as she sat down across his desk. This was good. Casual conversation. No fluttering in her chest, no warmth pooling in her stomach. "I guess I didn't convert you to cortados."

"I enjoyed the taste. But I've had a cup of black coffee every morning ever since I started university. It's a hard habit to get rid of. And the cortado…" His dark red brows drew together "It's rich. Indulgent."

"And you don't like to indulge?"

Dovraga.

She bit her bottom lip as the temperature of the room changed in an instant. Tension charged the air between them as their gazes met, held. The same flare of emotion she'd seen last night appeared in the dark blue depths of his eyes. But just like last night, he was still in control. His lips parted, no doubt to once again negate whatever was happening between them.

No. Now was the time to show both herself and Shaw she could keep things professional, too.

"My brother prefers his coffee black as well." She gave him a small, bland smile. "A touch bitter for my tastes."

Shaw's eyes narrowed. She met his gaze, striving for serene and unaffected as she waited.

At last, he nodded. "I spend money on some of the nicer things in life." He circled around his desk and sat. "I would be lying if I said I don't enjoy my home here in Edinburgh or driving a Rolls-Royce. But the clothes I wear and the car I drive serve a purpose. The people I work with, and the people I'm trying to work with," he added dryly, "respond to quality. To someone they think is like them."

Implying Shaw wasn't from their world. When she and Kirstin had researched his background in preparation for their proposal, there hadn't been much available on public record before he had enrolled at the University of Edinburgh for a finance degree. Given his preference for privacy, she hadn't bothered to dig further.

But now, as he sat there wearing his tailored suit as if he'd been born in it, a dominating force in his quietly luxurious surroundings, curiosity rippled through her. Who had Shaw been before he'd become a financial prodigy? What had driven him to create the Harrington Foundation?

"Are you not like them?" she asked quietly.

Darkness flickered in his eyes. "No."

The finality of the word told her that line of conversation was closed.

"Perhaps you should try a mocha, then. Coffee with just a bit of milk, sugar and cocoa powder. A touch of sweet, but not too extravagant."

His teeth flashed white as he let out a quiet laugh. The sound rumbled through her. For one moment, she saw him without the lines of tension in his forehead, without the weight he seemed to carry everywhere.

"Maybe one day." The smile disappeared as his face smoothed out. "Let's get last night out of the way."

Her shoulders tightened as she resisted the urge to shift in her chair. "All right."

"While I would still prefer to keep my life private, having read the article and better understanding where you got the information, I realize now that I overreacted."

Of all the things she had anticipated, acknowledgment of his own reaction had not been one of them.

"Thank you."

His eyes flicked once more to the picture frame on the corner of his desk. "When Zach made his choice to invest the funds, I didn't just lose an employee, I lost one of the biggest assets the foundation had. Zach made everyone feel like they were important, part of a mission."

Her heart ached for the trace of loss she heard in his voice. Even if he didn't want to admit it, she suspected that Shaw had thought of Zach as an acquaintance. Perhaps even a friend. Having one's trust broken was hard enough. Having it shredded by someone close hurt ten times worse.

"Zach choosing to 'make his mark' on the foundation, and his own ego without thinking through the ramifications of his decisions, has made it even more challenging for me to trust. And if I don't fix this," he added quietly, "even more people will suffer."

"You could hire a permanent PR rep now to—"

"No." He uttered the word firmly. "Eventually. But right now, I need to be the one to fix this. The Harrington Foundation is something I've been working toward ever since…"

A long moment passed. His brows knit together as if he were waging some internal battle. And then, slowly, Shaw reached out, picked up the frame and handed it to her. Eviana's breath caught as she stared down at the picture of the woman, at the joy radiating from her mega-watt smile, the familiar blue eyes and elegant features.

"Your mother," she breathed.

"She's the reason. For everything."

Eviana continued to stare at the photograph. She had so few memories of her own mother. But the few she did included laughter. Choosing the Kelna National Hospital as her first and primary charity had been because of her mother and the care they had given the late queen in her final days. Just those few years of memories had driven her. Understanding Shaw's motivation, even without the details of his life before, answered so many questions.

"How long has she been gone?"

"Twenty years," he said.

Her throat tightened. "My mother passed away twenty-one years ago."

When she looked up and their gazes met again, the arc that passed between them was not one of forbidden attraction but of shared grief. A bond she wouldn't wish on anyone else, but one that held some measure of comfort in knowing that she wasn't alone.

"You told me last night that people need a reason." He let a harsh exhale escape. "My mother worked herself to death. I don't want to exploit her sacrifice or her death for money. But I hope this provides some perspective on the importance of what we're doing."

She focused on the woman in the picture. Better than looking at Shaw and letting him see the emotion that must've been in her eyes. Heartache for what he must have suffered. Admiration for what he had done with his life. And tenderness for this newest layer he'd chosen to share with her.

Again, she had to remind herself, he hadn't shared that detail with her because of any sort of affection. It had been to help her understand the Harrington Foundation better. To help understand him and the kind of support he needed from an employee as he navigated a crisis.

Steel doors.

She pictured that warm glowing ball of tenderness, then envisioned throwing it behind the doors and locking them.

"Thank you." Eviana handed the picture back. "It does help to understand. I will verify any personal information in the future." She folded her hands together as she forced out the next words. "I also owe you an apology. While Roy Miles can be pretentious, the way I responded to him outside the Dome was unprofessional."

"Strong, perhaps," Shaw said with a shrug. "But I didn't find it unprofessional."

She blinked in surprise. "What?"

"I didn't hear everything Roy said. But I saw you give money to that woman. Based on your response and what I know of the man, I can only imagine what words of wisdom he tried to offer." He frowned. "If he had not been such a large donor, I would be divesting all ties with him. But what I heard was you stating facts, connecting the current situation to Roy's choice not to resume donations. Holding people accountable for their actions is not a bad thing."

"No," Eviana agreed. "I just sometimes struggle to find the balance of maintaining a professional facade and finding the right words."

"You didn't seem to have any trouble finding the words last night when you confronted Roy. Trust yourself more."

Eviana's eyes grew hot. "Back home…my family encourages a more sedate response."

"As I've stated, I'm not the best example of diplomacy." He regarded her for a long moment. "The moments where you let go of that mask you wear or you just let the words flow instead of thinking about everything you're saying beforehand…that's the PR pro I want to work with."

Eviana arched a brow, a casual action that hopefully covered how much of an impact his words had. How much they meant to her when almost everyone else in her life told her to prioritize propriety over her own instincts.

"Really? Because I could have sworn you were going to drag me out of that restaurant last night if I shared anything else you found inappropriate."

"I have some work to do," he acknowledged with a small smirk. "Had I let you continue, who knows where things might have ended with Roy. Which brings me to my last point. I'd like to continue working with you and Murray PR."

He held out his hand. Relief nearly made her sag in her chair.

"And I would like to continue to represent both Murray PR and the Harrington Foundation." She shook his hand, satisfied when she felt only the tiniest spark.

"Even though Roy did not commit to resuming his donations, last night was a good learning experience." Gears in her mind started to turn, puzzle pieces falling into place as she slipped back into work mode.

"It was," he said. "And we have another opportunity to try again. The other donor you identified, Olivia Mahs, has agreed to meet with us in London in two days."

"Olivia Mahs. The railroad heiress."

Shaw nodded in approval. "Yes. She's only in town for twenty-four hours for a meeting."

"Kirstin told me to focus exclusively on the foundation for the next couple of weeks, so I can make that work." Excitement trickled through her. Her one and only trip to London had left her with a feeling of whiplash as she'd been whisked from one royal event to another.

"Excellent. I'd also like for you to write up some scenarios."

"Scenarios?" Eviana repeated.

"Yes. Practice runs, so to speak, so I'm more prepared to engage with Miss Mahs."

"I think that's a great idea."

"Good." Shaw held up two slips of paper. "We'll have plenty of time to practice because Miss Mahs has generously provided us with train tickets to London."

"Train tickets?"

"Yes. She's in charge of launching a new passenger line that specializes in luxury train travel. A return to the olden days, if you will."

An image filled Eviana's mind of a train moving along a track curving through green pastures fluffy clouds of smoke puffed from its chimney. A peaceful sigh slipped past her lips. "I've never been on a train before."

"It'll be just under five hours. We leave the day after tomorrow at nine a.m. and should arrive just before two. Olivia gave us a three-hour window that day between five and eight. I'd like for you to make the arrangements as to where we meet."

"Done."

This part of the job was her favorite. Finding out what motivated people and what mattered to them, then tailoring a meeting that spoke to them, drew them in. Something that made an impact and encouraged them to volunteer, donate or engage.

"And then the scenarios, questions I should anticipate as well as what you think will help me be more personable," he said.

Eviana glanced at the picture frame, now back in its original place. Part of her wanted to ask Shaw to reconsider his stance on sharing the foundation's origins. Perhaps there was a way to rephrase it, to focus on his experiences while keeping his mother's name out of it.

But she would honor his wishes. He was trying to do better, and he had trusted her with a vulnerable piece of himself. A piece she suspected he rarely shared with anyone.

No, she would find other ways to put them at ease and let a little bit of his personality come through without placing him under a microscope. Knowing Shaw trusted her skills and even preferred the woman she had grown into these last couple of months made her feel seen. Confident. As if the shackles she had grown used to wearing had suddenly been ripped away and she could move with the same kind of freedom she had tasted working for Kirstin.

"We won't fail this time," she said.

"Ana." The subtle warmth in his voice froze her in place. "You didn't fail last night."

She didn't look up. Didn't want to see any sort of compassion, grace or other kindness that would make it that much harder to keep the doors shut on that infernal attraction.

"I appreciate the reprieve, but I disagree. Roy didn't agree to resume donations." She cleared her throat as she wrote something nonsensical in her notebook to at least give the appearance she was working instead of trying to resist her own foolish heart.

"Not yet. But you got through to him when I didn't. That wouldn't have happened if you hadn't been there."

Eviana waited a moment before glancing up. Thankfully he had refocused on his computer.

The worst thing about this man was that he moved through life all power and control and then out of the blue, he gifted her with words that touched on her deepest fears, soothed them, made her feel as though she could truly do this. Not just help the Harrington Foundation reestablish itself, but become a leader, someone Nicholai and Madeline and her people could depend upon.

Shaw Harrington was a dangerous man. The more she got to know him, the more she felt herself slipping down a dangerous slope. One she suspected that if she fell too far would result in her leaving broken pieces of her heart in Edinburgh.

CHAPTER THIRTEEN

Shaw

TREES AND GRASSY hills dotted with fuzzy sheep whipped past as the train sped through the Scottish countryside. It hadn't been more than a few months ago that Shaw had taken a train to London. On that trip, he'd spent most of his time on his computer, sifting through emails, evaluating reports from New York and, as always, monitoring media coverage on the foundation.

But today, as dark clouds scuttled across the sky and colored the landscape with shadows, he found himself looking out the window more and more. Noticing things he had missed, like the little stone cottage covered in ivy or the elegant manor house with horses grazing in the fields.

Although, he admitted as he tried to contain a small smile, Ana drawing his attention to various landmarks helped.

They were in the dining car, he with his laptop and she with her notebook. Her pen flew across the page, except for when something drew her attention out the window. Which seemed to be every three to four minutes.

Surprisingly, he didn't mind. In those moments when she looked out the window, he stole glances of her uniquely beautiful face that, every now and then, felt familiar. Something had changed for him the night of the dinner at the Dome. When he'd gone outside to wait for his car and seen her talking with Roy, his anger had propelled him down the sidewalk. Not just anger at her for continuing what he'd assumed was the earlier conversation without him present, but for the way Roy had looked at her just as he had the four-hundred-pound-an-ounce caviar.

But when he'd drawn close enough in time to hear her unleash her tirade against Roy, he'd stopped. What had transpired next had shot through his armor and left him defenseless long enough for his attraction to deepen. The proper professional he'd worked with for the past few days had vanished. In her place had been a stunning woman, fire and passion, who had taken a stand on someone else's behalf. Someone like his mother. Someone like him, or who he had been long ago.

As if that hadn't been enough, that moment on her front stoop had turned simmering warmth into a craving he'd nearly succumbed to.

Pulling back from kissing her had been the last thing he'd wanted to do. Which was why he had done it. He would not cross a line with someone who worked for him. But it had hurt, physically hurt, to see that embarrassment on her face. When she had shown up the next morning, the pressure that had tightened his chest as he'd walked away from her the night before had loosened.

She hadn't brought up their near kiss, so neither had he. Yet it lingered in his mind. Flared at the most inopportune moments. She appeared to have moved on once again quite easily. But he couldn't. Not with the memory of her voice vibrating with anger as she'd laid Roy Miles flat with her honest words. Not with the yearning that had shone in her eyes as their breaths had mingled in the summer air. The woman who intrigued him, the professional who impressed him and the fighter who surprised him had melded together until he couldn't ignore her or his own growing interest.

He could lie to himself and say he had shown her his

mother's picture as a gesture of goodwill. But after hearing her defense of someone Roy had dismissed, her last words reminding Roy of the work the Harrington Foundation did, Shaw had wanted to show her his mother's picture. Give her a glimpse of why it all mattered.

Ana might have thought she'd hidden her reaction well. But he hadn't missed the tightening of her fingers on the frame, the slight bob in her throat as she'd swallowed hard or the lingering glimmer in her eyes when she handed the picture back. That his divulgence had impacted her had been yet another blow to the walls he'd kept in place for so long.

Shaw watched out of the corner of his eye as she hailed a passing waitress to ask about the teas on the menu. Enthusiasm buoyed her tone. A genuine smile lit her eyes and made her gestures more animated. Just like that first morning when they'd met.

She continued to remain secretive about her background, but given his own penchant for privacy, he had no room to judge. Still, the questions lingered, grew as he spent more time with her. Where did Ana live? What family drama had spurred her to leave Southeastern Europe and come all this way? Was there a man in her life back home?

The last question twisted his stomach into a knot. Nothing could happen between them. Even if circumstances hadn't made a relationship between them forbidden, could he even open himself up the way a woman like Ana deserved? Trust someone with the darkest parts of himself?

A year ago, the answer would have been a resounding no. He enjoyed dating when his schedule allowed for it. He'd had a couple of relationships that lasted a few months, even reached a one-year anniversary with a prosecuting attorney in New York. But all of his relationships had run their course. Agreeable affairs that had ended amicably. He'd entered into each one knowing there was an expiration date.

But now, as he watched Ana, the thought of her returning home in a few weeks made the landscape outside seem even darker.

The waitress came back with a teapot colored dark blue and decorated with gold filigree and two matching cups. She set both on the table, dropped a sachet of tea leaves into one and poured. Steam rose as the fragrant scents of lavender and mint floated in the air. The waitress set the other cup in front of him.

"None for me, thanks."

The waitress smiled. "No, sir, the lady ordered you coffee, black. I'll be just a moment."

His eyes flickered to Ana. She didn't notice his glance as she raised the cup up, her eyes drifting shut as she inhaled. A serene smile curved her lips.

It struck him suddenly that out of the few relationships he had had, none of his previous partners had bought him coffee. A minor detail, one that seemed inconsequential. Yet in the span of a week, Ana had bought him coffee multiple times. She was an intern, living in a decent townhouse apartment, but nothing compared to his home in Edinburgh's elegant Greenhill neighborhood. While Kirstin had struck him as a fair boss, she was still building her own firm. Chances were she wasn't paying Ana much.

But Ana had spent some of those hard-earned pounds on him.

Her eyes fluttered open. Her expression didn't change, but a rose hue tinted her cheeks. She glanced out the window.

"Oh, look!" Her teeth flashed white as she pointed to a sprawling stone estate in the distance. "A castle."

"Yes. Another castle," he said dryly.

She rolled her eyes even if she shot him a teasing smile. "I know you have the luxury of seeing a castle every single day you go to work, but in a month, I won't get to see architecture like this anymore."

His jaw tightened as he forced himself to remain outwardly impassive. "Are you excited to go home?"

She looked down at her tea. "Yes and no. There are things I miss. People, like my brother and his fiancée."

"When are they getting married?"

"October. I'm the maid of honor."

"A role you want, or one you were forced into?"

She chuckled. "Very much wanted. Mad, my soon-to-be sister-in-law, is the sister I never had. And she's made my brother very happy."

He noted the hesitation, along with the genuine happiness she seemed to feel about her brother's upcoming marriage. He wanted to ask more, wanted an explanation for the secrecy.

Yet how could he demand more information when he was unwilling to give answers of his own?

Telling her about his mother, letting her hold the photograph, had been one of the hardest things he had done in recent memory, aside from giving the order to have Zach thrown out of his office in New York. Zach and a couple close acquaintances knew he had been raised by his mother and that she had passed a long time ago. But as he racked his brain, he couldn't think of a single person he had told the role his mother and his upbringing had had on his decision to develop the Harrington Foundation.

No one he had wanted to confide in.

Ana set her cup down and reached for her folder. "How about we run through a scenario?"

That was the last thing he wanted to do. No, he wanted to sit and listen to the bits and pieces of herself she was willing to share. Hear the melody of her voice, her excitement at a random sheep or hills covered in purple blooms.

"All right."

She flipped through her notebook.

"Have you thought about getting a computer?" he asked.

"Oh, I have one. I just like pen and paper." Her fingers flipped through the pages with practiced efficiency.

"Why?"

"It makes me slow down. Think. When I have a computer in front of me, it's so easy to let it do all the work." She shrugged. "Pen and paper feels more…me. Ah, here it is." She looked up and gave him a challenging smirk. "Ready?"

No. "Yes."

The first few questions were easy, standard ones about the foundation, the work it did, how the board of trustees chose what charities and individuals to give grants to. All standard information on the foundation's website. But as they walked through each of his answers, Ana made moderate tweaks to each one. Small changes that didn't change the essence of what he said but added strength and personability.

"What happened with the Veach investment fraud?"

The question came out of nowhere, a sharp departure from what she had been asking. But she'd done it on purpose, to throw him off guard, just as Olivia or anyone else might. He respected her for it, admired her calm presence. If she'd been nervous to ask the question, it didn't show.

"It's difficult to talk about." He paused.

"No, that's good. You don't have to share everything," Ana said quietly. "But even just that little touch of humanity and honesty shows me some of the man behind the foundation."

He gave her a quick nod. "Zachary White served the Harrington Foundation for five years. In that time, he did good work. Unfortunately, six months ago he made the choice to invest half of the foundation's assets into the Veach Fund. It was marketed as a real estate investment opportunity. It was a scam."

He could still remember Zach showing up in his doorway, white as a sheet, hands shaking as he'd closed the door behind him.

I need to tell you something.

It hadn't just been that Zach had disobeyed his order to not invest. No, it had been the betrayal. The realization that, unintentional or not, Zach had been the closest thing he'd had to a friend in his entire adult life.

"Zachary's actions were…foolish."

"Foolish or criminal?"

He narrowed his eyes at Ana, but she didn't back down.

"Foolish." He released a harsh breath. "But not criminal. While Zachary made a poor choice, and one that went against my wishes, his intention was to find a rapid way to expand the foundation's wealth and increase the number of organizations we were supporting."

"Does that absolve him of blame?"

"No." He heard the rigidity in his voice, the temper. Paused and collected himself. "His intention, however good, caused significant losses. That's why the Harrington Foundation released Zach from his contract the day he told us what happened."

"How will the Harrington Foundation…" Her voice trailed off as she peered at him. "Let's take a break."

"One more."

She looked as if she wanted to argue, but she obliged and glanced down at her notes.

"How will the Harrington Foundation ensure something like this will never happen again?"

This he could answer. "We've set new initiatives in place, a more rigid system of checks and balances regarding who has access to funds, the number of people who are notified when a request for a withdrawal of funds is placed."

As the words came out, he heard the banality, the lack of individualism. A rote answer that contained important details. But one that failed to sell even him on the idea that the foundation wasn't at risk of making the same mistake twice.

What would he want to hear if he were being asked to invest in something? What would reassure him?

Bluntness. Honesty.

"It's not perfect. I want to say we will ensure something like this will never happen again. I can't promise that. But I can promise that we are doing everything in our power to reduce the likelihood of it happening. And I fully believe in the board of trustees and my current team to make that happen, even as they understand and incorporate the additional oversight measures we've put into place."

Ana slowly closed her notebook and threaded her fingers together. Her eyes softened as she smiled. "That was perfect, Shaw."

He arched a brow at her, trying not to let her see how much the compliment affected him. "Even if I didn't make a promise?"

"You made a real promise. That's worth more than any perfectly crafted PR statement."

He leaned forward. "You've done this for a long time, haven't you?"

The dark clouds gathering outside and the dim glow of the dining car lights made it hard to discern details. But he could have sworn she paled at his question.

"What do you mean?"

"Before coming to Edinburgh. You worked in PR."

She slowly shook her head. "Not for a public relations firm, no. But I volunteered a lot. Worked with a hospital on fundraising, recruiting volunteers, that sort of thing."

"You were good at it."

Wistfulness touched her smile. "I was very good at it. And I enjoyed it. I got to work with the nurses and some of the hospital administrators. But I also got to know a lot of the patients. Hear their stories."

"Hence your preference for storytelling."

"Yes." She looked out the window again. Rain started to fall as the clouds pushed out the rest of the sunlight, making the landscape as dark as night. "I've met some amazing people and their families through the hospital. Ones who have agreed, or even volunteered, to have our committee share what they've been through. Numbers and statistics can go a long way, but the stories are what make the difference."

He wanted to tell her, he realized. Wanted to share why telling his story was so hard. Years of avoiding pain and eschewing connections made him stop. But what was the point in sharing? Of making himself vulnerable when nothing would come of it except more pain? There was no road out of this that left him intact. If he pursued anything romantic, he'd be breaching his own ethics. Even if he kept their relationship professional while sharing the hardest moments of his life and how much those events had influenced the foundation, Ana would be gone in three weeks, taking pieces of him with her he'd never intended to share. An act that almost seemed more intimate than a kiss.

The only logical road forward was to focus on the future and leave the past where it belonged.

"I think I'm going to head to my suite," Ana said as she stood. "I've been up late most nights working, and napping on a train in a thunderstorm sounds perfect."

"Of course." He followed suit and stood. "Sleep well." He waited until she was out of the car before he sat and scrubbed a hand over his face.

What was wrong with him? The more time he spent with Ana and saw the joy things like the scent of tea and the sight of a forgotten castle brought, the more he felt like he was emerging from a deep sleep, an existence that no longer seemed fulfilling. When he'd passed off the foundation's responsibilities to the board of trustees and a team of employees, he'd severed a bond. One that had kept him emotionally tied to something. Anything.

Was it the lack of emotional connections in his life that now made him respond so strongly to Ana? A susceptibility created by the stress of the past six months?

Or was it just Ana herself?

He shoved thoughts of Ana aside and pulled the shade down over the window. If he focused on his work, he could have a couple of productive hours before they arrived in London.

He kept his gaze on his computer and off the now empty seat across from him.

CHAPTER FOURTEEN

Shaw

SHAW STEPPED OFF the train and into the teeming rush of pedestrians streaming to and fro on the platforms of King's Cross Station. A ceiling of arched glass let in bright afternoon sunlight, a jarring change after the storm had followed them all the way to Peterborough. Languages rose and fell around him.

Past and present slammed together, melded. He saw himself sitting on a bench, watching as his mother tried to sell stems of wildflowers they'd picked along a roadside to get them back to Edinburgh. Saw the people hurrying past, faces turned away, collars turned up as they ignored the pleas of someone they labeled as just another beggar. Felt the scorching pain of his mother's embarrassment even as she squared her shoulders and did what needed to be done. To get them right back to where they had started with the bitter taste of fleeting happiness still lingering.

"Hey."

A hand rested on his shoulder, a comforting weight that yanked him out of the past. He looked down at Ana, saw the concern and compassion in her eyes. It wasn't hard to imagine her in a hospital, holding hands and offering words of comfort.

"You okay?"

"Yes." He gave her a small smile. "It's been a while since I've been here."

Just a couple years before his mother had died. Any time he'd come to London since then, he'd made sure to change trains so that he'd entered the city via a different station. Over time, it had become a habit. The painful memories of King's Cross had faded.

And now…now there was a sense of victory as they walked down the platform. Of not letting his past dictate his future. Of confronting it.

A taxi took them from the station to the Savoy. Shaw watched out of the corner of his eye as Ana took it all in, from the golden statue standing guard atop the canopy as they pulled up to the black-and-and-white-tiled lobby where they checked in.

"We're on the fifth floor," he said as they moved toward the elevators. "Two river-view suites."

As Ana pressed the button for the elevator, his phone rang.

"Shaw Harrington."

"Mr. Harrington." A smooth female voice with a British accent greeted him. "Olivia Mahs. I trust your trip went smoothly?"

"It did." He paused, then added, "I was very impressed. Your chef's smoked salmon with cream sauce was exceptional."

"Thank you."

Olivia's voice warmed with genuine pleasure. Out of the corner of his eye, he saw Ana give him a thumbs-up.

"I apologize for the late notice, but would it be possible to move our meeting to tomorrow? I've been held up in Madrid."

Shaw frowned. His schedule had been planned to a *T* around this visit. But Olivia had been generous since the beginning of the Harrington Foundation, donating what had amounted to nearly three million pounds over the years.

"Of course. What time tomorrow?"

"Would one work?"

"Yes. Let's still plan on the Savoy, and I'll let you know if the location changes." Shaw hung up and turned to Ana. "Olivia's been held up until tomorrow. I understand if I need to send you back to Edinburgh."

The elevator doors opened, revealing a vivid green carpet trimmed in gold.

"No, I'm fine. It gives us another day to prepare." Ana glanced at her watch. "I had initially booked dinner at the Savoy Grill for tonight, but with your permission, I'll change the reservation to the hotel's afternoon tea tomorrow. I think that will appeal to someone like Olivia more."

The doors closed as she talked, verbalizing ideas and making little tweaks out loud as the elevator carried them up. Shaw listened, once again impressed with her knowledge and strategy.

"Then I need to work on the donor dinner plan." She glanced up at him as he grunted. "I want to be prepared to move on it if Olivia says yes. I'd prefer to have both her and Roy on board. But even if we have just one, I think it's still worth a shot."

"It is."

It was just the idea of making small talk with people while trying to sell them on reinvesting thousands of pounds into a foundation that had lost a significant chunk of their last donation that unsettled him.

Ana glance down, then back up at him. "When we get back, I could reach out to Kirstin and see if there's something I'm missing—"

"Don't." He turned to face her. "Don't question yourself. Just because I don't like the idea doesn't mean it's not a good one."

She looked down at her feet. "I don't want to fail."

"You mentioned that before."

A stray lock of hair rested against her face. He'd resisted touching her once. But he couldn't anymore, not after everything that had happened the past few days. He reached up and brushed it away, his fingertips grazing her cheek. Her head shot up, her sharp inhale echoing in the small space.

But she didn't pull away. No, she just continued to stare at him with those jewel-toned eyes as temptation smoldered between them.

"Who made you question yourself like this?"

She stared at him, eyes searching his face. Then her lips parted. The elevator dinged and the doors slid open.

Shaw dropped his hand. He should apologize. Should. But he couldn't bring himself to. That single touch, feeling the warmth of her skin, seeing the way she looked at him… He couldn't regret any of it.

"I'll get to work on that plan." Her voice sounded husky, breathless.

"I'm in the suite next to yours if you need anything."

She nodded before rushing down the hall and disappearing around the corner. He flexed his hand. Tried and failed to banish the memory of her gasp when he'd touched her.

Perhaps finding another location to work in, somewhere that wasn't in the room right next to hers, would be best. The change in his feelings over the last few days had left him drifting through his normally well-ordered existence, unable to grasp onto his usual control and keep himself in check. Just this morning he had resolved to keep his growing feelings to himself. And here he was hours later brushing a stray curl off Ana's face.

He walked back into the elevator and pushed the button. Kirstin was coming back next week. It was probably the best possible thing to ensure that Shaw did not make a colossal mistake.

CHAPTER FIFTEEN

Eviana

EVIANA SCANNED OVER the draft of her event proposal. She'd rewritten it twice over the course of the afternoon. More, she suspected, out of the turmoil dancing at the edge of her mind than the plan needing much revision.

But it was good. Solid. A few phone calls had confirmed the restaurant she wanted was available. She'd emailed the plan to Kirstin, too, and was waiting to hear back. A productive afternoon.

Which was good because her morning had been anything but.

The train ride had started off well. But at some point she'd realized she was enjoying Shaw's company, not just professionally but personally. The surprise had been realizing he appeared to enjoy hers, too. Was she imagining the softening of his attitude? The lowering of his defenses? Was it all because of work? Or was he struggling, like she was, to keep things professional?

Nice didn't properly describe how wonderful it was to be around someone and just…be. No pretenses, no false faces. Just be herself.

Guilt invaded, creeping through her contentment and filling her with a sense of shame. Eviana was being herself. But she was still lying to him.

She'd already been on edge when they'd arrived at the Savoy. And then Shaw had shocked her in the elevator by sliding that stray tendril of hair back. That graze of his fingers on her skin had been more intimate than any of the handful of kisses she'd experienced in her life. She'd nearly run to her room so she didn't do something stupid.

The tension between them was becoming a problem. No matter how much she told herself it wasn't, it reared its head again and again. Except this time she knew without a doubt Shaw felt it, too.

Unsure of what to say or how to handle the situation, she'd attempted to review her notes on Olivia Mahs and her history with the Harrington Foundation. When the words had clouded together and she'd realized she'd attempted to read the same paragraph five times, she'd thrown on a coat and gone for a walk.

The walk had been a much-needed refresher. The last time she had been in London had been years ago, when she'd traveled with her father and Nicholai to England for the late queen's Jubilee. They'd stayed at the Ritz in a royal suite with gilded trim and bodyguards stationed outside the doors at all hours. She'd been excited for the Jubilee and to meet the queen. But every time she'd asked if they could go somewhere, do something other than the rigorously scheduled list of royal events, she'd been told no, it wasn't a vacation but a duty. As they'd ridden through the procession past Buckingham Palace, she'd been so focused on keeping a smile on her face and waving as people shouted and snapped photos that the whole thing had passed by in a blur.

Walking past Buckingham Palace earlier had been peaceful. There'd been the usual tourists taking pictures, but none of the cameras had been aimed at her. Even with her blond hair and reading glasses on for extra measure, no one had glanced twice at a random tourist.

By the time she'd made it back to the hotel, her mind had quieted enough for her to focus on work. She'd spied Jodi only once, passing by the reading room downstairs where she had set up shop. Working in her room would have made her tense, listening for sounds from next door, wondering if Shaw was going to knock on her door and finally confront the friction between them.

So she'd chosen a plush chair in the ivory-colored room just off the main lobby and gotten to work, first on her review of Olivia and then polishing her proposal for a private dinner for twelve of Shaw's former donors.

Her computer let out a soft chime. Kirstin had emailed her back.

Love it! Excellent work. Small scale, which will appeal to Shaw, I'm sure, but still elegant enough to attract the donors. The handwritten invite from Shaw is a great touch. Hope he goes for it. If he doesn't, I'll see what I can do. Mum's doing great this week—be back on Monday!

Eviana smiled. Even from afar, Kirstin continued to be her cheerleader.

Her eyes rested on the last line.

...back on Monday!

Having Kirstin back would certainly change the dynamic between her and Shaw. For the better, she reminded herself. Although perhaps they just needed to have a conversation. Get everything out in the open. Acknowledge the attraction and then move forward.

"Ana."

Eviana's head jerked up. Shaw was casually leaning against the black door frame.

"Oh. Hi."

Even though she hadn't said her thoughts out loud, it didn't stop the heat from climbing up her throat and into her cheeks.

"How was your afternoon?" he asked.

"Good." She cleared her throat. "Yours?"

"Productive." He moved into the room, eyes sweeping over the raised paneling on the walls, the plush emerald couch she'd claimed, the vase of elegant red roses behind her. "Cozy spot."

"Yes."

He looked at her then, that familiar intensity back again. "Why didn't you work in your room?"

She started to come up with an answer, something appropriate. And then decided to do exactly what Shaw had encouraged her to do and speak her mind.

"I wasn't sure how things stood between us after the elevator. I decided to keep my distance until I could figure out how to approach it."

He sat down in the chair across from her as she closed her computer. Then he gave her that slight smile she had come to enjoy so much. "I did, too."

"What?"

"Worked somewhere else."

She stared at him for a moment before sitting back and letting out a frustrated laugh. "We're a pair."

"Yes." He leaned forward, folding his arms as his face hardened. "Did I make you uncomfortable?"

"No! I mean…" The heat in her cheeks deepened. "No. Not uncomfortable. It's just…" She blew out a breath. "I find you very attractive."

His mouth curved up into a slight smirk. "Thank you."

"Working with you like this, so closely…" Her voice trailed off, and she ran a hand through her hair. "It's made it harder to ignore."

"I know. It has been for me, too."

The pressure on her lungs eased. "Good. Not that you had to ignore anything. Just… I'm glad it wasn't just me."

His blue eyes warmed a fraction. "It's not just you."

For a moment they stared at each other, endless possibilities drifting between them.

And then he sat back. "But we both know nothing can come of this."

She nodded, focusing on her sense of relief that they were on the same page instead of the hard ball of disappointment settling in her stomach. "You're effectively my boss. And I'm going home."

He started to say something, then stopped.

"What?" she asked.

"Nothing. I have no right to ask."

"Shaw, please," she said. "If we're clearing the air, we might as well as get everything out in the open."

"Is there anyone else?"

His words made her pulse pound faster.

"No. It's been a long time since I've been on a date."

"Me, too."

A different kind of relief coursed through her.

Even though it doesn't make a difference.

"I want to keep this professional for myself, my work ethic, and for Kirstin. She's done so much in such a short time," Eviana said. "I don't want to get involved with a client and have that come back on her down the road."

"Understood. I refuse to get romantically involved with an employee."

Silence fell between them. Soft conversations and the lilting notes of piano music drifted in from the lobby.

"So…what now?" Eviana finally asked. "Do we just keep our distance?"

"No," he said. "We go back to how things were without the underlying tension."

It sounded simple enough. And she felt more at ease with him than she had in...well, ever since they'd met. The attraction was still there. But now that it had been acknowledged with a mutual agreement that they wouldn't act on it, the tension had disappeared.

"I think I'd like that," she said.

"Good." He stood. "Because I'd hate to eat alone for dinner."

She grinned. "You seem exactly like the kind of person who would love to eat alone."

"Once in a while, even stuffy, private millionaires like company."

This was better. Much better. They could have dinner like civilized adults, converse, work together. And, she told herself as she followed Shaw to the elevators, over time, the attraction would fade. She would return to Kelna. Eventually she would find someone, fall in love, get married. The memory of her brief time with Shaw would be a pleasant one, something to return to and reminisce about on hard days.

It would be enough.

CHAPTER SIXTEEN

Shaw

ANA'S EYES WIDENED as they walked into the Beaufort Bar. "It's like stepping back into the roaring twenties."

Her eyes devoured everything, from the signature burnt-orange chairs with curved backs to the black walls decorated with strategically placed mirrors. Coupled with the soft lighting, the overall atmosphere was reminiscent of a glamorous speakeasy.

"Compared to the history of the Savoy itself," he said as he nodded to the maître d' he'd spoken with on his way down to the reading room, "a relatively new addition."

"It's incredible. This has to be the nicest bar I've ever been in."

"Do you go to bars often?" he asked with a slight chuckle as they were seated at a table for two in a corner of the room.

She laughed. "Actually, the first time I was ever in a bar was two months ago when I arrived in Edinburgh."

Shaw frowned. "You hadn't been inside a bar before?"

"No, my father didn't..." She stopped. Her eyes dropped to the table, then back up to his. "Image was very important to my father. And he had good reason," she added. "He had a certain esteem in our community. His image was a part of the work he did. I was a reflection of that."

Anger stirred deep in his gut. "That's a lot to place on a child."

"It was." The smile she gave him was sad but accepting. "It's hard to explain. It's not something I enjoyed. But it was a necessity."

"I flinch at the thought of a dinner with a dozen people. I can't fathom having to always be on alert."

The sadness in her eyes deepened. Just for a moment, but so heart-wrenching it made him want to reach out and touch her again, offer something that would chase the sorrow from her face.

Then it was gone as she broke eye contact and picked up the menu. "These drinks look incredible."

He wanted to pursue the topic, ask more questions and learn about the history she so carefully hid. But he also wanted to make the evening a happy one.

"What was your first drink?" he asked as he picked up his own menu.

"A beer."

"Was it any good?"

"Terrible," Ana said with another laugh. "I found a couple I've liked since then. But I definitely prefer wine and cocktails."

"Then you're not going to be disappointed tonight."

They ordered drinks. He went outside his usual parameters and ordered a whisky cocktail. She ordered a gin drink mixed with sparkling wine and violet syrup, topped off with a purple flower perched perfectly on the edge of the glass. They dined on grilled prawns, sourdough smothered in toasted cheese, and plump red grapes.

"May I ask you a personal question?"

Shaw looked up from the chocolate mousse they'd ordered for dessert. "Yes. I may not answer it, but you can always ask me anything."

She gave him a small smile. “Fair. You mentioned you hadn’t been to King’s Cross Station in a long time. You looked…sad.”

He set his fork down and picked up his drink. When she continued to stare at him, he quirked an eyebrow. “I didn’t hear the question.”

She rolled her eyes even as her lips tilted up. “What happened?”

Shaw took a sip of his cocktail, the smooth flavor of whisky melding perfectly with the sweetness of orange and ruby port. For the past few days, he’d wanted to know Ana more. To have her share a piece of herself. Yet he had done nothing to earn that trust. Had shared almost nothing of himself other than a couple of hints and a photograph.

“My father deserted my mother when I was two years old. I don’t really have any memories of him. Just her.”

The light in Ana’s eyes dimmed. “I’m sorry.”

“Don’t be. From what little my mother said, he was interested in her until I came along. They made it work for a couple years, but one day he just decided he didn’t want to be a father. So he left.”

Ana’s mouth twisted into a scowl. “Dobber.”

He smiled. Truly smiled for the first time in he couldn’t remember how long. “Precisely.” He used the stir stick in his glass to move the candied orange peel around, watching it dance among the amber liquid. “They weren’t well off, but he had told her to stay home with me. When he left, she had nothing. She was injured a year later when she was crossing the street on her way to a job as a maid at a hotel. Her leg was never the same, and it became difficult for her to work. We lived in Edinburgh for years.” He focused his attention on the bar, watched a bartender pour contents into a silver shaker. “When I was twelve, we came to London. There was a charity here that promised to get her set up with work, a place to live. And they did. We had two good years."

The best years. Years when his mother had gone to work as a receptionist for a doctor. When they had splurged on slices of carrot and hazelnut cake at Borough Market or visited the zoo every month. When his mother had laughed instead of cried herself to sleep when she'd thought he couldn't hear her.

"What happened?" Ana gently prompted.

His hands tightened around the glass. His fury at Zach and what he'd done was nothing compared to the rage that had consumed him all those years ago. Days after his fourteenth birthday, when the life he and his mother had come to know had been ripped away from them by someone else's greed.

"The charity that helped us with housing lost their funding."

A hand settled on top of his. Shaw stilled. Then, slowly, he turned his head and looked at Ana. There was no pity. No judgment or disgust. There was just Ana. Compassionate, kind, supportive. Grieving for a woman she'd never met and the boy he had been.

He breathed in. "We made it for a month or two. But without rent support, we had to move out of the apartment. It was too expensive to stay in London, so Mam and I came back to Edinburgh." His jaw tightened. "We took a train from King's Cross. We picked wildflowers along the way and tried to sell them in the station to earn some extra money. People…they weren't cruel, but they weren't kind, either. Just…indifferent."

Her fingers tightened over his. "Indifference can be its own kind of cruelty."

"Yes. Like we weren't even worth acknowledging."

Ana squeezed his hand once more before sitting back. He felt the loss of her touch as he curled his fingers into his palm.

"Thank you. For sharing with me."

Her voice was husky, raw, as if she were holding back

tears. That his confession had meant something to her made it worth it. Even if it had left him feeling exposed. Unmasked.

"I've never told anyone that."

Her shoulders rose up a fraction and she looked away. Uneasiness curled in his stomach.

"What?"

"I just…" She shook her head. "You told me something so personal. And I… I feel like I can't…"

"I won't betray anything you tell me, Ana. But it's your story to tell. And you did tell me something," he reminded her. "Your first time in a bar."

Her shoulders relaxed as she chuckled. "True."

"What else do you want to do?"

She gave him a quizzical look. "What?"

"What else haven't you done that you want to?"

The shy smile she gave him pierced his chest and lodged in the vicinity of his heart. "Have you ever been up in the London Eye?"

"The giant Ferris wheel? No."

"Me neither. I was only in London once before and didn't get to do much. Maybe I'll stay in London for a few days on my way home."

Impulse seized him. He pulled out his phone and pulled up the website. "You're in luck. The last rotation will start in forty minutes. We can make it if we leave now."

He held up his phone. The smile she gave him when she saw the e-tickets on the screen made him feel like he had just conquered a mountain peak.

After telling the waiter to bill the meal to his room, they hurried out of the bar and down to the main floor. A quick conversation with the concierge had a taxi ready and waiting for them as they walked out. Ana kept her eyes glued to the window as they passed the fountains of Trafalgar Square, the imposing facade of Whitehall and the timeless silhouette of Big Ben against the darkening sky.

As the taxi sped across Westminster Bridge, Ana tore her gaze away from the scenery and smiled at him. "Thank you, Shaw."

What he had said to her in the reading room, his promise to maintain his distance, now hung like a chain around his neck. He'd never before doubted his ability to stay indifferent, to keep himself removed from those around him.

Yet the woman next to him had him questioning everything.

The taxi pulled up to the curb. Ana started to pull out her wallet.

"Not a chance."

She narrowed her eyes at him. "You paid for dinner and for the tickets. The least I can do is spring for a taxi."

He swiped his card in the machine behind the driver's seat. Ana started to protest, but he slid out of the cab and held out his hand. She reluctantly accepted it, grumbling as he closed the door behind her.

"We're going to miss our ride if we stand here arguing," he said.

"I'm not arguing," she retorted as they moved down the sidewalk. "I just don't want you to think I expect you to pay for everything."

"The fact that you don't makes me want to."

She let out a confused laugh. "What?"

"I enjoy giving a gift to someone who appreciates it." He glanced down at her as they neared the ticket booth. "I want to do this for you, Ana."

Her steps slowed as confusion clouded her face. "Shaw—"

"Please."

She let out a small laugh. "How can I refuse?"

"I'm sold out of tickets," the attendant said as they approached.

Shaw held up his phone. "I believe I bought the last one."

"Oh." The attendant glanced at her watch, then smiled at them. "Perfect timing."

Ana's smile stretched from ear to ear as they walked up the queue. The wheel rotated continuously, so slow it was easy to step off the boarding platform and into the capsule. A giant bubble with a long bench in the middle and huge glass windows that provided 360-degree views of London.

"This is beautiful," Ana breathed.

Shaw's chest tightened. What would it be like to take joy in so many things, big and small?

As the wheel rotated higher, he tried. Tried to let go of the usual facts and figures he thought of and focus on his surroundings. A boat gliding across the water on the river below. The face of Big Ben glowed against a violet-colored sky.

Tension he didn't even realize he'd been carrying eased as he watched the world around him.

"When I go back home," Ana said softly, "I'll be taking on a much larger role in my family's organization."

Shaw stayed where he was, partly out of respect but also because a greedy part of him didn't want to spook her.

"I've always known I would be involved in it. But my father…" Her voice caught. She wrapped her arms around herself. "Logically, I know there's an end. But I always thought…"

He moved then, going to her side and wrapping an arm around her shoulders. He had never been swayed by physical touch. But the need to touch Ana was a living, breathing need inside of him.

"I thought the same of my mother."

She leaned into him. "We knew for some time that we were going to lose him. It gave us some time to prepare. But the weight of everything fell on my brother. He was going to be so wrapped up in it all that he was going to lose out on the chance to be with someone he really loved."

"Not to play devil's advocate, but wasn't that his choice? To choose work over his personal life?"

Ana shook her head. "It's…it's hard to explain."

That was what she had said about her father's expectations of her. What did her family do that would warrant such pressure?

"I understood why he was at the crossroads he was. So I offered to step up and take on a larger role."

His arm tightened about her shoulders. "Is it something you want to do?"

"Yes and no. I liked what I did before. This…it comes with so much more responsibility and expectations."

"To be someone you're not."

She looked up at him then, eyes wide and glimmering green beneath the soft lighting of the car. "That's what it feels like. Just before I came to Edinburgh, I made a mistake. One that made me question whether I'm right for the role."

"So don't do it."

The smile she gave him was bleak, almost hopeless. "It's not that simple."

"Why not? What is it that your family does?"

A shutter dropped over her face. She started to pull away, but he gripped her shoulders and turned her to face him.

"I didn't mean to pry. I just…you deserve more than that."

Slowly, one hand came up and rested on his. "Thank you. I know I sound hypocritical, telling you to share more when I tell you almost nothing about myself."

"One, you don't owe me anything, Ana. Ever," he said emphatically. "I want to know more about you, yes. But it's your choice, and yours alone, as to what you do and do not share with me."

Her brows drew together. "I appreciate that, but I've been pushing you to—"

"To share necessary information to get the donors who supported a charitable foundation a reason to trust me again."

As he said the words out loud, something slid into place, an understanding of what Ana had been trying to achieve. Logically, he'd heard her words, read her proposal. But now he understood the why.

"Never once have you pushed me to share my life with you. Even when I told you what I did about my childhood, you didn't press. You listened. You supported." He stepped closer as he moved one hand to cup her cheek. "Stop being so hard on yourself."

Her lips parted. His thumb drifted over her cheek, rubbing gentle, soothing circles across her skin. The air in the car changed, became charged with the tension they had both sworn to dismiss yet couldn't keep at bay.

Shaw stared down into Ana's eyes. Saw his own yearning reflected back to him.

Tomorrow he would make amends. But tonight…

He leaned down, savored her sharp inhale, the sight of her lashes drifting down as she closed her eyes.

And then he kissed her.

Eviana

The gentle pressure of Shaw's lips on hers filled Eviana with a warmth she hadn't even imagined possible. One that made her feel beautiful, cherished, wanted.

She rose up, pressing her body against him as she wrapped her arms around his neck. A groan sounded against her lips a moment before Shaw banded an arm around her waist and pulled her even closer, as if he didn't want to leave even a sliver of light between them.

Slowly, tentatively, she slid one hand up the back of his neck, her fingers delving into his hair. The feel of his silky hair contrasted with the hardness of his body against hers, sending a delicious shiver of sensation through her.

Joy filled her. Pure, unadulterated joy. She moaned softly, then smiled against his mouth as he angled his head and took her deeper.

She had been kissed before. But never like this. Never by someone she felt so connected to, who wanted to know the real her.

Except he doesn't.

The thought slammed into her, filling her veins with ice as her stomach dropped to her feet. She pulled back.

"Shaw..." She shook her head, trying to keep her tears at bay. "I... I can't."

He held her against him for another long moment, confusion and frustration evident in the lines of his face, the hardness in his eyes.

But he released her and stepped back.

"I'm leaving in three weeks. And this," she said as she gestured between them, "this isn't just some fling. This is..."

Embarrassed, she moved back to the windows. All of London was spread out before her, from the towering walls of Buckingham Palace to the dome of St. Paul's Cathedral. One of the most incredible views in England, and all she could think of was the man behind her. The man she was finally coming to accept would sneak past any defenses she erected simply by being himself.

"I know." She sensed him behind her, swore she could feel the warmth from his body at her back even though he didn't touch her. "It's the same for me."

She choked back a sob. In another life, they might have had something. If her father hadn't gotten ill, if she didn't have a life of duty waiting for her back home, if...

Too many ifs. None of them mattered. This was now, and nothing could change the trajectory she was on. Even if Shaw did accept who she was, their paths in life would never mesh. Her entire life would revolve around the kind of things Shaw hated. She had taken this sabbatical because she had struggled with the demands on her time and on her person. She couldn't, wouldn't, ask someone else to join her, especially someone like Shaw, knowing her role would slowly eat away at him.

But that didn't stop how she felt about him. How much her feelings had deepened in just a couple days.

The wheel continued to rotate, slowly taking the car back toward the ground. They stood in silence and watched London go by. She could see his reflection in the glass, the hard line in his jaw juxtaposed against the kaleidoscope of emotions in his eyes.

He'd given her so much tonight. Except she had been the one to pull back, to push him away.

Eviana vowed in that moment to tell Shaw the truth. Not now, when her heart was bruised and bleeding. But just before she left. She would tell him everything, including how much she was coming to care for him. He might be angry or disappointed. But at least she would tell him, and maybe one day, he would understand why she'd had to leave.

CHAPTER SEVENTEEN

Shaw

A LILTING MELODY drifted from the piano in the center of the Thames Foyer, a glass-domed atrium that hosted afternoon tea at the Savoy. China cups clinked as people conversed quietly, the occasional laugh sounding through the room. Tiered trays were delivered to tables with artfully arranged bites like artichoke tarts and blueberry scones, as well as plates filled with sandwiches like chicken, pickled cucumber and smoked salmon. An elegant afternoon spent at one of London's oldest hotels.

An environment Eviana had insisted would appeal to a woman like Olivia Mahs.

The woman in question sat across from Shaw, her gaze sweeping around the room. Tall with short, curly hair and round glasses, she exuded confidence and class.

Shaw kept his gaze focused on Olivia and off of Ana. A nearly impossible feat, given how incredible she looked today.

Focus, Shaw.

The rest of their ride on the Eye and subsequent taxi trip back to the hotel had been silent. As if they had finally tasted what could be yet knew nothing more could happen. They'd texted briefly that morning. But the first time he had seen her since bidding her good-night in the lobby had been when he had walked out of the elevator and found Ana conversing with Olivia.

For a moment, he hadn't been able to tear his eyes away.

In her red trousers, black silk top and white blazer, she had looked more confident and more self-assured than he had ever seen her. With her hair pulled up into a bun high on top of her head, the unique angles and planes of her face had been on full display.

He'd allowed himself one moment, just one, to drink in the sight of her. To savor the pride at seeing her wear bright colors once more instead of the bland black-and-white ensembles that had never seemed like her.

Like Ana. Bold, beautiful, kind.

And then he'd slipped back into his old armor as he'd mentally prepared for the battle in front of him.

"I'm curious, Mr. Harrington," Olivia said now as she raised her glass to her lips, "what you think you have to say that could persuade me to resume my donations to the Harrington Foundation given that nearly one hundred percent of my contributions from last year were lost to an investment fraud perpetrated by a man you personally nominated to be CEO."

Straight to the jugular, then.

"A valid question, Miss Mahs. But before I answer, I'd like to apologize."

Olivia blinked in surprise. "For?"

"Even though my role with the foundation is primarily ceremonial at this point, I created it. And you're right—I recommended Zach for the position because he had many of the qualities I lack."

Out of the corner of his eye, he saw Ana look down. For one moment, he wondered if he had screwed up. But then he saw the slightest upward tilt of her lips, felt her approval.

He took the strength she silently offered and continued. "I also did it because I wanted someone else to be the face. Had I not taken the easy way out and been more involved, this might not have happened."

Olivia regarded him over the rim of her glass for a long

moment. "Perhaps." She plucked a brioche bun off the tiered tray. "But men like Zachary White know just what to say. I should know," she said wryly. "He made quite the impression on me when we met in New York five years ago. Obviously, given that I became a recurring donor that same night."

"He was persuasive. But," Shaw continued, "I also had some concerns. Ones I pushed to the side because I didn't want to do the hard work or put myself out there."

Silence descended. Olivia watched him over the rim of her glass as she took a long sip of her rosé. As if baiting him to say something more, to see how long he could last while she evaluated him.

"May I add something, Mr. Harrington?"

He looked at Ana. She gazed back at him, a neutral expression and that subtle smile on her face. But her eyes…her eyes glinted with determination, conviction.

"Yes, Miss Barros. Please."

Ana turned to Olivia. "I've only been working with Mr. Harrington for a couple weeks. But in that time, I've come to see how much he cares about the foundation and the people it serves. When he says he didn't want to do the hard work, I have to disagree. He made a mistake that many have. You yourself stated you were swayed by Zachary. That Mr. Harrington was fooled, too, should not be held against him."

He blinked at the daring of her words. Whether Olivia Mahs would accept Ana's reasoning was one thing. But it didn't stop the pride that filled him at Ana speaking with this combination of professionalism and courage.

"That he's here now," Ana continued, "is a testament to how much he cares about the foundation and how much he personally wants to make things right."

Olivia regarded her thoughtfully. "Noted." She smiled at Ana before refocusing on Shaw. "Proceed, Mr. Harrington."

Shaw launched into the pitch he and Ana had worked on.

An international hiring process for a new CEO. New additions to the accounting department that would implement a series of checks and balances. Creating a public relations department to support the already strained marketing team and help better share the stories of the charities and people they helped.

"Even as our financial capabilities have plummeted," he said, "we've managed to sustain all of our charities in some capacity, with our board of trustees helping identify the ones who need the most urgent funding."

Olivia tilted her head to the side. "How have you been able to maintain your operations to that degree?"

Shaw glanced at Ana, who slightly shook her head. She hadn't said anything to Olivia about his contributions. But sometimes achieving something monumental demanded sacrifice.

"I have been making routine investments in the foundation since the crisis."

Olivia's gaze sharpened. "How much?"

"Three million."

She stared at him for so long, assessing, that he resigned himself to the inevitable. He hadn't done his job. Hadn't sold her on—

"All right."

He blinked. "Excuse me?"

"I'll resume my donations."

A slow exhale escaped as relief surged through him. "Thank you, Miss Mahs."

"Olivia." She smiled at him. "I admire and respect someone who believes in something enough he'll put his own money into it. Especially to right a wrong, even if he's not the one who perpetrated it."

"Your support will mean a great deal to the organizations we support."

She inclined her head. "That does come with the stipulation that if at any time I feel uncomfortable, I will cancel my donations."

"Of course."

"Miss Mahs," Ana said, "I know we've already asked a great deal of you, but—"

"Olivia," the older woman insisted with a gentle smile. "But?"

Ana launched into an overview of the dinner. Shaw watched as she rattled off the guest list, explaining the need for Olivia's support, drawing the event back to the need for reestablishing the foundation to meet the needs in the United Kingdom. The passion in her voice, the genuineness as she spoke about a specific organization that offered pediatric and maternal healthcare in rural communities the Scottish Highlands, drew him in as if he was hearing about his own foundation for the first time.

"Yes."

Olivia's voice yanked him out of his reverie.

Ana's lips parted. "Yes?"

"Yes," Olivia repeated. "I wasn't comfortable with canceling my donations to the foundation. But given that I had just been given the assignment of overseeing the final rollout of my family's railroad to the public, I was concerned that my choices would be under additional scrutiny." A frown darkened her face. "Personal reasons I should have thought about more before making such a drastic decision."

Shaw hesitated, then took a leap. "My mother and I relied on the services of a charity when I was younger. The CEO of the charity embezzled funds to purchase a house and travel. We lost everything because of it, as did a number of others."

He heard Ana's gasp. But he didn't look at her. Couldn't. Not when he had just revealed something so monumental.

"I'm sorry," Olivia said softly. "I had no idea."

"It was that experience that led me to create the Harrington Foundation. That and my mother." His chest tightened. "She persevered through some very hard times. When Zach told me what he'd done, I felt betrayed. A betrayal I'm sure you and our other donors felt, too."

"I already felt confident in my decision." Olivia lifted her teacup in a toast. "But now I'm certain of it."

Eviana

Eviana sat in the dining car, her notes on the dinner spread out before her. The meeting with Olivia had been an unprecedented success. Olivia had stayed for another thirty minutes, guiding the conversation to their experience on the train trip to London and asking for feedback on what could be improved. It had proven to be a very enjoyable afternoon.

Satisfaction bubbled in her chest. She'd done it—balanced speaking her mind with the professional calm Helena was always encouraging. It had been easy to be confident with Kirstin, to think she was improving while cocooned in the safe environment of Murray PR's office. But going out on a limb, with Shaw's encouragement, had been a test. One she'd forced herself to take on and passed.

She glanced out the window as houses gave way to pastures. Night turned the grass dark as stars winked into existence overhead. In just a few hours, she and Shaw would be back in Edinburgh. Returning to a completely different dynamic given what had transpired between them in London.

Whether it had been the exhilaration from their achievement or relief at finally having some good news, she and Shaw had managed to maintain a pleasant, albeit stilted, conversation on the taxi ride to the train station.

Now, as he sat across from her, fingers flying across his keyboard, she couldn't help but glance at his handsome profile. His sudden confession had rocked her. Learning last night of the struggles he and his mother had faced, followed by the betrayal they had experienced at the hands of someone who had promised to care for them, had left her speechless.

Even on her hardest days, she had never experienced such heartbreak. Which only made her respect him more. Respect and…

She swallowed hard. Feelings that went far deeper than she was prepared to deal with. Their kiss last night had left her wanting. Yes, she wanted to explore their physical attraction, but she also longed for something more. For the first time, she had tasted true desire: the need for a man who had accepted her, and wanted her, for who she was.

For who he thought she was.

Heat pricked her eyes. Not only was she still lying to Shaw about her identity, there was no future for them. Shaw's life was here, in Edinburgh. Or in New York, depending on what he decided to do. Regardless, it did not include a life with a princess. A life that would demand so much.

Too much.

"I'm going to go back to my suite."

Shaw glanced up at her and frowned. "Are you feeling all right?"

"Just tired," she said. "Like I ran a marathon."

His slight smile nearly undid her. "We essentially did." He glanced at his watch. "Two hours before we get to Edinburgh. I've arranged to have a car take you to your apartment."

This time Eviana didn't even feel irritated that he had arranged things. She was just grateful. Especially because she knew the coming days would demand more of her. The days between now and the dinner would be filled to the brim. Plenty to stay focused on and keep her mind off that amazing kiss.

"Thank you. I…"

There was so much she wanted to say. How she admired everything he had overcome. How deeply she respected him for putting himself out on a limb for what he believed in. How much she appreciated the trust he had placed in her. All professional feelings.

But it was the emotions that ran deeper, that were very much not professional, that held her tongue.

"See you in a bit," she said.

She walked out of the dining room and moved quickly from train car to train car until she reached her suite. Eviana darted inside and closed the door behind her, locking it with a quick twist before buying her face in her hands.

She'd known for some time it wasn't just a simple crush. But this…this awareness of him whenever he was in the room, the joy she had experienced on their dash across London and the first part of their trip up in the Eye, the ease of just being around him…

A knock sounded on her door.

She frowned. "Who is it?"

"Shaw."

His voice sounded through the door, deep and raw. She felt the need in his voice, closed her eyes as she stood on a mental precipice.

And then she unlocked the door.

Shaw filled the doorway, his breathing ragged, his eyes burning.

Did he move first? Did she?

Does it matter? she thought desperately as they crashed into each other.

His lips captured hers. She wound her arms around his neck, moaned as his hands pressed against her back and urged her closer.

It was as if they both knew this would be their last time. Their last kiss before they returned to Edinburgh, to real life. Here, on this train speeding through the twilight landscape, they had a few precious moments. Ones they greedily took as the kiss deepened, hearts pounding in tandem.

She should have pulled him into her suite. Kissing him in the doorway, when anyone could walk down the hallway, was risky.

But the greater risk would be inviting him in and closing the door behind him. So instead, for this one moment, she would throw caution to the wind and savor her stolen kisses.

Shaw slid a hand up her neck, his fingers giving one deft yank that sent her hair spilling over her shoulders.

"So beautiful, Ana."

She froze.

Eviana. My name is Eviana.

"Shaw..." She pulled back but selfishly kept her arms around his neck as she buried her face in his chest and breathed in his scent. "I..."

"I know." His touch gentled, his hand stroking over her hair.

"I want to ask you in."

"It's wrong."

She choked back a sob. He was speaking to his role as her boss. But he didn't know, couldn't know what was truly holding her back. The lie between them that had seemed so inconsequential in the beginning but now loomed like a phantom just outside her door.

"I want to come in," he murmured against her hair.

"I know." She squeezed her eyes shut. "I know you can't."

They stood there in the doorway, breaths mingling, hearts thudding, grief and longing filling the air.

He leaned down. His lips grazed her temple.

And then he slowly released her before he walked away, leaving her alone in the doorway. She watched as he stopped outside his door and slid a key into the lock.

He stopped, one hand on the key, his head turned slightly.

A tear slid down her cheek as she closed the door to her room and locked it.

CHAPTER EIGHTEEN

Eviana
Two weeks later

THE SECRET GARDEN room of the famed Witchery boutique hotel and restaurant lived up to both its name and reputation. Huge arched doors dominated one wall and provided a tantalizing glimpse of the patio. Dark stone and wood created an atmosphere of intimacy, enhanced by the candles flickering on the tables.

Private. Elegant. One of Edinburgh's culinary treasures.

Perfect.

Eviana circled the room for the fourth time, eyes sweeping over the table settings, the flowers. A table had been set up on the other side of the room with photos from some of the charities supported by the Harrington Foundation, along with letters from grateful clients, case managers and boards.

It had been her idea, one she hadn't been sure Shaw would like. But he'd agreed to it. In fact, he'd agreed to almost everything since they'd returned from London.

Her gaze darted to the stairs, then back to the room. Every meeting since their train ride had included Kirstin. By mutual unspoken agreement, they'd refrained from any situation where they might be alone. Instead, they'd both knuckled down—she and Kirstin with the upcoming dinner and public relations evaluation, and Shaw with the restructuring of the Harrington Foundation.

Eviana wandered over to the table with the pictures and letters. Her fingers drifted across a letter written in crayon. The child had written to thank the Harrington Foundation for helping find his father a job. He'd drawn a stick figure of his father pushing a lawnmower at his new job as a groundskeeper.

So many people. So many that had been given a supporting hand from a man who knew the value of helping others. A man who knew the pain of being left to flounder.

She turned away from the table. Shaw hadn't said any more about his experiences in London. Every now and then, she thought of his mother's photograph, wondered what happened between their return to Edinburgh and his mother's passing. What Shaw had gone through as he'd fought his way from poverty to the top of the financial world.

But it was none of her concern. Even after she finally shared with him who she was, he would owe her nothing. No more stories of his own past unless he wanted to share. At this point, she just hoped he would still talk to her after finding out she was a princess living incognito.

No matter what, she reminded herself as she adjusted a stack of brochures she'd worked on with the marketing department, she was going home stronger. Working with someone who had encouraged her to be herself, coupled with the success of their meeting with Olivia, had been nearly as freeing as coming to Edinburgh.

The doubts still circled. They probably would until she returned home. But they didn't rule her waking thoughts. When she thought of her snafu of a speech, she could think about it critically, analyze what had gone wrong and what she would do differently in the future.

Starting with writing her own speeches. Input from Helena and her team was fine. But if she was going to be a leader, she'd start by being the leader she realized she could be, not a puppet tailored to follow protocol.

As she walked across the dining room, awareness pricked between her shoulder blades. She knew even before she turned that Shaw would be walking down the stairs.

She faced him, giving him a polite smile even though the only other person in the room was a waiter lighting the last remaining candles. Shaw's eyes swept over her, warming with appreciation as he took in her dress. Pale blue, with one shoulder left bare and the other featuring a long length of wispy material trailing down her back, it made her feel elegant and just a touch daring.

"You look beautiful."

"Thank you." Hoping he didn't notice the tremble in her voice, she gestured to his dark blue tuxedo. "The tie was the right choice."

His smile set off a flurry of butterflies in her stomach. Despite the lingering tension between them, he had smiled so much more in the past two weeks. Enough that Kirstin had commented on it a couple days ago.

Maybe he has a girlfriend, Kirstin had said jokingly.

The thought of Shaw dating had left Eviana sick to her stomach.

"I certainly prefer this to the bow tie." He tugged on the end and slightly dislodged the knot.

"Oh." Without thinking, she moved forward and started to undo the tie before she realized what she was doing. "I'm sorry!" She started to step back. "I just… I do this—"

"It's fine." The huskiness in his voice slid over her, under her skin, leaving little trails of want behind. "It sounds like some guests are already here, so if you wouldn't mind…"

She focused on the material, trying to move quickly while tying with precision.

"You said you do this often?"

She smiled slightly. "For my brother. At least I used to. He'd get nervous before..." She stopped, swallowed her words. "His fiancée does it for him now."

Silence settled between them. She could feel his disappointment, his withdrawal as she finished tying.

So many secrets between them.

"Thank you, Miss Barros."

His words cut through her like a knife. But she was the one who had kept this barrier between them, who hadn't trusted him with her identity.

He stepped back, started to turn away. After tonight, she had one week left. One week before she returned to Kelna and most likely never saw Shaw Harrington again.

"Shaw."

His head snapped around. "Yes?"

She swallowed hard. "Tonight...after the dinner, could I..."

Voices filtered in from above. Shaw glanced toward the stairs, his shoulders going rigid.

"Sorry, what?"

"It can wait." She breathed in, resumed her mantle of professionalism as people began descending the stairs. "There's something I'd like to share with you tonight before you go."

He gave her a vague nod as he moved to the base of the stairs to greet the first couple. Eviana let out a harsh breath. She'd taken the first step. If everything went well tonight, she'd tell him. If it didn't...she would reassess then.

But it will go well.

She couldn't believe, after all the hard work everyone had put in, that at least some of the donors wouldn't agree to come back. She snagged a glass of champagne from a passing waiter.

Showtime.

The event kicked off with a cocktail hour. Kirstin, Eviana, Shaw and members of the board circulated among the guests. Shaw conversed and even occasionally laughed as he spoke with each donor. Pride filled Eviana's chest as he greeted people by name, shook their hands and remembered details like new grandbabies being born and recent graduations. Details that surprised his guests and left more than one watching Shaw with curiosity and appreciation. Even Roy and Victoria Miles had joined, although Roy had been unusually subdued.

Waiters served venison, barbecued halibut and grilled jackfruit for the vegetarians in attendance, alongside tomatoes dusted with grated pistachios, baked asparagus drizzled with hollandaise and burrata mixed with a garlic pesto and served on toasted brioche. Eviana dined with a banker from Switzerland and her husband. Besotted with their first grandbaby who had just turned one, Eviana was treated to numerous stories and a carousel of pictures featuring the lovely little girl in various stages of smashing a cake.

At one point, she looked up and saw Shaw watching her. He returned her small nod before turning back to his dinner companions. A museum curator from Spain and her sister, Eviana remembered. Watching both women converse, and the younger one subtly flirt, with Shaw tested her ability to focus. But she pushed through, keeping her eyes off his table as much as possible and on her dinner companions.

After the dinner plates had been cleared away and waiters brought in an array of desserts, from Scottish oatcake served with ginger chutney to chocolate torte topped with pear ice cream, Shaw stood. Conversations gradually died off as everyone turned their attention to him.

Eviana sat back in her chair, hands folded, pulse pounding as he glanced around the room.

"I hope everyone enjoyed their meal." He smiled as a murmur of approval swept through the room. "I'm glad. When I was a boy, I would walk by the gate for this restaurant. I'd see the people going in, never imagining that one day I would be one of them."

Eviana's heartbeat kicked up a notch as people exchanged confused glances with one another.

"Most of you don't know, but I grew up in Edinburgh. My mother and I occasionally had a roof over our heads. But there were plenty of times when we stayed in shelters or, one particularly hard time, in a car."

The room fell silent, save for the occasional crackle of a candle.

"I've never shared my history with anyone until just recently." He looked at Eviana again. Emotion flared in his eyes. Just for a second, but long enough to steal the breath from her lungs. "I know the Harrington Foundation has lost your trust. Why would you invest your money into an organization that just lost millions?

"I'm speaking to you tonight not as the founder, but as a man who for two years benefitted from the generosity of a charity in London. One that provided support for my mother to get a job she loved." He smiled slightly. "We didn't have much. But we had more than we'd ever had. Until someone serving on the board embezzled funds and the charity shut its doors."

Someone gasped as a quiet murmur swept through the room. Eviana kept her gaze trained on Shaw, strove for calm and collected even as her heart swelled in her chest.

"My mother and I returned to Edinburgh. I missed school half the time to help pay the bills. My mother was only forty-four years old when she passed away from a heart attack after working two shifts back-to-back as a maid and a waitress." His voice roughened, but he didn't falter. "Tonight I'm speaking to you as someone who knew a better life because of the generosity of others. Even though it was taken away, it motivated me to try harder, do better. As I've talked with each of you this evening, I've outlined our plan for doing our best to ensure this doesn't happen again. But I also hope that sharing my motivation to begin the Harrington Foundation will demonstrate my personal commitment and serve as the first step toward earning your trust back."

The quiet was broken by the sound of a soft clap. Eviana looked over to see Olivia Mahs slowly rising to her feet. Others joined in until the whole room was filled with the sounds of applause.

You did it, Shaw.

He had done it. She and Kirstin had helped, given him the tools and resources he'd needed. But he'd been the one to take that final leap, to listen to her advice and bare his soul to the people who had deserted him in one of his darkest hours.

Shaw stood motionless for a few seconds before nodding his head and taking his seat. When he looked toward Eviana's table, she managed to mouth *Well done* as she fought to maintain her composure. As people approached him, she excused herself and stepped out into the gardens.

The garden welcomed her, the floral scents made more potent by the settling of night. She breathed them in as she tried to calm her racing heart, tried to ground herself as she fully accepted in that moment that she was in love with Shaw Harrington. A truth she had denied, one that seemed almost impossible given they'd known each other for less than a month.

But it was there, beautiful and bright and heartbreaking. His confession to a room full of strangers, his commitment to doing the right thing and ensuring others didn't suffer needlessly, had cemented the emotions she had been powerless to stop since the moment he'd first spoken to her on the sidewalk.

"Going well?"

Eviana froze, then slowly relaxed as the voice registered. Jodi sat in a chair off to the side, partially eclipsed by shadows from the lanterns.

"It is." She gave her bodyguard a slight smile. "Very well."

"Good." Jodi paused. "It's not my business, but are you and Mr. Harrington..."

Eviana's cheeks flamed. "We're not lovers, if that's what you're asking."

Jodi held up her hands. "I just don't want you to get hurt."

Too late. Just the thought of leaving him hurts.

"I appreciate it, but—"

"Ana?" Eviana whipped around. Shaw stood just behind her, concern wrinkling his brow. "Who are you talking to?"

Her heart slammed into her throat. "I...no one."

He looked over his shoulder. His eyes narrowed. "You. You were at the Dome." A frown darkened his face. "I've seen you outside my office, too." His gaze shifted to Eviana. "But only when you've been there."

Jodi stood and moved to Eviana's side. "I'm a friend."

"A friend? Or a stalker?"

Alarm flared in Eviana's belly. "Shaw, it's not what you think—"

"Is that why you've been so secretive? Why you won't talk about home?"

O Bože, what had she done? Why hadn't she told him sooner?

"No, that's not it."

"Then what?" Shaw stepped closer, his gaze still fixed on Jodi's face, shoulders thrown back.

"She's my bodyguard."

It took a moment for the word to register. But then, slowly, Shaw turned to look at her. "Bodyguard?"

"Yes."

He stared at her. "Who are you?"

She nearly broke then. Nearly gave in to the urge to cry. But she squared her shoulders and prepared to face the consequences of her choices.

"Princess Eviana Adamoviç of Kelna."

CHAPTER NINETEEN

Shaw

SHAW SLOWLY TURNED his head to look at Ana.

No, Eviana. Princess Eviana.

He glanced back at the blonde woman standing off to the side. Her gaze was fixed on Eviana, her face blank. No, not entirely true. There was a trace of concern in her eyes.

"Princess?"

"Go, Jodi." The words were uttered so softly Shaw barely heard them over the noise of conversation and music from the restaurant behind them. "Please."

Jodi cast him a warning look as she headed inside. He returned it with one of his own. She'd known about Eviana's deception, had let a princess run around the United Kingdom with almost no supervision.

He thought very little of Eviana's bodyguard.

The door clicked shut behind her. Eviana moved away from the windows and wrapped her arms around herself, much as she had that night on the London Eye.

"How does a princess from the Adriatic coast end up in Scotland?"

She flinched at the ice in his voice. "I… I saw a picture of Edinburgh Castle. It reminded me of…" Pink appeared in her cheeks. "The palace back home."

The palace. Eviana lived in an actual palace. His hands

curled into fists at his sides as her treachery hit him with full force. Before he could give into it, he gestured for her to follow him. He stalked through the garden, not bothering to look behind him and see if she followed him to a darker corner far from the windows of the dining room. Each step grew heavier in tandem with his rising anger.

Once he was certain they were out of hearing distance, he whirled around and pinned her with his furious stare. "Was it all an act?"

Her brows drew together. "What?"

"Drop the pretense of innocence, An—*Your Highness*. The castle, the Savoy, the train ride…you acted so impressed, so excited—"

"Because I was," Eviana insisted. "I've never stayed at the Savoy, I've never been on a train and the castle—"

"You live in one, Princess." He bit out her title, his tone vicious. But he didn't care. Couldn't care. Not when the world he'd started to embrace over the past month was based on a lie. When the woman he had fallen for didn't exist. "I'm guessing you've flown on private planes and stayed in some of the most exclusive hotels in the world, too."

She looked away. "Everything I said…it was all true."

"Obviously not all of it. You knew how much honesty meant to me."

Her eyes glimmered with unshed tears. "I do. And I wasn't trying to—"

"But you did." He turned away from her, unable to see her face. A face he thought he knew. "Was the thing about your first time in a bar true? Your brother, your sister-in-law?"

"Yes." She sounded broken. Defeated. "My brother is Nicholai Adamoviç, King of Kelna. He and Madeline will marry in October, which is when she'll be crowned queen."

King. Queen. Princess. He'd paid for their tickets on the Eye, the taxi. She'd acted like it had meant something to her.

Just another lie.

"Did you at any point stop to think what ramifications your choices to play commoner could have?"

"What are you talking about?"

He steeled himself, then turned slowly to face her again. She stood in the shadows, her face hollow as she stared at the cobblestones.

"The Harrington Foundation has been in the spotlight for investment fraud." He stepped toward her. "How do you think it would look if it comes out not only that I hired a princess living in disguise to help with my public relations, but that I nearly had an affair with her, too?"

Her head snapped up. "But we didn't—"

"It doesn't matter what we did or didn't do." His voice whipped out as he latched onto his anger, chose it over the anguish trying to fight through and pull him down, pull him back toward her. "What matters is what people think. You know this. You're the one who's been telling me for weeks to be myself, to share a part of myself with others so that they'll trust me when all this time you've been lying to my face."

He'd gone to her that last night on the train, needing to see her, hold her one last time. That memory of her in his arms, the taste of her, the feel of her, had sustained him through the past two weeks. Had been a lifeline tonight as he'd bared his soul.

A memory that now seemed more like a nightmare as he stared down into the face of the woman he had come to care for.

A woman he didn't even know.

A tear slid down her cheek. "Shaw—"

"Mr. Harrington."

She bit down on her lower lip as another tear escaped. "Please… I wanted to…to have just a little bit of normalcy. And then I overheard Kirstin talking about offering an internship and thought I could learn something that might help me be a better leader—"

"So you used my scandal for your own personal gain?"

A fire kindled in her eyes as her chin came up. "No. And it's grossly unfair of you to accuse me of that."

"It's true," he shot back.

"I can understand your anger over everything but this. You're twisting this to push me even further away." Her voice softened. "I hurt you, and I—"

"I'm not hurt, Your Highness. I'm simply realizing the way I led my life before I met you was the better choice."

Her eyes widened. "That's not true and you know it."

"What I know to be true is that people like you don't get it."

"Like me?"

"People like you—people who have never struggled, who have never known instability or hunger or poverty—don't think. You don't think about the ramifications of your actions. You don't think beyond your own needs."

Silence fell. Eviana had gone unnaturally still, as if she been frozen to the spot. She didn't blink, didn't even appear to breathe. Then, slowly, as if she were coming out from under a spell, she tilted her head to the side. "People like Zach."

A dull roaring began in his ears. Only too late did he realize he had used almost the exact same words he had used to describe Zach the day he'd shown her his mother's picture.

The betrayal was still there. But he knew, even through the gnarled depths of his anger, that Eviana was not like Zach. To suggest such a thing had been more than a step too far. It had been a giant leap off a cliff.

"I didn't mean—"

She held up a hand, the movement smooth and regal. He realized now that all those times he had seen that serene calmness, he had been seeing Princess Eviana Adamoviç.

"I did lie," she said. "I lied about my name, and my vagueness and omissions were lies of their own. No, I did not think through the potential ramifications my actions could have on you and the foundation. For that, I am profoundly sorry."

He knew the words were true. But the lack of emotion in her voice, the emptiness in her eyes, clawed at him.

"The one thing I will not let you accuse me of is using your foundation for my own means." Her eyes hardened to emerald chips of ice. There was no fire, no passion. Only a cool detachment. "I meant to tell you tonight if things went well with the dinner, or tomorrow if they didn't. Tell you everything and ask if I could spend my last couple days in Edinburgh with you."

He remembered vaguely now, at the beginning of the party that felt like a lifetime ago. He wanted to say yes, to pretend like the revelations of the last few minutes hadn't just happened.

But even if he had gone too far in comparing her to Zach, it didn't erase that she had lied to him. A crime that so many committed on a daily basis. Yet one that hurt far worse coming from her, after everything he had shared with her.

She stepped away.

"Where are you going?"

"The party is almost over. I'm going home."

Alarm trickled in. "There's still work to be done."

"And Kirstin will do an excellent job for you."

His heart slammed into his ribs as she started to walk toward the covered archway that led back out onto the street.

She stopped walking but didn't turn around. That she wouldn't look at him added another layer of pain to the already heavy weight pressing down on his chest.

"I had hoped you might understand."

"Understand what?" he snapped. How could she expect him to understand her duplicity, her manipulations and clever phrases designed to conceal the truth even as she prompted him to open up?

She looked back at him then, eyes luminous in the glow from a nearby lantern.

"As a princess, there are thousands of people who depend upon me. Stepping into a larger role, that responsibility has grown tenfold." Her fingers tightened into fists, her knuckles turning white. "A princess who's been on the fringes of royal life all of her life because she was the second born. Someone who does what she can and does it well, but also accepted there was little expectation for her to have any large impact. And then her father…"

Her voice caught. He nearly went to her then, as he had in London. But then she was calm once more.

"Her father becomes ill. Her country expands much more rapidly than anyone anticipates. Her brother is left smothered under the weight of everything there is to do." A ghost of a smile played about her lips. "And then he falls in love, and his sister sees an opportunity to stand up, to do the right thing and be a leader."

He stared at her determined not to be pulled in, not to listen to her excuses.

"She does all right. She wasn't born with the expectation of taking on such duties. Even though her father and brother loved her very much, she spent more time with palace staff who constantly corrected her until she didn't really know herself at all."

Shock penetrated his anger. Even in the hardest times, he'd always had his mother's unconditional love.

"But she knows duty." Eviana's voice was barely a whisper now. "And she loves her brother. When duty calls, she handles her new duties. Until she doesn't. Until she starts making little mistakes. She struggles to sleep, struggles to figure out who she's supposed to be. She stumbles during a speech. She's drowning."

Her voice faltered. The images in his mind, of Eviana surrounded by people, struggling to smile, to talk, to do what she had committed to even as she spiraled, redirected his anger to the people who had placed so many demands on her even as they encouraged her to stifle the strengths that made her an incredible woman.

"Her brother recommends she take a sabbatical. One where she can rest and grieve. So she picks a place, one that reminds her of home, but it's still somewhere new. Somewhere she can be normal for just a few months." Her face softened. "She overhears a woman in a coffee shop talking about the kind of person she needs to help grow her business. And the princess thinks not only is this another way to experience life as almost everyone else in the world knows it, but maybe she can learn something. When she goes back home, the small lessons will end up forming the foundation of who she is expected to be."

Eviana smiled then. A perfect smile, one that didn't make her nose slightly wrinkle or her eyes dance. A royal smile.

"I guess I'll find out."

He almost said something, asked her to wait to talk. Pain and pride rendered him silent as she turned and disappeared through the arch into the night.

CHAPTER TWENTY

Eviana
Three months later

THE MORNING SUN bathed the waves of the Adriatic with a rosy glow as Eviana sat on her balcony with a steaming cup of tea. A lark flew by, gifting her with the soft trill of a song as it continued on. A cool October wind brought her the salty scent of the sea.

Home.

She'd started off most mornings like this since she'd returned from Scotland, giving herself half an hour to sit, read or simply enjoy the silence before the palace awoke. On days when her schedule seemed endless, she gave herself an additional fifteen minutes to soak in her tub. It always reminded her of the train ride to London. Most of the time she managed to focus on the nostalgia, reminiscing about the happy moments she had enjoyed on her sabbatical.

But then there were other days where happiness was far out of reach. Days like today when she was sad. Regretful that she had held on to her secrets for so long even as Shaw had slowly opened up. Wondering where he was and what he was doing.

She glanced at her phone, then tightened her fingers around the warm mug. She had made it six weeks and five days before she'd succumbed and looked up the Harrington Foundation online. The one and only article she'd read had been positive, touting the organization's comeback and Shaw's remarkable transformation into the face of the Harrington Foundation. Over ninety percent of the donors had resumed their contributions. The resulting press had led to a surge in donations from the general public in the UK and the States. A fact the newly formed public relations department, mentored by Kirstin Murray of Murray PR, had proudly highlighted. The foundation anticipated being back up to full strength by the end of the year.

Seeing the end result of a project she'd worked on had been gratifying and another boost to her confidence as she'd navigated her return to royal duties. But seeing Shaw's picture, that slight smile that had once made butterflies flap in her chest, had left her near tears. She'd dreamed of him that night, of standing in a capsule as the London Eye rotated. At first it had been wonderful, the dream so real she could feel his touch.

But then the dream had shifted, the Ferris wheel rotating faster and faster as Shaw had backed away from her, his face darkening with pain and anger. He'd looked at her, asking over and over again *Who are you?* as the wheel had spun so fast she could no longer see, no longer tell which way was up or down as the world spun out of control.

She'd woken up in a cold sweat, her heart hammering in her chest as she'd gasped for breath.

She hadn't looked up the foundation or Shaw again. There was no point in torturing herself further. The foundation was moving forward. The goal she had helped work toward had been accomplished. And now she was home. That should have been the end of it.

Except three months later, she still found herself thinking of him. Missing him and what could have been.

The wind blew harder, making the skin of her arms prickle

as coldness seeped into her veins at the memory of that night. She had walked through the small stone breezeway to the front of the Witchery and asked Kirstin to meet her outside. Saying she'd felt nauseous hadn't been a lie, but it had certainly been misdirection from the real problem. Thankfully Kirstin had simply told her to go home and rest. The walk back to the apartment had steadied her enough so that she could focus on what had needed to be done to get her out of Scotland as quickly as possible.

Her bodyguard had followed, had started to apologize, but Eviana had stopped her. Jodi had just been doing her job. If she had been honest with Shaw, had not let fear keep her from telling him the truth, none of this would have happened.

Jodi had helped her pack in record time, gone to the store for a box of hair dye and helped her achieve a brown close enough to her normal color until her real color grew back in.

She'd agreed to Jodi's recommendation of booking a private plane instead of flying commercial into Dubrovnik. Jodi had also suggested stopping off somewhere else along the way and using the last few days of Eviana's sabbatical to rest, recuperate. Somewhere like Paris or Lisbon or Zurich. But it'd been as if a switch had been flipped. All Eviana had wanted was to get home.

When she'd arrived, Nicholai and Madeline had surprised her at Kelna's tiny airport. Photographers had caught pictures of them hugging on the tarmac. They'd been splashed across Kelnan and Croatian newspapers the next day, and even a few American outlets, with the headline "The Princess is Home!"

There had been some speculation about where she had spent her nearly three months. She'd waited nearly a week for the axe to fall, for Shaw to reveal what she had been up to as punishment for her deception, or some zealous tabloid journalist unveiling all the sordid details.

But there had been nothing. Just silence.

She filled up her days despite Madeline and Nicholai's words of caution. No longer did she sit on the fringes, questioning every word that was about to come out of her mouth or if she wasn't portraying the right face for the occasion. She still exhibited diplomacy and compassion. But she had finally found her voice. And she used it.

She'd walked into the Witchery thinking she had conquered so many of her fears. Yet it had been surviving the rejection of the man she had fallen in love with that had given her the final push into completely embracing the woman she had discovered in Edinburgh. To truly embrace the leader she was capable of being.

Not that she was perfect. She'd still made her fair share of mistakes in the past three months. But unlike before, instead of analyzing each and every single one and worrying about it, she'd examined it, taken whatever lesson she could and moved on. No more lingering over old mistakes. No more focusing more on what people thought of her instead of what she could achieve with action.

Madeline and Nicholai had both noticed. So had Helena, even going so far as to compliment the speech Eviana had written herself to announce that the hospital would be adding a new neonatal wing the following year.

There were good things. So many good things. But on days like today, when she closed her eyes and could hear the long whistle of a train, smell spice and wood on the air, feel strong hands cradling her face as if she were made of glass…

On days like today, the good things were hard to find.

A knock sounded on her door. Eviana glanced at her watch and frowned. It was just before seven in the morning. She didn't have any events scheduled until after breakfast.

"Come in," she called over her shoulder.

"Dobro jutro, sestro."

She smiled as Nicholai's voice sounded behind her. He

walked out onto the balcony a moment later, dressed in trousers and a navy blue dress shirt.

"It's a quarter 'til seven."

Nicholai arched a brow as he sat down in the lounge chair next to hers. "And?"

She gestured to her bathrobe and fuzzy slippers. "You're making me look bad."

Nicholai chuckled. Despite the challenges of the past year—the losses, the country's explosive growth, the frenzy of media—she couldn't remember the last time Nicholai had looked so happy.

What would it be like to have the kind of relationship he had with Madeline? To have someone love you completely, the good and the bad, to find a compromise like the one he and Madeline had so that they could be together?

Her throat constricted. Even if Shaw had been able to forgive her, the life she led would have killed him. Her duty was first and foremost to her country, followed by her allegiance to her king and queen. She would not shirk it.

Not even if Shaw had returned her feelings.

Sadness tugged at her. She finally had her confirmation that she was committed to her role. She could mourn what that commitment meant and lean into the love and support of her brother and Madeline instead of keeping her regrets to herself like dirty secrets. She hadn't shared much of what had happened in Edinburgh. But they'd sensed her sadness and supported her.

She snuggled deeper into her chair and watched as the sun climbed higher.

"I think you have a better view than I do," Nicholai said as they watched another lark dip and swirl overhead.

Eviana smirked at him. "It's what I deserve for being second best around here."

She'd meant the words as a joke. But Nicholai frowned at her.

"Is that really how you felt?"

She started to brush off his question to make an excuse or a joke. But then she stopped. Honesty. Authenticity. There would be times when she would not be able to adhere to those concepts. Would have to abstain or dance around the truth. Such was the life of a royal.

But she had vowed when she had returned to be as truthful as she could.

"Yes."

Regret crossed Nicholai's face. "Did I make you feel like that?"

"No. I always felt loved by you and *Otac*. You two just spent so much more time together since you were the heir." She wrinkled her nose. "And the people I spent time with were more old-fashioned. Sit and look pretty, don't speak your mind, etcetera."

"You said last year that you didn't think I trusted you."

She nodded. "It felt like anytime I offered to help, unless it was with a charity, you didn't want my help. Our father was the same way until the last few years. Tradition has always dictated that the second born, and anyone after that, be focused on enriching the lives of Kelnans through charitable works. I accepted that, even if I didn't always understand it. I tried not to let it hurt me." She shrugged. "But sometimes it did. Other times I wondered if it was because I simply wasn't capable and I was overestimating my abilities."

"As Madeleine has reminded me countless times, the old ways are not always the right ones."

Eviana grinned. "I watch that video of her first press conference about once a week."

Nicholai rolled his eyes, but a smile lingered about his lips. "I almost had a heart attack in the moment."

"It was good for you."

"It was," Nicholai agreed, surprising her with his answer. "I got so used to doing everything on my own and, as you said, thinking about the way things had always been that I never stopped to think about how they could be." He looked at her then, his eyes sad. "I failed you. Not just before Madeline, but after."

Confused, Eviana set her tea on the table and turned to face her brother. "What are you talking about?"

"Before, all I could think about was tradition. Expectations. Everything that Helena drums into our heads. And then after..." His voice trailed off. A muscle worked in his throat as he swallowed hard. "After *Otac* passed, you being there to take on so many of the duties was a lifeline. One I abused."

She reached over and grab her brother's hand. "I told you that I wanted to do this. That I wanted to be more for our country."

Nicholai laid his other hand on top of hers. "I should have told you this months ago, but when you started taking on more, you were...phenomenal."

Tears pricked her eyes. She tried to blink them back. "I... I thought I..."

"No, *sestro.* You're incredible at speaking with people and forming connections. You jumped in and tackled everything that was thrown at you." A fond smile lit his face. "You and Madeline are so much alike in that regard."

Eviana grinned through her tears. "I'll take that as a compliment."

"You should," Nicholai said earnestly. "I laid so much at your feet in those months after *Otac* passed. I was so focused on the shipping port and the ballroom and the infrastructure assessment after the bridge collapse that I didn't stop to look at what it was doing to you."

"I thought..."

"I know. I should have said so much more."

Eviana blinked the rest of her tears away. "I know you told me I was doing well. But my own insecurities made me think you were just trying to be nice. And then I started making those mistakes—"

"Everyone makes mistakes."

She hesitated. "I overheard someone say after I ruined the chamber luncheon speech that you would never have made that mistake."

Nicholai's eyes hardened. "Who?"

"No."

"Eviana—"

"No, Nicholai. It hurt, but that person was entitled to their opinion."

"It was Helena." She froze. Nicholai grinned. "You still have a terrible poker face."

"Look, Helena and I don't see eye to eye…well, ever, but—"

"Helena and I had a long discussion while you were gone. Her practices, while admirable in their dedication to the crown, were rooted in how things used to be done. Even she acknowledged that you did well given how quickly you were thrust into it all. Especially right after losing our father."

A disbelieving laugh escaped her. "You're joking."

"I'm not. She was hard on you because she wanted you to succeed. But," he said firmly, "that's not the way things are going to be moving forward."

Eviana shook her head. "I just can't believe… Helena, of all people, giving a compliment."

"You were incredible then, and you're doing even more now. Have you seen everything you've accomplished since you've been back?" he asked when she started to shake her head. "The new wing for the hospital, representing the palace in I don't know how many meetings with ambassadors and dignitaries. Proposing the addition of a railway system to Parliament." He grasped her face between his hands and kissed her forehead. "You are more than capable, Eviana. You're a partner, an equal. It's not just Madeline and I who are fortunate to have you. It's our people."

"Even when I speak my mind?"

"You do so with grace. And you have good ideas. Great ideas. I wonder where you've been hiding them all this time."

She glanced away. She'd had plenty of time to think at night when she lay in bed, waiting for sleep to finally find her. Time to unpack years of memories and habits that had led her to those final days before she'd gone to Scotland.

"Do you remember when I was four and *Otac* was going to England for some conference?"

Nicholai frowned. "I think so, but I don't remember much about it."

"Do you remember me throwing a tantrum and attaching myself to his leg as he tried to walk out of the Grand Hall?"

Nicholai pressed his lips together in an attempt not to smile. "I do."

She sucked in a deep breath. "I remember after he left someone telling me to behave. To be like a princess. It was such a small thing, and it wasn't said meanly. But it stuck with me. Over the years whenever people would remind me to do this or say that instead of what I wanted to, it made me feel like the person I was inside was not…right. That I wasn't capable of being the princess I was supposed to be."

Nicholai's eyes glinted. "How did I not see any of this?"

"Because I didn't let you." Her voice trembled. "Because I wanted to make you and our father proud."

Nicholai looked away and stared out over the sea. "I wish I could say that I have never wanted you to be anyone but who you truly are. But the man I was before I met Madeline versus the man I am today…they're two very different people. I don't know how I would have reacted then if you had jumped in like you are now." He looked back at her, his eyes full of grief. "And for that I'm sorry."

"What matters is now." And she meant it. "Knowing that you approve of what I've been doing, before I left and now, means everything to me."

"I mean every word, Eviana. I don't know what happened on your sabbatical, but when you came back, it was as if you'd..." His voice trailed off as a reluctant smile tugged at his lips. "Madeline said it was as if you'd finally broken free. That you were letting everyone see the real you."

Warmth filled her chest. "She really is amazing."

"She is." Nicholai sobered. "But I still feel like there's something you're not telling me. You seem more yourself. But every now and then, you look...heartbroken."

Because I am. Because I fell in love and didn't trust myself enough to tell him everything when I had the chance.

"My time away had so many positives," she finally said. "Living on my own. Making a friend."

She thought of Kirstin, who had responded to the hastily written resignation letter Eviana had fired off the morning after the dinner party by calling her and demanding to know what was going on. Eviana had answered, more out of obligation than actual desire to talk to her mentor and friend. But it had been one of the best things to happen to her. When she'd told Kirstin the truth, the older woman had stayed silent for what felt like an eternity before finally blurting out, *So do I get to visit you at your palace?*

Mentoring the Harrington Foundation's new public relations department had taken up far too much time to allow for a visit. Until next week. Kirstin would officially be a guest of the royal family at Nicholai and Madeline's wedding.

"I'm glad I didn't know just how much living on your

own you were going to be doing until you got back," Nicholai grumbled.

"I know. That's why I didn't tell you," Eviana teased.

"And what about the not so positives? Come on, Evie," he said when she started to look away again. "I can tell something's wrong."

"Not wrong. It's been resolved. It's just… I made some really good friends. People I cared about. And I hurt them." Blue eyes rose in her mind. Warm with affection and longing. Then ice-cold with fury. Hurt. "One in particular."

"You are allowed to make mistakes."

"I know."

She thought back to the numerous times Shaw had expressed how much honesty meant to him. How much Zach's actions had hurt him. How many times he had told her he liked her for who she was. He'd made her feel like he was the first person to see all of her and like what he saw.

Yet there had been that insidious sliver of doubt that had been buried so deep inside her she hadn't been able to let go and fully let Shaw in. She'd made excuses, some of which had been valid at first when she'd barely known him. But as they'd grown closer, as he'd shared more of himself, she had done what she had accused him of and held back out of fear.

For that, she'd lost him.

"I hope whoever it is realizes how big of a mistake they made in letting you go."

Eviana shook her head even as she smiled. "I appreciate the sentiment. But I haven't talked to them since I came home."

A vice gripped her heart, squeezed tight for one painful second, then released.

One day at a time.

"I doubt I ever will again."

CHAPTER TWENTY-ONE

Shaw

THE SUN SANK behind Edinburgh Castle, giving the timeworn walls a glowing orange outline as day turned to night. Shaw stared at it, his chin braced in one hand.

Three months. It had been three months since Eviana had walked out of the restaurant and out of his life. Three months since he'd talked to her, heard her laugh, seen her smile. Yet every time he turned around, there was something to remind him of her.

Including an ancient castle right outside his window.

Frustrated, he turned away from the window and refocused his attention on his computer. The past twelve weeks had ushered numerous changes into his life. The dinner for the foundation's most prolific donors had exceeded his expectations. Olivia had made a public statement about her decision to renew her contributions, a statement that had been followed by a flood of donations.

Two months later, Zach had been convicted of embezzling funds due to investing far more than he had been approved for by the board. But the ruling had come with a lenient sentencing given all the evidence had pointed to Zach genuinely trying to improve the foundation's financial security.

Shaw had attended the sentencing. When Zach had seen him, he'd gone pale but faced him, regret etched into his face.

It had been in that moment that Shaw had accepted that Zach was going to face his punishment. Holding on to his anger did nothing but let a damaging emotion fester.

The picture of him shaking Zach's hand had gone viral, with headlines like "Founder of Charity Forgives Disgraced CEO." The resulting publicity and subsequent surge in donations had left the foundation with triple the amount of money Zach had lost.

The board of trustees had asked Shaw to consider taking the position permanently. He'd declined for the long term but agreed to serve until they found someone to replace Zach. He'd even taken leave from his firm in New York to focus on the foundation and see it through the upcoming transitions. Transitions like the addition of a new public relations department, one currently being mentored by Kirstin Murray.

His eyes darted to the side and fixed on the castle once more. He had everything he had ever dreamed of.

His life had never seemed emptier.

For the first few weeks after Eviana's departure, he'd managed to hang on to his anger, his wounded pride. But as the days had passed, morbid curiosity had sunk its talons into him until he'd finally caved and looked her up online. Oddly enough, he hadn't doubted her story. He'd simply been too hurt and angry to hear what she'd been saying.

When he'd scroll through the stories dating back to the weeks just before she'd come to Scotland—from her father's funeral to speculations about her weight, if she was sleeping well or feeling replaced by her brother's impending marriage—he'd gained a deeper understanding of the scrutiny she had faced. Everything she said, ate and did was analyzed and picked apart by the international press. He'd gripped the edge of his desk so hard he'd nearly snapped off a piece when he'd read one from just a few weeks ago speculating about Eviana's love life or seemingly lack thereof. The thought of another man holding her hand, getting to see her true smile, had him seeing red.

But there had also been the stories that had reinforced the image of the Eviana he'd known. The one that had lodged itself in his mind was a story of a bridge collapse the year prior. Many of the stories had focused on Eviana's future sister-in-law, mostly because a nurse had snapped a photo of the queen-to-be holding a child who had been injured in the collapse. But there had been other stories, too, ones that had highlighted Eviana's years of dedication and hard work to the hospital, including helping arrange fundraising events, galas and visiting numerous patients every week.

The photos of her with children in the hospital had hit him especially hard. His heart had twisted in at the sight of Eviana's beautiful face so happy as she'd sat and drawn silly pictures with a toddler. It had been those photos, the ones of her with the organization she had poured her soul into, that showed the Eviana he'd known. Happy, optimistic, content.

The others, however… The other photos had made him want to lash out. Photos of her dressed in pastel colors, her face blank as she attended dozens of events to merely serve as window dressing. He had been exhausted by his brief time under the microscope of the international press. Eviana had lived her whole life under one. Not just lived it, but questioned it, doubted it, even if she persevered and had tried to be the kind of leader she thought her country deserved.

Although, he remembered, the more recent pictures had been different. No more pastels or bland expressions. She'd been snapped in a bright red dress at a museum opening and a lavender skirt while out shopping with her sister-in-law. She hadn't looked vibrantly happy. But she'd seemed more confident. More herself.

A sight that had made him simultaneously proud and ache that he wasn't there to experience her renaissance.

Shaw scrubbed a hand over his face as he slammed his laptop shut. The more time passed, the more her absence pressed on him. He missed her sunny smile, listening to her ideas, sitting and working in the same space and simply enjoying her presence. She had woven herself into his life so deeply it was impossible to get rid of her.

And he didn't want to. He had been so focused on his own pain and pride the night of the dinner at the Witchery that he hadn't stopped to think. To listen.

As he stared out over Edinburgh, he finally acknowledged that this had been his problem for years. His obsession with doing better than the people who had let him and his mother down, of hanging on to betrayal and grief. It had blinded him to the world around him. His experience with the charity in London and the transgressions that had cost him and his mother so much had left him with exceedingly high standards. Important ones, but ones so high almost no one could reach them.

Something he had done out of fear. When everyone fell short and he had a reason to keep them at arm's length, no one could get close enough to hurt him.

Until now. Until Eviana had slipped in with her sunny smile and kindness tempered by that confidence that would carry her far if she would just trust herself.

As he should have trusted her.

The vise around his chest tightened. Slowly, he opened his laptop back up and pulled up the news site he'd been frequenting. An American reporter was in Kelna covering the week leading up to the wedding. The most recent article included photos of Eviana with the bride-to-be enjoying coffee at a local café. The bodyguard he'd identified, Jodi, sat at another table in the background, along with another man he assumed to be an additional bodyguard. The future queen, Madeline, had been showing Eviana something on her phone. Eviana had worn sunglasses, so he hadn't been able to see her eyes. The photographer had caught her mid-smile. But even with the sunglasses, he could tell it wasn't her usual smile. The one that made her eyes crinkle at the corners.

Was royal life weighing on her once more? Or did his rejection still linger, hurting her over and over again despite the months of no contact?

He reached out, traced a finger over her face framed by her dark hair. It had been a jolt the first time he'd looked her up and seen her with dark brown hair. Yet it had seemed more…her.

God, he missed her.

Shaw clicked out of the screen. Where would he even begin in mending the broken fences between them? Was there a point? Her life was, and always would be, in Kelna. His was…

He stopped. He had his house here in Edinburgh. A pleasant space, but nothing special. This building, his office—they were all simply there, tools to be used to further the mission of the Harrington Foundation. He'd barely used the office in the past three years as Zach had taken over so much of the duties. He had a small fortune earning interest every day.

None of it made him happy. The only thing in his current life that brought him pleasure was the foundation. When the new CEO took over, he wanted to stay involved, attend at least some of the events the new public relations team was coming up with. Wanted to visit the charities and people the foundation benefited, see firsthand what was going well and what could be done better.

But to let the Harrington Foundation truly grow, he would have to let it go. To trust others with more expertise and skill to nurture it.

Which left him with…nothing. Nothing except a small manor house in Greenhill and a luxurious penthouse in New

York City he hadn't thought of even once since he'd come back to Edinburgh.

What he had thought of, the one person who had never left his thoughts, even when his anger had been all-consuming, had been Eviana. She had brought out the best in him. And he missed her. He wanted her in his life. Wanted…

His heart slammed into his ribs. He wanted it all. A life with Eviana and all that entailed. Living in Kelna, marriage… Even though the thought of having children terrified him, it wasn't hard to imagine Eviana with their baby in her arms. Exploring a castle with a dark-haired toddler or riding a train to visit a new country with a redheaded child bouncing on the seat next to him.

It wouldn't be all sunshine. There would be hard times, too. Just the thought of having photographers constantly swarm around made him scowl.

But he'd stepped outside of his comfort zone numerous times over the past few months. Each time had gotten a little easier. Putting himself out there for the sake of the foundation had made it more manageable. If the price to pay for being with Eviana was to be in the spotlight, he would gladly pay it over and over.

"I love her."

Shaw said the words softly at first, then repeated them again. He was in love with a princess.

He turned back to his computer and pulled up flights to Kelna. That was how Kirstin found him when she walked in three minutes later, on the phone with his secretary and running an irritated hand through his hair. He shot her a glance and gestured for her to take a seat.

"All flights are booked?" he asked irritably.

"Yes, sir," his secretary said slowly, as if she hadn't just told him that exact same thing. "I've checked every airline.

There are no flights into Dubrovnik. People are flying into Croatia so they can travel into Kelna for the royal wedding."

He blew out a frustrated breath. "Fine. Look for anything into nearby airports."

"I'll try, sir, but it might not—"

"Just try." He stopped himself. "Please."

Shaw hung up.

"Where are you off to?" Kirstin asked with an arched brow.

"I'm trying to get to Kelna."

There was a beat of quiet. And then she exploded out of her chair, a huge grin on her face. "I knew it!"

"Knew what?"

"You're in love with Eviana!"

He sat back in his chair as he narrowed his eyes at her. "What makes you think that?"

"Oh, please," Kirstin scoffed as she sat back down. "One, I have eyes. Two, you've been a mopey mess ever since she left."

He scowled. "You said I was nicer."

"You are. But you're still walking around like you have your own personal thundercloud perpetually raining on you."

"Thanks."

"And," she continued as she shot him a smug smile, "because Eviana's been a sad mess ever since she left, too."

His breath froze in his chest. And then he leaned forward, his attention riveted on Kirstin. "You've spoken to her?"

She crossed one leg over the other. "Those four personal days I've booked? They're to attend the royal wedding as Eviana's guest. She even invited my mother."

His throat constricted. "How…how is she?"

"Well. She's made quite her mark on the palace since she came back."

"I read about everything she's doing." His smile was tinged with pride. "She's presenting a proposal on the addition of a new railroad to the minister and Department of Transportation."

"And continuing her work with the hospital charity, along with several others. We talk once a week. She thought I was going to be angry at her."

"But you weren't?"

"It bothered me for a few seconds. Then I realized it didn't matter if her name was Ana or Her Royal Highness Princess Eviana," Kirstin said with a shrug. "Or if she was a blonde or a brunette. She came through for me during a very difficult time in my life. She created an excellent campaign for you and achieved results. I'm getting new business because of the work she did. And I gained a new friend."

He looked away. If only he had been as understanding and forgiving instead of holding on to the familiar pain and pride that had guided so much of his adult life.

"She's sad," Kirstin said gently.

"I hurt her."

"You did. But I think she knows she hurt you, too."

"She did. It doesn't excuse my reaction, how I just let her walk away. But I'm going to rectify that. If I can..." His voice trailed off as inspiration struck. "How are you getting to Kelna?"

Kirstin leaned back. "Don't even think about it. I'm all for true love, but if you think I'm giving up my ticket when this will be the only chance I have in my life to attend a royal wedding—"

"If I can persuade her to forgive me and hear me out, you might be a bridesmaid in the next one."

Kirstin stared at him for a moment, eyes huge and round. And then she jumped up again, let out a loud whoop and ran around the desk to wrap him in an enthusiastic hug.

"She hasn't said yes yet—"

"If she doesn't, I'll help you come up with a plot to kidnap her or something like they do in the romance books until she admits she's in love with you, too."

He winced. "How about I just start with an apology and telling her I love her?"

"That works, too." Kirstin frowned. "But how are you going to get there if the flights are sold out?"

"That's why I was asking what your plans were. I've never booked a private jet for myself before, but I would prefer to have company if I'm going to spend the money on it."

Kirstin clapped her hands together. "I swear, this day just keeps getting better and better."

CHAPTER TWENTY-TWO

Eviana

EVIANA WALKED OUT of the small boutique on Lepo Plavi's main thoroughfare, a pale blue gift bag in her hand. Out of the corner of her eye, she spied two photographers with their cameras aimed at her. She smiled at Jodi as they walked down the sidewalk. "At least we're down to two instead of the four that followed us here."

"I can't wait until this wedding's over," Jodi growled.

Her bodyguard's furious expression made her laugh. Something she desperately needed. As much as she was looking forward to the wedding tomorrow, there would also be no shortage of relief once Madeline and Nicholai flew off to their honeymoon in Bora Bora. Hordes of tourists and paparazzi had descended on the capital. While Nicholai and Madeline were certainly the focus, Eviana had also become a target of random people wanting her autograph or to snap a selfie with a real princess.

It hadn't helped that one magazine had obtained a photo of from last month's hospital gala of her standing off to the side and watching people dance. The expression on her face hadn't been sad, but she hadn't looked joyful, either. The headline had read "Will Bachelorette Princess Find Her Own Prince Charming?"

The resulting media attention, not to mention a surge in

the number of men asking her out on dates to the museum, local wineries or one of Kelna's many restaurants, had left her wanting to hide in her room.

Logically, she should've been flattered. But she had zero interest in any of the men who had reached out. Not that they weren't interesting and accomplished, from an ambassador she had met last year to a professional football player from Croatia.

Maybe next year.

For now, she simply told everyone that her first and primary focus was supporting her brother and his soon-to-be wife on one of the biggest days of their lives.

She kept the part about having a broken heart to herself.

"Are you sure you wouldn't like me to call for the car?" Jodi asked as one photographer moved into the middle of the sidewalk and snapped a half dozen photos in a matter of seconds.

"As soon as I do that, they win. Besides," she added with a smirk, "maybe they'll catch a photo I could use on my dating-app profile next year."

Jodi stared at her for a moment before breaking out into a grin. "No disrespect, Your Highness, but I would pay to see your brother's reaction when you tell him you're going on a dating website."

Eviana was about to respond when she caught movement out of the corner of her eye. Awareness crackled across her skin as a man emerged from the Grand Hotel.

It can't be.

But she knew that determined gait, the thick red hair, the angular jaw covered by that closely trimmed beard. His head suddenly jerked to the side, and a deep blue gaze met hers. Fierce emotion flared in his eyes before he blinked and his familiar mask slid back into place.

She wanted nothing more than to turn away, to leave before she said or did something that would reveal her feelings. But she couldn't. Not with so many people milling about, so many photographers with cameras ready to document her every move.

"Your Highness," Jodi murmured, warning in her voice.

"I know." She gritted her teeth even as she smiled. "Just play along."

Shaw stayed where he was on the sidewalk as they approached.

Steady, she told herself. *You can do this.*

"Mr. Harrington."

His eyes narrowed before he bowed his head. "Your Highness."

She didn't burst into tears or fling herself into his arms.

So far, so good.

"I didn't realize you—"

"Your Highness."

Eviana's polite smile froze in place as Joseph Rexford, an ambassador from the States, emerged from the hotel and spotted her.

"Good morning, Ambassador."

"Good morning," he said with a friendly smile as he approached. "I'm looking forward to..." His voice trailed off as he noticed Shaw. "Shaw Harrington?"

Shaw turned his head, then smiled slightly. "Ambassador. It's good to see you again."

The two men shook hands. Even over the passing traffic and rise and fall of conversations around her, Eviana swore she could hear the click of the cameras across the street, down the block.

Smile. Smile.

"Small world," she said as politely as she could manage.

"Yes. Mr. Harrington and I met last month at a fundraiser at the New York Public Library. He was there with..." Joseph snapped his fingers. "Kirstin Murray. Getting ideas for upcoming events for the Harrington Foundation."

Despite the pain and heartache thumping inside her chest, Eviana smiled.

"The comeback has been impressive." She looked at Shaw. "You have a lot to be proud of."

Did she imagine the look in his eyes, the longing?

"How are you two acquainted?"

Eviana looked back at Joseph, who was now regarding her and Shaw with a slight degree of suspicion.

"Actually, I was introduced to Mr. Harrington by Ms. Murray," Eviana said with a light laugh. "I spent time in Edinburgh during my sabbatical and made both of their acquaintances there."

"I didn't realize that's where you'd been staying."

She lowered her gaze. "My whole trip was very private."

The ambassador's eyes widened. "Of course. I'm sorry."

"No need," Eviana said smoothly. "My brother and Madeline were gracious in giving me time off to rest and recuperate. But Ms. Murray and Mr. Harrington were also very generous to me with their time and sharing their experiences. It gave me a new insight into public relations and professional communications."

"Lessons I noticed you incorporated into your work here in Kelna these last couple of months."

Shaw's words sent a bolt of pleasure through her. Had he been thinking about her as often as she thought about him?

"Thank you."

"It'll be nice to have another familiar face at the wedding," Joseph said with a smile aimed in Shaw's direction.

"I'm not here for the wedding." His hesitation was so slight that Eviana wondered if the ambassador had even noticed it. "My timing is poor, but I'm here because after the wedding, I hope to meet with Her Highness and discuss the possibility of her presence at some of our events next year. Given her interest in supportive causes like mine, having a royal as an official patron would do wonders for the foundation."

Her pleasure evaporated. Blunt anger swiftly replaced it. Was that really the only reason why he was here? To use her?

"An opportunity I'm happy to discuss. Although," she continued as she fought to keep the edge out of her voice, "with the usual drop-off in guests at the last minute, we would be delighted to host you tomorrow for the wedding."

He inclined his head again. She wanted to scream at the formality of their interaction, playacting for the sake of the cameras. The exact opposite of what their relationship had been.

"I look forward to it," he said. "Thank you."

"Jodi will send a formal invitation over this afternoon." She glanced at her watch. "Speaking of, I have a gift that needs to be delivered to the bride-to-be. Ambassador, Mr. Harrington." She gave them each a formal nod. "We look forward to seeing you tomorrow."

She held it together down the street, not looking back, not faltering in front of the cameras.

Perhaps this was all a test. Putting her in another stressful situation, one where she had to come up with something on the spur of the moment with scores of people watching. No, it hadn't been a speech delivered to influential business leaders in the community. But there had been a different type of audience present, one far more intimidating and even, daresay, dangerous. The kind of people who snapped photos that could easily be taken out of context or twisted to fit a narrative to sell more stories.

"Call the car, please."

She felt Jodi's eyes on her. "I can have him kicked out of the country."

Eviana tried, and failed, not to smile. "As tempting as that offer is, I will have to pass. He'll come to the wedding tomorrow. There will be plenty of people there he can interact with. Especially if his goal is truly to use this event to expand the foundation."

"If it is," Jodi bit out, "I still have contacts in the Navy who I'm sure could—"

"I appreciate you, Jodi."

Out of the corner of her eye, she saw Jodi's look of surprise. "Thank you, Your Highness."

"You gave me a gift back in Edinburgh, one I'm not sure many would have. Being able to live my life the way I wanted to, on my own terms, to feel like I was just an everyday person. I desperately needed it."

"You're welcome." Jodi exhaled. "Although I still feel like I failed you."

"How so?"

"I failed to protect you from him."

Her heart twisted. "You didn't fail. It didn't have the happily-ever-after that I prefer, but I will never regret my time with him."

Even if it felt like her heart was being shattered all over again, leaving bits and pieces trailing behind her as she once more walked away from the man she loved.

"He's a fool," Jodi growled as a black car pulled up to the curb.

"On that," Eviana replied softly as another guard got out and opened the door for her, "we agree."

CHAPTER TWENTY-THREE

Eviana

THE DAY OF the wedding dawned bright and cool. Autumn in Kelna was truly beautiful, with beech and oak trees displaying a dazzling array of colorful leaves in shades of rich red, vibrant orange and cheery yellow. The sky seemed even bluer than in summer, especially when one got up early enough to enjoy the crisp mornings. It was usually one of Eviana's favorite times of year.

But now, as she wandered through the palace gardens on the morning of her brother's wedding, the only emotion she could find was grief. Grief that her father wasn't here to see his only son get married. Grief that their mother had passed far too soon to see either of her children grow into adults.

And grief for the man who probably still slept in a bed just a few kilometers away.

After she had run into him yesterday, Eviana had managed to make it through the rest of the afternoon and evening with a smile on her face. Mostly by sheer will, but she'd done it. She'd laughed and joked through the afternoon at the spa with Madeline, Madeline's mother and some of Madeline's friends from America. She'd conversed with countless people at the dinner following the rehearsal at the chapel.

It hadn't been until she made it into the privacy of her room that she'd succumbed to the need to cry.

He wasn't here to offer forgiveness or his own apology. To ask for just a little more time before they went their separate ways. No, he wanted to use her. Use her name and her legacy.

Her heart clenched. The woman in her wanted to say no to his request, wanted to cut off anything and everything to do with Shaw. She didn't know if she would be able to heal, to move on with her life with him always on the fringes. But the princess in her, the one who understood sacrifice and duty, knew how many people she could help by putting aside her personal feelings and agreeing to his request.

Wasn't that one of the reasons she had fallen in love with Shaw? His commitment to doing the right thing and, as she had later learned, striving to be better than the man who had let down him and his mother, along with countless others? A man who had taken a horrific experience and turned it into something good.

Although in this context, she thought glumly, his commitment was a double-edged sword. One that cut her deep.

Maybe after the holidays, she could take a short break. A week away, somewhere far flung where she could have another taste of being able to walk down the street and not be recognized…

Footsteps sounded behind her. Irritation cut through her melancholy mood. There were a number of people staying at the palace, including Kirstin and her mother. Mostly close friends and family, along with a few high-profile guests. It was only natural that somebody else would want to enjoy the pleasures of the gardens in the fall.

I just wish they could do it somewhere else.

She turned to greet the intruder. And froze.

Shaw stood just a few feet away, his gaze fixed on her. Hands clenched at his sides. "Good morning."

She swallowed hard. "Good morning, Mr. Harrington."

He took one step forward, as if testing the waters. "It's just us. You don't need to stand on pretense."

"I'm not."

His jaw hardened, an action that drew her eye and nearly made her miss the hurt in his gaze at her curt answer. An answering pain surged in her chest, followed almost immediately by anger. He had no right to be hurt. Not after what he'd said when they had last parted. Not after the reasons he had given yesterday of why he was here, especially the week of her brother's wedding.

"The last time we spoke—"

"Can we not?"

She abandoned all attempts at civility, at maintaining her emotional distance. In this moment, seeing him stand in her place of refuge, so near she could close the distance between them with a couple of steps and touch his face, was too much.

"I understand there are things you want to talk to me about," she said as she lifted her chin, "but they will have to wait until after the wedding."

"That's not—"

"Enjoy the ceremony, Mr. Harrington."

She turned and walked away as fast as her training would allow her to without actually running from him. She blinked back tears, needing the sanctity of her own room. Somewhere she could shut and lock the door against the outside world.

Eviana was crossing the lawn toward her private entrance when Shaw caught up to her, his hand engulfing hers. She hated that her breath caught, that her chest tightened at the contact.

"Don't." She glanced around. She couldn't handle it if a photo of them ended up in the news. The questions she'd have to answer, the renewed scrutiny of her love life. "Not here."

His fingers tightened around hers. "Eviana, please—"

It was the first time he had said her name, her real name, without pain or fury. It made her pause. Made her want to—

"No. You made your feelings perfectly clear back in Edinburgh." She let herself savor the pressure of his fingers, the warmth of his skin on hers one final time, then yanked her hand out of his. "I can't do this. Not now. I'm going to be standing next to my brother and the future queen of this country in four hours. I don't know why you're here or why—"

"I'm trying to tell you," he growled.

"And I don't want to hear it," she snapped back. "I have spent the last three months trying to move on. Then you show up and bring all of it crashing back. Today of all days I can't be weak, and you, Shaw Harrington, are my weakness."

With that pronouncement, she turned and walked off. It took a moment for her to realize she was walking in the opposite direction she had intended and was heading back toward the rose garden, but she didn't care. She just needed to get away.

The white pebbled circles of the rose maze beckoned to her. She passed under the stone arches, moved past the rose bushes that held on to their blooms thanks to the warmer Mediterranean temperatures. A still-bubbling fountain dominated the center. She slipped past it, her feet carrying her over the familiar stone path that led to a place that she had thought of as hers since childhood.

Even as hurt squeezed her lungs and made her breaths shallow, the white terrace built onto the cliffside eased some of the heartache. How many times had she snuck out here as a child, spinning around the terrace or leaning on the railing to stare at the sea below?

When the photos had come out of Nicholai and Madeline kissing after a royal ball, she had felt horrible for her brother. But the romantic in her had also thought there had been something telling about the location of where they had shared their kiss. The place she had once considered magical.

Now the magic lay in its comfort, its familiarity and offer of refuge.

She moved to the edge and placed her hands on the railing, staring down at the deep blue waves rising and falling against the cliffside. She'd handled that badly—all of her training gone out the window at the mere sight of him. She would've been angry with herself if she weren't so exhausted.

The soft crunch of gravel met her ears. Her body tensed a moment before his voice washed over her.

"Eviana."

It's better this way, she told herself as she stared out over the sea. *Get it out of the way so I can once and for all close this chapter of my life.*

"Say what you came to say and then leave. Please."

Warm hands grasped her shoulders and slowly turned her around. She looked up into his familiar face, into eyes so much like the sea.

"I was wrong."

She stood motionless, the distant roar of the sea indistinguishable from the roar of blood in her ears. "What?"

"I was wrong," he repeated, his voice vibrating with emotion. "I was shocked and hurt, and I let my foolish pride rule that conversation. I never should have let you walk out of that garden"

His hand came up, slowly, then settled on her face. A tremble passed through her as she closed her eyes and leaned into his touch. "Letting you walk away is the biggest regret of my life."

Eviana drew in a shuddering breath, then opened her eyes. She stood at a crossroads. One where she could do as he had done to her and push him away.

Or she could be brave once more. Be brave and give him the honesty she should have so long ago.

"My biggest regret is not trusting you sooner," she said.

"I don't know what it's like to be a royal. To have to guard my identity—"

"But that wasn't all of it." She had to be truthful, had to let him know everything. "In the beginning, yes, I didn't tell anyone because my whole reason for being in Edinburgh was to have a few months where I didn't have to be a princess. Where I could finally breathe. But as I got to know you, I wasn't worried so much about maintaining my anonymity as I was about how you would react when you found out who I was."

"Why?"

Honesty. Truth.

"Because I fell in love with you." His eyes widened, but she rushed on, not wanting to stop. "Because I wasn't confident in who I was. My feelings about the role I'm taking on were so conflicted, and knowing how you feel about being in the spotlight made any possibility of us seem hopeless. And when you said what you did about me being like Zach—"

"Which was a mistake," he cut in, his voice rough. "Something I said in a moment of pain and anger." He held her face in his hands. "You are nothing like him. That I even suggested you were is a guilt I will carry for the rest of my life."

"Still… I am sorry."

"I know. You apologized that night, and I should have accepted your apology. It took a moment to think and process what you told me. Most of all," he said as he rested his forehead against hers, "I should have realized then how much you mean to me. I'm sorry for so many things, including how long it took for me to realize how deeply in love with you I am."

She leaned back, her eyes searching his face. But all she saw was love, love and that deep longing she had glimpsed yesterday on the street but hadn't wanted to believe was possible. "You love me?"

"With all that I am."

He pressed a kiss to her forehead, one that made her heart swell. Then he stepped back. "You said you didn't care why I was here. But I hope I can change your mind."

There, on the terrace where she had dreamed of love and her own Prince Charming, Shaw dropped to one knee and pulled a box out of his pocket. Her hands flew to her lips as he opened it and unveiled a sparkling emerald set in a silver band.

"I never imagined myself falling in love. I never thought about getting married. Having a family. But I'm in love with you. The strong, confident woman who first ensnared me. The calm, elegant royal who guided me through some of the most challenging times I've ever experienced. Most of all, I love your kind heart. That and your ability to take joy in the little things." His blue eyes glinted. "You brought me back to life, Eviana, and I don't want to picture it without you in it."

How was it even possible to fall to the deepest depths of grief, only to be catapulted up into the most incredible moment of happiness she'd ever known?

Except...how could she accept him? Bring him into the life that had been such a struggle for her?

"Shaw..."

"Please tell me that's a yes."

"I want to say yes." Her voice broke. "I love you. You saw me for who I was, believed in me even when I wasn't sure who I was at my core. I want a life with you. But my life is here and—"

"If you accept me, I want to be here for you. I still want to be involved with the foundation," he added as she continued to stare at him, at a loss for words as he offered her everything she'd dreamed of. "But the rest of my life... It's not the same without you, Eviana. Everything I've done up to this point has been for the foundation. It does good work, but I want more. I know that I could do a great deal, not just for you but for your country."

Hope—beautiful, impossible hope—bloomed in her chest. "What are you saying?"

"You told me the reason you fled to Edinburgh was out of exhaustion. Out of fear that you weren't enough. You are enough. You are so much more than you give yourself credit for. But just as your brother faced too much, you do, too.

Your brother has Madeline. And I want you to have me. I know absolutely nothing about being married to a royal or what I'd have to do. But if I can survive the finance world of New York, an international investment-fraud scandal and," he added with a slight smile, "dinner with a dozen people who didn't trust me to take care of their money, I know I can be there for you. And what I don't know, I can learn. Want to learn," he added, his voice deepening with emotion, "for you."

His offer, what he was willing to sacrifice hit her like a freight train.

For one horrible moment, she faltered. "What if it's too much?"

"There will be days where it probably will be too much. But we'll have each other. That is worth more to me than any mundane existence could offer." His fingers tightened around hers. "Please say yes, Eviana."

"Yes."

Her answer came out on a whisper. But Shaw heard it, a smile breaking across his face as he pulled the ring out of the box and slid it onto her finger before he stood and pulled her into his arms.

And then he kissed her. A soul-searing kiss that had her seeing stars.

"How is this possible?" she murmured against his lips.

"Kirstin."

She leaned back and laughed. "Kirstin?"

"And Jodi."

"Jodi?" Eviana shook her head slightly. "But she..."

"Oh, she made her feelings clear when she called me last night."

Mortification mixed with amusement. "She called you?"

"Yes. Apparently it's very easy for a former intelligence officer with Kelna's Royal Navy to get information like a personal phone number. She also had some very creative threats on how she planned to remove me from your country. But," he said as grazed his knuckles over her cheek, "when I told her what I had planned and sent her a picture of the ring as evidence of my intentions, she helped me get into the palace this morning."

"Given how well this turned out, I suppose I can't be mad at her. In fact," she said with a small laugh, "I'll probably have to make her a bridesmaid."

His hold on her waist tightened. "How long do we have to wait after your brother's wedding?"

"There's not an official waiting period."

Eviana glanced around the terrace. She could see it now: garlands of roses and ivy wound around the railing. Lanterns flickering as the sun set. The people they loved celebrating their incredible journey.

And Shaw waiting for her at the end of a petal-strewn path, love shining from his eyes as he said *I do.*

"I wouldn't mind a spring wedding," she said.

Shaw lowered his head and captured her mouth with his once more. His low moan reverberated through her, stirring the desire that had nearly consumed them on the train. Her hands slid up his arms, over his shoulders, then up his neck, her fingers tangling in his hair…

The soft chimes of an alarm sounded.

With a regretful sigh, she pulled back to glance down at her watch, then did a double take. "I have to be in my room in five minutes!"

Shaw held up her left hand. "I suppose this will have to come off for the wedding."

"Probably," she said with regret. "I want today to be about Nicholai and Madeline. And given that there have been so many articles about my bachelorette status…"

"No more." Shaw's growl made her toes curl. "As soon as it's allowed, I want the world to know that you're mine."

She smiled up at him. "Now and forever."

EPILOGUE

Shaw
Five years later

A SHARP CRY pierced the stillness of early morning. Shaw sat straight up in bed, his heart thumping. There was an empty space next to him, the sheets in a tangle as if they'd been tossed back in a hurry. "Eviana?"

A moment later his wife appeared in the door, cradling a mound of blankets making soft, blubbering coos. "Just a hungry girl."

His heart swelled as Eviana sat on the bed next to him, her hair mussed as she gazed down at Lucinda Kirstin. At four months old, their daughter had demonstrated her healthy lungs on numerous occasions.

Although, he admitted as he reached over and stroked a finger over the tiny hand that had emerged from the blanket, the recent travel had not helped Lucy's sleeping.

In the five years since he and Eviana had married, they had managed to schedule several weeks off throughout the year where they traveled, mostly in Europe but even to places like Japan and Egypt. Those breaks had helped them both balance the long list of duties they had tackled as Kelna's newest royal couple.

He would never get used to the photographers, to having what he had for lunch at a meeting with an ambassador posted on a gossip website. But seeing the difference his and Eviana's work did, from the charities they supported to advocating for and working toward initiatives like Kelna's soon-to-be-opened railroad that would connect the country with the extensive Eurail system, had been far more rewarding than he had anticipated. Sharing duties with Nicholai and Madeline, who had welcomed him with open arms upon their return from their honeymoon, had made settling into royal life a much easier adjustment than he had anticipated, even allowing for him to stay involved with the continuously growing Harrington Foundation.

Still, he thought as Eviana scooted back and leaned against the headboard, the trip this year was very much needed. With the new addition to their family, they had returned to somewhere familiar. Somewhere they could still enjoy their time away but also savor every moment of new parenthood they could.

He glanced out the window. Mist swirled and shifted over the green hills as sunlight glimmered on the horizon.

"I think she's trying to compete with the hawk from yesterday," Eviana murmured as Lucy blinked at them, her face serene now that she had both her parents' attention.

It had been Madeline's idea for the royal family to travel to Scotland this summer, a trip that included Nicholai, Madeline, their three-year-old son, Asher, and their eight-month-old daughter, Sarah. They had found a secluded castle in the Highlands for rent, one with acres upon acres of rolling pastures, bubbling creeks and a full-time staff that included a stable caretaker and a hawker.

"Good morning, Lucy," Shaw said.

His daughter's head turned slightly, her eyes widening as they fixed on his face. Emerald eyes, just like her mother, but the little wisps of hair on her head were dark red.

"How about I hold her? Let you get a little more sleep?"

Eviana hesitated for just a moment before she gently laid Lucy in his embrace.

"Just a few more minutes," she said quietly as she lay back down.

"Take all the time you need," he murmured.

A moment later, Eviana's quiet breathing reached his ears. Lucy seemed to understand her mother's need for sleep as she lay quietly in his arms and stared up at him. When he and Eviana had finally decided to start a family of their own, he'd been excited and terrified in equal measure. The same emotions had coursed through him when he'd heard the steady thump of Lucy's heartbeat for the first time, and again when he had seen the little blob on the ultrasound.

But when the nurses had laid his and Eviana's daughter in his arms, it was as if the rest of his world, the last little piece he hadn't even known had been missing had slid into place.

He smiled down at Lucy. "Your grandmothers would have adored you."

Lucy's lips curved up into the tiniest of smiles. His heart stopped as his own smile grew.

"We're not going to tell your mother that your first smile was for me."

His daughter grinned as she let out a soft babble. His arms tightened around her tiny body as he laid a kiss on her forehead. "You are an amazing creature, Lucinda Kirstin Harrington."

Eviana's eyes fluttered. Her gaze slid between him and Lucy, a smile of pure contentment and love on her face. "I love you, Shaw."

"And I love you, Eviana."

Her eyes drifted shut once more. As Shaw sat next to his sleeping wife, with his daughter in his arms and the sun rising over the Highlands, he knew that he had truly found his happily-ever-after.

* * * * *

MILLS & BOON®

Coming next month

COPENHAGEN ESCAPE WITH THE BILLIONAIRE
Sophie Pembroke

Jesper was a stronger man than she suspected he'd ever give himself credit for. And it stirred up all sorts of feelings inside her chest that she really wasn't ready for.

She swallowed and looked away. 'So, tomorrow's a new dawn - what will that bring? What have you got planned for us next? Another message I assume?'

'Of course,' he replied. 'But I can't tell you what just yet.'

She jerked her head up to meet his gaze, only to discover that he was closer than ever. So close that, if she wanted, she could bring her lips to his without only the slightest movement.

If she wanted to.

Oh God, she wanted to.

Her throat dry, she tried to swallow before she spoke. 'You can't tell me?'

He shook his head, bringing his face ever closer to hers, the last of the sunlight shimmering off the silver in his beard. 'But I promise you it's magical.'

Magical.

That kiss at New Year had been magical - unexpected, with literal fireworks going off in the sky behind them. A gentle, but all-encompassing kiss that had suddenly opened up a world or a future she hadn't even contemplated before. That kiss had been her sunken church finding a new lease of life, her oceans meeting and crashing, her sunset before the sunrise.

And she could have it again, if she just leant in one iota.

She couldn't breathe with wanting it.

Continue reading

COPENHAGEN ESCAPE WITH THE BILLIONAIRE
Sophie Pembroke

Available next month
millsandboon.co.uk

afterglow
BOOKS

SCAN ME